By Heather Fawcett

Emily Wilde's Encyclopaedia of Faeries
Emily Wilde's Map of the Otherlands
Emily Wilde's Compendium of Lost Tales

Emily Wilde's Compendium of Lost Tales

Emily Wilde's Compendium of Lost Tales

A Novel

Heather Fawcett

 New York

Emily Wilde's Compendium of Lost Tales is a work of fiction. Names, places, and incidents either are products of the author's imagination or are used fictitiously. Any resemblance to actual events, locales, or persons, living or dead, is entirely coincidental.

Copyright © 2025 by Heather Fawcett
Penguin Random House values and supports copyright. Copyright fuels creativity, encourages diverse voices, promotes free speech, and creates a vibrant culture. Thank you for buying an authorized edition of this book and for complying with copyright laws by not reproducing, scanning, or distributing any part of it in any form without permission. You are supporting writers and allowing Penguin Random House to continue to publish books for every reader. Please note that no part of this book may be used or reproduced in any manner for the purpose of training artificial intelligence technologies or systems.

All rights reserved.

Published in the United States by Del Rey, an imprint of Random House, a division of Penguin Random House LLC, New York.

Del Rey and the Circle colophon are registered trademarks of Penguin Random House LLC.

Hardback ISBN 978-0-593-50022-4
Ebook ISBN 978-0-593-50023-1
International edition ISBN: 978-0-593-97682-1
Signed edition ISBN: 978-0-593-98326-3

Printed in the United States of America on acid-free paper

randomhousebooks.com

2 4 6 8 9 7 5 3 1

First Edition

Book design by Virginia Norey
Floral art by Alexandr Sidorov/stock.adobe.com
Ornamental frame by 100ker/stock.adobe.com

Emily Wilde's Compendium of Lost Tales

29th December 1910–cont'd

If there is one subject upon which Wendell and I will never agree, it is the wisdom of attempting to drag a cat into Faerie. Even if said animal is a *faerie cat;* even if we are merely returning her to the world whence she came, still it is the most frustrating process. Wendell and I had lost Orga twice already while navigating the rocky Greek coastline, as she went charging off after mice or gulls, and now, as we stood at long last at the threshold of Wendell's door, she had vanished again.

"Bloody thing needs to be leashed," I said, out of spite more than anything. I strongly suspected that if I approached Orga with anything resembling a harness, it would end with me wearing the cat on my head, likely with unfavourable results where my facial features were concerned.

Shadow was at my side, as usual, his snout buried in the fragrant coastal grasses, snuffling busily. He would never abandon me as Orga is so often abandoning Wendell. Dogs are proper companions, not the physical manifestation of caprice.

Wendell made no reply. He had gone still upon first sight of the door, so much so that he might have been some gilded illustration in a storybook, except that his cloak billowed at the hem, stirred by the salt breeze, which also tugged at the golden hair falling into his eyes.

I touched his arm, and he came back to himself, turning to smile at me.

"Em," he said, "she is a *cat*. You might as well expect Shadow to disregard your will as assume Orga to be governed by it. Remember her nature."

"Her malicious, untrustworthy nature," I said. Naturally the cat reappeared a heartbeat later, as if to spite us both, golden eyes glittering against her black fur, which rippled strangely, like smoke trapped within cat-shaped glass. Shadow, seated by my feet, gave her a weary sort of look and made his usual overture of friendship, nudging Orga gently with his nose. She arched her back and hissed.

"You should give up, dear," I told him, but the poor dog only looked at me blankly. Shadow's world was one in which all and sundry either fawned over him or kept a respectful distance from his intimidating bulk. Each time Orga hissed at him, Shadow seemed to assume it a misunderstanding, which grew increasingly improbable as these incidents accumulated, but still less improbable, in his view, than being disliked.

Wendell had gone back to staring at the door—savouring the moment, I suppose. I wondered if he would give a speech or something—after all, he'd spent more than a decade searching for the thing, and now here it was, folded snugly against the hillside like the bow on a Christmas gift.

I tapped my foot against a rock, feeling rather smug. Well, it had taken me only a handful of months to track the door down, hadn't it? I'd learned Wendell was looking for a door to his realm in November of last year when we were in Ljosland, and I'd begun researching the question in earnest in March, not long after we returned to Cambridge. And now—after a few twists and turns in Austria—here we were.

I considered and discarded several quips to this effect before deciding it would not be very magnanimous of me, and merely noted, "It's a pair with the one in St. Liesl."

Indeed, the door before us was nearly identical in shape and style—it blended into the Greek countryside perfectly, its wooden boards painted with a scene of pale, pebbly stone and sun-dried vegetation. A little patch of rock roses to the left continued into the painting, and these two-dimensional blooms tossed their heads in the breeze in time with their tangible brethren. Even more impossible, to my mortal eyes, was the doorknob, a square of glass enclosing a splash of turquoise sea. This nexus is truly the most peculiar variety of faerie door I have encountered in my career.[*]

Though I'd expected to find it here, one can never be certain of faerie doors, and there was relief mixed into my self-satisfaction.

I turned to scan the landscape, shading my eyes against the sun. It was my preference *not* to suddenly vanish from sight in view of observers, simply because it was easier that way—Wendell and I did not need any well-intentioned search parties following us into Faerie. Beyond a little salt-stained grove of cypress trees, the land stretched out in a series of pale commas that embraced a sea so blue it made my eyes water. A pair of two-legged specks moved across a bend of sand in the distance—that was all. The countryside was empty but for us and the wind.

"How will *they* follow us?" I said, trying to hide my trepidation.

---

[*] Unfortunately, my paper on the subject—currently under consideration by the *British Journal of Dryadology*—is still held up in peer review. It seems many scholars are not yet willing to accept the existence of faerie doors that connect multiple places, and it is possible that I shall have to gather additional evidence to override the skeptics, or perhaps convince other scholars to venture to Austria themselves to test my findings.

"Oh—easily enough," Wendell said absently. And he reached out with uncharacteristic hesitation and turned the knob.

We stepped through together, Wendell's hand closing around mine. I did not need his help, as I'd ventured through a few such impossible doors in my day without faerie aid, but I knew this was not his reason. His hand trembled lightly. I laced our fingers together and tightened my grip.

The little cottage beyond the door was empty, thank God—the winter faerie who owned it was now roaming the countryside, revelling in the delights of his season, as Wendell said such Folk were wont to do. The floor had been swept and the dishes in the washbasin put away, and overall everything had a very tucked-in, tidy look about it, as one might leave a home before a prolonged absence. I kept my gaze away from the mantel and the faerie's gruesome "art."

Orga and Shadow had followed behind us, Shadow giving the door a curious sniff before entering, but otherwise showing no sign he viewed this as any different from stepping through the door of my office at Cambridge. Wendell allowed it to close behind us, and we gazed at the row of six doorknobs on the inner side.

I wanted to ask him about those doorknobs—specifically, I wanted to investigate them further, as two were a complete mystery to me and I wished to know where they led—but I knew it was not the time. His fingers drifted past the knob that would open the door to the Peloponnese again—which was now at the top—and past the one for the Austrian Alps. This one had a large key in it that looked to be made from bone. Locked.

Wendell clicked the lock open—I pictured the little door shimmering into existence once more against the Alpine mountainside—then removed the key and set it on the table.

He lingered briefly on the doorknob decorated with a floral pattern before returning to the one covered in moss, which was now in the middle, for some reason. It had been lowest in the row when Ariadne and I had passed through the winter faerie's house in October. Wendell pushed the door open.

Light.

It was full morning, and my vision flooded with colour. Primarily green, but there was also the yellow of moss and lichened stone, the violet of bluebells clustered at the edge of the forest, the gold of sunbeams, and the rich azure of the sky. The door opened onto a hill in a small clearing, beyond which a wall of trees nodded their boughs in the wind, as if in greeting. The air was wet from a recent rain and heavy with the smell of green and growing things—all as I remembered.

Wendell pressed my hand to stop me from moving forward. His eyes followed Orga as she sniffed the air and then paced into the open. Her ears were pricked, alert, but the tension quickly left her body, and she sat back to nibble at a stalk of grass.

"I thought my stepmother might have this door watched," Wendell murmured. "If she lived."

"Or she might have sealed it," I agreed. "But then there is no reason to think she knew how Ariadne and I escaped, unless one of the common fae took note of our flight and told her."

Wendell nodded, but still he stood hesitating on the threshold. He looked pale and strangely young against the shadow of the winter faerie's home; he put me in mind of a nervous child hesitating behind a stage curtain, unwilling to emerge when his cue came.

I stepped into the sunlight, a welcome change from the dank chill of the winter faerie's house. A little shudder went through me, though whether it signified terror or excitement,

I could not tell. A part of me wonders if my fear of Wendell's kingdom, instilled by the many dark and unpleasant stories I have read of it throughout my career—not to mention my experiences here previously, which have faded into half-memories with the aura of nightmares—will ever fully leave me.

I gave his hand a playful tug. He looked at me, still pale, but something in my face seemed to steady him, and he allowed me to pull him through the door.

He took a few steps and then suddenly sank into a crouch, burying his face in his hand. Orga established herself at his feet, facing the forest warily. Shadow gave her what I can only describe as an approving look.

I strode up to the brow of the hill, both to give him a moment and to look for trouble. The hill was not high enough to afford a view over the entire forest, though I could make out the familiar glitter of a distant lake, over which rain fell in silver sheets. I leaned against one of the weathered standing stones that crowned the hill—as I did, there came a sort of startled skittering sound, and I caught a flash of a small foot disappearing under the stone, as if someone had been warming their toes in the sunlight.

Well, the common fae knew we were here. But that was unavoidable.

I made my way back down the hill. I expected to find Wendell enraptured by the bluebells and the forest—perhaps even the ghastly thing lurking at the shadowed edge of the clearing, one of the trees that gave Where the Trees Have Eyes its name. But no—he had brushed his tears away, and now had his chin propped on his hand, gazing at me with one of those enigmatic expressions I've not yet learned to parse, if I ever will. One of his faerie looks, as I think of them.

"What?" I said.

He rose, shaking the dew from his cloak. "You have that look."

He had mirrored my own train of thought, which made me scowl at him irrationally. "Which?"

"The one you wear whenever you outsmart me in some area," he said.

"Well," I began with a shrug, then stopped. My magnanimity was wearing thin, I'm afraid. "Haven't I?"

He laughed, a clear, bright sound, and then, before I knew what was happening, he had lifted me off my feet and spun me through the air, the greenery and shadow of the forest a whirl all around me.

"My beloved Emily," he murmured in my ear.

"Yes, yes, all right," I said, though I did not pull away. My smugness was back, together with a warm sort of satisfaction. It was pleasing to see him this happy.

The door swung open behind us, and suddenly the clearing was filled with noise. The guardians emerged first in a flurry of wingbeats, Razkarden in the lead. As they passed into the emerald light, they shed their glamours, transforming from pale owls to the most nightmarish creatures imaginable—still owls, at least in the main, but ragged and sinewy, eyes milky with cataracts. In place of feet, six massive spiderish limbs erupted from their torsos.

Razkarden alighted on Wendell's shoulder—or shoulders, for his legs would not fit on one—arranging his hideous limbs with surprising delicacy, and I was suddenly backing away from Wendell fast. Wendell, untroubled as usual, stroked Razkarden's beak and spoke quietly to the faerie monster. He took flight again, settling in the trees with the others.

Next came the trolls, by far the least unnerving of our motley army of common fae, their tools clanking in the packs on their backs. They burst into pleased muttering upon first sight of Wendell's kingdom, one marching up to a stump to rap on it, as if testing its suitability for building materials. Others seemed to be exclaiming over a pile of stones.

The tree fauns did not linger long in the clearing, which was a relief, but slunk immediately into the forest shadows, their feral hounds close at their heels. Now, the world holds enough Folk hideous to the eye, but in this respect I can think of none who surpass these fauns, with their scabbed and twisted horns and bulbous features.

Last came the *fuchszwerge,* streaming through the door in an auburn river, fox tails thrashing with excitement. Several dozen appeared to have volunteered to accompany us; the exact number is difficult to ascertain given how rarely the beasts stay still.

"*Finally,*" Snowbell crowed as he surged to the front of the pack. "Now the quest will begin! And it will be far more exciting than the last one, for there is only *one* mortal oaf this time." He settled himself at my feet in a proprietary sort of way and began to wash his face, pausing to snarl at any others who ventured near. Telling the fox-faeries apart remains difficult, but Snowbell is easy to identify, for he is always bragging about his role in my last adventure.

Wendell looked back at the trees, his reverence replaced with merriment.

"Shall we retake our kingdom, Em?" he said.

A shiver went through me at that. He had switched to Faie, which I had, of course, heard him speak before, but there was something discomfiting about the way he did it, abandoning the mortal tongue like an unsuitable cloak at the change of seasons. My hand strayed unconsciously to Shadow's head, and the dog butted at my palm, which steadied me.

"I suppose we might as well get on with it," I replied in the same language.

We found the path Ariadne and I had taken back in October at the bottom of the hill. I'd half expected it to be gone—why shouldn't faerie paths be as wayward as their doors?—but there it was, though it seemed to veer more to the north than I remembered.

I looked to the right, uncertain. "This way?"

Wendell followed my gaze. "I think not. The old ways will take too long. It's quite a distance to the castle, and I'd rather not tarry."

And he marched off into the dense tangle of undergrowth, making a sort of shooing gesture with his hand. Then—

A path unfurled at his feet, keeping pace several steps ahead of him, trees and grasses and stones simply drifting aside, as easy as waves retreating from a shore.

"Wendell," I said faintly.

He had already been turning to check on me, striding back up the path he'd made. I watched to see if it would dissolve again behind him, but it didn't, or at least not as quickly as it had appeared; the edges seemed to evaporate a little, greenery creeping back over the hard-packed earth.

He clasped my hands between his, his gaze radiating warmth and not a small amount of mischief. "We haven't much time for sightseeing, it's true—but let me show you what I can. Would you like that?"

He was teasing me, of course—he knew the answer as well as I did. The dangers looming before us, the trepidation I felt at my decision to venture here, to stay at his side—it was all abruptly subsumed by something much more familiar, which sent my heart skittering with excitement.

Scientific curiosity.

"Lead on, then," I said, taking the arm he offered me.

The path expanded to comfortably accommodate us. Shadow kept pace beside me, while Orga slunk in and out of the forest, appearing sometimes before us and sometimes behind, occasionally with some small, wriggling creature clutched in her maw. The others followed like a long and hideous train. I did not see the guardians, but from Wendell's unconcern, I assumed they were lurking in the canopy, watching us as they had during my first visit, though their intentions this time were less murderous—I hoped. Snowbell kept back, which he generally does when Wendell is near me. I believe he has the same terror of him that Poe does, though Snowbell expresses it in a rather more disturbing manner. I have heard him speculating more than once with his fellows about the quantity of blood Wendell would shed in retaking his kingdom, whether there would be leavings for the *fuchszwerge* to enjoy, and if so, what these might taste like.

Wendell talked as we went, pausing every few moments to point something out—he has a great deal of botanical knowledge when it comes to his realm, which I can only assume he was born with; I cannot imagine him acquiring it any other way. When I took out a notebook, he beamed at me—I had intended to spend our first day in Faerie observing rather than compiling facts, but he was so pleased whenever I lifted my pencil that I found myself recording a great deal. My concentration was somewhat hampered by the looming peril, but in no way did I need to feign enthusiasm, and I asked many questions, though his answers were not always helpful and tended towards the nonsensical. I will here record a select few insights.

✦ ✦ ✦

On the geography of Where the Trees Have Eyes

This is composed primarily of a mixture of woodland and heath, with a scattering of boggy regions and a mountain range that bounds the realm to the east. These mountains are known as the Blue Hooks. There are three lakes: Muckle, the largest; Silverlily, beside which sits the castle; and Lower Lake in the south, a dark place within the lands claimed by the hag-headed deer, where we would not be venturing.

Asking Wendell to help me sketch a map of the realm proved largely fruitless, which did not surprise me. It is a widely acknowledged truth that Faerie has all the spatial integrity of a dream; a mountain may be in one place on a Tuesday and decide to spend Wednesday in a more favourable locale. At different points during our conversation, Wendell informed me: that the lakes and the mountain range were fixed points; that the Blue Hooks had once encircled the realm entirely, and were known to stretch themselves on occasion; and that Lower Lake had a contrary streak and sometimes switched places with Silverlily.

On the faerie snails

After my unpleasant run-in with these uncanny denizens during my previous visit—I can still feel their shells breaking beneath my hands and knees, and hear their tiny screams of agony—I desired to know more about them. Wendell, though, would only shudder and advise me against making enemies of them. Apparently, they possess a crude intelligence and value their dignity above all things; as such, they spend most of their lives occupied with revenge quests. While their vengeance may be slow in coming, they always have it in the end.

On the bloody trees

I do not wish to write about these. But what sort of scholar of the Folk would I be if I hid from every horror?

No. I cannot do it.

But I must. Lord, what a mess of blotches and crossings-out this entry has become. Let us get this over with as quickly as possible.

The trees that give Wendell's realm its name are known as attentive oaks, a typical example of faerie euphemism. They are scattered here and there throughout the woodlands, though more often than not they lurk in the darker folds of the forest, the better to catch one by surprise and provide ample material for nightmares, I assume. Had each tree only a single pair of eyes, perhaps they would be bearable, but there are hundreds, if not thousands. For each leaf has an eye staring out of it, which may be creased in rage or widened in surprise, heavy-lidded or bloodshot, as if there is a unique personality trapped within every one, and all move to stare at you as you pass, rustling wetly.

Wendell, naturally, takes a philosophical view of these monstrosities. "Have you not seen worse in Faerie, Em?" he said. "Only leave them be, and you shall have nothing to fret about. Give them no reason to take offence."

"How does one avoid offending a tree?"

He began ticking things off on his fingers. "Don't insult them. Don't remove their leaves. Don't go tearing them open to see if there is a faerie king more agreeable to your tastes hiding inside."

I did not deign to reply to this. "That's all?"

He thought it over. "Mind your step in the autumn months."

God.

As we went on, I could not help noticing that the path Wendell made for us was a much cheerier one than Ariadne and I had followed; we traversed sunny glades and bluebell meadows, and sections of bilberry-studded moor open to the sky, often boasting impressive standing stones. Silver baubles sparkled in the treetops, about the size of globes and light as air, which sometimes drifted from one tree to another with the wind. Wendell informed me that these were, in fact, a kind of faerie stone, which contained enchantments meant to provide comfort to travellers. He warned me against breaking them, though, for some had been tampered with by bogles, and could no longer be trusted.

"Are you purposely keeping me from the darker parts of your realm?" I enquired, as the path brought us to an expansive view of Muckle Lake. "I have been here before, you know. I'm aware it is not all sun-splashed meadows and harmless archaeology, so you needn't act like a nervous suitor on his best behaviour."

He gave a surprised laugh, and I knew I had guessed close to the mark. "Can you blame me for wishing to impress you a little? Besides, the darker groves are home to some unpleasant bogles and beasts. I suspect they would bow to me, but I would rather not risk any unpleasantness. We will have plenty of that to go round once we reach the castle."

All the while, he used his magic carelessly in a way I have not seen from him before, like an aristocrat tossing coins from his carriage, pressing his hand to trees to quicken them or make them flower; summoning hosts of bluebells in meadows he complained were lacking in colour; and at one point ordering a craggy hill to move to one side so that we would not have to clamber up it. I watched him, my mind running through several theories.

We paused after an hour or so to take refreshments—his suggestion, of course—beside a stream that flowed through a sunny clearing. Wendell knocked upon a standing stone, and out rushed a pair of tiny brownies clutching a silver tray piled with lightly steaming scones. They placed them upon a rock at the edge of the stream, bowed to Wendell, then with nary a word spoken darted back behind the standing stone.

For a moment, I stood blinking at the place they had vanished. Then I shook myself.

You shall encounter stranger things than that *in this place*, I reminded myself sternly.

I settled beside Wendell, who had summoned one of the silver faerie stones and broken it against a rock, whereupon the shards transformed into a glittering tea set. He scooped stream water into each cup, gave it a swirl, and it was tea, piping hot and smelling of honey and wildflowers.

More magic, I thought, making another mental note.

"How far to the castle?" I enquired, sipping the tea—naturally, it was delicious, sweet and sharp together. "Will we pass through the barrows?"

"I'd rather not." He was swishing his hand absently through the rushing water, looking as pleased as a cat in a sunbeam. His beauty seemed to me to have assumed an even more ethereal quality since we'd stepped through the door—was it my imagination? His hair was like dark gold lit by firelight. "Most of the barrows encompass villages," he continued, "each with their own lord or lady."

I nodded. We'd agreed that the best course would be to

avoid alerting whoever held the castle to our presence, or any nobles who might use the information to their advantage.

"I hope we'll arrive before nightfall," he said, tearing off a piece of scone. "We must get past Muckle Lake, and I've no doubt we shall encounter dangers along the way. Beyond that—"

I waited, but he only made an expansive gesture that someone who didn't know him as well as I did might have found enchantingly mysterious. He finished, "We shall see."

I gazed at him for a moment, digesting this.

"You don't know where we are," I said in flat disbelief.

"Roughly, roughly." He looked puzzled by my consternation. "Well, what need would I have had to venture this far into the hinterlands? Of course, that isn't to say I never left the castle grounds when I was growing up. Many of the nobility are exceedingly fond of the Hanging Pools, where the river Brightmist spills down a ravine and forms a series of crystalline ponds, perfect for bathing in. And then there is the forest of Wildwood and its bog, hunting grounds forbidden to all but the monarchy and our chosen companions, where one finds uncommonly large boars and the rarest species of deer, which possess antlers of pure silver . . ."

He continued his rhapsodies concerning the bathing pools and hunting grounds. When at last he paused for breath, I said, attempting to keep my voice level, "Wendell. We are here to conquer your kingdom. This will be difficult if you do not know the way to the bloody *throne*. Now, answer me one way or the other—are we lost?"

"Oh, Em," he said fondly. "You worry too much—remember that we are in my kingdom, not some Godforsaken ice court or mountain wasteland. No, we are not lost, not in the sense you mean. I know where the castle is—what does it matter where *we* are?"

On that infuriatingly nonsensical note, he was off to rap on the standing stone again, this time after a little jam for the scones.

Lest any assume that Wendell and I marched into one of the most dangerous Faerie realms on record without any strategizing whatsoever, I assure you it was not so.

"We should review the possibilities," I had said one late October night as we sat by the fire in Wendell's apartments. It was a week or two after our return from Austria.

He had looked up from the book he'd been reading—some silly romance or other; he doesn't read much, and when he does, his taste is questionable. "Hmm?"

"For whom we might be facing when we return to your realm," I said. "If your stepmother is dead, who might have stepped in to claim the throne? Who would have the standing, the influence, to earn the loyalty of the nobility? Perhaps your stepmother's half-brother, Lord Taran?"

"Taran?" Wendell tilted his chin back, thinking it over. "He never struck me as particularly power-hungry. I suppose it's possible, though. As I said before, Em, I had little to do with him, and he with me. My uncle is ancient, and would have viewed me as a silly child, beneath his notice."

I felt a prickle of frustration. "Well, who else is there? Had your father any siblings?"

"Oh—a brother or two." He thought. "Two. He had them executed long before I was born."

"Good Lord," I muttered. I'd known Wendell's court was a nest of vipers, but I was beginning to suspect the stories were, if anything, rosier than the reality.

"Who else?" I pressed. "Cousins? A well-liked advisor? Friends?"

"My father's only true friend was my mother." Wendell's gaze drifted towards the fire. "He always said so. They were everywhere in accord, their opinions and preferences so similar. Only she was of *oíche sidhe* blood, but one would have thought he too was descended from the little housekeepers. I suppose that is partly why he married her, despite the taboo. Everything had to be meticulously clean, under my father's roof. And he and my mother would sew and weave together, combining their magics to produce such kingly attire as has never been seen before . . . not only clothes, but hunting nets that could snare the most formidable quarry, and pennants so intricately woven and bright it was said that my father's enemies could not help staring at them even in the heat of battle." He gazed into the flames. "After my mother died, I don't know that he was close to anyone. My eldest sister, perhaps. But she is gone too."

He shook himself and reached for his teacup. Though his subsequent exile pained him, I have rarely had the impression that Wendell is much touched by his family's murder, something I have generally put down to his faerie nature. It is less troubling that way, which is not to say that it *isn't* troubling. At a fundamental level, the Folk are not like mortals, a fact which, at times, I still struggle to connect with Wendell. I waited to see if he would go on, but he did not.

"You said your stepmother had children," I pressed. "That she wanted to see her own flesh and blood on the throne."

"Yes—once she'd finished with it," he said drily. "She and my father had one daughter, who was a child when her mother decided to murder her father and half-siblings." He rubbed his forehead. "Deilah. She would still be very young—it's hard to imagine the nobility taking her seriously. I don't know. I've no doubt there *are* plenty of Folk with designs on my throne. But I know so little about politics."

I shook my head. "Surely your father gave you some form of a political education. Surely you learned *something,* watching him."

"Em—" Wendell closed his book, his expression taking on a pained quality. "I was barely nineteen when I was exiled. At that age, Folk are viewed as near infants, at least as far as our wisdom goes. We are expected to attend revels and balls, and more revels and balls, and cause a variety of minor troubles for our parents, and that is the extent of it." He sighed. "I was perhaps more fond of parties than the average youth. My father could not have had a lower opinion of my political capabilities. Besides, I had five brothers and sisters between me and the throne, and even given my kingdom's penchant for assassinations, few thought I'd get anywhere near it."

I paused as the weight of what he was saying sank in. "Then—you haven't the slightest idea how to rule a kingdom."

"Does anyone?" He took my hand, discomfort shifting suddenly into earnestness. "We will learn together."

"Oh God," I said faintly.

He studied me. "Is it that bad? You already know more about faerie kingdoms than any mortal."

"Stories," I said faintly, drawing my hand back. "I know *stories.*"

He gave me an odd look. "And have you ever needed anything else? Have you not shaken a kingdom to its foundations, found a door to a distant otherland, overthrown a queen? Hand you the right storybook, and you are capable of anything."

Well, I doubt I need describe how little comfort I took from his absolute faith in me. I've always known Wendell squandered much of his youth, but I assumed he had learned *something* about his court, about what it meant to wield power. Now I understood the truth: he knew nothing about kingship, and yet, on the eve of claiming his throne, viewed this fact as largely immaterial, if it had even occurred to him before. Small wonder some dryadologists believe all faeries are mad.

"I am a *scholar*," I said. "I observe. I record. I don't—no one will ever see me as a queen."

"No?" He opened his book again. "More fool them. I suppose I could simply follow my father's playbook and send Razkarden to pluck out my enemies' eyes and entrails."

I could not tell if he was joking or not, which put paid to my desire to pursue the discussion. And that, more or less, is where we left things.

Though I did not stop thinking about it.

I thought about it as we walked, the weight of my bag shifting against my back. I had packed four books—two of which I smuggled out of the special collections section of Cambridge's dryadology library,[*] which grates at my conscience, but I cannot see what else I could have done; one cannot mind library due dates in a world where time is liable to rearrange itself—all of which deal with the politics of faerie courts, what little is known of them. While it has long been assumed that the lords and ladies of Faerie rule primarily through might, the nobility being more skilled at enchantment than the rest of the courtly fae, recent scholarship has done much to challenge the notion that faerie monarchs are inept at strategizing or other conventional leadership skills.[†] And, indeed, the

---

[*] *The Irish Monarchs: Tales of Fayerie Kings and Queens from the Pre-Christian to the Modern Era*, by John Murphy, 1772; and *The Mirror King: A Speculative Biography of Scotland's Oldest Faerie Lord*, by Douglas Treleaven, 1810.

[†] See, for example, Anna Queiroz's recent article on the two faerie kingdoms of Madeira, one of which has long been depicted in local folklore as a grey and unpleasant land ruled by a rapacious king, while the other is ruled by a king and queen who, among other things, hold regular tribunals to resolve disputes and regularly abduct mortal musicians to write propaganda ballads about their

rise of Wendell's stepmother, a halfblood, to the throne offers more evidence to bolster this perspective.

I have not said much to Wendell about this, because the project is at present only a half-formed idea, but I have begun taking notes on the principles of faerie leadership that I have gleaned from my readings. It goes without saying that no dryadologist before me has actually *witnessed* the ruling of a faerie court from the throne itself, and thus no one has ever been better placed than I to write a book on faerie politics.

Even thinking those words sends a frisson of anticipation through me. If Wendell's stepmother has us slain before I have a chance to contribute to the scholarly debate, I will be very disappointed.

A great deal of whispering followed Wendell and me as we made our way through the forest. I had the sense of being regarded by many pairs of eyes, but no Folk, either courtly or common, dared to greet us.

"If only we could glean some news," I said. The frustrating truth is that we know next to nothing about what we will be facing. I have spoken with Poe, who has proven himself an uncommonly good source of gossip due to the volume of visitors he receives from disparate faerie realms, but he knew only that Wendell's kingdom fell into chaos after I poisoned its queen. Wandering Folk, according to Poe, tend to avoid realms in such states of turmoil.

Wendell looked around. "Why not ask her?"

"Who?"

Wendell just kept on staring at a branch. "You needn't cower. I am not going to harm you."

I waited, but no response came from the forest, nor any

---

reign; their kingdom is much larger, and home to some of the most fantastical revels known to scholarship, generally a marker of a prosperous faerie realm.

sign of movement. Wendell made an exasperated sound and plucked the faerie off the branch—the faerie that I had not seen, who wore a cloak of woven moss. With the hood drawn up, crouched as she had been, she was merely a bend in the bough, an inconsequential vagary in the forest's pattern.

The brownie gave a panicked squawk before going still again. She could not have been more than a foot high, with a cherubic face half covered in moss and the all-black eyes that are commonplace in creatures of her type.

"Your Highness!" the brownie cried in her small voice. "I did not see you! Forgive me!" As soon as Wendell set her down, she threw herself onto her face at his feet, jabbering something I could not make out—more apologies, I believe, only she also mentioned moss a great deal, making or mending it, I think, perhaps to give to Wendell as a present? The logic was difficult to glean.

"Please stand," Wendell said. "I am not anybody's Highness at present, so you needn't—oh, this is tedious."

The annoyance in his voice seemed to penetrate the faerie's desperation more than his words. The creature stood, shivering.

"We are not going to harm you," I repeated, but she only looked at me miserably. I felt a surge of pity.

Wendell swept his cloak to one side and crouched before the faerie. "Now," he said, "answer me quickly, and you shall return to your moss-den all the sooner. What has happened to my realm?"

The faerie began to jabber again, coupling this with a great deal of hand-wringing and elaborate gesticulations. Again I could make out very little of what she was saying, despite my fluency in Faie; the brownie mumbled and spoke in a dialect that seemed to have a great deal of Irish mixed in. After listening for a moment, Wendell held up a hand.

"Nothing particularly useful," he said to me, standing. "The little ones have been greatly troubled of late by Folk charging about on their steeds, trampling their burrows. Battles have been waged, and a great deal of magic expended, sending brownies like this one into a panic. Some have fled into the mountains, abandoning their homes altogether." He looked genuinely upset. "But they do not know what is happening, nor the players involved, only that their lives have been made very unpleasant. What a mess!"

He rubbed his hand through his hair. "It began with my stepmother—her decision to enlarge her kingdom by conquering the neighbouring realms; not an event appreciated, it seems, by all the inhabitants, who send regular raiding parties to harass our Folk. Things have grown only more unstable since your visit."

I addressed the brownie. "Does the queen live?"

More gesticulating and dense dialect. This time, even Wendell looked confused.

"Yes?" he said. "But there's something else—she says my stepmother has fled. Though the little one uses an odd word for it. One that describes how a fallen leaf decays into soil, becoming part of the forest floor."

We looked at each other, and I saw that we were in agreement; something in this boded ill. "Anything else?" I said.

"There is a battleground near—the little one offered to show us. We may learn something there."

"All right," I said, and we set off, the faerie a green ripple of movement on the path ahead.

30th December

Well! I have a great deal to recount since I last opened this journal, and I scarcely know how to feel about any of it. Hardly a new sensation since taking up with Wendell.

The battleground was an area of moorland beside a marsh, an offshoot of Muckle Lake, I think. Small embers of light floated here and there—the remnants of magic expended during the battle, which looked a great deal like will-o'-the-wisps.* There were also several inexplicable elements, foremost of which was an ivied staircase leading to nothing, and what I can only describe as a giant fox frozen halfway into the process of transforming into a tree. An attentive oak had been cleft perfectly in two, with a neat passage between, though

---

* Possibly the most widely misidentified faerie species. Even experienced dryadologists have been known to mistake natural phenomena, fireflies, or indeed other forms of faerie activity for will-o'-the-wisps. Found in old-growth forests throughout the world, these nocturnal trooping faeries are barely two inches in height, and most of that is their mothlike wings, which dwarf their tiny bodies. They were once believed to be bioluminescent, but Sofia Wagner's 1822–24 field study in Belgium demonstrated that, in fact, each wisp carries a glass lantern with a tiny flame inside it, which Wagner posited is used for communication (a theory supported by Brendan O'Reagan, whose 1906 book, *Fireglass*, attempted to decode this language of magical Aldis lamps). Contrary to popular belief, stories of errant mortals led into the wilderness by drifting lights can generally be attributed to bogles, not wisps, which are notoriously shy; if they perceive they are under mortal observation, they will usually flick their lights off and vanish into the nearest knothole.

this did not seem to have killed the thing, unfortunately. Occasionally there came a sort of roaring sound, which seemed to emanate from beneath the earth. On the whole I was content *not* to have witnessed the enchantments that had been cast during the heat of the fighting.

There were no bodies, either dead or wounded. The only movement came from the wind brushing calmly over the ferns that spilled out from the forest's edge. A great many theories seek to explain what happens to the bodies of the Folk after they die; scholars have documented the remains of a fair few species of common fae—indeed, some are housed in Cambridge's Museum of Dryadology and Ethnofolklore—but not of the courtly fae. The leading theory among mortuary dryadologists is that, for most of the courtly fae, there is an evanescence of some sort, perhaps after a period of time has elapsed. The stories do not agree on this point, however, and it remains one of the questions that, for reasons likely pertaining to my own weaknesses, I have avoided asking Wendell.

"The worst of the fighting took place beyond that rise," Wendell said.

"You go," I said, eyeing Shadow, who had bent his head to drink from a creek. He had been lagging behind for the past hour, requiring us to slow our pace. "I'll remain with him. I believe he will appreciate the rest."

"Poor dear," Wendell said, bending to rub Shadow's ears. "When I retake my throne, I shall dedicate a fleet of servants to his needs. They shall make for him a velvet bed in every room, with a fire burning beside each one, and the bones of my enemies will be preserved for his enjoyment."

"That started off well, but I did not care for the ending," I said.

Naturally, Wendell only laughed at this and set off for the hill. I had one of my moments of existential panic, in which

I question everything that has led me to this point, before burying it under thoughts of a more practical nature, as I always do. If I one day erupt into uncontrollable screams and go charging into the woods, tearing at my hair, who but Wendell will be to blame?

I dug out the salve I use for Shadow's arthritis and rubbed it into the dog's ankles. He closed his eyes in contentment and rolled onto his side, enjoying the sun on his fur, though this did not lessen my worry. He is too old for such long walks now, preferring to spend the majority of his day napping by the fire.

"All right, my love?" I murmured, rubbing the dog's ears.

Shadow gave a huff and thumped his tail against the grass.

Our little army did not join me in the clearing, but lurked in the shadows of the forest—I am uncertain if this was preferable for my nerves, but at least I didn't have to look at them. With the exception of Snowbell, of course, who hopped onto my lap and gave me an expectant look. I scratched behind his ears warily—an enjoyable experience for him, I suppose, but less so for me, given that the fox-faerie tends to tire of affection without warning and lunge snarling at my fingers.

"I know the best way to the castle," Snowbell complained, flicking his tail. "It would be faster if we went *my* way."

"You tell that to His Royal Highness, then." I knew the creature would do no such thing, of course, and was merely boasting for the sake of it.

"Your coat is marvellously shiny today," I told him, just to forestall any more tedious complaints. Sure enough, the faerie sat up straighter and hopped onto the ground to preen in a patch of sunlight, the better to show himself off.

I spent a contented half hour or so finishing the previous journal entry. I was just opening my pack to locate a book when Lord Taran came striding into the clearing.

"There you are," he said in a dismissive manner, as if we had been at tea and I had wandered off for a moment.

I started to my feet with a smothered cry, my journal and pen spilling onto the grass, and backed away from him. He stopped and regarded me calmly, cool and collected as could be in spite of the massive sword he carried, its blade dark and wet, not to mention the stains upon his silver-threaded tunic and spray of blood across his pale face. It was abundantly clear that he had played a significant part in the battle in this grove.

I, on the other hand, was far from calm. Lord Taran was not a large man—his height was average for the courtly fae, who tend to be a little taller than mortals—but his presence had a weight to it that made it difficult to look away from him, much as I wanted to. Sometimes, when I blinked, I beheld from behind my eyelids a creature as skeletal as branches, covered in glittering moss like tattered finery. He had reminded me of the Hidden king when last we met, but when I looked into the Hidden king's eyes, I had seen towering glaciers and snowy wastes; when I met Lord Taran's gaze, I saw the impenetrable darkness at the heart of an ancient forest.

"I—my apologies, my lord," I stammered, sketching a hasty curtsy. "I did not expect you to grace me with your—"

"Never mind that," he said, pushing the dark hair off his brow. "Did our dear departed prince not deign to accompany you this time? Or are you here to make off with another cat? He had only the one, you know."

There was amusement in his gaze, but it was not a friendly thing—far from it. I sensed a fundamental cruelty in the mordant way he examined me, held in check by something I did not understand.

I did not know what sort of reply would please him, so I simply went with my instincts. "One cat is more than enough for me, thank you. I have come for a throne this time."

He smiled, and my legs wobbled with relief.

"Have you?" he said. "Well, why not? This kingdom has been ruled by halfbloods and housekeepers; a mortal queen is hardly going to lower us further."

And just like that, I was on solid ground. *Solider*, at any rate; whatever else this man was, he was every bit as snobbish as the majority of the courtly fae.

"Why not take the throne yourself, if you are so bothered by the pedigree of its previous occupants?" I asked, which was brazen, but then many of the courtly fae are charmed by boldness in mortals, in much the same way that we coo when a kitten bares its teeth.

He snorted. "I value my neck, that's why. Which I have managed to keep intact for many centuries—far longer than those who covet power in this bloody wolf's den of a court."

This was so far from what I had expected that I was silent for a moment. "Wise of you," I said.

The malicious amusement was back. "Thank you—I cannot tell you how highly I value the opinions of mortals, particularly young girls who cannot stop themselves from stumbling into violent faerie realms."

"It's not necessary to be rude," I said, nettled. "And for your information, I am thirty-one years old." I was feeling much calmer now, because I no longer felt it likely that he wanted to harm me; not out of any sense of morality, but because— I sensed—I was providing him with enough amusement to stay his hand.

"We are capable of wisdom, Professor Wilde," he said. "Some of us. Now, where is Prince Liath?"

I don't know how I kept my composure at that. Of course I knew that Wendell had another name, but I have never asked for it—I suppose because part of me does not wish to think of him as anything other than Wendell. I also knew, because

Wendell had told me, that the Folk rarely refer to each other by name, not even by the shortened form of their true names, which has no magic.* I had inferred from Wendell's vague explanations that to do so is seen as rude, not unlike a mortal using the Christian name of someone they do not know very well. Instead they prefer to use "Uncle," "Weaver," "Lady," and so forth. It is a fascinating example of faerie etiquette, no doubt springing from their aversion to giving away their true names; I can think of at least four possible approaches to tackling the question in a research paper.

"If I knew where he was, I would have told you already," I said, after only the slightest of pauses. "I have not been prevented by my enthusiasm for conversing with powerful Folk covered in blood."

"He will come when you call him," Taran said, almost gently.

I studied him—I don't know what I expected to glean from doing so; it was like trying to interpret the motives of a god. I took a breath and shouted, "Wendell!"

For a moment, I just felt silly. A very short moment, because I had not drawn half a breath before Wendell stepped out of a tree.

I wish I could say that I have grown used to him doing this, but in truth, I have not, and I had to stifle a childish shriek. There is something about the manner in which he does it that is deeply troubling; perhaps if there were a puff of smoke, or

---

* "Rumpelstiltskin" is, of course, the most famous story of a faerie foiled by his own name, but plenty of others exist, notably "Old Erenondalen" (Norway) and "Lammy Boggs" (Britain). Due to the rarity of scholarly encounters with the courtly fae, and the offence many common fae take at enquiries regarding their names, little is known about the actual power these have, and whether knowing a faerie's full name would be tantamount to holding them in thrall. Those few common fae who have entrusted scholars with their names have given them only a piece, sometimes the first half and others the second, and sometimes, as with Lewis Hartland's henkie, Wattle, a childhood nickname.

a tremor, or *something* to denote there is magic afoot, it would not be so bad, but he simply steps out of trees as if they are empty doorframes.

He looked from me to Taran, showing a complete lack of surprise but plenty of hostility. He was holding a sword, which I assumed he'd obtained from the battlefield. "What are you doing, Uncle?"

"Talking, my dear," Lord Taran said. "What does it look like?"

"It *looks* as if you are looming over my betrothed with a sword."

"Wendell," I said, suddenly alarmed, because his expression had begun to take on a quality I had seen before, a malevolent sort of calm. I was decidedly of the opinion that we did not want to make an enemy of Lord Taran if we did not need to, nor of his friends, who I doubted would appreciate it if Wendell flew into a rage and decapitated him.

But Lord Taran only tapped his sword idly against the ground, looking Wendell up and down. "How touchy you are!" he said. "Your grandmother's temper has skipped a generation, has it? Your father didn't inherit it, bloodthirsty as he was at the end. And, of course, your mother was more likely to take her frustrations out on the laundry, like most of her kind. But you prefer swords to brooms, do you? How conventional."

"Wendell, he helped me," I said quickly. "He helped *us*. He showed me a way into the castle. I doubt I could have healed you if he had not."

Wendell merely gave me a puzzled look, as if unclear why this would be relevant.

"I did, didn't I?" Taran said. "That was more Callum's idea than mine, though; he has always disliked my sister for the wars she is so fond of starting. He would prefer to see you on the throne, Prince, despite your youth. He believes that returning to the former king's line would offer the realm more stability." He spread his hands. "Now, I prefer to stay out of politics, but as someone who has always valued his neck, I cannot find fault with this argument, and anyway I am generally inclined to give Callum whatever he wants, regardless of whether I see the sense of it. But, ah! There is the little matter of my oath to your father." He gave a wince that seemed calculated to appear as insincere as possible. "You see, the old king had little love for his firstborn—your eldest brother, Prince— who was rather boorish and stupid, and besides that quite unskilled magically. So the king made me swear that I would not allow anyone to ascend the throne who was not stronger than the king himself. I believe he wished for me to murder his firstborn, so that his second—your eldest sister—would be first in the line of succession. No doubt he was surprised when I stood back and allowed my own sister to murder her way to the throne, but then, I was only fulfilling my oath, was I not? She proved herself to be stronger than her husband, in her own way."

He heaved a sigh. I had the distinct impression that he was enjoying himself, that cruel amusement lurking behind every sorrowful gesture. "Now we have come to the crux of it, Prince—you see, I cannot let you leave until you have proven yourself stronger than your father. If you return to the castle and win back the throne, I will have broken my oath."

Wendell did not seem nonplussed by any part of this absurd speech. He appeared lost in thought, his head tilted slightly. He turned and gave me a look I did not understand, something measuring. I know now that he was looking not at me, but my cloak.

"We should—" I began. I don't know what I meant to say— whether I had any actual advice to offer, or if I simply wished to stall, to give us time to think our way out of this new peril. It didn't matter, because in the space of a breath, Lord Taran had gone from leaning casually on his sword to driving it towards Wendell's chest.

Wendell swore and dove out of the way. Even I started backwards, though I was nowhere near the blade—the speed and ferocity of Taran's movement was unlike anything I'd seen before. Wendell landed in a clutch of ferns, vanishing into the greenery as if it were a deep pool—a fraction of a second later, Taran's sword had lopped the heads off them.

"Your father could not beat me," Taran said, turning to scan the glade, for Wendell had not reappeared. "He was the greatest swordsman I have ever fought, yet in the end I always triumphed when we played at swords. So, Prince—simply disarm me once, and I shall consider the matter settled. You will have proven yourself stronger than your father."

"Wendell, this is ridiculous," I cried. Shadow, at my side, was growling low in his throat. I stood, trying to work out where Wendell might be. "We can negotiate our way out of this, surely."

"I'm afraid not." Wendell reappeared from a tree on the other side of the stream. He was eyeing Lord Taran warily, which made me still, because Wendell with a sword is normally the picture of self-assurance. "His life is forfeit if he breaks his oath."

Lord Taran nodded. "As I said—I value my neck."

"Oh, for—" I began, my voice hitching, because I could not believe that it might end here, after everything. Surely there was something I was missing, some other way out—

Taran charged, but this time, Wendell was ready. Their swords met in a flurry of silver, the sun striking the blades and throwing flashes of blinding light across the clearing. Dark spots flitted across my eyes, but I forced myself to watch—little good it did me. They moved so quickly that I couldn't follow it at all; it was like trying to map the diamond scatter of sunlight on a heaving sea. When they broke apart, Wendell was on the other side of the creek, Taran gazing at him from across the bank.

"You are—" Lord Taran paused. He did not appear surprised—I wonder if he is still capable of such an emotion—but there was new interest in his gaze. "It is like fighting your father again."

"No one has ever beaten me at swords before," Wendell said, almost absently.

"Nor me," Taran said. "I suppose that is why your grandfather, the old king, named me his general. And his mother before him. Your father tried—but I am done with war."

He spoke with neither malice nor amusement now, only a fathomless tranquillity, and for a moment I felt I could hear the aeons echoing through his voice. Wendell is uncertain how long his father's reign lasted by mortal reckoning, only that it was centuries, not years. And Lord Taran had seen at least two monarchs rise and fall before him?

"Wendell—" I tried again as dread settled in my chest.

But again, Lord Taran did not allow me to finish. He was across the water and forcing Wendell back before even the splashes made by his boots had fallen into the stream. Wendell parried and dodged with impossible grace, but he was losing ground. He stumbled, and Lord Taran moved to take advantage of his distraction, but then suddenly Wendell was under his guard, slashing at Lord Taran's side.

Taran laughed. He fell back, pressing his hand to his ribs. When he lifted it, his palm was red. "Your father's son, indeed," he said, and for the first time, there was warmth in his voice.

Wendell was breathing rapidly, his hair in disarray. I had

seen him fight before, but I had never seen him fight like this—superficially, he still looked like Wendell, and yet at the same time he seemed to have shed some part of the human façade that he wore. If I'm honest, it was terrifying. There was a moment when some animal part of me lost all interest in who won, and simply wished to be *away* from these otherworldly terrors.

But it wasn't enough. Wendell was clearly spent, and needed a moment to rest. Lord Taran did not give it to him.

His sword met Wendell's with such force that I expected the blades to shatter. Wendell parried, barely, and then leapt into the tree behind him. Lord Taran lifted his sword—

And sliced the tree in two.

It was almost a casual movement. One moment, the tree was whole. The next, its trunk wobbled and began to fall forward. Lord Taran moved aside unhurriedly, already scanning the grove again, and the tree toppled behind him with a thunderous crash. Several faeries about the size of my hand darted out from among the branches, wailing and dragging little satchels of clothing and what looked like tiny drums behind them.

Wendell emerged to Lord Taran's left, his sword already flashing, and the other man was forced back towards the stream. Momentarily. I had the terrible impression that the character of the fight had changed, that Lord Taran had solved something in Wendell, and was now merely drawing things out for the sake of it.

My supposition was proven correct moments later, when Lord Taran's sword slashed beneath Wendell's guard. It caught only the edge of his cloak, but Wendell was truly off-balance this time, and abruptly, Taran's sword was swinging at Wendell's head.

I screamed. But before the sword could fall, there was a

flash of black, a shadow rising from a hollow in the ground. Orga twined around Taran's feet, and he staggered, falling onto one knee. His sword sliced harmlessly through the air by Wendell's shoulder.

"What's this?" Taran demanded. Then, to my astonishment, he added in a tone of affection, "Betrayal? I kept this one fed during your absence, Prince. I have always liked cats. It seems she has changed her mind about me, though."

"Orga cares even less for my enemies than I do," Wendell said unevenly. "After this, you can expect her to spend the rest of her days orchestrating your demise."

Lord Taran did not shrug this off as easily as I expected him to. In fact, he looked quite disturbed. But then he shook his head.

"So be it," he said, and their swords clashed again. I thought, for a brief moment, that Wendell had recovered his strength, for he parried with his usual agility—but then there was a flash of light sailing across the clearing, and I realized it was Wendell's sword, caught in the sunlight as it rotated around on itself.

Wendell stumbled back. For a brief moment, Lord Taran looked disappointed. But then it slipped away, replaced by something ancient and inscrutable, and he was lifting his sword again—

And I was running, yelling God knows what—something about oaths, I think, for I had been scouring my memory during the entirety of the duel, searching for a way out. I had come up with three or four possibilities, the most compelling of which pertained to an Irish tale in which a rural baker makes an ill-advised pledge to a faerie lord in exchange for eternally soft loaves.[*]

---

[*] "The Laughing Stove," which can be found in J. P. Gillen's *Anthology of Irish*

At the same time, Wendell shouted, "Your cloak, Em!"

My mind was like a sword in that moment, honed by terror, moving more quickly than I was conscious of, and I understood what Wendell wanted and why. Lord Taran's words reshaped themselves to fit the pattern of a dozen stories, and I saw the door in them—the way out.

I wrenched my cloak off my shoulders and flung it at Wendell. He caught it one-handed, and for a moment held it between himself and Taran like a shield.

It was a ridiculous gesture to my eyes, but Taran didn't seem to think so; he fell back a step, his brow furrowed. Wendell gave the cloak a shake, like the gesture one might make to unroll a carpet, and the hem of the cloak spilled across the clearing, a black and rippling shadow.

Lord Taran recoiled. "What have you done? That isn't—"

"It is," Wendell said. He was still breathing unevenly, but he no longer looked liable to collapse from exhaustion. "A fragment of the Veil, which I sewed into the hem. A window, if you like. What better ward is there against the Folk?"

"That should not be possible," Lord Taran said, which represented perhaps the only moment in which we two would understand each other. He was not looking at Wendell, but at the cloak, tensing each time it fluttered in the wind.

Wendell shrugged. "You said I must be stronger than my father. But you did not specify by what measure, when you made your oath. Indeed, my stepmother could not have beaten her husband in a swordfight—her strength is of the mind. Well, I have the stronger eye for needlework. You no doubt saw the garments my father made and mended—I already know that you never saw the equal to this."

Lord Taran was silent. He was not so difficult to read now—

Folklore from the Viking Era: A Cross-Cultural Analysis, 8th ed., 1908.

there was real trepidation in his eyes, and I remembered what Wendell had said about the Veil, and that all Folk fear it.*

Wendell straightened with a wince, supporting himself with a branch. I went to his side to put my arm around him, not caring, in that moment, if Lord Taran decided to slice through *me* to get to Wendell, because I had noticed that he was bleeding—at least a dozen small slashes along his arms and side.

"He is correct, of course," I said to Lord Taran. "Faerie oaths have a great deal of loopholes, but yours seems particularly open to interpretation."

"Yes, yes," Lord Taran said, sheathing his sword hurriedly. "I am satisfied. You can—put that away now."

I was not enthused about putting *that* away; I had known Wendell had enchanted my cloak in myriad ways, but I hadn't known there was a window to some hellish otherworld sewn into it, and now that I did I was more inclined to light the thing on fire. But Wendell looked pleased, as if Lord Taran had given his workmanship a great compliment, and a part of me felt a kernel of smugness amidst the terror of owning so fearsome a garment, so I allowed him to help me back into it. The hem rippled and shrank until it was once again an ordinary—though immaculately tailored—cloak.

"You could have asked for my cloak first instead of duelling him," I pointed out. I felt lightheaded with relief, and also as if I might burst into hysterical giggles, which I preferred to avoid in front of Lord Taran.

"I thought I could win," Wendell said. He did not seem put out by his defeat, but almost cheerful. "And anyway, I have al-

---

* After an exhaustive search, I have come to the conclusion that no academic literature exists concerning this mysterious "Veil," a Faerie realm that only monarchs may access. I believe I am the only scholar to learn of it, or at least the only surviving scholar.

ways wanted to duel my uncle. He is said to be the best swordsman in the realm. It's been a while since I had so much fun."

"He nearly decapitated you!" I exclaimed.

"Yes, but *besides* that, Em," he said patiently.

Lord Taran retrieved Wendell's sword and handed it to him, hilt-first. Wendell accepted it with a look of regret.

"I would like for us to do this again," he said.

"God," I muttered.

"Not *to the death,* obviously."

"As you wish, my king," Taran said. He pronounced the word with a grimace, as if it had a sour taste. "Back to the rule of housekeepers, it seems."

"Shall we have some refreshments?" Wendell said, and they strode back to the stream, talking of tea, as if they had not just been trying to kill each other.

Orga, though, was not so easily appeased. After Lord Taran had settled himself elegantly on a flat stone, she crept up behind him and slashed at his ankle.

Lord Taran swore, pulling up his trouser leg to reveal a line of bright red. "Yes, it is clear that our friendship is at an end," he said, sounding regretful. "Not that we were ever the best of friends; I can recall only two occasions when she deigned to let me stroke her. Come to think of it, you are the only person I know to have formed such a bond with the cat *sidhe*."

Wendell waved a hand. "My Emily has a grim."

Lord Taran examined me, and then Shadow at my side, new interest sharpening his gaze. "A mortal?"

"Are you so astonished by my mortality that you must mention it every other minute?" I said, because, like Orga, I was not so ready to forgive him. "Your husband must find this tedious."

Lord Taran laughed. I did not have the sense that the cruelty in him had faded, only that he had sheathed it somehow, as he had his sword.

Conscious of the absurdity of the situation, I removed the leftover scones from my pack, as well as the teacups from the faerie stone. There was a third cup in my pack now. I handed one of the scones to Lord Taran.

"Thank you," he said. "These look excellent."

Wendell scooped water from the stream into one of the cups and handed it to Lord Taran. I watched very closely, but still I could not pinpoint the exact moment when it turned into tea. It seemed as if a shadow had fallen upon it, and then it began to steam.

"Ha!" Lord Taran took an appreciative sniff. "That's the one. Your father used to call for it on Harvest Market mornings."

"Now, tell me," Wendell said, once we all had our tea. "What has become of the rhododendron meadow?"

I could not believe he was asking about flowers, what with everything else we had to worry about, and opened my mouth to tell him so, but he only touched my hand and said, "It's an important matter, Em."

"You know my dear sister hated the place," Lord Taran said. "She ordered the gardeners to neglect it. And, well—I'm afraid it's been claimed by the Deer."

"One more thing for the to-do list," Wendell said with a sigh.

"What on earth does that mean?" I said.

Wendell looked apologetic. "All lands claimed by the hag-headed deer are—unfriendly places. They have a tendency to go feral."

While I contemplated what feral rhododendrons might look like, Lord Taran said, "Enough small talk, Your Highness—you must satisfy my curiosity. We have heard all manner of rumours about you over the years. You are employed at a mortal school as a common labourer, some say; others, that you have been in the north, harassing one of the winter kings."

"Oh, that," Wendell said, and launched into an account of our adventures in Ljosland, the bulk of which consisted of hyperbolic descriptions of snow and cold. Lord Taran seemed particularly interested in the concept of glaciers, and asked a number of questions. I waited, tamping down my impatience, until there was a break in the conversation.

"Whom were you fighting before we arrived, sir?" I asked, using a respectful form of address for the courtly fae, which they use to address one another, but not the *most* respectful form, which is used by brownies and the like. If Lord Taran took issue with this, I did not particularly care. The word has no direct translation, but shares a root with the Faie word for *musician,* an intriguing quirk that has been the subject of much scholarly debate.

"Oh, it was invaders from—" He used a word I had not heard before. The rough translation is *Where the Ravens Hide*.

"One of the realms conquered by my stepmother," Wendell explained. "Scholars call it the Silva Orchis. Unpleasant place—bloody mountains everywhere." He looked thoughtful. "I wonder if I could order the mountains in my realm to depart? We have hills enough—what more does one need?"

Lord Taran shrugged, evidently not much interested in the matter. "Anyway—the battle began with the invaders. But then some of the queen's soldiers leapt into the fray—her personal guard remains loyal to the death and have generally been making a nuisance of themselves. They organized a performance last night in the castle gardens in which a dozen singers and flutists serenaded us with tedious ballads about disloyalty being the seed of decay; traitors must be put to death, etcetera. They kept at it all night; I slept very poorly. So I formed an alliance with Where the Ravens Hide and slew the moralizers instead." He paused, seeming to consider. "I wonder where the invaders got to afterwards?"

"Good Lord!" Wendell said. "Flutes and minstrels—could they not have hired a harpist or two?"

"That's just it—one cannot expect good taste from the warrior class," Taran said.

"Who holds the throne now?" I interjected. Navigating the conversation was beginning to feel like swimming against a tumultuous and mercurial current.

Lord Taran sipped his tea. "Yesterday, it was one of the old king's advisors. The day before that, the head of the queen's guard tried to make himself regent in the queen's absence. Thankfully, he was slain before he could make us sit through any ballads. Today—oh, who can say?"

"And where is my stepmother?" Wendell said.

Lord Taran spread his hand. "Dead, I presume. Well, she was dying when last I saw her. The poison caused a rapid deterioration in her health—you were perhaps overgenerous in your dosage, my dear." He gave me a smile that I did not find pleasant. "She had her guards spirit her away somewhere before she could actually expire—I expect it was to spite you, Your Highness. You would have had an easier path to the throne if her death was irrefutable; now, though, those loyal to the queen will have an excuse to stay loyal."

Wendell looked downcast at that, but then he shrugged. "I will fight them, I suppose."

"And you will win," Lord Taran said. "Of that I have no doubt. But there are so many contenders for the throne that it will be a long and tedious business. Many of the queen's inner circle, as well as the old king's, share my opinion that you are too young to rule. Others dislike you for the same reason they disliked your mother, the old queen—they do not wish to be ruled by one descended from the small Folk, particularly the *oíche sidhe*. It is unnatural."

"Actually," I said, as I leafed through the stories in my mind, organizing them like papers on a desk, "the real worry is that your enemies may *not* attempt to fight you. Instead they will smile and bow and make pretty speeches, and behind your back hire assassins or poisoners. It is, after all, one of the things your court is known for."

Wendell groaned and rubbed a hand through his hair. Then he seemed to take note of something in my voice. He examined my face, and began to smile. "You've had an idea, haven't you, Em? Please say yes."

"I think," I said slowly, "that we need your court to fear you. Enough that they will be too afraid to stand against you."

"Well, of course; everyone is afraid of children," Lord Taran said. "And what a fearsome reputation this one has! They say he was almost always the last to leave a party. Now he returns with a rumpled little scholar at his side! His enemies will be quaking."

Wendell had not taken his gaze off me. "How?"

"Your trick with the cloak has given me an idea," I said, resisting the urge to straighten the wrinkles out of my skirt.

Lord Taran's smirk vanished. "You cannot think to throw us all into the Veil, my lord. You will have no one left to rule over. Well, spare me, at least—I am on your side."

"Are you?" I snapped. "Forgive me, sir, but you do not seem much enthused by the idea of Wendell taking the throne."

"Oh dear," Lord Taran said. "It seems we've misunderstood each other. Indeed, I believe my nephew will make a terrible king. We might as well offer the throne to one of the gardeners and see how they fare. But I couldn't care less who the king is. I am on your side because it will make Callum happy."

I did not trust him one bit. "That's all?"

He smiled. "Naturally that is all, because what else matters in life?"

Wendell was nodding. "I am glad there will be another mortal at court. In fact, I believe I will invite others to join us. Perhaps we should have an equal number of them on our Council, Em. What do you think?"

"You say that as if it is out of the goodness of your heart," I said with a snort. "Really it is because you find mortals easier to charm than other Folk."

He gave me an amused look. "Ah, but there you're wrong—I prefer the company of those who are difficult to charm."

Lord Taran finished his tea and stood, setting the cup carefully on the rock. "I will go on ahead. Naturally, everyone is expecting you to appear at some point, and so a number of the queen's soldiers are lying in wait for you at various places around the castle grounds. I will get them out of the way, at least. Then you can sweep in and terrify us all with your sewing kit, my lord."

I glared at him, and he raised his eyebrows innocently. "No? Broom collection, perhaps?" And, laughing at my expression, he marched off into the forest.

"Good riddance," I muttered. I turned to find Wendell smiling at me fondly.

"We are fortunate to have my uncle on our side," he said. "He is sometimes called *Eldest*, for he is possibly the oldest person in the entire realm, and widely feared."

"He is insufferable."

"He's also correct," Wendell said, unperturbed. "It is no easy task to frighten my court. We are too used to monsters. And none of them have ever viewed me as a fearsome figure."

"Your magic is growing stronger," I said bluntly. "I have been watching you. You have never used it so freely, and it does not seem to tire you."

"I—" Wendell blinked. For a moment, he looked as he had when he stood at the threshold of his door—slightly lost. "I hadn't noticed."

"I believe it is a good sign," I said. Also an unnerving one, but I did not bother to mention this. I had not accompanied him to Faerie only to lose heart and sit quaking in some corner, had I? Shoving my anxiety to one side, I sat up straighter and continued, "Several of the oldest stories suggest that the realm recognizes its rightful lord or lady. I can only hope your court is ready for an unorthodox display of power."

31st December

We reached the castle at dusk.

We had tarried another day in the forest—partly because Wendell needed the time to work, and partly on account of Shadow, whom Wendell and I felt the need to fuss over. Wendell located another standing stone with some helpful brownies living in it, who came racing out with a plate of dog biscuits this time. Shadow devoured the lot and collapsed upon a patch of moss, falling into a deep slumber. When he awoke in the morning, there was a spring in his step I have not seen in years.

We approached the castle from the east rather than the route I had taken in October, through the gardens. Here the path around the lake widened into a broad promenade used by lords and ladies arriving by carriage, as well as the monarchy when they wished to make a grand return from some battle or hunting expedition.

In other words, it was perfect.

When I had explained my idea to Wendell, he began to laugh. "Well?" I said as he wiped his eyes. "Is it that ridiculous?"

"No, Em," he said, taking my hand. "It is better than anything I could have come up with. And much less work than bursting in on everyone with my sword flashing."

"You don't have your needles, though," I said.

"Of course I do. You thought I would leave them behind?" He snapped his fingers, and one of the guardians alighted on his shoulder, making me start back with my heart thundering. Slung across its back was a leather satchel, and within that was the collection of silver sewing needles that Aud, the headwoman of Hrafnsvik, had gifted Wendell a year ago.

I was not idle as he worked, though my contribution was necessarily limited. Few scholars know any Words of Power, and I have acquired two, one of which—the more ridiculous of the pair, naturally—was well-suited to our circumstances.

I wandered a little way into the forest and spoke the Word. At first, nothing happened. I recalled there had been a similar pause the previous time I had invoked its magic, beside the Hidden king's tree amidst the snow of a Ljosland winter.

Then something came sailing out of the forest gloom and smacked me in the forehead.

I staggered back a little, more out of surprise than pain. I stooped and picked up the button from where it had fallen among a clump of ivy.

It was a lovely little thing, made from some sort of pale blue crystal that flashed even in the leafy shadow, carved in the shape of a rose. Emboldened, I spoke the button-summoning Word again. This time, I managed to catch the button before it hit me in the face, though I fumbled it immediately, and almost lost it in a hollow. This button was of silver, unadorned but so delicately made that I feared it would break if I held it too tightly.

Snowbell, who had followed me into the trees, watched with interest. "How can a mortal oaf work our magics?" he said.

"Anyone can use the Words of Power," I replied. "The difficult thing is tracking them down, as many have been forgotten." I glanced at him, suppressing a smile. "It is true, though; I am only a mortal, and my eyesight is poor. I fear I may lose the buttons as soon as I find them."

"Hum!" Snowbell's tail twitched in excitement. "*My* eyesight is excellent!"

And so, I spoke the Word more than a hundred times, and after each utterance a different button would come sailing out of the forest. They came from all directions, and some took longer to arrive than others, as if they had crossed a great distance. I managed to catch a few, but most hit me in the head and bounced off somewhere, at which point Snowbell or one of the other *fuchszwerge* would give a yip of delight and chase them down, snarling at one another as they fought to be first.

"Good Lord!" Wendell cried when I showed him my eclectic little hoard, which I had collected in my skirt. He was leaning over a strange pile of dark fabric that rippled in the breeze, his sewing needle flashing. "Where on earth did you find them?"

"People are always losing buttons," I said. "The Folk are no different. Of course there would be a quantity of them scattered throughout the forest like dropped coins. I had only to call for them. The question is, are they useful?"

Wendell stuck his needle into the mushroom he seemed to be using for a pin cushion and ran his long fingers over the buttons.

"Oh, Em," he said quietly. "They're perfect."

His confidence in me was heartening, though later I found my confidence in *myself* on the verge of shattering as we made our way up the promenade with the castle looming ahead.

It was not just Taran's *rumpled little scholar* remark—though I will admit that stung—but rather the overall pattern into which it fitted. Perhaps if the majority of my life had not been spent failing to fit in to most environments; perhaps if I were a little less well-read when it came to folklore, and thus a little less aware of how far I deviated from the type of mortal who ordinarily draws the attention of faerie royalty—yes, perhaps then I could have felt some of Wendell's triumph in that moment, which was, after all, also my triumph. But I was too focused on keeping my head up, and walking with something that I hoped approximated elegance, and, above all, praying that I would not stumble or otherwise embarrass myself. I had decided that I would try, as much as I was able, to make myself into the sort of mortal who would play this role in a story. To that end, I had asked Wendell to place a glamour on my dress—it was now black, to match with him, layers of silk with silver brocade in a pattern of bluebells.

Over the glamoured dress I wore my tailored cloak, the train unfurled so that it stretched behind me as a vast, rippling darkness, as if my shadow had been swapped for that of a giant. I had been reluctant to allow Wendell to alter it further, as I like it the way it is, but I knew I had to cut an impressive figure somehow, ridiculous as that is to imagine. And so he had swapped out my old sturdy hood for one with stars woven into it.

I wish I could say that was metaphorical, but Wendell informed me—in as matter-of-fact a manner as he tends to use in such circumstances—that he had gathered up the starlight reflected in a forest pool and stitched it into the fabric. The lights framed my face like a ghostly crown, some constant, others flickering; every few moments, one would blaze across the hood and disappear among the trees, sometimes to a chorus of squeals from the brownie spectators we had accumulated as we went. I tried not to jump when this happened.

Wendell had also insisted that Shadow dress for our arrival.

"Orga will not have it," he said. "But at least one of them must be appropriately outfitted. They are to be familiars of the king and queen, after all."

Now, Shadow has never been fond of clothing, but he seemed to sense the importance of this particular imposition on his dignity, and held still while Wendell measured and draped him in iterations of what became a fine coat. It was a soft, velvety black, embroidered with a kingly amount of silver, which Wendell somehow made from a handful of the silver buttons I had found. He had decided to make Shadow intimidating—to which I did not object, knowing this would lessen the dog's embarrassment—and so he had taken tendrils of fog and attached them to the cloak like billowing ribbons, so that Shadow seemed to carry a mist with him everywhere like the spectral beast that he is. Together with the glitter of the silver, the effect was—well, mythic.

And as for Wendell? I wish I could adequately describe it.

Though I watched much of its construction, I could not say how he made his cloak. At times he seemed to reach down and gather a shadow from beneath a tree, at which point it became a solid thing, or solider, an undulating darkness not unlike my own cloak. Sometimes he would stride into the forest and come back with an armful of pine boughs or birch bark, which would, from one moment to the next, turn into something like fabric. Occasionally he would dip the cloak into the lake as he worked, and when he removed it, it would have taken on a subtly different shape.

The resulting garment was black, of course. But it was like no fabric I'd ever seen before, liquid and faintly glimmering. He had ordered each of his guardians to donate several of their feathers, and these he had woven into the material. They were not *visible* exactly, except as a suggestion of wings when the cloak caught the wind. It was a garment that needed no adornment, for it was like something snipped out of a dream, and he gave it none, apart from the row of buttons. I would have expected him to pick the finest of those I had gathered, but instead he chose a selection that would represent all the regions of his realm: silver from the Weeping Mines and the lower tributary of the Tromlu River; carved oak from a dozen different corners of the forest; rare bone from the antlers of one of the hag-headed deer; coloured marble from the Blue Hooks. The effect was more impressive than if he had adorned himself in jewels, for together the buttons possessed an enchantment that made strange images flit through my mind when I looked upon them, memories of places I'd never seen. A shadowy grove around a narrow standing stone; a flash of mist-shrouded water tumbling down a sheer cliff.

The train of the cloak was where things became—unsettling.

I had not known he could do this, of course. I had merely said that whatever he created should be frightening. I had thought that perhaps he would weave another fragment of the Veil into it, but instead he had put in something *alive*. The cloak grumbled and growled, a guttural noise so resonant I felt it beneath my feet. It also had an appetite—according to Snowbell, it had devoured two of his kindred when we weren't minding it; Wendell had to command it not to eat anybody else. I had no idea what the creature was, and even more disturbingly, neither did Wendell.

"I found it in a hollow log," he said with the self-satisfaction of a shopper who unearths a hidden gem at a flea market.

I am going to be honest: I tried to avoid looking at it.

Behind us trailed our miscellaneous little army. The trolls were at their most intimidating, stocky and muscular, marching along with their hatchets and scythes over their shoulders—and while I knew these were implements used for their industry, still the picture they presented together made me shudder. Snowbell and his brethren came next, snapping and snarling at anything that moved, a red river made of teeth and claws. And, last but certainly not least, the hideous fauns crept silently in our wake, their dogs, which were closer to dog-sized rats, leashed at their sides.

As for the guardians, they flew overhead, close enough for me to feel the wind from their wingbeats. Razkarden rested on Wendell's shoulder.

We were noticed instantly, of course. Soon after we emerged from the forest onto the promenade, we encountered a castle guard on horseback. I barely saw him, so startled was I by his mount's enormous size and thundering hooves that I staggered back. He was more alarmed by us, though, for he gave a shout and fled immediately—back towards the castle.

"Your horses are too large," I commented inanely—my heart was still racing. "Thornthwaite would be delighted."

Professor Thornthwaite specializes in all manner of faerie horses, the stranger the better. Why I was bringing up Thornthwaite then, I didn't know—I suppose it was because Cambridge felt so distant in that moment, painfully so, that I wished to cling to any thread of connection, no matter how tenuous.

"You needn't worry about our horses," Wendell promised. "You will ride a drayfox—they are slow, elegant creatures used by much of the nobility. In fact, I was thinking that I would give you Red Wind, whom I learned to ride as a boy. I hope she still lives."

"I will ride a fox," I repeated distantly. "Well, of course I will."

Wendell had been walking along at a leisurely pace, entirely at ease, stroking Razkarden's beak and occasionally exclaiming over the fruit trees that lined the promenade or the view of the castle through the branches. Now he turned his gaze upon me and stopped.

"Em," he said, taking my hand. "You will not have to ride Red Wind if you do not wish it. In fact, once I have retaken my throne, you will not have to do anything if you do not wish it. If you desire to sit in some corner of the castle hunched over your books and notepaper, bestirring yourself only to demand a tour of some brownie market or bogle den, then it will be done."

I let out a trembling breath. "And what sort of queen would that make me?"

He looked perfectly earnest as he leaned in to kiss my cheek. "Mine."

I could not help laughing. My heart was still galloping, but I felt a little calmer. "Perhaps we should secure your throne before I go about demanding any tours."

"Oh, yes," Wendell said. "First things first."

And so, that is what we did.

I had expected more complications, I confess. Particularly given Lord Taran's warnings. But then, Lord Taran had not known about our army, or Wendell's ability with a sewing needle.

We continued on our leisurely stroll, coming upon several more guards, all of whom reacted much as the first had—I felt almost sorry for the former queen, that her loyal servants should be so lacking in courage. But then we rounded a corner, and the castle came into view, windows gleaming in the twilight like coins. The gate was so obvious that I wondered at my inability to locate it on my previous visit, but then I had been without Wendell's protection, muddled by the magics of Faerie.

Even now, though, I felt as if I were not fully *grasping* the castle, somehow. Oh, I could see its towers and parapets well enough, and the forested hillside behind it, several of the treetops connected with silver bridges. But I found I could not hold on to the image when I looked away—the memory blurred like a dream.

I could not stare long at the castle, though, for three of the queen's guards had been braver than their fellows and regrouped to await us.

We had attracted an audience at this point. Not only brownies, but courtly fae had begun to line the forest paths that ran parallel to the promenade. They were mostly in shadow, but the silver glitter of their finery gave them away. It was difficult to determine if the overall mood of the crowd was friendly or hostile; its character was perhaps best described as inconsistent. A handful of Folk screamed and fled as we passed; there were several cheers; some called Wendell's name in tones ranging from delight to fury. One man shouted "Murderer!" and "The queen will have her vengeance!" over and over until Razkarden chased him shrieking into the woods. The larger percentage simply stood and gawped.

"Wendell," I said as we neared the guards. They sat atop their massive horses, brandishing their swords and generally looking terrifying—*I* certainly did not wish to draw any nearer. But before Wendell could reply, a curious thing happened: the horses began to tremble, and the lead guard fumbled his sword. They backed up, keeping pace with us as we advanced, and then as one they turned their horses and thundered chaotically into the woods, nearly crashing into one another in their haste. As they fled, they knocked over an entrepreneurial little brownie balancing a reed basket atop its head that held a variety of cheeses and biscuits, which he seemed to be selling to the spectators. A seed biscuit bounced into our path, and Shadow snapped it up with a pleased *whuff*.

"Good!" Wendell said, evincing only vague satisfaction at the terror he was striking in our onlookers. "I have no appetite for swordplay tonight. How wearying travel is! Even through one's own realm. I think I shall do everything on horseback from now on. Look there, Em—*that* is the bridge that leads to the Royal Observatory, a balcony where one can see for miles and miles, all the way to the Singing Caves. Now, I doubt I will have much success in convincing you of the merits of sunsets, but..."

He continued to chatter excitedly, pointing at this or that, and I believe I may have made some reply, but in truth I barely heard him—my attention was otherwise occupied.

Before the castle gate was a broad courtyard of cobblestones lined with ivy-wreathed lanterns and benches around the perimeter—from which lowlier Folk could admire the nobility as they paraded about, I assumed, but nobody was sitting there now. One of the many disturbing qualities the Folk possess is that, when one encounters them en masse, they appear to blend together, as if one is seeing them through mist, or through the interpretation of a painter who has chosen to give only the impression of a crowd. Perhaps it is my human inability to comprehend their strangeness, I don't know— I noted several beautiful faces, some wild-eyed with panic and others twisted into a hungry sort of delight. There was also a musician dressed all in grey who set a massive harp upon the cobbles and began strumming a merry tune—it formed an odd contrast with the fraught quiet of the courtyard, which was a susurration of crying, mutters, and occasional half-stifled screams.

One woman in particular made me start—she wore layers of dark silks like the gradient of a winter twilight, and her hair was a river of black feathers down her back. She was frowning at her pocket watch but seemed to sense me staring; she looked up, smiled wickedly, and faded back into the crowd.

Then the castle doors swung open, and out strode Lord Taran. At his side was Callum Thomas, whom I had also met before, and I nearly fainted with relief. It was not Callum himself—I barely knew the man—but rather the sight of a mortal face amidst the wonder and horror of Faerie. I had not known, until that moment, the strain it placed upon me.

Lord Taran might not have been at all conscious of the current of panic surging through the crowd, nor of our intimidating retinue. To me he seemed bored, though this was mostly hidden behind an expression of polite deference. The boredom vanished abruptly, though, as Orga came charging into his path.

As she drew between him and Wendell, she seemed to grow. And grow, until she was a monstrous shadow towering over Lord Taran—a shadow with only the barest of shapes, that being mostly mouth, yawning with fangs. I gave a choked cry.

"The Beast of the Elderwood!" someone shrieked. There was a little stampede as some onlookers to our left decided their curiosity had been adequately sated, but most of the Folk stayed put, riveted to the scene unfolding before them—the return of their exiled king, met by their ancient general, brother of the old queen. Which way would it go? I was as helplessly fascinated as any of them.

Orga shrank back to her customary size almost immediately, settling at Wendell's feet, whereupon she began to wash her face—I suspect she'd merely wanted to make Lord Taran flinch. He had fallen back a step, his hand upon the pommel of his sword.

"I would prefer not to spend the remainder of my existence looking over my shoulder for you, dark one," he said, giving the cat a scowl. "Perhaps this will redeem me somewhat."

He swept his cloak aside and knelt at Wendell's feet, pressing one knee to the ground and laying his sword across the other. Callum did the same after flashing me a quick, bright smile.

Lord Taran's gesture moved through the crowd like a sigh after a long-held breath. Folk fell to their knees, some more energetically than others. A few more screams ensued, and another clamour of footfalls, though it seemed to me that less than a handful actually fled—those who deemed their necks most at risk, I suppose, or perhaps they had especially nervous dispositions. The only person who did not change his position was the harpist, who strummed louder, his playing taking on a sanctimonious character. The cheese-wielding brownie returned and began circulating among the courtly fae as they rose to their feet, joined by another wearing what looked like a lily pad for a hat and clutching a basket of roasted chestnuts.

Lord Taran made a gesture and a half dozen Folk—a mixture of courtly and common, all dressed in silver-threaded grey—emerged from the shadows of the castle, each dragging a small wagon behind them. These were covered with silk, hiding the contents, which rattled over the cobblestones.

One of these Folk bowed to Lord Taran and passed him a hand mirror. It was wrought from pure silver, its frame an intricate and uneven scalloped pattern, as if it had lain upon the sea floor for years and accumulated all manner of shells and barnacles. With another bow, Lord Taran gave it to Wendell.

"Thank you," Wendell said. He gazed into the mirror, then turned towards the crowd, absently tapping the glass against his opposite palm. The motion scattered diamonds of reflected light across the courtyard. It was odd, but he reminded me then of the first time I had watched him present at a conference. Had it been five years ago, or six? The subject had been the folklore of Provence, and while I had been skeptical of his claims and annoyed by the offhand showmanship with which he delivered them, I could not help being awed by his effect upon his audience. For Wendell in such moments has a gravity about him that has nothing to do with enchantment, and nor is it like the Hidden king's; it is something warmer, good-natured, which makes one wish to lean in, not cower away.

"What's this about?" I muttered.

"Oh—just a little tradition. To mark the passing of the throne from one monarch to the next," he said, his gaze roaming hungrily over the castle and the hillside beyond.

"Look, Em," he said, pointing to the drifting lights overhead. "Fireflies! Yes, I remember—they always came out at this time of the evening."

"You're enjoying yourself," I noted.

"I am." He turned to kiss me. "My dearest Emily! I am home at last. And all because of you."

"You had a bit to do with it," I said drily, though it was difficult to stop myself from smiling. I have often found Wendell's happiness infectious, particularly now; it seemed to radiate from him like morning sunlight.

He laughed. "Now all I want is a good, hearty meal and my own bed. But let us give them a show first, hm?"

He stepped forward, still emanating good cheer, and I sensed the crowd relax further. I wondered if they'd expected him to simply unsheathe his sword and start beheading people—probably. Violence came as naturally as drawing breath to monarchs of the Silva Lupi.

"My stepmother is dead," Wendell said in a carrying voice. "Or will be, soon enough. To those who loved her: know that she served our realm well, with courage and devotion. To her enemies: I invite you to celebrate with me tonight, and with your new queen, who slew her with her own hand."

Folk grinned at this, their teeth flashing in the lantern light, and I suppressed an urge to step behind Shadow. A woman with a hedgehog perched on her shoulder burst into hysterical sobs.

Wendell turned to me, holding out the mirror. "Would you care to do the honours? It is our custom to smash all mirrors in the castle when a monarch passes, so that we are rid of everything that bore their image. This was among my stepmother's personal possessions."

"You do it," I said, for I was a little thrown by this and did not want to misstep somehow.

Wendell nodded. He drew Shadow out of the way, then hurled the mirror against the side of the castle. It shattered into a hundred tiny shards, which transformed into fireflies and soared into the air to join the others.

The crowd erupted into cries of delight—even those who had seemed most afraid were cheering now, and several more harpists joined the first. The frisson of terror began to melt, and the evening swelled with music and laughter.

Lord Taran made another motion, and the silk coverings on the wagons were removed, revealing an assemblage of mirrors of all shapes and sizes. Above the tumult of the crowd, Wendell shouted, "Who will celebrate?"

Folk surged forward, snatching up mirrors from the carts, some common fae hoisting mirrors larger than they were and stumbling about clumsily under their weight. There was a great deal of pushing and shoving, and small fights broke out, for there were not enough mirrors for everyone. The sound of shattering glass sparred with the harps' strains, and innumerable fireflies floated into the night. The silver faerie stones amidst the treetops began to glow like floating lanterns. Folk went charging through the gate, shrieking with excitement.

"They will roam the castle tonight, searching for mirrors," Wendell told me. "As I said, it's a very old tradition. Some get carried away—no doubt a few windows will also be shattered, particularly those in my stepmother's rooms."

I drew towards him, overwhelmed. I could not tell if my fascination outweighed my fear in that moment. "I—" I began, though I did not know what I meant to say.

"I know," he said quietly, his arm encircling my waist.

He led me towards the castle gate, an unnervingly massive thing with doors of heavy oak several times my height and carved with what I had taken for an abstract floral scene, but which, up close, was revealed as a head encircled with brooklime, leaves spilling from its eyes and mouth.

Lord Taran stood to one side, Callum to the other. The auburn-haired man gave me a smile as Wendell and I passed.

"Welcome back, Professor Wilde," he murmured. "Or should I say Walters? You certainly know how to make an entrance."

1st January 1911

A new year.

Not that one would know it in Faerie—the Folk pay no mind to human calendars, or, in some cases, to the concept of linear time. It is odd—I never gave much thought to the passing of years, in the mortal world. Certainly I never bothered celebrating them, as others do. Yet here in Faerie, where I am quite possibly the only person to know that one year has faded into the next, I find myself wishing to mark the event in some way.

But I am rambling.

(How on earth have I gotten myself into this? How will I convince anyone that I am a queen, and how did I believe it would be a good idea to try? This is utter madness. I try to stamp these thoughts out of existence, but they will not leave me be.)

I woke this morning in a manner to which I have become accustomed of late: with Orga perched upon my chest, kneading at the flesh below my throat.

I sat upright with a gasp, dislodging her and the dreadful prickling of her claws, so close to my jugular vein. She has never once woken Wendell in this manner; I suspect she is making some sort of statement.

Shadow, stretched out at the foot of the bed, awoke with a grunt. I glanced over at Wendell—naturally he was still asleep, buried in blankets as always; he only mumbled something when I touched him and rolled onto his stomach so that his face was engulfed in pillow.

I could not remember much of the previous evening, not because of enchantment, but because I had been so exhausted by our long trek—and the weight of the strangeness around me—that I had been almost asleep on my feet. We had dined in a banquet hall open to the sky, with glassless windows through which the ivies and mosses crept. I say "dined," but Wendell kept being interrupted by Folk who wished to bow and talk to him and give him presents—chiefly jewels and silver trinkets, though one lady presented him with a wooden chest that released a swarm of colourful butterflies each time it was opened. Folk charged hither and thither, smashing mirrors and the occasional window, and there was a great deal of shrieking and—I think—violence, though this was distant, and I could not tell who was fighting whom. Overall it was nothing short of chaos and served only to exhaust me further.

After I'd eaten a little, Wendell led me up to his rooms. He returned to the party, but not for long, I don't think—I woke to the sound of him falling into bed beside me, muttering about "tedious courtiers not even giving me a moment to sip my tea" and then seemed to fall immediately asleep.

I pushed the blankets back and stood. Wendell's cloak grumbled at me from the floor. It was strange to be here again, in the bedroom where I had poisoned the queen, but Wendell would not hear of taking over his stepmother's more majestic chambers, and had been set on returning to the familiar wing in the castle he had occupied in his youth.

"Well?" I said to Shadow, who was eyeing me. He *whuffed* and jumped to the floor beside me.

I went to the window and drew back the rich black curtains. The weeping rowan stirred and slowly drew its sharp leaves across the glass, as if seeking entry. I do not think I will ever like the look of the thing, with its clusters of blood-coloured berries, but at least it is not an attentive oak.

I paused beside Wendell, considering whether to wake him. We had, in fact, woken once already, earlier that morning, and then spent an hour or two very agreeably occupied—I blush now to write these words—before falling asleep again. He had declared his intention of properly expressing his gratitude to me, and—well, I had not been disinclined to allow him the opportunity.

I decided to let him sleep.

Wendell's bedroom was no longer in the state of dilapidation I had witnessed on my previous visit. It had been cleaned and freshened, the wooden floors scattered with soft rugs, the smell of mould replaced with that of pine and wildflowers. New mirrors in silver frames had been placed upon each wall, so that I could behold endless reflections of my inelegant self frowning sleepily amidst the gentle glitter. A part of me wondered when the renovations had occurred—after his stepmother fled, or upon his arrival yesterday evening? Either way, I suspected *oíche sidhe* involvement; the walls and furnishings had that slightly-too-polished look about them, and I doubted I would find a single speck of dust in the entire place, not even beneath the wardrobe.

Within said wardrobe I discovered a variety of dressing gowns, all ridiculously elegant and mostly black, and selected one of the simplest, which was of plain brown silk.

Orga wound herself around my legs, purring in an insistent sort of way. She butted her forehead against me as if trying to draw my attention.

"What have you got there?" I took the scrap of midnight-blue fabric from her mouth and examined it. The brocade was a silver pattern of leaves and tiny deer. "This looks like the cloak Lord Taran wore at dinner yesterday."

Orga rumbled her agreement and rubbed enthusiastically against my legs. I noted the many tooth punctures in the fabric.

"You wish me to help you murder Lord Taran, is that it?" I said. "No, thank you. I'm fairly confident that one could turn me into a slug with a wave of his hand. And anyway, Wendell is fine."

Orga growled in such a way that I understood this was insufficient grounds to pardon her nemesis. Clearly witnessing Wendell being nearly decapitated had awakened some aspect of her nature that I did not fully understand, and that I hoped would never be directed at myself.

"Come, Shadow," I said. Now that I had slept, my scholarly curiosity was back, and I wished to undertake a proper investigation of Wendell's rooms—I barely remember anything about the castle from my previous visit, so muddled was I by magic.

Initially, I thought the rooms were arranged in a line, because on my right hand was always a window overlooking the lake and gardens. I paused for a moment to admire the silver shine of the waves cresting in the sunlight. But then I recalled that I had taken the door across from the bed, which should have led *away* from the view, at which point I tried to stop thinking about it.

The first room I entered was a magnificent bathing room tiled in river stones, with a full bath one stepped down into, like something from Roman times. This was steaming and honeysuckle-scented, and I availed myself of it with pleasure, using up two of the leaf-shaped soaps on my dishevelled hair before continuing my search.

The next room was illuminated by skylights and a row of tall casement windows. It was also the dining room, and it was full of Folk.

They were a half dozen or so in number, and upon first sight I thought they were *oíche sidhe*. But no: while they were drab and greyish, with the same spindly hands, these creatures were smaller and stouter, with perpetually red faces. They were bustling about the table, which had two places set and was filled with silver dishes of fruit, buttered bread, jams, sausages, and some manner of spiced porridge with cream poured over top.

Most of the faeries froze in surprise when I entered, but the one nearest to me, who seemed quite young, gave a shriek and dropped the platter of eggs she was holding, which struck the floor with a wet sort of clang.

"Your Highness!" another faerie said in a hoarse voice, after a fraught moment in which we stared at each other in mutual panic. "Would you care to—"

"No, thank you," I said, overloud. Then I turned and fled.

I regretted this instantly—not only because it was undignified, but also because my stomach was rumbling noisily. But I was faced with a conundrum as I regained the bathroom—if I returned and apologized, they would think me contrary and strange, if not outright mad. Or, worse, unfit to be their queen.

Well, naturally I am unfit to be anyone's queen. But I had no desire to make this more apparent than it already was.

Shadow and I returned to the bedroom (Wendell had not moved) and went through a different door. We passed through two rooms of uncertain purpose, which were cluttered with trunks and wooden crates and the odd piece of furniture. I assumed that the castle servants were in the middle of furnishing things, and indeed, I heard muffled voices and thumps in an adjoining room, followed by the sound of hammering.

I realized I was clutching the coin in my pocket instinctively, as I'd done in the Hidden king's court, and forced myself to release it. My mind was clear, I reminded myself, my sense of direction also—this in spite of the seemingly impossible configuration of the apartments.

I opened a different door and walked through. And halted midstep.

This room was filled with wooden shelves, as well as a number of stacks, such as one finds in libraries. The ones against the wall were full, while those in the centre of the room were mostly empty, as if awaiting their purpose.

And what did they hold? Journals. Dozens upon dozens of journals.

These were in a variety of shapes and sizes, some bound with wood boards decorated with silver and jewels, others with leather. Many were elaborate; others were plain. The shelves ended at the ceiling, which was several times my height.

I blinked stupidly. Shadow gave a huff.

Perched upon stools at a workbench in the corner were two faeries hunched over piles of leather and blank parchment. One—the more wizened of the two—clutched an awl, with which she was gesticulating as she lectured the younger, smaller one, who sat with tears in his eyes and a pile of tangled thread in his lap.

"Flakes, flakes, flakes!" the older faerie was snarling. "You pay no mind to allowing the glue to set, do you? Look at this! We cannot present it to Her Highness in this state. It will sully her hands whenever she writes in it—and your thread is far too large; look how the spine bulges. This is the last time I hire family, mark my words. You are every bit as incompetent as my daughter and—"

I must have made some noise, for they both turned to gawp

at me. The elder one sprang to the floor and bowed low, crying "Your Highness!" in a voice that creaked like an old hinge.

The faerie had the look of a book goblin, which I have encountered only once before. She was small—the top of her head just reached my waist—with a hunchback and a severe, squinting look, black eyes nearly obscured by heavy wrinkles and the curtains of bristly hair that fell over her face. Dangling from a chain on her neck was an odd glass sphere that I took for a monocle.

"Please allow us to give you a tour, O Exalted One," the faerie said, clasping her ink-stained hands together in excitement.

"I— Thank you," I said, blankly staring. "But I will be late for breakfast."

And I hurried out, pulling the door closed behind me and leaning against it, as if the little faeries might give chase.

Good Lord! How had this room come to be? Wendell had ordered it, because of course he had—but when?

I blundered off, too discombobulated to pay much heed to where I was going. My thoughts kept returning to *O Exalted One,* as if it were a sharp seed caught in my throat, driving me to distraction. I *thought* I had chosen the door that led back to the bedroom, but instead I found myself in a narrow hallway ending in a closed door, sunlight streaming through a row of windows. Orga—I hadn't realized she had followed us—gave a trill of satisfaction and flopped onto her side in the sunbeam.

Naturally, the view out the windows was of the lake, painted with tree reflections and morning sunlight, even though, according to my senses, this should be an interior section of the castle. I paused and tried to catch my breath. As I did, I became aware of a breeze.

The breeze came not from the windows, which were shut—

it meandered out from the crack below the door at the end of the hall, smelling of rain.

It was not raining outside.

Now, I knew full well that the wiser course would be to wake Wendell and investigate this together. But how often have I thrown wisdom aside in the face of faerie mysteries? I was flummoxed and full of half-formed anxieties, but I also felt like a hungry child who, presented with a cake, cannot stop herself from devouring it whole.

I went to the door and pushed it open.

Morning light spilled into the hall at an angle that contradicted the light of Faerie. I was presented with a view of a green hillock at the edge of a forest. A little whitewashed cottage perched atop the hillock, which was strewn with mossy rocks and purple with heather. Behind the cottage, a fine waterfall tumbled down a rise in the wooded landscape, and this gave off a mist that, coupled with the drizzling rain, gave the scene a spectral atmosphere.

Impossible as it was, what I saw relaxed me a little. Here at least was a simple faerie door to an otherland—it was, of course, madness that an otherland should be found just off my bedchamber, and I would certainly be speaking with Wendell about it—but at least it did not contain hordes of Folk desperate to oblige my whims.

I closed the door—after grabbing Shadow by the scruff and hauling him back, for he had shoved his snout into the otherworld and was sniffing voraciously—and went back the way I had come. But I'd become turned around once more, not by enchantment but my own blundering, and while I was correct in intuiting the direction of the bedchamber, I ended up—to my dismay—in the dining room once more.

I could not stop myself from swearing. At least the servants had left, and for a blessed moment I thought I was alone with the platters of lightly steaming food. But then I heard the creak of a chair against the wall behind me.

"Your Highness?" a woman said. To my infinite relief, she was mortal, a tall, pretty woman with dark brown skin and black hair cropped close to her scalp. She seemed to be blind, and held a simple cane made from willow reeds, but I caught the flash of silver woven into the construction. Her dress was of plain dark silks, but there too was a subtle silver stitchery along the cuffs. I understood from this that the woman possessed some status among these Folk.

"How did you know me?" I said.

She smiled. "I have lived among Folk for thirty years, by the mortal reckoning. I am used to the sound of their footfalls. Your tread is different."

I let out my breath and sank into a chair. "One of the common fae is fond of referring to me as a blundering mortal oaf." I gave a shaky laugh that perhaps went on too long.

She had stopped smiling and now looked concerned. "Are you all right?"

I rubbed a hand over my face. "Who were those Folk with— with the papers and awls?"

"The bookbinders? The king summoned them to court last night. They have been hard at it ever since. Does their work not please you, Your Highness?"

I made an inarticulate sound and poured myself a cup of tea. "Please don't call me that."

"Oh, thank God." My words—or perhaps the raggedness of them—seemed to break the tension between us, and she sank into a chair across from me with a sigh of relief. "I had to be certain you weren't one of those mortals who had grown big-headed from finding favour with faerie royalty, and would toss me into the dungeons for presumption. Do you know me, Professor Wilde?"

I examined her—I saw nothing familiar in her face, but it did not take me long to work it out. "You've spent thirty years in Faerie," I murmured, mentally thumbing through the list of scholars who had vanished into the Silva Lupi. "You are not Dr. Proudfit? Niamh Proudfit, of the University of Connacht?"

She grinned. "Steady on. You would think *I* was queen of this realm. You need not be impressed by me."

"I'm sorry," I said, trying to get my emotions in hand. "I have never seized the throne of a faerie kingdom before. I'm afraid I find the experience somewhat trying."

She laughed—it was a rich, warm sound, which, coupled with her boisterous manner of speaking, gave an impression of conviviality and open-heartedness. I recognized in her a particular variety of professor, the sort most likely to receive glowing student reviews, who displays an infectious enthusiasm for her chosen subject and an easy command of a podium. Now, as this sort is furthest from my own type—my reviews are decidedly mixed—I tend to view such individuals with a touch of resentment, but I felt none of this now. My relief at meeting a fellow scholar was too great.

"You were a friend of Farris Rose's, were you not?" I found myself asking, though we had more important things to talk about.

Her face brightened, and I sensed that she was just as pleased as I to speak of academic matters. "We co-authored an article on the Black Hounds of Cumbria! How is he getting on? Has he grown dignified and venerable with age? When I knew Farris, he was still stammering during speaking events."

We spent several minutes discussing Rose; I gave Niamh an account of his career since her disappearance, and she told me a story of how he had once locked himself outside his boardinghouse before a conference and had to deliver his presentation in his slippers. She was also fascinated to hear of our association with Danielle de Grey and Bran Eichorn, two other famously vanished scholars. Both have returned to academia—to fanfare I doubt I need describe, other than to say that they are, unsurprisingly, now the most talked about dryadologists in all of Europe—with Eichorn following de Grey to her old alma mater, the University of Edinburgh. I confess I am not disappointed that they decided against remaining at Cambridge; our relations at present could best be described as polite but frosty. With Eichorn, this can be explained as being in harmony with his nature, but regarding de Grey, I have at times had the impression that she resents how intertwined our names have become, given that I am the one being credited with her rescue (Wendell asked that his role in the whole business be omitted). She seems the sort who prefers being at the centre of things.

"Most of academia has given you up for dead," I told Niamh. "This is the Silva Lupi, after all. But what are you doing here, in their court? You are not a prisoner?"

"Not at all," she said. We had tucked in to breakfast, and Niamh paused to wash down her toast with some tea. Several of the red-faced servants had returned, unobtrusively keeping our plates and cups filled. I felt more comfortable with them now that I was not the only person being waited on.

"I was the old king's scribe," she said. "That means right hand, here; the head of his Council and general fixer. The queen sacked me, of course, when she had the royal family murdered and took Prince Liath's throne—King Liath, I mean."

I was impressed; not only by her position, but that she had survived the queen's purge. "How did you—"

"Keep my head?" She laughed again, though there was a brittleness about it that undercut the irreverence. "The queen always liked talented mortals. She appreciated my intellect—she said so, anyhow. She continued to consult me occasionally on political matters, but by and large she let me be, which suited me well enough. I have been able to focus on my research these last few years."

I examined her again. Niamh Proudfit had been thirty-six when she vanished, and she looked barely older now. She may not have experienced as many as thirty years in Faerie, but to see no change whatsoever—

"Yes," she said, seeming to comprehend the nature of my pause. "As you know, the Folk have ways of extending mortal lifespans—for those they value, in any case. So long as I remain in Faerie, I shall age very slowly. Callum Thomas is the same—the man is nearly two hundred years old! I doubt I shall linger here so long, but certainly there is no greater gift to a scholar than the gift of time. I shall stay at least until I have completed the book I am working on."

I was delighted. "What is the subject? You specialized in Faerie temporality, did you not?"

"I did—a rather tricky subdiscipline, given that human mortality and Faerie time are as compatible as oil and water. But my focus is primarily ethnographic—I wish to understand how the Folk perceive time, which I believe will prove more illuminating than the clumsy comparisons one often gets from temporalists."

I forgot my anxieties as we discussed her work thus far. Having the old king's favour had given her access to Folk who might not otherwise have deigned to speak with her, and he had aided her research in other ways, including by casting an enchantment that made all books in the realm transform to braille at her touch. Niamh questioned me about my current projects, and I told her of my idea for a book on faerie politics.

She grew animated at that, and provided me with numerous suggestions regarding parameters and scope, which were so helpful that I pulled out a notebook to scribble them down. In the midst of our scholarly enthusiasm, Wendell made his entrance. His golden hair was sticking straight up in the back, and over his silken pyjamas he wore a night-coloured robe that gleamed with tiny green jewels at the cuffs. He stopped short at the sight of us, his mouth falling open.

"Niamh!" he exclaimed. "Good Lord! I assumed she had killed you."

"Hello, dear," Niamh said warmly. "You've grown taller, haven't you? I can see a little," she added to me. "Light and shapes. And you sound like a proper man now. When last we met, you were still a half-formed teenager."

They embraced and began to chatter in Irish. Wendell broke off with an apologetic look in my direction.

"Isn't this wonderful, Em?" he said. "It seems my stepmother has not destroyed everyone I cared about. Niamh is the only member of my father's Council who ever paid me any notice."

"In the Council's defence, your talent for shirking responsibility was unparalleled," Niamh said, shaking him gently by the shoulder. "On the rare occasions you were summoned to a meeting, you didn't bother to show up. But you were kinder than your siblings, I noticed—not a trait much valued at this court, but we mortals appreciate it."

Wendell gazed at her fondly. "Do you know? It was you who inspired me to embark on a career in academia when I fled to the mortal realm. She was so wise, Em, when it came to our stories and ways. I thought: perhaps dryadology will lead me to my door."

"Then the rumours are true!" Niamh exclaimed. "I never

believed the Folk who said you'd turned professor. I simply can't imagine you putting in the effort. Emily, what was his research like?"

"I wouldn't know," I said drily. "As he faked most of it."

"Of course," she said with a laugh. Wendell scowled good-naturedly at us.

"I will have you know that a great deal of effort goes into inventing a convincing field study," he said, seating himself at the table. Instantly the servants were upon us again, appearing out of Lord knows where, bowing and filling his plate and cup. Many seemed to be trembling, whether with terror or delight at Wendell's arrival, I could not say.

"Thank you," Wendell said. He took a sip of his coffee and gave a groan, closing his eyes for a long moment.

"Good grief," Niamh huffed, giving him a playful shove. The servants looked scandalized. "It's just coffee."

"Two words that don't belong in the same sentence," Wendell said. Turning to the servants, he added, "Which of you is in charge?"

More trembling and bowing. Finally a short creature, easily as wide as she was tall, stepped forward and fixed her glittering black eyes upon Wendell's feet. She had a grease stain upon her apron that she seemed to be trying to conceal behind her clasped hands.

"Thank you for the excellent breakfast," Wendell told her. "You could have fled, as others have done, for mayhap you loved my stepmother; instead, you have remained and offered me your services on short notice, though you hardly know me. I realize this has been a trying time for all small Folk. Your loyalty will be rewarded—your pay will be doubled, for one thing. And you must inform me when you are in need of anything. Won't you?"

The servants stared at Wendell in blank astonishment. The

leader seemed to make an effort to speak, but then she burst into tears.

"Thank you, Your Highness," she sobbed. "My apologies." And she dashed from the room, trailed by the others, who tossed looks at Wendell over their shoulders ranging from awe to terror.

"Is she all right?" I said, for I was also taken aback—though less by the servants' reactions than by Wendell's uncharacteristic speech.

"I don't think I heard your stepmother direct a single kind word at the help," Niamh said. "I'm not certain she even glanced at them."

"I have a mind to be charitable where the common fae are concerned," Wendell said. "They have been so useful to us. Also I believe I will enjoy gaining a reputation for benevolence. What do you say, Em? You approve, surely."

"Yes," I said dubiously, my surprise lessening somewhat. I wondered if I should point out that the merits of charity were somewhat lessened when one anticipated praise at the end of it, before deciding the effort unlikely to yield any fruit.

"You should be careful in that regard," Niamh said. "Plenty of Folk dislike you for your mixed blood. Open kindnesses directed towards the common fae will only serve as a reminder. I suggest you refrain from further benevolence until your rule is secure."

Wendell smiled. "My father always valued your advice. Do I take it from your presence here that you would be willing to take up the mantle of scribe once more? Emily?"

"I think it an excellent idea," I said, trying to sound dignified rather than overeager.

Niamh's face brightened. She seemed more pleased than surprised by Wendell's suggestion, and I thought Wendell had guessed right—she had come to us in the hopes of being offered the position. "You do not wish to consider other candidates?"

"Not particularly," I said. "You were loyal to Wendell's father, which makes you less likely to scheme against us—I say *less* rather than *un*likely, given the character of this particular realm. And I remember Farris speaking highly of you. If it will not be a distraction from your book?"

"I must confess that I have more than one book underway," she said with a rueful smile. "The second is a memoir of my years in the Silva Lupi."

I let out a breath of laughter. Last year, I became the first scholar in history to visit Wendell's kingdom and escape with my life; it is not only one of the deadliest Faerie realms, but the most enigmatic. "That *will* create a sensation," I said.

"That's the hope," Niamh said. "So you see, I have no objection to being named your scribe; it will only add interest to the memoir."

"Scholars!" Wendell exclaimed. "What do I always say? You are a mad lot. Taking up careers that could easily get you killed simply to have something to write about. You will be at the top of the assassination list, Niamh, if I am overthrown. Still, it is hard to argue with you—I want you on my side too badly."

"That's settled then," Niamh said with self-satisfaction. At that moment, a different servant entered with an auburn-haired mortal man in tow—Callum Thomas, looking wary, but also as if he were trying to mask it behind a polite smile.

"Oh, it's you," Wendell said. "Good! Sit down and help yourself to breakfast."

"Thank you, Your Highness," Callum said. His expression did not change, but I saw his shoulders relax. His carefully concealed discomfort was of a character I recognized; it was what I felt whenever I conversed with a member of the courtly fae who was not Wendell.

"You are welcome here," I told him. "I understand we have you to thank for Lord Taran's allegiance. Not a small thing, that."

Callum smiled, seeming to relax further at the mention of Taran's name. "It did not actually take much convincing. He never liked his half-sister much. In fact, I recall he spent more time arguing with me over our silverware when I suggested we change it."

I glanced at Wendell, who raised his eyebrows at me. "Why?" I said.

"It was a bit garish," Callum said, buttering a roll.

"I didn't—"

"I know what you meant." He put the knife down, his smile becoming a wince. "You ask why I helped you."

"You have helped me more than once, in fact," I pointed out.

"This realm is a hell for mortals," he said simply. "All but a favoured few. A place of violence and torment. Whenever I have the chance, which is far less often than I would like, I endeavour to make it less so."

"And yet it is your home," I said, examining him.

He gave the faintest of nods. "And yet it is my home."

"Oh dear," Wendell said sympathetically, touching his hand. "I have no doubt you've seen things that upset you greatly. My father used to round up the mortals who stumbled into his realm—those who didn't amuse him in some way—and set them loose in Wildwood Bog for the nobility to hunt."

Callum nodded. "A tradition continued by your stepmother."

"She would!" Wendell said. "Well, no such base pastimes

will be allowed under our reign. I haven't the heart for brutality or violence."

I bit my tongue at this.

"We have heard rumours of you for years," Callum said. "And of *you*, Professor Wilde. Your stepmother had spies watching you, you know. It was said that our exiled king had become taken with some scholar. Few Folk could believe it."

"And from this," I said, "you believed that Wendell deserved your loyalty? That seems a gamble. And we mortals can be tyrants too."

"It was a gamble," Callum agreed. "But he could scarcely be worse than Queen Arna."

A chill touched my neck like the brush of a cold breeze. Wendell had never spoken his stepmother's name. The surprise of it made me feel superstitious, as if saying it might summon her.

"The trouble is, *all* of Faerie is a hell for mortals," Niamh said, waving her fork. "We scholars like to rank things; it gives us additional subjects to argue about. Yes, some realms have claimed more lives than others, but the Folk are, at the core, unfathomably powerful creatures governed by caprice. You might as well argue over which sea is more dangerous to the mariner."

Callum smiled faintly. "As always, I wish I could be as philosophical on the subject as you, Niamh."

She immediately looked regretful. "My apologies, Callum. Your sister—I did not mean to imply—"

"You didn't," he said with a sigh, running his hand through his hair. "Please don't worry about it, Niamh. I am always quick to quarrel when I have not had much sleep!"

"Your sister?" I repeated, too interested to realize until a moment later that Callum did not seem to wish to discuss this.

Wendell touched his hand again. "Callum's sister was stolen away by one of the nobility when she was a small child," he told me. "The Lady of the Clawed Barrow, I believe. He came in search of her, but it was too late."

Callum had gone back to buttering his roll in smooth, precise strokes. "The Lady abandoned Nora in the forest—she must have tired of caring for a human child. The guardians came upon her. I suppose they were in want of sport that day." He put the food down and rested his hands briefly on the edge of the table. "I would likely have suffered the same fate, if Taran had not met me while on one of his wanders, and fallen in love with me."

"The poor child," Wendell said. "I am glad Taran dealt with the Lady as she deserved."

Niamh looked unimpressed by this, and gave a huff through her nostrils. "Yes, sometimes justice is meted out," she said. "If the right mortal is affected."

"I have come to say that a great queue has assembled in the King's Grove," Callum said, and even I understood he wished to leave the subject behind.

"We will change the name," Wendell said. "The Monarchs' Grove, as it was known before my mother died."

"Of course, Your Highness," Callum said after a pause. "As I was saying, there is a great crowd, and they grow increasingly restless. Many have come from far and wide to speak with you—some seeking favours, while others, I suspect, merely wish to fawn or gawk. There are musicians and cooks seeking employment, lords and ladies wanting curses undone, wandering assassins hoping to offer you their services, and various other mendicants."

"I have no interest in that now," Wendell said. "What has become of my realm?"

Callum stopped short. "You've noticed."

"I've noticed." Wendell drew one of his knees up as he

played absently with a strawberry. "I wasn't certain, at first. I thought perhaps it felt different because I have been away so long. But this morning, as soon as I awoke, I knew. What has my stepmother done?"

Callum grimaced. "Perhaps you should ask Taran for the story. I don't know that I understand it well enough to do it justice."

"What is this?" I said, new dread rising within me.

"There is a sickness here," Wendell said. "I feel it burrowing into the roots of the forest and heathlands."

"Good Lord!" Suddenly the *shush-shush* of the leaves as they brushed the windows took on a sinister cadence. "Has the old queen placed a curse upon the land?"

Callum shook his head. "I know not how to answer that. In the chaos last night, Taran apprehended two members of the queen's guard who were lurking about the castle grounds, attempting to sow discord. They confessed that the queen lives, though weakened, and is in hiding. Through some dark enchantment, she has transferred the poison in her veins into the land itself, or perhaps she has allowed her own body to be absorbed into the forest, infecting it—I am unclear on the particulars."

"What is the nature of this sickness?" I asked. "Are the trees dying?"

"In a sense," Callum said. "They die, but some corruption in them lives on, twisting them out of shape—any small Folk who touch them perish."

"Fire," I said immediately, for my mind had been sifting through the stories even as he spoke. Callum stared at me. Wendell smiled.

"Have you tried purging the sickness through fire?" I elaborated. "If it is in the trees—"

"We have, in fact," he said. "Taran sent scouts out last night, and they located two infected groves. Both were burned, which seems to have banished the corruption."

"Good," Wendell said. "But it is *not* banished entirely—I feel it still, like the chill in an autumn wind." His gaze grew distant, and then he seemed to shake himself. "Tell my uncle to send more scouts. Where is he, anyway?"

"Rather busy," Callum said drily. "Your stepmother's heir—your half-sister—organized an assassination attempt on you last night, which he only barely managed to thwart. It involved several members of the nobility and a few hired thugs. Taran threw the girl into the dungeons for now, but unravelling the web of co-conspirators is taking time."

Wendell sighed. "Good Lord! How tedious children are. I suppose I must work out what to do with her."

"You must meet with the Council first," Niamh said. "Most of the queen's Council has fled or been killed in the chaos following her defenestration—I recommend you summon those who live, as well as your father's senior councillors."

"More important than the Council is tracking down the queen," Callum said. "Also, the realm is at present in a state of instability, with invaders from conquered realms crossing our borders. Nobody is doing anything about them, because most of our soldiers have abandoned their posts."

Wendell fell back against his chair, looking faint. "What a mess! And I am to deal with all this today? It is not possible. For one thing, I was planning to take Emily to the Broken Meadows for a picnic."

I recognized the desperate gleam in his eyes and said quickly, "The challenges are not insurmountable provided they are set in order and dealt with accordingly. I agree that we must hunt down your stepmother; she must not simply be allowed to *lurk*—I doubt I need point out that this never ends well, in the stories. Your uncle will send more scouts. In the meantime, you must be seen by your subjects, and you must appear intimidating—that is the best way to discourage more assassination attempts. We will visit this Grove and hear our supplicants." I paused. "Tonight we will have our picnic, if there is time."

Wendell's face broke into a smile so bright it was as if his former distress had never existed. "Em, you will adore the Broken Meadows. It is a veritable garden of streams and wildflowers. The *coirceog sidhe*[*] live in great numbers there, which means endless brownies for you to interrogate. The honeymakers have strange and secretive ways."

He began to tell me about them, with occasional asides from Niamh, and so we talked no more of dark things that morning, nor of the manifold dangers lurking before us, and in every corner and shadow.

---

[*] A species with which I was wholly unfamiliar, though eventually I recalled a passing reference—the only one in scholarship, I believe—in *The O'Donnell Brothers' Midnight Tales of the Good Folk* (1840), specifically, "The Midwife's Lost Apprentice."

1st January–late

The place once known as the King's Grove is located in the forested hillside behind the castle, accessed by a lantern-lined path, one of many that winds through the royal forest. It comprises a half-dozen massive oaks, including one taller than any tree I've seen, with great spreading branches that form a little clearing around its circumference. Between roots that rise from the earth like the ribs of a terrible giant are two thrones, both relatively unadorned and made from strange, twisted bundles of wood, which I eventually realized were more roots that had forced themselves up through the earth from unknown depths. I did not enjoy sitting upon my throne, though it was made comfortable with several cushions, in part because I could not help envisioning those roots eventually growing tired of bearing a tedious mortal like me and dragging me into the earth. The throne smelled of deep, dank caverns and icy springs that have never known sunlight.

I had wondered if Wendell might feel strange issuing commands to his subjects; at Cambridge, he generally relied on charm and deception, rather than his position of authority, to get what he wanted. But I need not have worried. He delivered his judgments with an offhand and good-natured sort of imperiousness, seeming to have accepted his new role—which, I suppose, was not entirely new, as before his exile he'd held the throne for a brief period—as easily as he accepted any other luxury that came into his life, whether it was a sumptuous feast or fine garment. Namely, as if it were as natural as the earth beneath his feet.

Yet while Wendell's mood started off cheerful, as the day wore on, and the queue of supplicants seemed barely to diminish at all, he began to indulge in a great deal of sighing and rubbing at his hair.

And there were all manner of supplicants.

These included courtiers, of course, who mostly came to bow and congratulate Wendell on ridding the realm of Queen Arna, whom, the courtiers assured us through simpering smiles, they had always abhorred. I did not trust a single one of them, though Wendell accepted their allegiance carelessly. And there were also brownies and trooping fae with complaints, many revolving around the invaders who trampled their homes and disturbed their industry, though some had other concerns that I could not understand—one seemed to be involved in a dispute with the morning dew?—because of their thick dialects. One of these was a dishevelled little clap-can who seemed to have lost all but one of his bells.[*] His feet were covered in a sticky grey substance like the webbing of some oversized spider. Upon his skin were several weeping scabs that made Wendell swear and leap up from his throne. He healed the faerie with a single touch, but the creature would answer no questions after, merely muttering in a desperate voice, "Must keep going," before fleeing into the forest.

"Bloody invaders," Wendell said to me, rearranging himself on his throne in a slouch.

---

[*] This I found more concerning than anything else, for clap-cans carry their bells wherever they go, and are said to protect them with their lives.

"You think they were the cause of his injuries?" I said.

"I've never seen a wound like that in my realm." Wendell shook his head. "They have strange magics in Where the Ravens Hide."

I opened my mouth to question him further, thinking of Queen Arna's curse—and yet, hadn't Callum said the poisoned groves had been burned? But then the next faerie was coming forward, and I was forced to redirect my thoughts.

Several Folk, including one bedraggled member of the queen's guard, who looked as if he had not stopped drinking since Wendell's return, challenged him to duels. Wendell won each of these handily, though he refused to fight the drunken guard, and merely lifted his hand and turned the man's sword into a stick, at which point the guard broke down sobbing and had to be led away by two servants.

I wished to take notes, but restrained myself. It was not required of me, of course, for Niamh sat to Wendell's left, tapping away on a braille typewriter. The matter-of-fact clack-clacking of the keys was calming, but on the whole I felt awkward and uncomfortable for the entire afternoon. I wore the simplest of the dresses the servants had offered me, deep green with small yellow flowers embroidered into the bodice, beneath my star-strewn cloak, but naturally this did not make me feel any more a queen of Faerie. I sat up straight, feigning equanimity, trying to behave as mortals in such circumstances do in the stories—they are generally portrayed as plucky, down-to-earth creatures unimpressed by the glitter and elegance of Faerie. I do not believe I had much success. Most Folk, if they looked my way at all, eyed me with disdain or suspicion.

Wendell, on the other hand, could not have looked more like a monarch of Faerie. He was luxuriously but simply attired in all black, a row of small silver buttons the only adornment on his tunic, which naturally he had tailored to perfection himself, and a pair of sharp-toed riding boots. In place of a crown, leaves and flowers had been woven into his hair, plucked fresh that morning and then glazed by the royal silversmith, a particularly extravagant tradition, as the process needed to be repeated each day with fresh flora. (I had refused a similar headpiece, knowing my hair would resemble a bird's nest by day's end.) He had on his terrifying cloak, of course, the hem draped over the arm of the throne and onto the forest floor. Occasionally, it would stir and grumble to itself, or slither towards a terrified courtier, growling, before Wendell yanked it back.

Completing the picture was Razkarden, who perched upon the back of Wendell's throne, his many legs digging into the wood as he fixed his ancient, malevolent gaze upon the assembled Folk. He attempted to settle on my throne once, but Wendell, with a quick glance at me, called him back.

I could not stop my gaze from sliding to Wendell throughout the day. I am used to him in mortal clothes, against mortal backdrops, and while he was even more beautiful in his native context, I also at times had the impression that he had faded into the wonders around me, becoming part of them, as if something about him had lost its definition when seen through my mortal eyes. At one point I realized I was fantasizing about seizing his hand and dragging us both back to the mortal world. It was partly homesickness for Cambridge, I believe. It kept jabbing at me like a knife. Particularly the memory of my office: the snug proportions and neatly organized papers and bookshelves; the morning light streaming over the desk and the tidy greenery of lawn and pond beyond the window.

As I was contemplating this, he met my gaze, then waved the courtier before us away.

"I'm all right," I said.

"Em," he said, leaning close, "even the most fire-breathing of dragons is allowed to tire of its occupation sometimes. I've had enough of this. Haven't you?"

"Yes," I said, sighing with relief. To my astonishment, the sky was beginning to take on a lavender hue, the afternoon blurring into twilight, and the lanterns along the path were flickering to life against the dark trees.

"Where have the fauns got to?" I asked. The *fuchszwerge* I caught glimpses of here and there, watching us from the trees, while the trolls, I understood, were building themselves a series of workshops somewhere down by the lake, but the fauns had disappeared the previous evening.

"Oh, I have given them a new assignment," he said.

I frowned, suspicious. "What new assignment?"

He laughed. "Nothing terrible, I promise. Not that they wouldn't deserve it, the little beasts. Now, shall we—" He stopped, his gaze drifting back to the Grove.

A woman of the courtly fae had stepped out of the trees, ignoring the still-lengthy queue, the foremost members of which grumbled and glared at her. Her eyes were much too wide-set and her nose too large for her face, but she was beautiful, the unusual, arresting variety of beauty that many of the Folk possess. Her hair was a spill of dark feathers, her dress a dozen shades of black. I remembered her immediately—she had been one of the more disturbing members of our audience last night.

"Your Highnesses," she said, bowing at us both, before rising with a malicious smile. She carried a sword at her side.

"You again," Wendell said, frowning. "You will have no luck here, Lady. I advise you to put your sword down and return to the trees uninjured."

"But I have waited an age," the woman replied in a voice much older than her face. "My hunger for vengeance grows like ivy, strangling my heart with each passing season. I thought your stepmother had denied me my chance."

"Very well," Wendell said. "I would lift your curse, if I could—but I can see no way through my father's magics."

"I want nothing from you," she spat. "Only your blood on my sword."

I had no idea what was going on, but this faerie looked every bit as unhinged and dangerous as she sounded. "Please tell me you are not going to fight her," I said in disbelief.

"Don't worry, Em," he said, for naturally this was exactly what he was about to do. "This poor wretch will not trouble us long."

Sighing, he stood and picked up his sword. He and the raven-haired faerie circled each other for a few moments—Wendell did not seem enthusiastic about another swordfight. Eventually, she charged, sword flashing. The Folk in the queue, as well as the various courtiers who had gathered in the forest shadows to watch the proceedings, cheered and clapped.

The woman was more skilled than any other Wendell had fought that day—she ducked and wove like a dancer, her midnight skirts twirling about her. There was a pause in the fight, and Wendell heaved another sigh. I realized he had been hoping to win without exerting himself particularly. When the woman charged him again, he met her with an impossible series of parries, and then—I did not perceive the moment he disarmed her—her sword was sailing over our heads and into the forest. Two courtiers ran after it, giggling. Wendell put his hand on the raven-haired faerie's shoulder as if in commiseration. Then, with his other hand, he drove his sword into her chest.

A strangled sound escaped me. Wendell had angled the sword slightly upwards, the motion calculated and precise, and I realized with a shudder that it must have been to ensure that the woman did not linger. He murmured briefly in her ear and stepped back.

The woman's face was twisted in a peevish sort of scowl, as if he had done nothing worse than beat her at a hand of cards. She collapsed against the moss, and her body began to contort, bones snapping and shrinking and feathers bursting through her fine silks. A heartbeat later, a crow hunched in her place, and then it launched itself into the air, flapping at Wendell's head before Razkarden chased it into the forest.

As I stared in mute silence at the place where the woman had lain, Wendell plucked a feather from his hair and fell back into his throne.

"She will remain that way for as long as my reign lasts," he said, twirling the feather idly between his fingers. "It is her curse, placed upon her by my father long before I was born. The magic releases her from her crow form only briefly to challenge each of my father's descendants when they ascend the throne. To break the curse, she must slay one of us, else she is returned to the treetops."

Good Lord. It was nonsensical even by the standards of Faerie. "And what was her crime, that your father doomed her thus?"

"Oh, I don't know," Wendell said. "It was so long ago that most Folk have forgotten. I suppose her fate must have made sense to him; he enjoyed constructing elaborate punishments for those who angered him. I remember him of an evening, chuckling to himself by the fire. Poor thing!"

"I see," I said noncommittally—the fate of the vengeful faerie woman was appalling, but I could summon little sympathy for her. I found I had trouble focusing my thoughts. It was as if I had been holding my composure in place by a thread, and this final bizarre incident had snapped it.

"What a wearying day!" Wendell exclaimed, though he'd

spent most of it lounging upon his throne, sipping an array of coffees supplied by the eager red-faced servants, who seemed to be having a private competition over which blend he would prefer. He waved away the next petitioner, a faerie woman who pouted prettily at him. "I'd almost rather be in a lecture hall," he said. "Well, I refuse to exert myself further. I look forward to having all of this"—he waved a hand vaguely—"sorted out, so that I can spend most of my days at leisure, as one should."

"Your stepmother kept herself busy starting wars," I pointed out.

"Ah, but that was merely her way of amusing herself. My father enjoyed receiving supplicants, but that was because he always liked holding court. He very rarely resolved anything, and often made the situation worse."

I mulled this over. Kaur has theorized that most faerie monarchs rule through a sort of capricious neglect, and that their true role is as an animus for the magics of their realm, rather than a head of state in the human sense.[*]

He stood and offered me his hand. "Let's go home."

"You wanted a picnic."

"That can wait. Come—the servants will see the rest of these Folk off."

As soon as we left the Grove, Wendell led me off the path and through a screen of tall ferns, which thickened behind us, growing so tall they blocked even the lantern light.

"Where on earth are we going?" I groused.

Wendell turned and clasped my hands between his. He looked so anxious and dejected that it brought me up short—I'm not certain I've ever seen such an expression on his face before.

---

[*] Naya Kaur, "Towards a Less Anthropocentric View of Faerie Governance: Examples from Wallonia," *Journal of Social Dryadology,* 1905.

"Do you wish to return to Cambridge, Em?" he said. "Because if that is the case, you need only say the word. I suppose I could return to teaching—perhaps I could do both, or install a regent here, to rule in my stead. If there is one thing I will not stand for, it is for you to be unhappy—"

"No, indeed!" I exclaimed. He appeared to have worked himself up into a proper speech, so I put my hand over his mouth. And then—my initial thought was that this would be more efficient than arguing with him—I pulled his face to mine and kissed him.

As I had guessed, he forgot all about what he had been saying, and pulled me closer. His lips tasted like the salt the servants had sprinkled onto the coffee—quite agreeable. I stopped thinking, something I rarely do, and for a moment there was only the hum of crickets and rustling of night creatures in the trees.

He drew back and touched my cheek, his dark eyes searching mine. A flickering, moon-coloured glow had appeared above us—he had summoned a light.

"I mean it," he murmured. So not quite so forgetful, then. The light caught on the silvered flowers in his hair and made him look even more inconveniently otherworldly than he already did, but I found that when I focused on small, familiar things, like the way his mouth came up slightly higher on the left side, and how his green eyes leaned more yellow than blue, I was able to disregard this.

"I know," I replied. "I have brought myself here, Wendell—I am not some poor maiden who stumbled unawares through a ring of mushrooms. You can trust me to tell you if I change my mind."

"All right." He swept his gaze over me, then pulled me into his arms almost matter-of-factly. "That's enough of that."

"Enough of what?"

"You're shaking."

To my astonishment, I realized that I was, and had been for some time. He held me until I was still, gently combing through my hair, and I leaned my forehead against the curve of his neck. I could smell the wildflowers in his hair.

"I don't know what I should call you," I mumbled into his shoulder.

He gave a breath of laughter and drew back. "You haven't been worrying about that, have you? It doesn't matter what you call me, Em. You may choose whichever name you like. You said you didn't want my true name."

"I still don't," I said. The idea of having that sort of power over him filled me with disquiet. In the stories, whenever a mortal is granted such power over the Folk, she will always be forced to use it. "I would prefer to call you Wendell."

"Good!" He kissed me again. "Do you know? That name is more comfortable to me now, after all these years, than Liath is."

I felt suddenly worried that I hadn't been understood. "It's not that I dislike your name. I don't dislike your realm, either—quite the contrary. But even after all my studies, after all I've learned over the years, this is so much— What I mean is, even to compare it to the Hidden king's realm, it is, well—"

"So much," he finished.

I let my breath out. "So much."

"I thought it might be," he said. "Let me show you something."

He seemed so pleased with himself that I was instantly apprehensive. "Please let it not be a dress that mutters to itself, or contains anything other than fabric."

He laughed. "Far better than that."

We returned to the castle, where we were met by servants who trailed unobtrusively behind us. I found that I had a firm grasp of the layout, as if I carried a map in my head, despite my also knowing, somehow, that it was likely to shift at the whims of its occupants. The main level was a series of large galleries, some empty and moss-floored, others elaborately furnished sitting rooms or displays of art and statuary. In one gallery, a group of ladies sat at tea, twilight streaming through the windows as tiny brownies serenaded them with reed pipes. They beamed at us when we passed and waved us over, but Wendell merely called out a merry greeting and swept me along. In another room, several mortals admired paintings of village scenes that seemed human-made, beautiful but mundane. Throughout the place, the light shifted oddly, and shadows of leaves and wind-tossed branches scattered the floor, as if it were haunted by the ghosts of the trees that had stood there before the castle was built.

We mounted the largest of the five staircases to the uppermost floor, where we found Shadow sprawled across the landing, keeping a woebegone eye on all who passed. As soon as he saw us, he leapt upon me, then Wendell, tail lashing so hard he generated a breeze.

Lord Taran awaited us in Wendell's reception room, perched upon one of the window seats and looking resentful. "It has been a very long day, Your Highnesses," he said in a complaining tone, gesturing towards the small crowd of courtly fae gathered at the other end of the room, who eyed us nervously. At the centre of these was a woman with brown skin and tangled white tresses that trailed upon the floor, woven with bits of grass and leaves.

"I have no doubt of that," I said, before Wendell could speak. Recalling what Callum had said that morning, I added, "Thank you, Lord Taran. For everything you have done for us."

This seemed to bring him up short, and he blinked at me

for a moment. "Yes, it is a great deal of work, keeping you two alive," he said. "I wonder if it is worth the effort."

"I shall not presume to try to influence your opinion on that score," I said. "I wish only to express my gratitude—and Wendell's—and to say that I am aware of how fortunate we are to be assisted by the most venerated person in the realm. You could easily have chosen otherwise."

"And I may yet, if I am forced to endure your childish attempts at flattery," he said, and yet some of the irritation drained from his eyes, replaced by the familiar glint of amusement. I was reminded, unaccountably, of Snowbell, and I had to press my lips together to suppress my smile.

"I have summoned a Council for you, my king," Taran said, nodding to the other courtly fae. "Most of these served your father, or your grandparents before him. Choose who you like, or discard the lot; it's all one to me."

"Oh, good," Wendell said blithely. "I'll speak with them momentarily. Emily, this is the Lady East Wind—she is the only one I like. Well, Lord Wherry is all right, I suppose; or so I thought before I heard it was he who murdered one of my brothers."

I thought I could guess who Lord Wherry was from the greyish pallor his already pale face took on. The Lady East Wind—she of the radiant white tresses—stood and offered me her hand. When I placed my palm against hers, she bowed her head and kissed my fingertips. "Your Highness," she said gravely.

"Emily," I corrected her inanely, my surprise getting the better of me.

"Queen Emily," she said, gazing at me with a hungry sort of interest that made me wish to run away. I found myself longing for the dismissive looks of the courtiers in the Grove. Fortunately, Wendell took my hand and drew me away.

"I shall await you in the garden, Your Highnesses," the Lady East Wind said. "I grow more weary of confinement with each passing year."

"As you wish," Wendell said, flashing her a charming smile. She smiled back, and then abruptly vanished. A heartbeat later, a wind stirred our hair and blasted the window open, rustling the branches beyond as it went.

"Wait a moment," I said, staring at the window, which swayed gently on its hinges. "Is that—is she *really* the East Wind?"

"I suppose it's possible," Wendell replied, as if he had never given the matter much thought.

Another prospective councillor stepped forward and inclined her head. She, too, seemed to take more interest in me than I was used to, which I disliked even more than the Lady East Wind's attention. Because I had noticed this immensely intimidating faerie before—at the banquet last night, and this morning, watching Wendell and me in the Grove. According to Wendell, she was an exile from another court, and her name was unknown to him, even in part; she was referred to by her usual attire, a crimson cloak. This cloak left a trail of what looked like blood behind it wherever the Lady went, as if she had recently come from a gruesome murder scene. Her skin was the variegated colour of birch bark, her hair waves of burnt gold, and she was as beautiful as a summer's twilight, though she would have been more so, in my opinion, if she did not also have blood in her hair, and upon her hands.

"It would be an honour to serve you both, Your Highnesses," the Lady in the Crimson Cloak told us, her gaze lingering upon me.

I nodded in reply, silently willing her to turn back to Wendell. He meanwhile smiled at the Lady as if she were not at present leaving ghastly stains upon the carpeting and said, "It is dull work, but you have our gratitude. Excuse us."

He led me from the room. I muttered, "I doubt I will ever associate the feeling of gratitude with that horror. Must we put her on the Council?"

"Not if you object," Wendell said. "Do you?"

"No," I said, after a pause. There were a great many monsters in Wendell's court—I was going to have to get used to them at some point. "Only you know so little about her. What court is she exiled from? What was her crime? And what about this Lady East Wind—why did she stare at me so?"

"I know little about most of them," Wendell replied with a sigh. "As I said, I did not spend my youth in the most productive manner. Those old and venerable enough to serve on our Council were not exactly part of my social circle."

I opened my mouth again, but before I could get another word out, Wendell continued in a warning tone, "It was thoughtful of you to praise my uncle, Em. But if you believe him to possess a kindly nature beneath all that spite, you are much mistaken. As general, he took great pleasure in torturing my grandparents' enemies—not for reasons of loyalty, but because he relished the opportunity to invent creative forms of pain. I may not be well acquainted with many of the respectable Folk of my realm, but he at least I can warn you against befriending."

A little chill went through me. "Noted," I said.

Wendell pulled me on, through a room filled with crates and a jumble of furniture, and down a corridor that ended at a door I recognized.

"The bookbinders!" I said. This was not the bookbinders' door, but it made me remember my ill-fated exploration that morning. "Wendell, all those journals—did you—"

"Ah, you found them!" He turned to smile at me. "You needn't thank me, Em. That was but a small wedding gift."

"Small!" I exclaimed, remembering the dozens of journals, all beautiful beyond measure—so beautiful, in fact, that I could scarcely imagine despoiling them with my inelegant handwriting.

"I mean for you to have everything you could ever want," he said. "While we're on the subject."

He gave me a smile that filled me with foreboding, it was so mischievous. But he was already opening the door and pulling me through, Shadow at my heels.

The view was as I remembered—the misty waterfall, the treed hillside, the little stone cottage. But I had only had a quick glance that morning, and I realized that I made an incorrect assumption on one rather key point.

"This isn't Faerie," I murmured. "It's—"

"Corbann," Wendell said. "Well, the edge of Corbann, in County Leane. It's a pretty village, as mortal villages go. This door was once located in the woods beyond Silverlily Lake. I used it myself once or twice when I was a teenager. I couldn't have opened it from *this* side, for my stepmother had used an enchantment to seal it against me, but that was easy to undo last night, from the Faerie side. And then I simply moved the door into the castle."

"Yes, that all sounds perfectly straightforward," I murmured.

The last vestiges of daylight filtered through the mist that drifted off the waterfall—it was a chilly winter twilight, but welcome nevertheless. Welcome, because it was somehow distinctly *mortal*. For a long moment, I simply stared. Wendell waited, looking pleased but anxious, as does one who gives a gift that involved a great deal of guesswork as to the recipient's desires. Shadow, meanwhile, snuffled happily at a patch of clover, either unaware or uncaring that we had been abruptly returned to the mortal world; but then, to him, all the worlds are merely one vast canvas of smells.

"Why have you brought me here?" I said at last.

"I thought it might be helpful. For most mortals it takes time to become accustomed to living in Faerie—even those under royal protection. It can be very wearying. Niamh seems comfortable now, but I know those first years were a trial for her. I felt it would be additionally trying for you, perhaps, given your previous sojourn in a Faerie court. So! I decided to offer you a bolt-hole of sorts. Here you may come to escape from courtiers and common fae alike, or simply to have a quiet place to scowl at your books. Do you like it? I would have preferred something more grand for a queen of Faerie, but then I know your preference for rustic accommodation."

There was another moment during which I could not speak. "But when did you do all this?" I finally demanded weakly. "The bookbinders—this portal? I cannot imagine you accomplishing all this last night."

"You needn't look so astonished," he said, unfolding his collar against the damp. "As I told you before, Em, being disinclined to exert oneself overmuch is not the same as being incapable. Now: I must tell you how it works."

He spun me around, facing the direction whence we came. I didn't need to ask what he was indicating, for the faerie door was as clear as day to my trained eye. Within the grasses, half covered in moss, was a scatter of flat stones. Most mortals would have taken them for a natural formation, as that sort of speckled stone was everywhere. But I could see that they formed a rough little path that bent towards a grove of oaks.

"Any mortal could stumble into the private chambers of faerie royalty," I said, an absurd laugh rising in my throat.

"I doubt it," he said. "Few villagers come this way. They believe that waterfall there to be faerie-haunted—which is only a little inaccurate, for certainly a great many Folk from my realm have made use of this door over the generations. And one must tread upon each of the stones to pass through, which is difficult to do by chance."

As I stuttered and fumbled my words—I think I was trying to thank him, but another part of me wished to protest all these indulgences—he leaned forward and kissed me.

"Don't tarry here too long," he murmured against my lips. "I shall miss you too much, and come to regret this." He turned and stepped from stone to stone as if they were little islands in a rushing stream. And then, as he moved from one stone to the next, he vanished.

I turned back to the cottage, feeling as if I were in a dream. It was winter, but this was Ireland, and one of the southernmost counties at that, so everything was still very green. I was not cold in my cloak, though a scarf would have been nice, for the damp breeze had a chill. My initial thought was that the countryside reminded me a great deal of Wendell's realm, but with fewer trees and a welcome sense of the mundane about it. Oh, it was beautiful, but the trees here were *trees,* not leering monstrosities, and none of the landscape features seemed inclined to change position on a whim. It was coherent, unambiguous, and immensely restful to my eyes.

Moving slowly, I made my way up the path to the cottage. A dry stone wall enclosed a little garden—a vegetable patch and a few clay pots of flowers, leafless and slumbering in the January evening. A mountain range loomed in the distance, snow adorning a few of the higher peaks. Far gentler than the towering heights of Austria, of course, but pretty in its own way.

The door was unlocked, but as I turned the knob, I had a moment of misgiving. Someone was moving about within—

I heard a clanking sound, then a series of thumps, as if they were in the process of preparing a meal. Had Wendell installed a fleet of servants in the place to cater to my whims? It seemed likely, and I wondered if it would be possible to send them away; cooking my own supper would be preferable to being waited on and having to work out their expectations of me, where I would no doubt fall short.

I looked over my shoulder, and for a moment I considered simply going back. It was not only the idea of servants; I did not like that there was now a world between Wendell and me. It filled me with a foreboding that I did not care for, though I could not guess what it signified. In addition to that, Wendell's realm was still a threat to him, with enemies everywhere, and I had little faith in his sense of caution.

The faerie door glimmered faintly—with damp, a mortal would assume, but I knew better. I turned from it with a sigh. I did not want to spurn Wendell's gift, particularly given the thoughtfulness behind it. I would remain in the mortal realm for an hour or two, then return to Faerie.

I pushed the door open. Warmth and light spilled over me, together with the smell of stew and baking bread. The main room of the cottage was low-ceilinged and cosy, a fire burning merrily in the hearth, before which were several comfortable armchairs. On the other side of the cottage was the kitchen, and through the open door I saw a pretty, dark-haired woman with a curious scar upon her forehead. She was chopping carrots at the table, pausing occasionally to tuck her hair behind her ear or toss a comment over her shoulder at her companion, whom I could not see. The cottage was full of their voices and laughter.

I removed my cloak and boots, my hands trembling slightly, and hung the cloak on the hanger by the door. Then I stepped into the kitchen.

Margret looked up from the carrots and gave a cry. Lilja, who was peering into the oven at a tray of buns, let the door swing shut with a bang.

"Emily!" she exclaimed, springing upon me with a delighted laugh. Margret circled around the two of us, alternately patting me on the back and crying, "Let her breathe, dear, let her breathe!"

I drew back, half convinced I had stumbled through yet another faerie door. "What" was all I could get out.

"Oh, dear." Lilja guided me over to a chair. "Wendell said he wanted to surprise you—I see he went through with it."

"Here, drink this," Margret said, pouring me a cup of tea, then adding a liberal splash of something from a bottle. "You look like you need it!"

I took a sip. The *something* turned out to be rum. I downed the lot and set the cup back down.

"There we are," Margret said with a laugh. I laughed along with her. Now that my shock was fading, I realized how happy I was to see them.

"You'd best explain yourselves," I said. "After the day I've had, I'm afraid I'm ill-equipped to deal with surprises, even agreeable ones."

"Wendell wrote to us, of course," Lilja said. "When was it? November, I think. He wished to know if we would like a little holiday—how did he put it? Oh, yes: 'Where winter is a peaceable, rainy season, and one need not insulate oneself with dead animals to venture out of doors.' You know, I don't think he will ever take to Ljosland."

"He might also have mentioned that you would be visiting us from time to time," Margret said, poking the silver-threaded lace on my gown playfully. "When you desire a reprieve from running a faerie kingdom. We arrived last week, and I believe we shall remain for another month or two."

"We never had a proper honeymoon," Lilja said. "We've simply been too busy—it's a great deal of work, running one's own house! So we couldn't possibly have said no, particularly when we heard we would see you again."

"And—" I glanced about me, taking in the shelves of neatly stacked pots and pans, the brushed stone floor and the vases of flowers on the windowsills. "And this place is—?"

"It's a mortal cottage, not something faerie-conjured," Lilja said. "Wendell told us it was abandoned long ago, and that Folk would stay here sometimes when they visited the mortal world. It was in decent shape when we arrived, just a little musty. We've done some cleaning and minor repairs—the villagers lent a hand there. And Wendell came by last night and did—well, I'm not sure what. He only swept the floor and did a bit of tidying up, but afterwards it seemed a new place." She pointed to a vase of lilies. "He also brought these—they've not lost a single petal. In fact, I think they've grown bigger."

"I quite like it here," Margret said. "It's ever so peaceful not having relatives knocking on your door at all hours, and the village is only a short stroll away. And there's a lovely path up to the waterfall; you must join us for a walk in the morning. Lilja was chopping wood in her shirtsleeves yesterday—not once have we needed to shovel any snow."

They chattered on about their stay thus far—evidently, it was the first time either of them had ventured beyond Ljosland, and they were almost as awed by the experience as I had been by my first visit to Faerie. I had the sense that they had a great many questions they wished to ask, but also that they were holding back, allowing me the respite of sitting quietly and listening, voicing only murmurs of interest or agreement.

"Well, what do you think?" Lilja said, flashing me a smile as she rose to remove the buns from the oven. "Do you like what you've seen of the place so far? Wendell seemed anxious that you should be happy here. He asked me to make note of anything I thought could be improved."

"Yes," I said, mostly succeeding in hiding the wobble in my voice. "I like it quite well." And we tucked in to our supper.

2nd January

I slept late this morning, rising with the sun at around half eight. The cottage was hushed, Lilja and Margret being still abed, and Shadow too seemed inclined to laze amongst the blankets, rousing himself only when I reminded him of the fine steak awaiting him downstairs. Wendell, in another uncharacteristic fit of initiative, had written to the local merchants in Corbann in advance of Lilja and Margret's arrival and arranged an unlimited tab with which we three could purchase whatever we desired. I hoped he planned to pay them in mortal currency and not faerie coin, which is merely glamoured leaves or pebbles or other bits of rubbish, and eventually returns to its original state as the enchantment fades,* which would be unlikely to endear us to the locals.

The cottage is snug, perhaps a little smaller than our accommodation in St. Liesl, but larger than the Hrafnsvik let. Upstairs are two bedrooms and a bathing room that I sus-

---

* Danielle de Grey's article "A Landscape Model for Classifying Faerie Currency: Case Study of a Highland Market" (*British Journal of Dryadology*, 1857) argues that this form of faerie trickery varies by country and region. Glamoured leaves, which tend to be favoured in the South, maintain the illusion of coinage for a few days, on average, while the hardier pinecones and pebbles more commonly employed in Scotland and Northern England may hold on to their glamours for years.

pect Wendell has enchanted, for the water is hot and gushing to a degree that is generally alien to creaky, rural cottages. As for the downstairs, the layout is simple, merely a sitting room with hearth and the kitchen, divided by a little hall with the staircase at one end and the door at the other. The place is bright even in winter, for the windows appear larger from within than from without—which is certainly possible, until one realizes that there are also *more* windows inside the cottage, which is not. A handful of feral cats with odd, all-black eyes include the garden in their neighbourhood patrols, keeping the mice away. Lilja and Margret say that the villagers are much mystified by their appearance, as prior to this winter, none were to be found within five miles of the place beyond a fat housecat or two.

I cooked up a simple breakfast of omelet and toast, tucking some away in the oven for Lilja and Margret when they awoke, and then I wandered around the cottage, looking out the windows. Around the back was a door leading down to a cellar, which my friends had stocked with provisions. The sun was bright that morning, and it was almost warm, or warm enough with a coat and scarf. I settled myself on the wooden bench in the garden and spent a happy hour there, taking copious notes for my book on faerie politics or gazing out at the landscape, lost in thought.

I found myself regaining my excitement for my project and the opportunity for scholarly discovery presented by my presence in Wendell's kingdom. Given the peril that surrounded us, this may seem a little mad but—well, actually, I have no defence for that. It is nigh impossible to find evidence to support the wisdom of taking up a throne in any of the Faerie realms, particularly during a time of political conflict; yet this thought shrinks to almost nothing when I imagine how my research will benefit the scientific cause, our understanding of the inner workings of Faerie. The opportunity is monumental.

When I think how often I despair of the irrationality of the Folk!

I paused in the sketch I was making of Wendell's throne to watch a robin poking about for worms. The mist from the waterfall settled over the grasses, gilding the places the sunlight touched. Lilja and Margret came to find me a moment later, and we walked up the hillside to where the water began to cascade down the steep, ferny slope, which offered a view of the pastoral landscape. I could see two lakes, similar in shape to Muckle and Silverlily. The village was a scatter of perhaps two dozen dwellings along a cobbled street, with farms beyond that stretching to the mountains with their light dusting of snow. We talked of ordinary things—the health of Auður, who was doing a little better these days, though still far from her old self; Margret's newfound fondness for baking bread, which she had taken to selling at a tidy profit to sailors who passed through the Hrafnsvik harbour—as well as my time in Faerie.

"And you have not changed your mind?" Margret said, after I'd unravelled the tale as far as the previous evening. Lilja put a hand on her arm, and the two exchanged a look before turning the subject to other things. Not for the first time; I sensed they had a great deal to say about my decision to take up a Faerie throne, as well as my faith in Wendell, whom they have always liked, particularly given their gratitude to him. But I am coming to understand that this is not the same as saying that they *trust* Wendell—perhaps this distinction holds true for all the villagers of Hrafnsvik, given their troubled history with the courtly fae.

We returned to the cottage after our walk and I collected Shadow, who would not have enjoyed such a steep hike. He yawned and stretched, his bones creaking a little, and I felt a stab of melancholy familiar to all those who care for old dogs. I would speak to the servants—perhaps they had a more beneficial salve for his joints than the one I relied on.

"Would you care to come back with me?" I asked as we stood by the gate. "I could show you the castle."

Margret and Lilja exchanged another look. "It's kind of you," Lilja said. "But we are content to remain on this side."

Instantly, I regretted my words, recalling what they had suffered at the hands of the courtly fae of their country. Before I could apologize, though, Lilja touched my arm and smiled.

"You will visit again soon, I hope?" she said.

I promised I would. Then I turned and went through the faerie door.

The stones were slick underfoot, almost slimy. I had just stepped onto the third stone, my left foot halfway to the fourth, when I found myself standing in the familiar castle hallway, the door open behind me.

Shadow gave a pleased huff and trotted off down the hall. I knew he was in search of Wendell, for he seemed disappointed when each room we passed was empty or revealed only a servant or two, who bowed hastily when they noticed me. The bedchamber was similarly abandoned, apart from Orga, who was curled up among the tangled blankets—I guessed that she had not permitted the servants to make the bed. To my surprise, she greeted me with a chirp and rolled over, purring, allowing me to pet her stomach. Shadow made a lumbering hop onto the bed to commence his customary midmorning nap; Orga ignored his existence entirely, which represented a marked improvement in their relations.

Ordinarily, I spend little time on my appearance, but the idea of donning one of my plain shifts and throwing my hair up into a knot here in Faerie made me uneasy. Someone had added another wardrobe to the bedroom, and in this I found a dozen dresses in a range of colours and styles, as if someone—the servants, I supposed—had chosen to offer me a selection in order to assess my tastes. Naturally, they were all far too luxurious, too brightly coloured or with odd accoutrements; a green dress had vines attached to the bodice that had to be untied before I could put the thing on, while one of white lace had the silliest sleeves I had ever seen, with what looked like silver bracelets dangling off them. I eventually chose a black one, which at least didn't have any adornments, though it *did* have five layers of skirts embroidered with silver that sparkled as I walked.

After some hemming and hawing, I summoned a servant and requested a hairdresser. This creature—a brownie with a wrinkled grey face held in a permanent scowl—yanked my hair into an elaborate plait atop my head and wove it with silvered flowers, primarily poppies. Once everything was in place, I felt awkward and slightly sweaty, though the dress was light, even with its many layers.

I cast a longing look at the simple brown dresses I had brought with me, which I had hung in the wardrobe alongside the finery. They pressed together like poor relations at a lavish ball, who on the whole would have preferred not to have been invited.

"Right," I said, eyeing my appearance in the mirror apprehensively. Then I set to work.

My first task, I had decided during my ponderings that morning, would be to speak to the *oíche sidhe*. I knew the creatures did not like to be seen, even by other Folk, and also that they preferred to work at night, and thus were most likely at rest now. But there was nothing for it.

I found several servants in the dressing room. They were tailors, hard at work assembling garment after garment from the rich silks and linens—mostly black, naturally—that were scattered everywhere, though two were presently adorning headless mannequins with tunics. I glanced about for a moment, overwhelmed.

When I asked if the faerie woman in charge, who was of the courtly fae, might escort me to the *oíche sidhe,* she gave me a horrified look and darted from the room. Before I could decide if I had offended her or if my request had been so strange that she had panicked and fled, she was back, and behind her was another faerie.

"The head housekeeper," the faerie woman said, and then she and the other tailors departed, leaving us alone in a room full of expensive fabrics and scattered measuring tapes and thimbles.

I almost didn't see the new arrival at first, strange as that may sound, because he was so grey and unexceptional that he blended into the flagstones of the dressing room. He was small, but not so small as most of the common fae, the top of his head reaching my shoulder. His fingers were many-jointed and far too spindly, his eyes black, and his hair fell to his chin in dust-coloured wisps. He wore a belt with a single grey rag dangling from it, which his hand went to frequently, twisting it about his fingers in an absent-minded way. He was, unsurprisingly, painfully neat in every respect.

"Hello," I said hesitantly. "I apologize if I disturbed you."

The faerie sank to his knees and lowered his head. "Your Highness," he said in a rough voice that made me picture the bristles of a brush.

"Oh, no," I said. "No, please stand up."

The faerie rose gracefully to his feet, pausing only to smooth the wrinkles from his trousers. "As Your Highness desires."

I gazed at him, feeling oddly tongue-tied. Wendell's grandmother had been of the *oíche sidhe,* and he had taken their form briefly, when he and Aud had rescued me from the Hidden king's court. He had looked a great deal like this creature—nearly identical, in fact, and I guessed that the vagueness of these faeries' appearance also applied to the degree of difference between them. It was unsettling.

"I would like to ask a favour," I said. "Somewhat unusual, perhaps, given your occupation."

I half expected the creature to make some wry remark, as Wendell would have done, but naturally he did not. "As Your Highness desires," he said again.

"You see," I began, not knowing how to phrase my request in a politic manner. In the end, I simply allowed myself to be blunt. "I am in need of spies. Information. Mortals often overlook their housekeepers, who come to learn a great many of their secrets. I doubt the Folk are any different."

"Worse," the faerie said quickly. I had the sense that he was pleased by the direction the conversation had taken, and even eager to speak on the subject. But this was merely a guess; discerning any emotion in the creature's subdued expression was difficult.

"Then you have served both mortals and Folk?" I said.

"I have served," he agreed in his sparse manner.

I nodded. Here was a creature with as little use for small talk as I. "Do you know of anyone who might wish harm to either Wendell—the king, I mean—or myself?"

"Yes," the creature said. And then he began to provide names and specifics.

When he came to the end of the list I found myself standing very still and staring at him. I shook myself and said, "I—thank you. That was—" *More illuminating than I guessed it would be,* I thought. "Thorough."

"Your Highness." The faerie bowed.

I pressed my lips together, uncertain. "You have placed yourself in danger by helping me. Do you desire compensation? I mean—of course I shall compensate you. Only tell me—"

"I have helped His Highness," the creature replied. "I am compensated."

The faerie had spoken softly and flatly throughout our exchange, but this remark seemed to have real emotion behind it.

"I see." I considered him for a moment as I ran through what I knew of the *oíche sidhe,* which was a great deal, or at least more than most dryadologists, for I had made them a priority in my studies since I'd learned of Wendell's lineage. "And I suppose it was you who ensured his rooms were ready upon his arrival. Quite speedy work you made of it, for you could not have known he would prefer his old wing."

"He is one of ours," the creature said.

I gave a slight nod, and the faerie seemed to take this as a dismissal and bowed himself out.

Wendell was not difficult to locate. I simply followed the swirls and eddies of servants and courtiers flitting through the galleries on the castle's main level. Most of the nobility seemed to be availing themselves of the gardens, and of the sunny portico that gave onto them, and thus the servants hastened between there and the kitchens, bearing cups and trays piled with delicacies. I stopped one and took a cup of coffee and a biscuit for myself. It looked plain but tasted of sugared almonds and impossibly tart strawberries.

I found him standing alone near the centre of the gardens upon a hill festooned with lilies and foxgloves. At the summit was a bench shaded by several neat rows of cherry trees and—to my dismay—an attentive oak. It was smaller than the wild-growing ones I'd seen in the forest, but it glowered and gawked at me all the same.

Wendell rested his hand on one of the cherry trees in an absent sort of way, gazing over the landscape. The tree began to flower, buds bursting forth in a riot of purples and blues, and the leaves grew so green they resembled crushed emeralds. It matched Wendell's expression, somehow, as he swept his gaze over the view, a contentment that seemed to radiate from him, cheering all in his vicinity. Two servants carrying what looked like a newly minted silver mirror stepped more lightly, their faces brightening, and a fat leprechaun sprawled against a nearby boxwood chuckled in his sleep.

Wendell turned and saw me standing there, and if anything, the happiness in his eyes only grew. "Em!" he exclaimed, and I am certain he would have seized me and spun me around again, if not for the cup in my hand. "Well? Did you enjoy yourself? By that I mean, did the cottage provide the correct ambience for devouring stacks of old tomes and scribbling away in journals?"

"Yes, thank you," I said. "Though you might have told me about the guests."

"To tell the truth, I was a little nervous about your reaction. I felt you would enjoy seeing Lilja and Margret again, but last night I wondered if you wouldn't have preferred solitude more."

"You needn't look like that," I said, laughing a little at the worry that had stolen over his face. "I was indeed happy to see them. And I am glad you took the initiative of offering them a holiday."

He smiled. "Well, how could I not, the poor dears? What a misery winter is in that accursed place! I don't know how anyone stands it."

I doubted he knew how anyone stood *any* clime different from his native realm, but I was not about to waste my breath on this. We had far more important things to discuss.

"We must go to see this curse your stepmother has inflicted upon the forest," I said. "It is far more important than any other problem we face—I am embarrassed I did not recognize it immediately. I know the stories of deposed faerie monarchs quite well. Working out what she has done must be our sole priority."

"Emily," Wendell said after a little pause, during which the only sounds were the wind moving through the leaves and the bloody oak blinking moistly at us, "as we have established, your thought process moves apace; I often struggle to keep up. You must learn to explain yourself."

"'The Tale of the Bard's Stolen Dirge,'" I said. "'The Robin Lord's Reckoning.' Just to name two examples—there are a dozen more. Don't you see?"*

"I know my stepmother must be dealt with," Wendell said. "My uncle has sent scouts—"

I shook my head. "That's not good enough. We must see what your stepmother has wrought, and without delay."

Wendell gave a breath of laughter. "Well, naturally we will, then."

"Oh, and you must remove the Lady East Wind from your Council," I said. "And, if possible, banish her from court. She had a series of clandestine meetings with the head of the queen's guard before he was executed. Apparently, she helped

---

* Both of these Irish stories recount the gruesome revenge wrought by deposed monarchs. "The Robin Lord's Reckoning" is perhaps the less disturbing of the two; the Robin Lord, likely the king of the northernmost Irish realm, the Montibus Ventus, is overthrown by his son, and hides himself away for three years. During this time, he abducts his son's beasts one by one—hunting dogs, horses, and falcons—enchanting them with an insatiable blood lust. He then lets them loose upon his son's court, where they devour the usurper, his family, and everyone who ever aided him.

your stepmother plot the assassination of your father and siblings."

"What!" Wendell exclaimed. "But we won't have an even number now. I shall have to find somebody to replace the Lady with, and there is nothing more tedious than dealing with councillors, as I have recently discovered. I am out here hiding from them, in fact."

"You should also banish Lord Carlin and someone who calls herself the Keeper of the Secret Brook," I said. "They too are plotting against you."

"How I hate politics!" Wendell heaved a sigh. "Oh, well. All this is useful material for your book, is it not?"

I could not help smiling at this. "Indeed, though I would rather said material did not come in the form of people wishing to kill you."

He made a noise of agreement. "Well, Em, I am now convinced that your stay in Corbann has done you good. You are quite yourself again, ink-stained and full of schemes to burden me with, as if I do not already have enough to do."

I paused. "You do not wish to know how I came by this information?"

"Yes, but only because you clearly wish to tell me," he said, smiling.

I blushed under the warmth in his gaze. "The servants proved exceptionally knowledgeable," I said. "The *oíche sidhe*. I have asked their leader to report to me should they learn anything else of note. I believe this should solve the assassination threat. The courtly fae either ignore the little ones or treat them with condescension, particularly the servants. That they might be listening in on their conversations seems barely to cross the minds of the nobility, even when they are plotting regicide."

Wendell stared at me, and then he began to laugh. "Of

course," he said. "The common fae have come to our rescue again, have they?"

"The head housekeeper," I said after a short pause. "He—seemed to feel some affection for you. He said you were *theirs*."

Wendell's amusement faded, and he looked momentarily disturbed, then a little lost. "Did he?"

"Have you had any contact with that side of your family?" I said.

"None. It was not—" He sighed. "Well, I suppose I could make excuses and say that I never knew my grandmother. She died long ago. The *oíche sidhe* are prone to injuries, given the nature of their work, which compound with age and wear away at their health. But the truth is that I never wanted to know them. It is not usual for my kind to mingle our bloodlines with the common fae. The resulting children are aberrations." He amended, "That is how most Folk see us. Of course, as one in line for the throne, I was insulated from much of this sentiment. Few dared insult me to my face. Generally it was a thing that most at my father's court went out of their way to ignore."

"Which is not the same as saying it was accepted," I noted.

Wendell shrugged, looking moody and unsettled. "It is kind of so many of the common fae to help us."

"You are their king, too," I said.

He seemed not to know what to do with this, and I reminded myself that it was uncommon for the courtly fae to bestow any consideration at all upon the small Folk of their realms. Had Wendell, over the course of his life, had additional motivation to avoid giving them much thought? I decided to change the subject.

"Have you been to see Deilah?"

"My sister?" Wendell wrinkled his nose. "What has she to do with this? Yes, I visited her this morning—briefly, but that was long enough. The brat merely spewed insults and laughed in my face when I suggested she renounce her wretched mother and swear fealty to the new king and queen. She's convinced her mother will have her revenge upon us somehow. My uncle wants to execute her, naturally—that is his solution to everything."

"In this case, it is sound advice," I said. "She attempted to have you assassinated, after all. But I am glad you haven't taken it. In many of the Irish stories, faerie monarchs who murder innocents are punished for it in some way. It would strengthen your stepmother, more likely than not."

"I wasn't thinking of *that*," Wendell said, frowning at me. "I haven't killed her because she is a child, Em. Let her stew in the dungeons a fortnight or so, and we shall see if her vindictiveness holds."

"I have another idea," I said.

Wendell groaned and put his face in his hands.

3rd January

We assembled at the stables in the early morning, as soon as the dawn light began to spill over the lake—Wendell, Lord Taran, Lord Wherry, and I, together with half a dozen guards and one of Lord Taran's scouts. I had left Shadow to sleep in, for I sensed he had not yet recovered from our long trek through Wendell's realm. With us instead—poorer substitutes there never have been—were Razkarden, perched above us in the tree-shadow like a waking nightmare, and Snowbell. Against my better judgment, the little fox-faerie had convinced me to carry him on my shoulder. I suspect he took his inspiration from Razkarden, for whom he has a twisted sort of reverence; Snowbell, though, cut a rather less intimidating figure than the spectral owl, despite his oversized teeth. I thought it likely that Farris Rose would not long be the only one-eared Cambridge scholar on record.

There was also one less willing traveller in our party.

Wendell's sister sat atop one of the monstrous faerie horses, a guard stationed to either side. She looked to be about fourteen or fifteen, with enormous, jewel-blue eyes rimmed by long brown hairs like moths' antennae, and golden tresses that were remarkably like Wendell's, though Deilah's reached her chin and floated about her face in becoming waves. She was barefoot, and her dress was dirty and ripped—I understood from Wendell that she had torn it herself, and refused to change. She presented a miserable picture with her tear-stained cheeks and downturned face, though she sat up straight in the saddle, as if to prove herself unbowed by her distress.

Wendell did not even spare his sister a glance, but strode into the stables with Lord Wherry, who had been invited as a representative of the Council. I stood there awkwardly for a moment, wondering how on earth I should navigate this particular thicket of brambles, long enough for Snowbell to bore of me; he hopped to the ground to preen in a patch of sun.

"Hello," I said, my voice sliding up at the end, as if it were a question. I felt unaccountably nervous, addressing this forlorn child. But then, I had never met any of Wendell's blood relatives before. He had none to meet, apart from Deilah.

It was that thought that led me to add, softly, "I am sorry that we should meet under such circumstances."

The girl turned to me, and her inhuman eyes widened in astonishment. "Such a plain little mouse!" she exclaimed. "I had heard my brother had strange taste, but I wasn't expecting *this*. And they have dressed you up like one of us—how embarrassing for you."

She began to snicker, and to my dismay, I felt my face grow hot. "I merely came to see if you were comfortable," I said stiffly.

"How sweet!" she said, her eyes glittering with amusement. Her voice, though, was kind as she added, "Well, since you asked, if you could fetch me one of those flowers, I'd appreciate it ever so much. I would like to have *something* to wear in my hair, as my brother hasn't let me have my jewels."

I looked down at the flowers she was indicating. They lay by the side of the path and resembled a meadowsweet, but in a vivid shade of red. I gave her a suspicious look, thinking she meant to kick me, but the flowers were just out of range of her boot. I knelt and plucked several blooms, and as I did, I felt something brush the top of my head. Thinking it was merely one of the errant leaves scattered by the wind, I rose and handed the girl the flowers.

"Thank you," she said, pressing her hand to her mouth. It was only when I had gone to sit upon a bench to wait for Wendell that I felt something wriggle in my hair.

Choking down a shriek, I yanked the thing out, coming away with several strands of my hair at the same time. It was a fat, spotted centipede. A shudder wracked my body as I tossed it aside.

"How on earth did she get her hands on that?" I grumbled to Lord Taran, who had come to see what I was fussing about.

"Hold still," he said with a sigh, and plucked three more centipedes from my hair. "There."

"Thank you," I said, my cheeks hot.

"Perhaps, my queen," he said in a dry voice, crushing the insects under his boot, "you might enlighten me: why we are bringing that charming little moppet along?"

"We cannot kill her," I said. "Doing so may harm Wendell. And yet she is Wendell's main rival for the throne, and has already come close to assassinating him once, so we must destroy the risk she poses to us *somehow*. Therefore, I would like to try to win her to our side. Perhaps if we show her evidence of her mother's wickedness, and the damage it has done to the realm, she will reconsider her loyalties."

"My," Lord Taran said, "just listening to that has given me a headache. That is the benefit of old age—one loses all interest in politics."

I examined him, his glossy dark hair and smooth skin, the perfect bow of his lips. He looked to be a man in his early twenties—an age at which there remained a hint of boyishness in his face, and I wondered if he had chosen it as a joke. "How old are you?" I said, just to see how he would sidestep the question.

To my surprise, he said simply, "That question doesn't apply. I am from an era before time."

It took me a moment to comprehend what he was saying. "You are—older than this realm?"

"I am older than any realm." His gaze slid to my cloak. "Save one."

I had to remind myself to breathe as dozens of questions swarmed through my head. "You cannot mean that."

"Can't I? Well, I suppose you're right, Professor Wilde—you can never trust the Folk." He raised his eyebrows in mock innocence and turned to attend to his mount, a towering black stallion. I stared at the back of his handsomely tousled hair—surely it was impossible. Wasn't it?

"Yet you are not so old as to be above tormenting scholars," I muttered.

He gave a surprised laugh. "You know," he said musingly, "I was not enthusiastic at the prospect of my nephew inheriting the throne, and for the most part, I remain unimpressed by him, even if he is not quite so feckless as he once was."

"He will make a better ruler than his stepmother," I interjected. "A kingdom perpetually consumed with war is no kingdom at all. Your soldiers were dying; the small Folk were terrorized night and day. Do you truly not care about such things?"

He adjusted his horse's saddle. "I truly do not. As I was saying—as highly as you esteem your husband, I have never seen anything exceptional in him. As a child, his magical talents were ordinary, and certainly there were many wiser and braver—and less indolent—candidates for the throne, including at least two of his siblings. But you, Emily—you appear to be an entertaining queen."

"I am not truly a queen, for Wendell and I are not married yet," I said, flustered. How I wished this man would simply ignore me, like the rest of his court! Perhaps his attention would have inspired less anxiety had I not recently watched him cleave a tree in two with a single blow.

Something in my tone summoned that familiar malicious gleam in his eyes. "Oh dear," he said. "Does someone have cold feet? Is our king perhaps a disappointment in other respects?"

"*No*," I said, growing only more flustered. "My feet were never warm to begin with, on the marriage subject. It has nothing to do with Wendell."

He made no reply to this, but I could see from the delight in his gaze, like a cat spying a wounded bird in the grass, that this was not the last I would hear on the matter. *You've put your foot in it now*, I thought with a sense of impending doom.

I turned to look at the lake; we stood beside a path that rambled down to its shore, where there was a beach of sand and stone. Sun sparkles danced blithely upon the water, as if it too were laughing at me.

Wendell finally emerged from the stables. Behind him came two servants, one of which was leading a creature that, it was only too clear, was my intended mount.

"Oh God," I said faintly.

The fox was smaller than the faerie horses—not a comfort, I assure you, given that it was still far larger than any fox had a right to be. Its coat was a rich auburn, lighter on the chest and belly, and its massive ears flopped like a dog's. It was a heavyset beast, a saddle encircling its rounded belly, but its legs were thickly muscled.

Snowbell clambered back onto my shoulder with an appalled squeak and gnashed his teeth in the creature's direction. "Stop that," I admonished. "I will put you down."

"What do you think, Em?" Wendell said, smiling. "Does Red Wind meet with your approval? I promise she will give you no trouble whatsoever. But you may have your pick of the horses, if you prefer."

"That—that's all right," I said. Now that the initial shock had passed, I found myself relaxing a little. The prospect of riding Red Wind was at least tolerable, unlike the thundering faerie horses, who were perhaps more alarming in how they confounded my expectations. I had no expectations where horse-sized foxes were concerned.

Wendell patted Red Wind's flank, and the massive creature yawned—her teeth were the length of my hand—and blinked her liquid black eyes at me. After a moment's hesitation, I reached out to rub her forelock, and she leaned into my hand with a guttural snort that made me start.

"As for you," Wendell said, turning to gaze at his sister thoughtfully. He wore black riding boots and gloves, and had exchanged his horrible grumbling cloak for a non-sentient one of darkest green, a match for the silvered leaves the servants had woven into his hair that morning, which sat so naturally amongst the golden waves that they might have sprouted from his scalp. He needed no crown to signify his title—even the trees and grasses seemed to bend towards him—and I could see that even his sister sensed it, which perhaps accounted for the ferocity of the glare she levelled at him.

"The kindness of your queen has granted you a respite from the dungeons," Wendell told her. "You are being given an opportunity to regret your loyalty to our mother. Thus, good behaviour on your part is not an expectation, but a requirement."

"Blah, blah, blah" was the child's reply. "You're as boring as one of *them* now. Like a mortal pretending to be Folk. Why don't you just go back to their world, brother?"

Wendell's eyes narrowed. "You, on the other hand, have only grown more like the old queen. Or, rather, a poor copy—plenty of spite and jealousy, but lacking her imagination."

The girl's face went white. "The *true* queen will have you quartered and hung from the battlements, along with those stupid mortals you care so much for."

"Your opinion of mortals is so low," Wendell said. "Yet one of them was your mother's undoing. How does it feel to be proven a fool?"

"My mother is not dead," she spat, and for a moment I thought she was going to lunge at him. "She cares too much about the realm to—to—"

"To die?" Wendell gave a quiet laugh. "If only there were protection in that! Alas. Our father cared a great deal for the realm, too. But then, you were too young—I doubt you remember him much. Well, let us go and see what our mother's malice has wrought upon her beloved realm, and then we shall see if there is anything in you but her worst qualities."

He turned his back on her. She seemed to be struggling to come up with a retort, and instead stuck her tongue out at him. I could see, though, that she was holding back tears.

"Was that necessary?" I muttered as he came over to me.

He sighed, looking vexed. "Children are so tedious!"

It seemed to me that Deilah was uniquely adept at eroding his good humour, but I did not point this out. "Wendell, if we meet your stepmother—"

"You shall not have to deal with her again, Em—leave her to me." He examined my face. "What is it?"

I shook my head. I had read through several dozen Irish

folktales the previous evening, comparing and contrasting; I did not care for the pattern that I saw emerging here, that was as much as I knew.

"Nothing," I said, trying to quell the foreboding. "Only I wish your stepmother was already dead."

"It would be tidier," he agreed. "But she is far too complicated a person to make things easy for anyone, even on her deathbed."

All the guards were saddled and ready, and so Wendell helped me onto Red Wind. Then he mounted his horse, and we were off.

At first we followed a broad path, wide enough for two mounts to walk abreast, but as we drew farther from the castle the path narrowed, and we travelled single file. Red Wind was so wide that the boughs brushed against her sides, until Wendell flicked his hand and added another foot or two to the path.

I did not much care for my drayfox. I did not say so to Wendell, but I began to think I would have preferred one of the faerie horses after all. Red Wind did not bump or jostle me, as a horse would, and therein lay the problem: her gait was too smooth. I felt as if I were being carried upon a well-tempered cloud, albeit one prone to sudden, violent sneezes and wet snorts.

I found myself noticing familiar plants and features as we travelled through the woods. Some brownies, for instance, had stone dwellings built into the earth—closer to cellars than houses, to my eye—roofed in densely interwoven fern fronds. Doubtless others dwelt in the canopy, for when I looked up, I saw the telltale silver gleam of impossibly narrow bridges connecting the trees like spiderthread. But as we moved away from the castle, I saw less of this glittering architecture, and more of the humble, cellarlike variety. I also noted that I was growing increasingly adept at spotting moss-brownies, as I had begun to call them in my head, for the mossy caps they wore. These small, black-eyed creatures, whose bodies were often covered in moss as well, could be seen peeking at us from behind branches, or sometimes in plain view upon a green stone or bough, where they were surprisingly difficult to detect.

I realized, to my amazement, that I was beginning to grow *comfortable* here. In the Silva Lupi! Farris would never approve.

I could not fully appreciate any of this, however; I was too anxious about what we would find in the forest. And so I availed myself of the opportunity provided by Red Wind's uncanny lope to work on my book.

I had not been scribbling in my notebook for five minutes before Lord Taran advanced his mount to ride alongside me, the path expanding to accommodate him.

"What on earth are you writing?"

"A book," I replied shortly.

"A book!" he cried. "With a kingdom to rule, and a vengeful rival on the loose, our queen is occupying herself with trivial matters of scholarship?"

"Yes," I said, and pointedly made another note.

He smiled and drew his horse closer to me, affecting polite interest. "What is the book about?"

"The politics of faerie courts," I said, wishing very much that he would leave me alone with my trivial scholarship.

He wrinkled his nose.

"I apologize if it is beneath the interest of an ancient faerie lord," I said.

Unfortunately, I seemed to have amused him again, and instead of going away, he said, "But what is the point of it all?"

I gave him a blank look, pretending I did not comprehend. Really I just didn't want to be drawn into an epistemological debate with him—or a debate of any sort, really. I suppose it was unscholarly of me; I should have leapt at an opportunity to interview such an exemplar of the courtly fae. But the man had tried to kill Wendell, much as the two seemed to have forgotten about it.

"Your profession," he clarified. "And Niamh's. The projects you two are always scribbling away at."

"Perhaps you should ask Niamh. She might enjoy the conversation."

"Oh dear," he said. "We *have* gotten off on the wrong foot, haven't we?"

"I can't imagine why." I sighed and tucked the pen into my notebook. "The *point* of my scholarship is to understand the Folk. To the extent that we mortals can."

"It has never struck you as a futile endeavour?"

"No more than any other branch of science." I gestured at the sky. "What can mortals learn of the stars, given that we cannot walk among them? Yet we try." I opened my notebook again. "Others have argued that it is the endeavour itself that is the point of scholarship. I am not so certain of that, for I can never stop yearning for new discoveries. Even the smallest are as precious jewels to me."

I could not be certain he understood me. After a moment, he said, "Why must mortals always be solving mysteries? What is the point of life if everything is pinned and labelled in some display case? You scholars should aim to discover more mysteries, not untangle them."

"How sibylline," I said. "That is ever so helpful, thank you."

He gave a delighted laugh, and then, to my immense relief, he rode on ahead, leaving me alone in the sanctuary of my research.

It should have been a lengthy journey. Instead, we reached our destination before a single hour had elapsed.

"This should not be," Lord Taran said, frowning as he leapt from his horse. "The corrupted grove should be fifty miles from the southern lakeshore—we have come ten, if that."

"A new outbreak?" suggested Lord Taran's scout, a severe man with two crossed swords upon his back and a scar that divided his face from temple to chin.

"I don't see anything," I said. The countryside was mixed woodland and moor, somewhat more open than the lands Wendell and I had passed through on our way to the castle. Rain so fine it was almost mist drifted through the trees like crowds of ghosts. I saw nothing but green flora, and heard only birdsong and the occasional snort from my mount. Something was off—though I could not pinpoint what it was.

"What a stink!" Snowbell said from my shoulder. He pinched his nose and added in a nasal voice, "I will not go near *that*."

"Near what?" I said, frustrated by my limited mortal senses. Snowbell made no reply, simply hopped to the ground and slunk into a foxhole.

Wendell slid gracefully from his horse and strode ahead. He pushed aside the bough of an attentive oak, which blinked furiously and glared at him, and disappeared through the trees.

"Yes, go marching into danger alone," Lord Taran muttered. "Like father, like son." He dismounted, motioning to Razkarden and two of the guards, and together they followed Wendell.

Lord Wherry remained sat on his drayfox, looking anxious. He seemed to be in his fifties; the Folk can appear any age they choose, and some prefer to look wise. Naturally, his lined face was still beautiful, his greying brown hair thick and long enough to wear in a plait. It was difficult to imagine him killing anyone, for there was a boyishness about his large eyes and round face that belied his apparent age, but in the opposite direction than was usual for most Folk.

I dismounted to a chorus of disgusting snorts from Red Wind. I paused beside Deilah, who had been surrounded by the remaining guards. "Would you like to come with me?"

"What does it matter what I want?" she said, turning her chin aside. Her eyes were red and swollen, as if she had been crying the entire journey. "Imprisoned princesses have as much say in their destinies as leaves in the wind."

Good grief. This girl had Wendell's talent for melodrama, that was clear. "Very well. Then I will choose for you: help her down."

The guards obliged me, and together we followed Wendell and Taran up the little rise to a grove of yew trees. At first, I thought it was mist before me. It hovered over the forest floor, and wisps of it climbed the trees like ghostly ivy. It seemed thicker than mist, however, unpleasantly so; I felt certain I would become stuck wading through that, like an insect in syrup.

The trees, meanwhile, looked ghastly. Their trunks were covered in scabs and strange protrusions, like infected sores. Wendell was frowning at them, absently twirling a lily he had plucked from the forest path.

"Lilies make charming wedding bouquets, Your Highness," Lord Taran said in an innocent voice, while smiling snidely at me behind Wendell's back.

I treated him to my most heartfelt of glares. Wendell blinked at his uncle, then examined the flower. "They do, don't they?"

"What has happened here?" I said pointedly.

"My stepmother, it seems," Wendell said. "She has come here, to the dooryard of my court, and placed a curse upon this grove. More specifically than that, I cannot say."

"It is like the others," the scout said, looking disgusted.

"We burned the others," one of the guards said. "This—whatever this place has become—will not ignite on its own, but if we set the neighbouring trees ablaze, and drive the flames towards this grove, it will eventually catch."

He raised his sword and hacked at the sticky mist. His sword sank deep and then stuck there; he had to wrench it free with a wet smacking sound.

"Don't," Wendell said, putting his hand out. Stabbing at the substance had produced a strange reaction; it shuddered and twitched like a wounded beast. It was then that I realized what was niggling at my senses. It was not anything in particular, but rather an absence. I should have been able to hear the minute rustlings and footfalls of brownies and other common fae, watching us from the green forest shadow, indistinguishable from nature's ordinary soundscape to most mortals, but not to me.

Panic rose within me, as well as horror, but it would be a lie to say these were not alloyed with excitement. I pulled out my notebook and began a quick sketch.

Lord Taran gave a huff of laughter. "What a peculiar little thing you are."

Wendell, meanwhile, was pacing back and forth, examining the grove with increasing distress. "It is a ruin," he said. "The trees—the flowers. Every burrow and den. I can't—"

He lifted his hand and made a sweeping gesture. Something passed over the grove—a ripple of light, smelling of summer and tasting of rain, impossible and wondrous, a cleansing sensation. And then it was gone, and the grove was unchanged.

I rocked back slightly. A part of me wanted to ask him to do that—whatever he had done—again. It was the childish part that was half afraid and half delighted whenever he performed some feat of magic I hadn't known he was capable of.

He did not repeat the enchantment, though, merely gave a curse and ran a hand through his hair. "Wendell," I said suddenly, gripping his arm.

Two brownies sat in one of the cursed trees, watching us. At least, I think they were watching us. They too were wrapped in tendrils of the uncanny mist, which seemed to be animating them somehow, like puppets, for it was evident that they were dead; their eyes stared but did not *see*, and their bodies had a slight translucence. Together, they turned and faded back into the corrupted forest.

"Gather up the deadfall and start the fire," Lord Taran ordered the guards. "Actually—"

He flicked his hand at a cluster of ferns, and they burst into flame—it was smoky and malcontent, because of the damp, but it burnt brightly. The mist stirred, and then it detached a thick tendril and smothered the fire with a gentle burbling sound.

We all fell back a step.

"It did that before," the scout said. His face was so pale the scar looked livid, almost fresh. "We must light it away from the margin—once the flames pass a certain size, the corruption cannot defeat them. Come."

He and two of our guards disappeared into the trees. I turned to where Deilah stood with a guard on either side of her, thinking that I would order them to take her back to our mounts. But Deilah was no longer there. Instead, I found one guard blinking at the space where she had been and the second pinned to the ground beneath a deara, which was both like and unlike the creature Ariadne and I had met: the faerie had roughly the same shape, something halfway between a man and a toad, but it too was dreadfully scabbed, and its body seemed more mist than substance. Yet this had no effect on its ability to do violence. Indeed, the guard was no longer moving—the creature had opened her throat with its teeth.

It had happened so fast that I did not even have the wherewithal to shout, but Wendell did not hesitate. He lunged after Deilah, who was being dragged into the forest by two other corrupted deara. I could not follow exactly what he did, for he moved far too fast, but I saw the aftermath well enough: two heads went tumbling past me. He shoved his sister back, for another deara had lunged at him out of the mist, and she tripped and rolled down the hillside after the heads.

Lord Taran, meanwhile, was driving his sword into a creature I did not immediately recognize, which looked like a deer gone scabby and ethereal, like the others. The mist, meanwhile, was roiling like water in a heated pot.

I ran to Deilah's side and helped her to her feet—the girl was gasping and clutching at her throat, which was developing a nasty bruise from the deara's grip—and then Lord Wherry was there, dragging the both of us down the hill.

"Wendell—" I cried, still half stupefied. I kept thinking, *Too fast. This has come apart too fast.*

"The king can take care of himself, you silly creature," Lord Wherry said. "We must get you two back to the horses."

But we had travelled only a few paces before Lord Taran caught up with us. I thought for a moment that he'd joined us in fleeing the scene, but then, to my astonishment, he dealt Lord Wherry a backhanded blow that sent the man sprawling.

"What are you doing?" I cried. "He's helping us. There's no need—"

"Oh, but there is," Taran drawled. "I have a great curiosity to see how this phenomenon affects the nobility. Councillors are easily replaced, my queen."

Lord Wherry shrieked and tried to flee. Taran gestured, and a gust of wind knocked Lord Wherry off his feet.

"We can't have that, my lord," he said, and then, in a motion as casual as the one he'd used to crush the insects, he lifted his boot and stamped on Lord Wherry's leg. A sickening crack resounded through the grove.

Deilah screamed—I pulled her to me and pressed her face into my neck. Just in time, too: though there seemed to be no need for it, for Lord Wherry lay still on the forest floor, moaning, Taran lifted his boot again and broke his other leg.

I choked down my own scream, bile rising in my throat. Lord Taran seized the blubbering Lord Wherry by the collar of his cloak and dragged him easily through the trees, and then he tossed him into the rippling dark.

Lord Wherry's cries were abruptly silenced.

I felt as if I were rooted to the forest floor, staring dumbly at the place where Lord Wherry had vanished. The breeze smelled of smoke, and through the trees came a bright flickering. The guards had started a fire, but how long would it take to reduce this cursed place to ash? Wendell finished dispatching the deara, as well as several corrupted brownies, and left the remaining guards to handle the other spectral figures who rose up out of the mist.

"We've seen enough," he said, raising his voice to be heard over Deilah's sobs.

I nodded, because even through it all—the horror of the grove, the greater horror of Lord Taran's brutality, Deilah's blubbering—I found a theory surfacing in my mind, like a single bright fish rising through troubled waters.

"I think—" I began, but what I had been about to say next twisted into a shriek.

Lord Wherry had risen from the dark. He too was draped in mist now, his eyes unseeing. I could not make sense of it. Only moments ago he had been a living, breathing person, one whom I had been speaking with; now it was as if the vitality and substance, the very *personhood* had been drained from him, leaving behind only the outline of what once had been, like a shed snakeskin.

Wendell turned quickly enough to meet Lord Wherry's sword—I use that word only loosely; it had the translucence of ice. That was the most terrifying thing about these wraiths—my rational mind kept telling me that they should not have been able to touch us; the mist seemed to transform them into itself as it claimed them. They should have been like the monsters under a child's bed, a presence that could frighten but not harm.

Wendell parried and thrust his sword into Lord Wherry's chest, and the man collapsed back into the mist.

"My curiosity has been sated," Lord Taran said grimly. "Our kind is not immune to the corrupting influence of this grove. As I would prefer not to become an unthinking puppet in my dear sister's revenge plot, I suggest we depart."

It was as he spoke the last word that I heard a *whoosh* of air, and felt something solid strike me. Solid—and slightly bony. I rolled down the slope, having little idea what was happening. It was only when I came to a crashing halt against a tree trunk that I understood: Deilah had leapt upon me, sending the both of us tumbling down the hill, and sparing me from probable decapitation, for the *whoosh* had come from a sword.

I felt something warm slip down my forehead, and pressed my hand to it. I stared at the bright red staining my palm—the sword had cut my scalp.

"Emily!" Wendell shouted, horror sharpening his voice. He had locked swords with the person who had tried to maim me, and sent her reeling back. It was the guard who had been killed by the deara—the corruption had claimed her as she lay forgotten where she had fallen.

"I'm fine," I called, trying to reassure him before I was even certain it was true. Fortunately, as I took stock of myself, I found I was right—the cut was shallow, though it was bleeding a great deal.

"Here." Hiccupping a little, Deilah pressed a silk handkerchief to my head.

"Thank you," I said.

Her lip trembled. "I want to go home," she said. Then she burst into tears.

"Shh," I said, patting her back. Guilt pricked at me; I had been the one to bring her here. And yet her mother was the cause of this. Shouldn't she witness it? Hadn't that been my intention?

I gave up arguing with myself and simply huddled there with Deilah as Wendell fought. The guard seemed to possess some skill with a sword—or perhaps it was the curse that lent her strength—for she managed to deliver a shallow slash across Wendell's side. Only the one, though, for in the next instant, Wendell knocked the wraith's weapon aside and drove his sword into her chest. Then he drove it in again. And again.

"Wendell!" I shouted, but he seemed not to hear me. Eventually, Lord Taran, who had been distracted by another wraith, simply kicked the thoroughly dead guard out of Wendell's reach.

The earth shuddered.

I had been in the process of picking myself up, because it was abundantly clear that, as poor Lord Wherry had noted, there was no need for Deilah or me to be there, getting in the way, but the tremor threw me to my knees. A new spectre had risen from the mist, towering over the others. It was a drayfox—which, I have since learned, can grow as large as cottages in their old age. The mist swirled about it and through it, only half obscuring the scabs poking through its spectral fur. It was then that my mind cleared.

The scabs were like those on the tree fauns' horns.

My thoughts took off at a gallop. I remembered what Callum had said about Queen Arna—that she had taken the poison within herself and somehow infected the realm with it, as a mortal might pass on a cold. It was a mad idea, of course, and yet simultaneously—as is often the case in Faerie—there was a sort of logic to it. Monarchs of Faerie do not merely inhabit their realms; they are thought to be intricately entwined.* It was both a threat to Wendell's rule and the perfect revenge against him. He who had evaded the same poison was now forced to watch it consume his realm.

The theories kept churning. The poison that had sickened this grove had come from the tree fauns. Had the common fae possessed by it also been possessed by the fauns' malice?

Wendell crouched at the edge of the darkness, leaning on one hand; the other he pressed against his side, blood dripping through his fingers. When he looked up, I saw that he was lost. His expression was devoid of anything other than the all-consuming fury I had witnessed only a handful of times, and had rather hoped I would not see again.

"Brother, do not touch it," Deilah cried through her tears. She ran towards him, and I seized her arm and dragged her down the hill, or tried to—she fought me, her elbow connecting with my stomach, and the breath left me in a wheeze.

Wendell, still possessed by his mindless fury, marched into

---

* Wentworth Morrison's *Folk-Lore of Scotland, Volume III: Thrones of Faerie* (1852) remains the definitive resource on this topic, but Farris Rose's exhaustive investigation of Cornish faerie stories (in particular his *Atlas of Tales*, 1900) provides additional insight. Cornwall holds the record for the sheer number of interactions between mortals and monarchs of Faerie (Rose's "Comparative Analysis of the Faerie Markets of Bodmin Moor," published in *Dryadological Fieldnotes* in 1902, offers several intriguing theories as to why this might be so). In many of the tales recorded by Morrison and Rose, a faerie monarch's power is also their Achilles' heel: while they control the landscape and weather, they can be defeated by being trapped and removed from their homes, as a flower dies when uprooted from its soil.

the swirling mist as if we had not just watched it possess everything that it touched. Horrified, I screamed at him to turn back, which produced absolutely no effect. But the mist did not rise to cover him as it had Lord Wherry; it shrank back. It closed behind him, but not in the places where his blood fell upon the earth. There the grasses and underbrush of the forest grew lush and green, shaking off the curse.

This I noted.

The curse did not seem to appreciate Wendell's determination. Dozens of wraiths rose out of the darkness—it sickened me, the sight of so many small Folk destroyed by this dark magic, even as I quaked in terror of them.

Lord Taran had no such conflicted feelings, and even seemed to be enjoying himself. His sword flashed as he hewed and stabbed, often moving so fast that he was little more than a dark wind to my eyes. I clutched Deilah to me—to comfort the child, who was still crying, though I suspect it was as much to comfort myself.

Wendell, meanwhile, had neither slowed nor slackened his pace, no matter how many monsters the mist threw at him. Two of the guardians swooped in to help him—not Razkarden; no doubt he was too wise—and he killed them without pause, or any sign of recognition.

When he reached the spectral drayfox, which had only grown in size, he drew back his sword and hurled it in a glittering arc. It plunged into the spectre's eye, and a gust of wind enveloped the grove, the ground trembling beneath our feet. The spectre sagged backwards, and then it collapsed.

Wendell had caught his sword, or summoned it somehow, and was now hacking at the mist itself, there being no more wraiths to challenge him. Eventually, Lord Taran, stepping gingerly through the mist, which was beginning to dissolve, met Wendell's sword with his own, disarming him with a series of impossible strikes. At that, the fury seemed to leave Wendell like an exhaled breath, and he gave Lord Taran a puzzled look, as if there had been nothing at all strange about his murderous rampage, nor any reason for him to stop.

The disintegrating mist expanded towards Deilah and me, and the girl tore herself out of my grasp and ran pell-mell into the forest, shrieking. Wendell swore and took off after her, vanishing into one tree and then stepping out of another, where he caught his sister and hauled her back towards our mounts. She seemed torn between beating her fists against his chest and sobbing into his neck, which slowed their progress somewhat. The grove was brightening, and I coughed on the smoke clogging the air. One of the guards came hurrying towards Lord Taran, soot smeared across her cheek.

"We've surrounded the grove with pyres, my lord," she said. "These trees will soon be up in flames."

Lord Taran sheathed his sword and came towards me, which sent me scuttling backwards on my hands in instinctive terror before I forced myself to stop. He helped me to my feet, catching me with unexpected gentleness as my legs wobbled. And then I was dragged away.

9th January

It has been too long since I've written. Several times after our journey to the yew grove I have picked up my journal, readied my pen, and then simply stared at the blank page—a symptom of a condition with which I have intimate familiarity by now: namely, stupefaction brought on by some manner of faerie misadventure. In addition, I had only a page or two left in my old journal, hardly enough space to recount anything in detail.

Eventually, I visited the bookbinders, still hard at work filling the shelves in my journal room, and selected this ridiculous paper confection. It has pages enough, but also an enchanted lock—which I do not bother with—and intricate silver engravings of overlapping circles of fern fronds, which I am beginning to recognize as a common artistic motif in *Where the Trees Have Eyes*. The top of every page is illustrated with a little landscape sketch, a gentle brook or a moorland vista, and if one stares at these long enough, they become a tiny window to the place where the artist must have stood. It is all completely frivolous and unnecessary.

But. I am writing again.

I reached Dublin's Trinity College three days ago via

a carriage from Corbann to the train station one village over, then two additional trains. Since then I have been ensconced in their Natural Sciences Library—in which is housed their considerable collection of dryadological journals and folklore—from dawn to dusk. I would sleep here if the librarians would allow it, but while most of them have received me with kindness and welcome, the head librarian is a tyrannical sort, and seems already to disapprove of me and my many requests, even seeing fit to lecture me for leaving the special collections room in disarray, so I doubt such a request would be well received. One would think books existed simply to be looked at and occasionally dusted, the way that man carries on. And if the filing system differs from Cambridge's, is it my fault if this occasionally leads me to misplace things?

I have been dreadfully scattered of late. I sat down to provide an account of my doings since the grove, and here I am, griping about librarians.

Wendell has written me three letters already, despite the short period of my absence. I had the below waiting for me when I arrived at my rented lodgings.

To: Dr. Emily Wilde
11 Scholars' Square, Trinity College
Dublin

From: Wendell Bambleby
Faerie via Corbann

Dearest Emily,
I do not like this promise I made to you, that I would match the passage of time in my realm to that of the mortal world.

Surely you would not object to me speeding things along a little, so that I should only have to wait another hour or two for your return. And anyway I am half convinced that the enchantment has gone awry somehow, for surely it has not merely been a day since you left. How dull it is without you! At least I have Niamh to talk to, and I have even taken to summoning my uncle every so often to keep me company, which he does not seem to appreciate, surly old recluse that he is. I have had some good conversations with Callum, and I seem to be making progress in convincing him that he need not be afraid of me. My dreadful sister has been following me about, but I do not count her as company, for all she does is mope. And what reason does she have to carry on so? I have endured a great deal more hardship than she, and yet here I am, engaging in all sorts of industry and enduring tedious demands upon my time; nor have I had one word of sympathy from her. I don't know why she has suddenly chosen to inflict her presence upon me; I even woke this morning to find her curled up outside my door under a blanket, asleep. I attempted to talk to her kindly, which I knew you would appreciate, as you seem to have some sympathy for the wretch, but she only spat insults at me. Is this situation better or worse than when she was trying to kill me? Worse, I think. I could throw her back into the dungeons if she were up to no good. You will only be angry with me if I do so otherwise.

 Anyway, Em, I am sure you are happily ensconced in your native habitat, that dreary monument to mortal rumination that is the library, no doubt thinking of me hardly at all. Well, why would you give a thought to romance or the faerie kingdom that now belongs to you as much as to me when you have a limitless supply of dusty old tomes to mutter and scowl at? I see now that my downfall as a suitor lies in my ability to offer you only a castle, great quantities of faerie silver, and various enchantments to dazzle and provoke you, instead of the full bound collection of Dryadological Fieldnotes.

Please return tomorrow, or the day after at the latest.

Love always,
Wendell

And the next day:

To: Dr. Emily Wilde
11 Scholars' Square, Trinity College
Dublin

From: Wendell Bambleby
Faerie via Corbann

Dearest Emily,
You have not heeded my request to return today, I see. Will you be back tomorrow? Surely you will have exhausted the supply of relevant tomes by then, given how quickly you devour them.

I know you are annoyed with me for pestering you with letters, when you have only gone away in the first place to unravel the threat to my kingdom, but Em, do you truly believe the answer to my stepmother's curse may be found in a library? Particularly when you consider how little scholarship understands about my realm. After all, you once thought it quite a fearsome place, did you not? Now you know how exaggerated such accounts are.

(I gave a strangled snort at this.)

Well, if there is one person who could unearth the proverbial needle in the haystack that is the esoteric ramblings of thousands of scholars, it is you, but if you do not find an answer, please do not sit there sulking among the stacks, or waste time harassing the poor librarians, as you were wont to do at Cambridge. Just come home.

Yours, always and ever,
Wendell

Today I had a much longer letter from him, which included an update on Orga's campaign against Lord Taran—she somehow obtained entry to the wing of the castle he shares with Callum, whereupon she shredded half of his boots, namely the left half of every pair, a remarkable display of efficiency. There were also the usual demands for my return and complaints about his sister, and the news that he had fired half the Council ("the more insufferable half") and replaced them with mortals, which he seemed convinced I would be delighted by, though I did not have the sense that he had applied any criterion in the selection beyond a lack of faerie ancestry. It would be nice if he would include something useful in his missives—the queen's curse is spreading every day, but how much? Perhaps he does not wish to alarm me, though it is also possible that he does not consider the information as relevant as his visit to Margret and Lilja, including an update on Margret's progress in mastering traditional Irish baked goods.

This morning I made my way from my rented rooms to the library, stopping only to take a quick coffee and buttered scone at one of the campus cafés. (I was once able to make do without breakfast, but I have fully succumbed to the habit now, it seems.) Trinity is smaller than Cambridge, though elegant in its own right, a mix of gothic architecture jostling good-naturedly with modern brickwork, and a great deal of green lawns and quiet promenades. The library is particularly admirable, with a vaulted ceiling and warmly lit atrium, off which one may find innumerable reading rooms and shelves stretching from floor to ceiling. Though the task before me is a grim one, I have found these homely surroundings to be a balm upon my anxieties.

Yesterday I made a discovery that I believe will be of immense help in our plight, and today my goal was to cross-reference the tale in question with stories from other Irish realms. I claimed a desk and switched on the electric lamp, then took up my notebook, in which I had jotted down the shelf number and location of several volumes. Shadow, meanwhile, settled in for a nap under the desk. One of his many talents is his ability to make himself scarce; dogs are rarely welcomed in libraries, but he seemed to blend into the shadows in that corner of the room, and I did not think he would be noticed unless one looked closely.

I had to visit the special collections room again—an experience I was not anticipating—but thankfully the man who had taken such offence to me before was not working that day, and I was assisted by a kindly old woman who not only located the volume I required, but suggested I consider another book of folktales, similar in theme, which I had overlooked before, having assumed from the title that it was written in Irish. Such is the way with librarians, who are almost as unpredictable as the Folk, some minatory and persnickety, others overflowing with warmth towards humanity at large. I thanked the woman, hefted my stack (ten books in total), and made my way carefully back to my desk, sweating a little.

I did not note the passage of the hours at first. However, shortly past midday, an older scholar wearing a bowtie and carrying a handkerchief he kept wiping over his bald head established himself at the desk across from mine, despite the abundance of empty space elsewhere. Naturally, he then proceeded to hum softly under his breath as he paged through the bound volume of journals before him, occasionally muttering criticisms, usually pertaining to the shortsightedness of the authors. Glaring at this oblivious person had no effect; indeed, he only seemed to grow more loquacious, as if desiring to further impose his presence upon my sanctuary. Well, it was not as if I were trying to rescue a kingdom from destruction, and might need a little peace and quiet to think. It was like sharing office space with Professor Walters again.

After a quarter hour of this I decided I had earned a stroll upon the green; with any luck, the man would be gone when I came back. I woke Shadow, switched off my lamp, and placed my library card with its Cambridge seal upon it atop the books as evidence that I would be returning, to ward off any overindustrious shelvers. Then I wandered outside with Shadow padding at my heels.

The wind was chill, but for once it was not raining. I drew a deep breath, savouring the sense of homecoming. No, Trinity College is not Cambridge, but there is an essence shared by great universities that always puts me at ease; entering the campus grounds had felt like donning an old, cherished jumper. I adjusted my scarf and headed towards the open sunny expanse of the neighbouring green, where several students were seated on benches, taking advantage of the miserly winter warmth.

I paused for a moment in the sunlight, but the chill lingered. Now that I was away from my books, the thoughts rushed back like a flock of dark birds. I missed Wendell with a sudden and painful ache that left me short of breath, a sensation that would have surprised me had I not been experiencing it regularly, even when he'd been there beside me.

For two days after our visit to the yew grove, I'd buried myself in Irish folklore, and there I'd found the answer I sought, in all its horrifying simplicity. I'd had an inkling—of course I had.

Wendell's death would lift the curse. Nothing more, and nothing less.

I had not known how Wendell would react when I came to tell him my theory, my hands stained with ink and my eyes red from rubbing at them. I'd found him gazing out the window of one of the castle's many galleries, this one filled with curious wooden statues of dancers in various positions, some perfectly balanced on tiptoe, others with skirts twirling about them and arms uplifted. They looked like ordinary mortals, dressed mostly in peasant clothes, and some gave off the impression of mortal clumsiness too, even in their frozen states. I certainly *hoped* they were artistic renderings and nothing more sinister. Wendell does not know their origin; they have been in the castle since long before he was born. Naturally, they move when you are not looking. Just slightly, as if they are still caught in the dance, only time has slowed for them to the merest of trickles—a single finger might uncurl, a heel lift up, but that is more than enough to make me avoid the room as a general rule.

In any case, Wendell had not been in the least perturbed when I confided in him. He had nodded, and told me he had guessed as much, for he could feel the curse seeping through the realm, farther and deeper, and he had watched his blood heal the grove in the places where it fell.

"Well," he had murmured, gazing at the forest. "At least I have seen it again."

He must have seen my reaction in my face, for he added quickly, "Em, it is only a last resort. We will find our way out of this somehow. Have we not navigated such dangers before? I have no desire to give my stepmother the satisfaction of killing me, and still less to leave you." He smiled. "Though I would not be surprised if you proved more adept at ruling a faerie kingdom alone than with my help."

I was in no mood for jesting, and his calmness troubled me; I had obviously been expecting *some* reaction, most likely dismay, but annoyance and exasperation at the very least. I wished I could put into words the terror that had gathered within me since I worked out his stepmother's true plot, how it only seemed to grow and grow until I feared it would take over every inch of me.

He had not needed me to explain. He had merely drawn me into his arms and held me for a long time, while the green shadow shifted beyond the window, and the dancers moved ever so slowly around us.

As I strode down the path beyond Trinity's library, lost in unpleasant thoughts, something blue moved out of the corner of my eye. To my astonishment, I turned to see none other than Dr. Farris Rose in a navy peacoat, seated at one of the outdoor tables of the library café, waving at me.

"What on earth" was all I could sputter when I reached him.

He laughed and motioned for me to be seated. "Well, Emily!" he said, extending his hand to give Shadow a pat. "Have I surprised you? You've given me quite a turn yourself, you know. I've been here four days, enmeshed in research—when did you arrive?"

"Not three days ago," I said. It was, I realized when I thought it over, more of a surprise that our paths had not crossed before now. No doubt Farris had also spent much of his time at this same library. "But what brings you to Dublin?"

"Ah." He sipped his tea with a rueful sort of grimace. "Our meeting is perhaps not so much of a coincidence as I implied. I did not know you would be here. But Ariadne—well, something in your recent letter to her piqued my academic interest. And what better place than Trinity to research the Silva Lupi?

Naturally the lion's share of scholarship on the Irish realms is held within those walls." He gestured at the library towering behind us.

"Ariadne shared my letter," I repeated. I did not know whether to be annoyed or embarrassed—should I have written to Farris as well? Our relationship has come a long way from what it was before Austria, but someone like Farris Rose will never *not* be intimidating, and I confess I cannot imagine writing to him of my troubles, as I would a friend. What if he took offence at the presumption? I have ever been a poor judge of such things.

"We were spending the day on the huntsmen project when the letter arrived," he explained. "The girl was much perturbed by its contents, and could not help but share them with me."

"I see." Following our Austria expedition, Farris took Ariadne on as one of his research assistants—quite an honour; he ordinarily has two or three assistants, but never has he employed an undergraduate before. Currently, they are working on a paper on the hunting patterns of the elder huntsmen, which the four of us had the misfortune to meet in St. Liesl.

Farris flagged down the waiter, who brought me a cup and refilled the pot. Farris waited until he had gone back inside before continuing, "I suspect you left out many of the details of what you are facing in Bambleby's realm. Am I correct?"

I looked away. Yes, I had given Ariadne only an abbreviated version of what had transpired since Wendell and I returned to Faerie. I had made it sound as if Queen Arna were more of a temporary nuisance than a threat, to avoid worrying the girl.

I could tell that Farris was holding back questions. The lines in his face—scholars' lines, mostly between the brows and around the eyes, from frowning down at books—were sharper with suppressed tension, and suddenly I wanted nothing more than to tell him everything. And so I did.

Farris listened intently at first, then held up a hand with an "If you don't mind?" He rummaged around in his pockets until he unearthed his glasses, settled them on the bridge of his nose, and opened the little notebook he'd placed beside him on the table.

"Please continue," he said.

He did not attempt to steer the direction of my tale, though I went off course several times, providing far too much detail on extraneous matters (the ghastly oaks being one of these); he merely listened, jotting notes in his shorthand. Occasionally he would ask me to clarify something, but that was all. He might have been taking notes at a conference. I felt oddly comforted by the whole thing.

"This curse," he said when I came to the end of the story. "It is worsening, then?"

"Every day it spreads to a new grove or moor," I said. "Those that are not promptly burnt only grow larger. If we cannot put a stop to it, the realm will become a wasteland."

Saying it out loud had an effect upon me that was like hearing Queen Arna's name for the first time; it was a destabilizing feeling, like standing on the precipice of a great height. I realized that I had not said it before, the potential consequence of our failure, not even to myself. It did not feel real. Wendell and I had worked so hard to find a way back to his world—that all our efforts should have brought us to this!

I wished Wendell were with me, which was completely irrational, of course—he would not be of any practical help, and was needed in Faerie.

"The central problem," I said, "is that the realm has *two* monarchs. Queen Arna has not formally abdicated the throne, nor has she been killed. As a half-mortal woman, she is no match for Wendell, but as a monarch of Faerie, she has access to magics other Folk might not even comprehend. Thus the strength of her curse."

"Fascinating," Farris said. I did not take offence to the excitement in his voice, recognizing it for scholarly enthusiasm and nothing more. "Other realms have fallen into states of decay due to curses and suchlike, but this situation strikes me as unique."

I frowned as a thought occurred to me. "You must have left Cambridge directly after reading my letter."

"Naturally!" he said, becoming preoccupied with the sugar. "What could be of greater scholarly interest than the inner workings of the Silva Lupi?"

If I hadn't known him better, I would have thought he was being dismissive; but Farris, I know now, often gives off an impression of rudeness when he is flustered. I looked down at my own cup, blushing a little and feeling dreadfully awkward. He had abandoned his own research, as well as the graduate seminar he was teaching on Renaissance faerie art, and come all this way in the hopes of assisting me, and he had done so at the drop of a hat. And here I'd been worried about whether I would be taking liberties in writing him a letter.

"It is—an intriguing conundrum," I finally said lamely.

Farris affected not to notice. "Indeed! Your travails in the Silva Lupi are rivalled only by Blake's wanderings in Orkney."

And just like that, we were back on ground more comfortable to the both of us. "Poor Blake," I said. "It is a pity he never finished his book."*

---

* William Blake (a distant cousin of the poet of the same name) was a Scottish dryadologist born in 1655. Dryadology was in its infancy then, particularly in this corner of the world, and little was known about the Scottish faerie kingdoms, at least eleven of which have been documented today. In 1690, Blake had the misfortune to stumble into the darkest of these, the Oram Pluvia, which to this day has been so little studied that some scholars argue its existence remains in question. There the mad queen took a fancy to him and made him her consort, forcing him to share her throne. From his letters to his sister Jane, also

"We should locate Ariadne," Farris said. "She would be disappointed to be left out of this conversation."

"She's here?"

"Naturally. Since your foray into the Silva Lupi, she has become something of an expert on the subject—reads everything she can get her hands on. She is talking of specializing in Irish dryadology, though I have warned her against deciding on such things so early in her career . . . Anyhow, I could not very well leave her behind, all things considered."

He made a dismissive gesture at the end of this vague statement, and I understood. Ariadne too had been eager to help me! Here I had thought that Wendell and I were navigating this path alone, with his magic and my ingenuity our only defences against a realm teeming with monsters. Yet here were two people who had crossed a sea to assist us.

I took a swallow of tea. "Where *is* the girl, anyway?" I said in a gruff voice.

"The museum," Farris replied. "They have a fine collection of faerie stones and other artefacts—she had an idea that the stones might function as weapons against this Queen Arna. Several stories from that part of the country feature them, and why leave any stone unturned, pun intended. Let us go and seek her out."

---

a dryadologist, which he managed somehow to smuggle out of Faerie, Blake seems to have initially viewed his capture as a triumph for scholarship. As the years passed, however, he attempted escape multiple times, sometimes with the assistance of the mortals of the region, finally succeeding in 1699. He spent a year travelling much of Europe, speaking of his experience at the most august institutions. His health, however—both mental and physical—had declined to such an extent that it is difficult to know how much of his account is truth, for he often contradicted himself, weaving elaborate tales of both revelry and torment that he would later disown. Against the urgings of his friends and family, Blake returned to Orkney in 1700 to collect faerie stories from the locals, likely in the hopes of refuting his critics. He spent a comfortable night at an inn on Orkney Mainland and departed the following morn for a "short stroll" in the countryside, from which he never returned.

+ + +

It took only a quarter hour or so to locate Ariadne—Trinity's Museum of the Good Folk is a tall, narrow building* of stone and ivy a short walk from the library, with an entire floor dedicated to the realms of the country's southwest. The girl was hunched over a notebook on a flat bench across from the faerie stone display, a pensive look on her round, freckled face. She gave a cry of delight and astonishment when she saw me, and needed several reassurances that I had arrived by train, in the human fashion, and had not stepped out of one of the dozen or so faerie doors on display in the museum.

"Come," Farris said, "let us go somewhere more private before we continue our discussion."

We made our way to Farris's lodgings in Scholars' Square. He had been given one of the larger suites, as is customarily afforded to the most eminent visiting scholars, which included a sunny reception room facing another handsome library, this one dedicated to literature and the humanities. Ariadne had a childhood friend studying at Trinity, and was staying in her flat.

Farris made tea in his small kitchen—we had just had it, of course, he and I, but I made no objection and sipped mine gratefully, warming my chilled hands against the cup. "So," he said, settling himself by the fire, "these corrupted groves may be healed with a little bloodletting. Well, that has precedent in the literature, doesn't it? 'The Winding Ways of Tatty Tom,' for instance."

"That is a Scots tale," I said. "It is often attributed to the

---

* The building's construction was predicated on an old belief that the Folk dislike stairs, which likely arose from the fact that many household brownies in Ireland sleep in the walls adjacent to the hearth, which is generally found on the ground floor.

Irish due to its erroneous inclusion in Baker's *Evergreen Ballads*.* Wendell's blood will not heal his realm, for by now there is too much corruption in it, and each time he heals one grove, his stepmother will poison another."

Farris's wiry white eyebrows had pushed closer and closer together until they were touching. "You are not thinking of 'The Shoemaker and His Lost Queen'?"

"I am," I said. "As well as 'The Winter Gardener.'† In theme, the two tales are nearly identical, despite their differing origins—Wendell's situation makes three. It seems clear that the only way to end the curse the old queen has inflicted upon Wendell's realm is for him to sacrifice himself. To die. A little blood may heal half an acre; only his life will heal the realm."

There was a silence.

"It is a neatly constructed vengeance on Queen Arna's part," Farris said slowly. "One cannot argue with that. The faerie rulers of old would applaud her."

I gave a ghost of a laugh. It was relief I felt, more than any-

---

* First edition: Cambridge University Press, 1741.

† Both tales are commonly told throughout Ireland, though "The Winter Gardener" is thought to be a French import. In "The Shoemaker and His Lost Queen," a humble but talented shoemaker is abducted into Faerie by bogle-like creatures before being rescued by the queen of the realm, initially out of admiration for his craft, though they eventually fall in love and are married. The queen's realm is dying, however, for in her youth the queen had denied hospitality to a travelling peddler, who later revealed himself as a powerful and ancient member of the courtly fae and placed her realm under a curse. Initially, the queen's kindness towards the shoemaker seems to lift the curse, but eventually the queen tires of him for shallow reasons and casts him out. At this point, she learns that the shoemaker was only another guise for the vengeful traveller, who had returned to see if the queen had improved her character. He informs the queen that only her death can lift the curse now, and so the queen takes her own life, which heals the realm.

"The Winter Gardener" is a similar tale, with the titular gardener replacing the shoemaker, but in this story, the gardener is merely a mortal woman who does not possess a secret identity. After the queen sacrifices herself to save her realm, the gardener plants a snowdrop over her grave, which grows as large as a tree and scatters its seeds across the realm; the tale is often used as an explanation for the perceived advantages of Irish snowdrops over those of other countries.

thing else, to be able to discuss this ghastly revelation with my fellow scholars, as if it were merely some academic riddle to be scribbled upon a blackboard and coldly analyzed. "I have no doubt."

"I suppose, as she has somehow tied herself to the land, she would be healed as well," he continued in a musing voice. "And, with her stepson out of the way, free to assume the throne once more."

"That I cannot say for certain, but it is plausible."

"It cannot be," Ariadne burst out. She had been watching Farris and me, seeming to grow more and more astonished by our detachment. "Professor Bambleby must be able to heal his realm some other way. He—" She broke off, biting her lip.

Now, Wendell is not really a professor anymore; though he was granted leave from Cambridge, supposedly to conduct an in-depth investigation of the Hidden Ones of Ljosland— a plausible story, given that he and I were the first scholars to conclusively document their existence—this was mainly to provide an explanation for his eventual disappearance from the mortal world, hopefully preventing anyone from going looking for him. But I did not correct her.

"I don't believe he can," I said. "In fact, Wendell has come to the same conclusion—that only by giving his life will he drive out his stepmother's poison, and stop it from destroying the realm."

Farris rubbed his face. "Then there is no other way for the curse to be lifted."

"I do not believe that is the correct concern," I said. "Yes, Wendell's life is the antidote, but what is more effective than finding antidotes?"

Ariadne's face lit up. "Stopping the poisoner."

"Precisely. The problem is that Queen Arna has spirited herself away so effectively that none of our scouts have been able to track her. She is somewhere within the Silva Lupi, of course, or she would not be able to damage it so, but the Silva Lupi is vast, and not merely in the mortal sense, for it is full of shifting landscapes and layered in enchantments. It would take Wendell years to scour it all. So that is the mystery I am attempting to unravel: Where has she gone? How can we find her?"

I opened my briefcase and removed the book I had smuggled out of the special collections section. (I am aware that I am getting into a bad habit with this sort of thing, but I would be returning the volume before I left Dublin; also, I looked through the records, and not one scholar has requested it in over a year.)

"I have been combing through the folklore of County Leane, from which we have most of our tales of the Silva Lupi," I said. "It took some time, but I believe I have come across a tale that describes a situation similar to our own. From what I have been able to glean, it was first recorded in 1480 by a theologian named Geoffrey Molloy—this was before the invention of dryadology as a discipline, as you know, and thus many of our sources are from the Church."*

I handed Farris the book, and he opened it to the page I had marked. "The only problem," I continued, "is that Molloy was recording from the oral tradition, and many such tales are fragmentary. Including this one."

"'Kinge Macan's Bees,'" Farris read. "I'm not familiar with it."

"Few are, I suspect. But I must try to track down the complete version; perhaps more fragments have been preserved by another theologian."

---

* Due to the medieval belief that the Folk are rebel angels who managed to escape from Hell.

"Hm!" Farris said. He adjusted his glasses on his nose and peered at the book. Ariadne read over his shoulder. There followed a few moments of quiet, the only sounds coming from Shadow snoring by the fire and the boards creaking overhead as another lodger walked about. I restrained myself from tapping my foot in impatience.

"Interesting," Farris said at last. He handed Ariadne the book so that she could continue reading. "I see why it caught your interest. The curse, the former monarch being chased out by a new one, etcetera—it certainly follows the pattern of current events. Then you think it might provide you with some clue for locating Queen Arna?"

"That is the hope," I said. "You know the importance of stories to the Folk."

He murmured assent. "Well! We shall see if we can't find the rest of it."

"I should—you need not—" I began, stumbling to a stop. At last I said simply, "Thank you."

"Thank yourself!" Farris said, smiling. "Our foray into the Alps has advanced our understanding of Faerie by a decade or more; I should be pleading with you to allow me to help. I am beginning to feel, Emily, that simply following you about from place to place would afford me enough scientific discoveries to make my career all over again. Well, Russell-Brown and Eliades had their hangers-on, did they not?"[*]

I affected interest in stirring my tea. Certainly I am proud

---

[*] Robert Russell-Brown (1832–1880) proposed the classification system for the Folk that is still in use today, took the first photographs of a faerie market, and stole a goblet from one of the kings of Yorkshire, among other exploits, though today some argue his contribution to scholarship has been exaggerated due to contemporary admiration for his derring-do. Nikos Eliades (1551–1610), considered by many to be the father of dryadology, was the first scholar to establish a working relationship with one of the Folk, a dryad named Lani, who gave him several faerie stones and a poem written in Faie, among other enchanted trinkets, all of which are currently housed in Athens's Museum of Faeries.

of my achievements, but I am no Russell-Brown or Eliades, and the idea that Farris placed me in the category of those luminaries was overwhelming. I decided to assume, for my own comfort, that he was flattering me.

Ariadne had been watching both of us. She had not touched her tea and was wringing her hands in her lap. I looked at her, waiting. Finally, she burst out, "But you *must* tell us about the Silva Lupi!"

I laughed, surprised. "You have seen it yourself, Ari!"

"I know," she said, laughing sheepishly along with us. "But—I only saw it from a distance, if you understand me."

"I do." I took up one of the biscuits on the tea tray and tapped it absently against my cup. "Where shall I begin?"

11th January

Well! I have poured myself a glass of wine to celebrate, for I have completed my work here, and sooner than I thought I would, thanks in large part to Farris and Ariadne. A light rain, mixed with sleet, is falling beyond the window, but I have not drawn the curtains, for my view of the lantern-lit campus is charming in the winter night's gloom. I must be concise, for my train departs Dublin early on the morrow. I would return to Faerie tonight if I could, but the trains do not line up, and I would just end up spending the night in Limerick.

Ariadne and I spent most of the last two days in the library, while Farris came and went; he was of more use in leveraging his connections among the Trinity dryadologists, of which he has a fair few.

From one Professor O'Connell he managed to obtain a rare book so obscure there is no record of it in any academic library, an authorless volume of folklore from Counties Leane and Clare, likely dating to the early eighteenth century, which is merely called *Village Tales*. It contains another version of "King Macan's Bees," overly concise (*Village Tales* seems to have been written for children) but more complete than other iterations.

Farris even succeeded in identifying several scholars who are familiar with the tale, or have heard similar versions of it. The celebrated Professor Malik, who has been active in the field of Irish dryadology for the last half-century and is now semi-retired, was particularly helpful. Despite her age, her memory is impeccable, and she informed Farris that she had heard the tale some decades ago from an aged grandmother in a little village called Fenrow on the Leane coast. She had recorded it at the time, having thought perhaps to include it in one of her books, but the tale being so obscure—and, she suspected, invented by the grandmother in question, who according to her children had a habit of such things—she had culled it. Malik was able to provide Farris with the journal in which she had written the tale as it had been told to her by that now long-dead matriarch.

Ariadne, meanwhile, managed to win over the obstreperous head librarian with her unique combination of unconscious charm and youthful enthusiasm. Not only did he inform her that several relevant volumes of Irish tales were in the process of being re-bound, but he allowed her to peruse these at her leisure, provided she was careful to wear gloves and put everything back where she had found it (this last statement being delivered with a pointed look in my direction). In one of those volumes, we found another version of "King Macan's Bees," enigmatically titled "The King's Revenge."

And thus, in fits and starts, and after having been met with various dead ends and false signposts, we have managed to stitch the tale together, to the extent possible. Missing pieces remain: What motivated Macan's wife to betray him? Was she mistreated, as mortals in Faerie so often are? What is the nature of the bees, and are they symbolic of anything in particular?

I could go on. But in any case, here is the fruit of our research, such as it is.

King Macan's Bees

There was once a minor faerie lord who dwelt in a mound known locally as King Macan's tomb for reasons no one could remember. The mound was a natural feature long inhabited by the Folk, who also used the flat top for their summer revels, not an ancient, mortal-made monument to some dead king. Over the generations, the faerie lord came to be referred to as King Macan by the mortal inhabitants of the nearest village, which pleased him greatly. The faerie was not a king, and his castle within the mound was strange and dilapidated, but like all Folk, he saw himself as perfectly deserving of mortal veneration.

King Macan, being even more vain than the average faerie, had a great love of guests, for they gave him the opportunity to show off both his castle (which he thought very fine, despite its topsy-turvy architecture) and his appropriated title, which he had inscribed upon every lintel. This would prove his undoing, for one winter's night a wandering peddler came to his door. This peddler, despite his humble appearance, was in fact a faerie prince who had unsuccessfully challenged his older sister for her throne and been chased out of the kingdom in disgrace. Though he had fallen on hard times, even being forced to make his living peddling trinkets to puffed-up nobodies like King Macan (so the prince regarded him), this had not made him humble. The prince, in fact, still wanted a throne, and he decided that an imaginary one was better than none at all.

After welcoming the peddler prince into the castle and

giving him a tour, King Macan invited him to dine at his table and sleep a night beneath his roof. The prince acquiesced happily, and after all had retired for the night, he snuck out of his room and into the king's chamber. With the help of King Macan's wife, a mortal woman called Mona, the prince tied King Macan to his bed and bludgeoned him with his crown, which the king had made himself and inscribed with his false title. Thinking the man was dead, the prince threw his body into the river that flowed past the castle, placed the bloodied crown upon his head, and declared himself King Macan the Second. Then he announced his marriage to Mona[*] and they retired together without so much as changing the bedding.

Unfortunately for Macan the Second, Macan the First had not been killed, only grievously wounded. He crawled up onto the riverbank, and there he cast a powerful curse upon the mound and all who dwelt there, fed with his heart's blood and tears. For as long as the old Macan lived, the river in which he had nearly drowned would eat away at the foundations of the castle, making it teeter and shake ominously, while the bed in which he had been beaten, along with every other bed in the castle, would fill their occupants with nightmares so foul that some were driven insane.

Mona and her new husband knew they had to find the old Macan and kill him properly, for until they did, his curse could not be undone—his bitterness and hatred only fed the magic. Yet they could not work out where the old king was hiding; they found his blood upon the riverbank downstream, but after that he appeared to have slipped back into

---

[*] An ancient faerie custom first documented among the pine dryads of Greece in the early 1700s. While many Folk marry in elaborate ceremonies, not unlike mortals, some of the older tales depict such unions occurring via a simple declaration of mutual regard.

the river and drifted away. They began by questioning the servants, who were at first loath to be involved in the dispute, having love for neither of the Macans, the first being vain and stingy, the second bloodthirsty and rapacious. But, eventually, they convinced the man who prepared the king's baths to talk. This servant informed them that Macan the First had a secret castle that he disappeared to when he wished to be alone with his books, for the old king was a great reader, though preoccupied primarily with histories of his family and race. This castle was smaller, and hidden by magic—the servant knew not where it was, but he said that whenever the old king returned thence, he had bees tangled in his hair, which the servant found drowned at the bottom of the bath.

Next, the conspirators questioned the kitchen hands. Finally, one of the servants that stocked the larder confessed that whenever Macan the First returned from his hideaway, he would bring with him a handful of snail's head mushrooms to cook for his supper.

Mona and her new husband were certain they were close to tracking the old king down, but none of the other household servants could be convinced to speak with them. It was Mona who realized they had not yet questioned the gardeners. These Folk were as disinclined to cooperate as the rest, but one eventually directed them to a boggart[*] who was living in a folly beside the vegetable patch. The boggart agreed to help, but on one condition: that he be allowed to take up residence in the castle, a request that Macan the

---

[*] While originating in Scotland, boggarts are the ultimate wanderers and have appeared in faerie stories throughout the British Isles and France, and in several disputed tales from Spain. Yet, as is to be expected with the Folk, they are also full of contradictions; once a boggart has found a home it likes, it rarely stirs therefrom, and many stories depict the bodiless creatures as bound to crumbling ruins, either unwilling or unable to part from their homes.

First had long denied. To this the conspirators agreed without much thought, for the castle was large and had plenty of space for a boggart, who in any event spends most of its life asleep, like a cat.

The boggart then gave them the final clue they needed: long years ago, an age before Macan the First had married Mona, he had ordered a bridge built over a stream, which was now hidden by overgrowth. The boggart led the pair to this bridge, and once they crossed it they found a winding little path. This they followed, but still they would not have found Macan's secret castle had they not noticed the patch of snail's head mushrooms at the edge of the path and followed it into the forest. And still they might have missed the castle had they not seen an immense tangle of honeysuckle filled with drowsy, overfed bees, for once they pushed their way through the vines they found King Macan's other castle.

Macan the Second told his bride to await him outside, and then he went into the castle and slew Macan the First without a great deal of trouble, for the man was weak from his injuries and the effort of maintaining the curse.

As soon as his life's blood finally ran dry, the river waters subsided and the castle stopped its ominous shaking, and all who slept within its beds dreamed of gentler things, or as gentle as they had dreamed before. And that is how Macan the Second lifted the curse upon his kingdom.

But, alas—once Macan the Second exited the castle, he was swarmed by the bees, who had formed a friendship with Macan the First. Macan the Second was stung so many times that he died of the venom later that night.

After the death of the Macans, the boggart took up residence in the castle, as was his right under his bargain with Macan the Second. It is doubtful, though, that the man had guessed the boggart's true aim; boggarts are cunning and cruel, which the old Macan had known well. There being no claimants for the title of King Macan left alive, an event the boggart had doubtless foreseen, he declared himself the owner of the name as well as the castle. Mona continued to reside there with him, fuming over her misfortunes, but after a few years had passed her practical nature reasserted itself, and she agreed to the boggart's offer of marriage. She and King Macan the Third lived together in relative harmony through the passage of two ages in the world of mortals, and had many children, each more unsettling than the last, for they were half boggart and half human, an unfortunate combination.

This is as much as we have been able to piece together. The story grows entirely fragmentary beyond this point, seeming to turn its attention to the deeds of one of the halfblood children, who likely will be made to suffer for her parents' sins in some way—I see hints of that familiar pattern. But this is the material concatenation of events, and it is what I will bring to Wendell.

I know how to find the queen.

12th January

I had the most unexpected conversation with Farris this morning. I am grateful to have this time on the train, which bears me back towards County Leane and the cottage where Lilja and Margret are residing, to mull it over. At present I am unsure what to make of it.

My train was due to depart Dublin at ten, which gave me time for breakfast with Farris and Ariadne. But when Shadow and I arrived at the café, I found Farris seated alone at a table, looking grim.

"Oh dear," I said, pushing my hood back. It was one of those still winter mornings when the world is all shades of white—the sky like eggshell; the vines creeping up the stone buildings limned with frost. "Has something happened? Where is Ariadne?"

"Nothing has happened," Farris said. "I asked Ariadne to join us in half an hour. I wanted a few moments to—confess something."

I was not much heartened by this, given the seriousness of his expression. He drummed his fingers on the table and then said abruptly, "How is your book progressing? The politics of Faerie—an excellent topic."

"Yes," I said, a little annoyed, but deciding to allow him

to come to the point in his own time. He looked almost ill. "Though I have had a change of heart about it—I wished to focus on politics because I wanted to get at the *structure* of Faerie. What makes it tick, in other words. Yet I have realized that I am going about it wrong. The politics of Faerie—indeed, everything about the place—revolves around stories. Stories shape the realms and the actions of those who dwell there. Some of those stories are known to mortals, but many others have been lost, both to us and the Folk."

Farris nodded. "Then your book will be about the Macan tale?"

"That will be a piece of it," I said, leaning forward as I warmed to the topic. "I thought I would create a compendium of tales told by the Folk of the Silva Lupi. I mentioned that crow woman, bound by an ancient curse laid upon her by Wendell's father. I have met a dozen such creatures in Wendell's realm, enmeshed in stories every bit as fascinating as hers. If I can gather enough of them together, I believe we scholars might come close to grasping the true essence of the Silva Lupi—which is, like all of Faerie, an intricately woven tapestry of story."

He smiled. "It is a most intriguing idea. Brilliant, even—no scholar has ever had the sort of access to the Folk that you have."

"It is partly inspired by you," I said. "Your Sandstone Theory. You have always argued we should pay more attention to the stories the Folk tell of themselves if we wish to understand Faerie."

He murmured agreement. I noticed that his ear—the human one; the other was a strange, silver construction that he attempted to hide behind his lionlike white fringe—was now slightly pink. He seemed to steel himself for something, then opened his briefcase and took out a book. After a brief hesitation, he passed it to me.

The book was old and battered, the leather cover so worn it had become floppy. I flipped through it and found that it was not a book, but a journal, filled with someone's small, precise hand. The writing was legible, but even at a cursory glance I noted many instances of shorthand abbreviations that I suspected would prove troublesome. There was something oddly familiar about it.

I flipped to the first page and was astonished to find, tucked in the corner of the inside cover, the letters E.W. They were of so similar a character to how I write my own initials—the same matter-of-fact crossed W, the same slight lean to the E—that for a moment I wondered if I wasn't looking at one of *my* journals, which someone had taken and filled with their own writing. And yet—the hand was similar to mine. Neater, perhaps; it is more accurate to say that it was like mine when I take the time to make my writing legible to others, which I do only on rare occasions.

That was when I understood.

"This belonged to my grandfather," I said, simultaneously baffled and intrigued. My grandfather Edgar Wilde, while not a dryadologist himself, had been fascinated by the Folk, and had amassed a small library of folklore over his lifetime that had been, in part, what had inspired me to pursue this field of study. "But how on earth did you come by it?"

Farris grimaced. "I should have told you this a long time ago, Emily: I knew your grandfather. I was concerned that this fact might affect our professional relationship."

"You knew him? But why would that have any effect upon our relationship?" When he did not immediately reply, I thought over what he had said, and my memory of our conversations, searching for connections. Once I understood, my mouth fell open.

"He was your friend," I murmured. "The one you told me

about in St. Liesl, who died from exposure in Exmoor. The Folk killed him."

"Yes." Farris gazed absently into the fire. "Not just a friend; Edgar and I were like brothers. We grew up together, and remained close through many of life's vicissitudes. It was he who held me together after Catherine passed—my wife."

"But—" I was still struggling with the revelation. "I was told my grandfather died from heart failure."

"I believe that was the medical explanation," Farris said. "Yes, he did have trouble with his heart, but he could have lived many years longer than he did. I'm not surprised your family kept the full story hidden, given that it was somewhat—indelicate. Not only because Edgar was still married to your grandmother when he ran off with that faerie woman, but—well. The circumstances."

I did not need clarification. Farris's childhood friend—my *grandfather*—had been cruelly abandoned by the wandering group of Folk who had taken him in. When he had pursued them, still desperately in love, they had tied him to a tree by his beard, and there he had hung for hours before he was found.

"Good Lord," I said, staring down at the book in my hands. I tried to recall my grandfather—I'd been only thirteen when he died, and the few memories I had of him were in relation to his fantastical library, as I'd seen it. He'd never cared much for children, and I have no recollection of conversing with him, though he did tolerate me looking at his books, because I was careful with them.

An image rose in my mind: an old man—so he had seemed to me then, though he would have been only in his fifties—with his back to me, shirtsleeves rolled up as he hunched over a book at a desk. The man himself was blurred; I had the vague impression of a lanky frame and jutting ears, but no other details. Around him rose shelf upon shelf of books;

those near the desk were brightly lit, while the rest faded into shadow.

"I did not know he journalled," I said. "I take it these are not his law notes?"

Farris shook his head. "As you know, Edgar was something of an amateur enthusiast of the Folk, yet one who attempted to maintain professional records whenever he investigated a barrow or other rumoured faerie site. He prided himself on it, in fact; he wanted to leave accurate records for any dryadologists who might wish to further investigate his findings."

I nodded. While some dryadologists take a snobbish attitude towards hobbyists, the latter have been instrumental in a number of significant discoveries.*

"Unfortunately, your family had his other journals destroyed," Farris said. "But this—" He looked sheepish. "Well, I took it. It was among his belongings when he was found in Exmoor and brought with him to the hospital. I intended to return it to your grandmother, but when I learned what your family had done to the rest of his writings—"

"I understand." I set the journal down on the table, for abruptly I did not wish to be touching it. "Then it is a record of his last days."

"Not quite," Farris said. "He appears to have given up on

---

* Ursula Waldron is perhaps the best-known of these. In the late eighteenth century, Waldron questioned the efficacy of a protective practice dating to the medieval period, namely that of stuffing one's pockets with day-old bread before venturing into regions frequented by the Folk. The method was once thought as efficacious as salt circles or turning one's clothes inside out in warding off unfriendly faeries, and was particularly popular in the post-plague generations, a period of greater mobility in rural regions. Perhaps this is why so many peasants were abducted during this era, as Waldron proved, through a series of interviews with the trooping faeries of Wiltshire, that the Folk are not only unharmed by stale bread, but have been known to approach mortals with especially fat pockets to see what they're about. Waldron, a retired blacksmith who taught herself to read and write in her later years, was eventually appointed to the post of Honourary Lecturer at Cambridge, despite the grumblings of the traditionalist set.

journalling at some point during his stay with the Folk. Perhaps a few weeks before they abandoned him? It is difficult to be certain. And the first half of the journal is preoccupied primarily with a separate investigation he undertook earlier that year. But it is indeed a record of his final adventures."

I sighed. At that moment, the waiter brought us a fresh pot of tea—I hadn't touched mine, but Farris had polished off the lot. I waited until he was gone before saying, "This is another one of your warnings, then."

"No," Farris said firmly. But then he amended, again a little sheepish, "Not entirely."

"I thought you did not wish to play the gloomy sage."

"I will not tell you how to live, Emily," he said. "I would not do you the disrespect."

I gave a short laugh. "Then what is this?"

"The journal belongs to your family by right," he said. "Your grandmother has passed, so why should you not be the one to decide what is to be done with it? You might donate it to the Library of Dryadology, or put it to some other purpose. Or destroy it, for that matter."

"We are in accord on the matter of ownership," I said. "It is more the timing of this revelation that I question. You know that Wendell and I will soon be married."

"I believe you should have all the relevant information before you commit yourself to one of the Folk. Or accept one of their *thrones*."

"Relevant," I repeated. "My grandfather did not fall in love with Wendell. It was not Wendell's people who murdered him on that Exmoor heath. Your definition of relevance seems somewhat loose, Farris."

He gave a small shrug. "Then you can have no objection to reading it."

"Very well." I felt he had gotten the better of me somehow,

and it put me out of humour. And did not Farris recognize that I had more pressing concerns than this decades-old family secret? Nevertheless, I slid the journal into my briefcase. Whereupon it largely left my thoughts; Ariadne arrived shortly after, and together we finished our breakfast. They walked me to the train station and we said our goodbyes.

Since boarding the train, however, I have not been so incurious and have found my thoughts straying repeatedly to the journal. I have removed it from my briefcase and placed it on the seat beside me, where it now sits unopened, putting a damper on my sense of triumph at having come up with a plan to find Queen Arna. But why should this be so? I meant what I said to Farris—I am fully aware of the danger involved in marrying one of the Folk and do not need him to rescue me.

I keep feeling as if the bloody journal is glaring at me. Or not *glaring* precisely, but brooding in a sullen and self-righteous way, as if it knows as well as I that I should not be ignoring my grandfather's last testament. I think I will put it away again.

12th January–late

I arrived in County Leane after sundown, my last train having been delayed. With nothing to occupy me on the carriage ride to Corbann but my grandfather's journal—or, rather, with plenty to occupy me, all of it worrying—I spent the time perusing its contents, reading the last entry first and then moving backwards to the beginning. I am not entirely certain why I did so, only that the idea of reading it sequentially made me uneasy. I suppose that when the ending is so unpleasant, one does not wish to leave it looming. I need not have feared, however, for it is as Farris said: my grandfather's last entry merely describes a night of dancing and feasting, one of many he experienced among the Folk. He never recorded his abandonment, or anything that came after. The last words he wrote: *To-morrow I shall walk down to the sea.*

Interestingly, there is no point at which he *chooses* to run off with the woman in Exmoor—one day he encounters her bathing in a stream; the next, he is taking tea with her. After that comes a series of impossible banquets under the stars, complicated dances amongst the night mists whose patterns he can never remember afterwards, and nonsensical conversations with various Folk, all described in his ordinary, matter-of-fact tone, as if he were recounting a visit to the post office. Occasionally he mentions a mysterious "she" whom he describes as "beauty incarnate," "ethereal wanderer," and other fawning terms. But then in the next sentence he is looking forward to telling his wife about the "wondrous cakes" served at dinner, or to writing to Farris to tell him of some strange species of common fae he encountered. I think it likely that he was unconscious of the danger he was in.

I was not able to make sense of it all in the time I had, as the shorthand he employed is difficult. Also—need it be said?—it is an unsettling thing to read. I know Farris meant for me to be unsettled by it, which only increases my resentment. I threw the journal down several times, only to pick it up again, helplessly drawn in by the unfolding tragedy, the unanswered questions, and the uncanny echoes of myself. It was not just our handwriting or initials. My grandfather was as obsessive about his research as I, and seemed as skilled at giving offence. He was even quarrelling with a librarian!

Madame S— can write me all the letters she desires, he wrote at one point. *I am not returning it until I have finished my research. Where is the need? Not one person borrowed it in over three years— I consulted the catalogue. That she would threaten to send the county sheriff after me! As if she does not have better things to do. Well, let her try to find me here. Ha!*

I never did learn which book he was so determined to keep.

My first thought upon my arrival in Corbann was to return immediately to Wendell's realm through the stepping-stone door; however, I could not pass by Lilja and Margret's cottage without stopping to greet them. They invited me in to supper, so curious about my visit to Trinity that their enthusiasm was like a current sweeping me along, and I wondered how I could excuse myself.

Fortunately, before I had time to worry about it, there came a knock at the door, and there was Wendell, looking eager and impatient. I was so relieved to see him, alive and well and not somehow overcome by his stepmother's curse in my absence, that when he stepped towards me, I beat him to it, flinging my arms around him and nearly knocking him over on the doorstep.

"Emily!" he exclaimed, laughing. "This is only the second time I can recall that you have greeted me with enthusiasm. Are you well?"

"Good grief," I said, glowering to cover my embarrassment at my display. "Surely *second* is an exaggeration."

"Now, that is a look I am more familiar with." He placed a finger beneath my chin and tilted it up, then kissed me softly.

"Are you going to stand there letting in the cold, or are you staying for dinner?" Margret called from the kitchen, grinning at us and not looking at all embarrassed to be interrupting. Lilja wore a smile too, though hers was more guarded.

"Only if you will allow me to assist," Wendell called back gallantly. He swept inside, as merry as I'd ever seen him—and, I thought, relieved, as if this were a welcome respite from something unpleasant.

That sent a shiver through me. What had he left out of his letters?

"Wendell?" I said, but he was already storming about, scooping up plates and cutlery. Shadow awoke with a snort and promptly leapt all over Wendell, and he paused to pet and coddle the dog into submission before helping Lilja set the table.

Supper was a noisy affair, for Margret likes to talk almost as much as Wendell when in familiar company, and Shadow was delighted by the presence of so many of those he loved, and snuffled up to each of us by turns, whining excitedly. Wendell was off on one tangent after another, mostly amusing stories about Folk he had known in his youth who were, apparently, still getting themselves into a variety of adolescent troubles, including one individual who had made herself so drunk one night that, on a dare, she cast an enchantment upon herself that turned her into a patch of lichen whenever she sneezed. I did not volunteer to explain my findings at Trinity, nor did Wendell mention his stepmother's curse, and nobody asked; we had all made an unspoken agreement to speak only of lighter things.

I had little appetite, which Wendell must have noticed, for he did not tarry after the plates were empty, as he would ordinarily have done, but made our excuses and offered to clean the kitchen before we departed. Margret chased after him with a dish rag, good-naturedly protesting this indulgence—which, I sensed from the despairing look Wendell had given the moderately disordered countertops, was less an indulgence than a necessity on his part. Shadow trailed after, for this was also the route the plates with their scraps had taken, and Lilja and I were left alone.

"Would you care to see my carvings now?" Lilja said, and I agreed. She took me to the little workspace she had created at the back of the cottage, a long table facing a window with a view of the waterfall, its glass damp from the mist. Upon the table was a pile of untouched wood as well as a series of carved figures in varying stages of completion. A hobby from her youth, she had told us, which she had not had time to practice until now.

"But these are marvellous!" I said with perfect sincerity. My eye was drawn first to the raven, an intricate construction of proud beak, talons, and windswept feathers, before I noticed she seemed to be attempting to conceal something from me.

"Is that—?" I began, astonished. Laughing, she handed me the carving.

"It's not finished," she said. "I forgot to put it away. I was hoping to surprise you with it."

I was holding a life-sized carving of Poe—or the top half of him, at any rate; the rest was unworked wood. His face was rough but recognizable, skeletal with a great deal of teeth. Somehow, in its roughness, Lilja had managed to suggest something of Poe's ethereal quality, the sense that he is both *here* and *not here*. She had made a start on his needle fingers, several deep scores in the wood as long as his arms.

"I will admit," she said, "I am not as fond of the creature as you are. Much as I wish it were different, I cannot stop having nightmares about him! And I am always worried he will accidentally slice off one of my toes and not even notice."

I laughed and set the carving down. How I miss Poe! He gave me a key so that I might visit him, but it is a magic that works only in lands where winter is more at home than it is in Ireland.

Lilja showed me the rest of the carvings, which were also very fine, though she claimed each needed various improvements. Watching her, I realized it was not my imagination—she was distracted, but whether this pertained to myself or something else entirely, I couldn't have said. Ordinarily I attempt to suppress the impulse to be blunt, but Lilja does not take offence to me. "I think you are upset," I said. "I would like to know what has caused it."

She gave a small laugh. "Oh dear! I'm sorry, Emily. I have been trying to find the words, but—I'm afraid I would be interfering where I shouldn't."

"You needn't worry," I said. "I am not the best judge of the bounds of friendship; therefore you are unlikely to overstep with me. You are concerned for my safety—is that it?"

She looked troubled. "That is putting it mildly. Dear

Emily—you have taken one of their *thrones*. Can you truly not guess how worried I have been? Thora too, and Aud—she writes me weekly to ask for news of you."

I felt relieved. Not to be having this conversation, but to know that I had not angered her somehow, or otherwise caused her to question our friendship. "You know that I am one of the foremost living experts on the ways of the Folk," I said. I was not worried about bragging, for this was a simple statement of fact.

"That is the problem," Lilja replied. "Yes, I know that you *know* the Folk, but there is a difference between knowing and feeling. Those of us who live among them would never trust the tall ones. For all you have read about and studied the Folk, you have never truly lived with them, dear. They are like—like nature. Can you understand the feeling of a winter night, or a spring wind, if you have only read about it?"

This was an uncomfortable echo of something Farris had said to me once. I pursed my lips and replied, "All right. Let us accept for the sake of argument that you possess a truer understanding of the Folk than I, that books and academic knowledge are secondary to lived experience. What then would you have me fear?"

She hesitated. "Power," she said at last. "In our stories, it is the great ones—the lords and ladies, the monarchs and generals, that one must avoid above all else. They are the true monsters lurking in the night."

This again! I thought. Aloud I said, "I have heard a similar opinion recently from another friend of mine, who seems to think Wendell will abandon me to die of exposure or some such, I suppose when he becomes tired of me."

"Oh, no!" Lilja said. "That is not what I meant—I don't believe for a second that Wendell would harm you. But I worry there will come a day when you no longer recognize him. And what hurt is worse than that?"

I could not reply to this. There was something in her gentle manner that sent a spear of panic through me that Farris's words had not, much as he'd clearly been trying to make me uneasy. Somehow, it laid bare the many times I'd voiced a similar fear to myself, before immediately burying it beneath other things.

Lilja seemed to regret her words, which naturally only made them keener. "Don't mind me," she said quickly. "You are the best judge of your heart, and of his. I am your friend, but that does not make me all-knowing."

She seemed upset, but I did not know how to correct this; the conversation had gone beyond my ability to navigate. I could only say, "I will think on what you have said."

She nodded, and we went back to the carvings. A few moments later, we heard Wendell calling me, and made our way to the front door with Shadow. There we took our leave. Lilja, I thought, hugged me longer than she ordinarily did.

The night was cold, the wind tossing sheets of mist from the waterfall into our faces. Wendell and I crossed the stepping-stones, but I stumbled in surprise when we emerged into the Silva Lupi, nearly tripping over Shadow.

"Where are we?" This was not the castle; we stood in the forest, possibly near the royal gardens—the grass held a scattering of daisies, whose seeds drifted from their beds into the neighbouring woods.

Wendell grimaced and looked about him. "The door has returned to its original location. A number of enchantments have been going awry like that. My stepmother's curse is spreading—this way."

Shadow and I followed him through the trees—it was a deer

trail, nothing more, but he widened it with a gesture, opening and then closing his hand. "I must tell you what I've discovered," I said.

"Yes," he said over his shoulder. "Momentarily, Em."

I felt a flicker of annoyance that he had so little interest in my research. Did he assume I had failed? "But I've found a solution to your stepmother's curse."

"I know you have," he said, a little question in his voice, as if wondering why I'd bother to state something so obvious. "But you will only have to tell the story again for Niamh, and my uncle, I suppose, so let us wait until we can summon them."

I was mollified.

"Wait," I said. "You were skeptical before about whether I might find an answer in the old stories."

"Not really," he said, sighing. "I only didn't want you to go away. I never do, but I feel especially guilty in this circumstance. I thought I would be showing you everything my realm has to offer—the lakes, the gardens, the brightest and the darkest parts of the forest. I thought I would be summoning strange and terrible Folk to dance before you, or give you presents, while you scribbled away in your notebook... Instead, we are forced to contend with my stepmother's treachery. I'm sorry."

"You say that as if you have dragged me into something," I said. I regretted the change from his good mood, and added, "I'll have you know that I find all of this—your stepmother's treachery included—fascinating. I am making good progress on my book."

He laughed, and the forest around us seemed to brighten. "Read me some of it later, Em."

The leaves rustled as some small creature, faerie or otherwise, made its way through the canopy. My attention was caught by a line of flickering lights drifting along the forest floor, parallel to our path—initially I thought they were fireflies, but upon closer inspection I saw that they were trooping fae the size of my thumbnail, each carrying a lantern. Warm hearthlight glimmered from knotholes in the trees, and occasionally I heard distant, rowdy voices, as from a packed tavern. The branches in this part of the forest, near to the castle, where the concentration of common fae was greatest, looked as if they were strung with innumerable glittering spiderwebs, but these were only the small bridges used by brownies and suchlike, which clinked softly like bells whenever one of the creatures dashed across, moving so quickly I saw only the bridge swaying afterwards.

Wendell stopped here and there to examine a tree, pressing a hand to those he thought sickly or dull-looking and unleashing a burst of new growth, while worrying aloud about the state of the cottage in Corbann. It seemed he had been much perturbed by the disarray he had seen—wood shavings from Lilja's carvings scattered about, rugs left unshaken—and wondered if he should assign a few of the *oíche sidhe* to put things back in order. At least, I think that's what he was on about—I was too busy admiring the forest, which at night is such a perfect match for my childhood fantasies of what a faerie forest should look like that it left me breathless.

"What is it?" Wendell said after I again failed to respond to one of his silly complaints with more than a *hm!*

"What is what?" I said peevishly. My annoyance was not directed at him in particular, only I was wearied from the long day of travel and talk, not to mention worrying. "I'm merely thinking. Why do you assume something is the matter?"

"Em," he said, "I am quite accustomed to the cadence of your silences by now. I know the difference between thinking and brooding. You may hoard your misgivings in your usual dragonish manner if you wish, but I will work them out eventually, you know. Spare me the trouble?"

I eyed him sidelong. It seemed wrong to confide in him what Lilja had said—and yet, now that I thought about it, I no longer saw why. This was *Wendell,* not some wicked faerie in a story. So I told him all.

I did not know how he would react, but I certainly wasn't expecting him to look pleased. "It's a kindness that she shares her concerns with you," he said. "Lilja is a good friend."

"A kindness!" I repeated. "Is that really what you think? She is not much better than Farris, who thinks you will have me strung up in a tree."

"Naturally she worries about my feelings for you," Wendell said, passing his hand absently over the tall ferns that bordered the path. "Think of the source. Lilja suffered greatly at the hands of the Hidden Ones—it would be strange for her to trust me."

I did not find this a satisfying answer, particularly given the disquiet Lilja's words had aroused in me. "That is all you have to say? You yourself told me that you were worried the throne would change you. And it does seem true that, in many tales, power corrupts those Folk who wield it." I did not mention my ambivalence regarding this interpretation, for it has always seemed to me more likely that power only draws out the amorality inherent in all Folk, giving it free rein, rather than instilling a preference for wickedness.

"Yes." Wendell came to a stop, frowning as he rubbed at his hair. "I do wish you would allow me to give you my name. Then if one day I *do* turn into a vengeful monster, as my stepmother has—or that bloody ice king of yours, wasn't he a terror!—you can simply speak one word, and I will be under your command, free to become whatever you want me to be. Would it not ease your worries?"

Well, how on earth was I supposed to respond to this? After blinking at him in silence for a moment, I said, "I would prefer you not to turn into a monster in the first place. One murderous fiancé is enough for me."

"*More* than enough," Wendell said with such passionate resentment that I snorted with laughter. His expression changed as abruptly as sun breaking through cloud.

"Where would I be without you, Em?" he said. It was an old joke of ours, but it wasn't a joke now, the way he said it. I did not reply, merely straightened the hair he had mussed, brushing it back into place. He took my hand and we kept going. Soon, the castle came into view—its light was visible first, a glow that silhouetted the nearby trees. Wendell stilled.

"What?" I said, instantly on my guard.

"It wasn't here when I left," Wendell murmured.

"*What?*" I repeated.

He hurried forward, and I followed him, Shadow giving a huff of displeasure at the length of this walk, when by rights he should have been abed already. It was several moments before the trees thinned enough that I could see what Wendell did.

In the forest behind the castle, stretching all the way to the brow of the hill, and laterally for as much as an acre, perhaps, was the same dark mist we had seen in the yew grove. The trees seemed shrunken and indistinct, and the silver bridges that draped this part of the forest, crowded with common fae, had vanished entirely.

What was more, the curse had consumed part of the castle grounds. At least two of the gazebos had been reduced to dark, skeletal things, like slashes of ink put to canvas by an impatient artist. The path that had led to the Monarchs' Grove was gone—and was the Grove as well? I couldn't be certain.

"The gardens," Wendell murmured.

"What is the extent of it?" I said. My voice was shaking. "Is it growing?"

"I don't know."

I took his hand before he could fly into a temper—violence would not serve us now; there was nowhere to direct it.

We needed to find the queen.

"Let us see for ourselves," I said. "Quickly."

13th January

We convened before sunrise in the sprawling banquet hall. Niamh had suggested we meet here, where the court could see us. I had not fully understood what this meant, for I had imagined, given both the importance of my research and the likelihood that the queen's spies still haunted the castle, that our discussion would take place in private, with only those we trusted in attendance. But, in addition to being open to the sky, the hall had many glassless windows so long and tall one could simply step through them from the gardens beyond, which meant we had an audience of innumerable eavesdroppers, courtly and common alike. Most did not even bother to conceal what they were doing; I saw several boyish-looking courtly fae setting up a table for playing cards just outside the closest window, and another brownie selling nuts from a basket on his head wandered along the wall (only the basket and two long-fingered grey hands were visible). A troupe of ghoulish-looking bogles dressed in rags perched upon the roofless walls, gawping down at us with their hollow eyes, occasionally catching hold of insects and tossing them into their cookpots. Nobody seemed to think any part of this strange; as far as I could tell, this was simply how court business was conducted in Where the Trees Have Eyes.

I was dressed once again in my queenly attire, much as I missed the simple shifts and cardigan I had worn at Trinity. The cardigan in particular, shapeless and scholarly as it was, had large pockets at the front that could hold my notebook and an array of pencils. Today's gown—black again, with intricate silver lace across the bodice in the shape of flowering vines, which extended up my neck—had pockets, but I did not wish to use them. They seemed to be under a similar enchantment to the cloak I had obtained from the Hidden Ones; whenever I put my hand inside, I found some new trinket, or sometimes a piece of fruit or handful of sugared nuts. I worried that if I stored my notebook there it would vanish—or, almost as bad: become sticky.

Callum Thomas was present, as was Lord Taran, who leaned his head on his hand, looking bored, his dark eyes gazing absently up towards the sky. Niamh Proudfit sat across from them at the oak table, tapping at her typewriter and occasionally muttering inquiries and instructions to her personal attendant, a merry-faced spriggan.* In addition to these was Wendell's half-sister, whom he kept ordering away, after which the girl would simply sneak in through a window and crouch somewhere out of sight, until he eventually gave up and ignored her. There were also two members of the Council—which had dwindled in numbers due to many councillors having fled the castle in terror of the queen's curse. One was a poet, and solely referred to as such, an elderly mortal man who spent much of his time dozing off, which was no

---

* A broad category of brownie that goes by various names in different cultures, always described as hunchbacked and grandmotherly in appearance. Faeries of this type are so unnervingly cheerful they are used to frighten children into good behaviour in some parts of Eastern Europe ("Go to bed, or I'll send you to grandmother *iele* to mind," is the refrain in the well-known Romanian tale "The Youngest Brother's Folly"). Spriggans often serve the courtly fae as personal attendants or bodyguards.

great loss, for when he did speak it was a largely incoherent jumble of metaphor that gave the impression of consequence. I assumed this to be the result of too much time spent in Faerie, yet his speeches often had an air of affectation. The second was—unfortunately—the Lady in the Crimson Cloak. I preferred not to look at her, and she seemed to feel the same where I was concerned, though I suspect our reasons differed somewhat.

Wendell was pale. His hand was bandaged, for he had driven the queen's curse back from the castle with his own blood. The corruption still lurked within the royal forest, but we were not at present in danger of being devoured by it. His fury had faded, but he was in a state of constant agitation, pacing back and forth and regularly going up to one of the windows to stare out into the forest. I found it very distracting and wished he would sit down.

"Now," Niamh said, "give us the tale again."

I had already told them the story of King Macan's bees, but I respected her wish to be thorough. I repeated the tale, with which I am now so familiar that I could likely recite it backwards. I had to raise my voice a little, for the usual background rustle of the forest was even louder that morning, though it was not windy. I assumed the trees were as agitated as ourselves.

"It's good," Niamh said with a nod. "The story has many echoes of our present troubles—the usurper, the vengeful monarch, the curse. There is even a treacherous mortal queen." She smiled in my direction. "I don't know why we couldn't make use of it. So, you propose—what? That we question the servants?"

I nodded. "In the story, the new king has no need to search for the old one, because Macan the First's hideaway is known, or partly known, by those servants who were closest to him.

So it is likely that there are three servants among the castle staff who each know a different clue that will lead us to the queen."

"The queen holds each card—the deck is mist, and the jesters dance with royalty," the poet declared, which was to be his sole contribution; thereafter he dozed off again. How he had attained a position on our Council was beyond me, until I remembered that Wendell had merely rounded up a handful of mortals at random, under the misguided assumption that this would please me.

"Let us interrogate the servants immediately," said the Lady in the Crimson Cloak in her imperious manner. "With threats, if necessary." She motioned to an attendant standing by the wall, and the faerie darted away, followed by three others, all looking wide-eyed with fear; the lady's gesture had been vague.

"No, wait—" I said, but the attendants were already gone. I quelled a sigh. Nothing in this court, it seemed, could be accomplished without some amount of chaos.

"We should start with Queen Ar—the old queen's ladies-in-waiting," I said. "In the story, the first clue came from a servant who ran the king's baths."

"Most of them have fled," Wendell said from his position by a window. He wandered back to the table and began to pace behind my chair, driving me to distraction.

"Or they've been killed," Lord Taran said. "Oops."

"We will look for any that remain," Niamh said, motioning to the spriggan at her side. The little creature grinned wider—she was always grinning, which I found off-putting, but I did not doubt Niamh had reason to trust her—and hurried off.

"Has anything else of note occurred during my absence?" I enquired. "I would particularly appreciate *good* news, if there's any to be had."

"The realm may be slowly disintegrating," Lord Taran said, "but the invaders have left. My scouts have informed me they have fled back to Where the Ravens Hide. Apparently they do not wish to be cursed along with the rest of us."

"Thank you," I snapped. "You consider that good news, do you?"

He gave me an amused look. "Not particularly."

Callum murmured something to him, and Taran rolled his eyes, slouching in his chair with his hands folded, and went back to examining the walls. Wendell, meanwhile, was still pacing energetically. I was perhaps thirty seconds away from strangling him. Fortunately, an idea occurred, and I pretended to forget about Wendell's coffee cup as I rearranged my notebook on the table. My elbow struck it, and the cup overturned. As I'd hoped, Wendell stopped pacing, seizing one of the napkins and applying it to the spill.

"Forgive me," Callum said, "but I feel as if I've fallen a few bars behind. I understand that stories are an important part of Faerie, but—"

"Not a part," Niamh said, pausing at her typing. "They are the very foundations of this world, and all the others. As such, they may be used as compasses. Guiding stars. Choose whatever analogy you like."

"Yes," Callum said after a little pause. As if seeking reassurance, he glanced at Lord Taran, who gave him a smile that I had never seen from him before, in that it was entirely devoid of malice. "I suppose what I am wondering is," Callum continued, "why *this* story? Are there not others that may be useful to us?"

I bristled instinctively, as I would at a conference when an audience member questions my methods. Part of it was that I had worried over the same question myself; after all, I had spent only a few days at Trinity. Had I truly exhausted all the possibilities? "Other stories may exist," I said, "but I assure you, 'King Macan's Bees' is the likeliest candidate I could unearth."

Wendell was still preoccupied with removing the coffee stain from the table, rubbing at a crack in the wood with a napkin and some of the lavender water from the finger bowls. "It is the right story," he said, and though he did not elaborate, there was something in his voice that swept away my lingering doubts.

"Yes," Taran said, running his thumb over the back of Callum's hand. "Don't worry about that part, my love. The real concern is whether we can locate my sister before her curse devours the castle, along with everything else. Our new queen may have discovered this answer too late."

"Your confidence is much appreciated," I said tightly. "But you need not be so grim about our prospects."

"I am not," Lord Taran said. "Should this poison continue to spread, I shall be taking Callum and fleeing to another realm, even if it be Where the Ravens Hide. I am more powerful than any of their nobility. They will be unable to do anything about it."

I did not bother mentioning that most in Wendell's realm could not do the same; apart from a few wanderers, Folk do not flit from realm to realm in the manner Lord Taran was proposing.

But Callum sighed, and somehow, that slight sound transformed Taran's expression. He gave Callum a look that was half affection and half exasperation, and added, "But, naturally, I will do whatever it takes to stop my sister. She deserves a lingering death, as do those who have helped her, which I would be happy to administer. I guessed she would throw a tantrum once she lost her grip on the throne, but I did not anticipate her destroying her own kingdom in pursuit of vengeance. Truly, I have never known her to be so uncouth."

Niamh made some reply to this, but I could not make out all the words, for the rustling of the leaves had grown so loud as to drown out most sounds—it was almost a roar. "Good Lord!" she yelled. "What has possessed the forest? Are we under fresh attack?"

"It's the attentive oaks," Lord Taran said. For some reason, he was looking at Wendell, so the rest of us did, too.

He glanced up—he had finished cleaning up the coffee spill and was now scrubbing obsessively at the inlaid carvings on the lip of the table. I would not have been surprised if he soon wore holes in the wood. I put my hand on his arm.

"What? Oh, yes." His face went abruptly blank, as if he had stepped out from behind it and gone—elsewhere. This gave me the same dreadfully unsettled feeling as when he used trees as doorways. "The oaks," he said. "They know."

"Know what?" I didn't much like the idea of those things knowing anything.

"That I'm—they can sense—" He ran a hand over his face, and then he closed his eyes. "If I can calm myself, I think they will stop."

He kept his eyes closed for a moment while we stared at him like jittery attendees at a seance. Gradually, the rustle of the oaks lessened, and then, finally, the noise sank to little more than a whisper.

Wendell opened his eyes. "My apologies," he said, then poured himself a fresh cup of coffee as if nothing had happened.

We continued to stare at him. Even Lord Taran looked a touch unnerved, though he paired it with a smirk. "That's a sinister trick, Your Highness," he said. "Not since your great-grandmother's day have I seen a monarch rile the oaks with a thought. I am not overfond of those trees."

"Thank God," I muttered. "I thought I was the only one."

"Oh, no!" Lord Taran made a face. "You have not experienced all their delights until you have ventured out for a walk on a crisp autumn morning, and come home to find one of their leaves in your hair."

Niamh's attendant returned and muttered something in her ear. Niamh nodded.

"We have located one of the old queen's personal servants," she said. "This one did not draw her baths, like Macan's, but she helped make her breakfast every day."

I was already standing. "She has information about the queen's refuge?"

"She did not say this," Niamh said. "But as soon as she heard we were questioning the servants, she fled."

"That's an encouraging sign," I said.

"You go," Lord Taran said, knitting his fingers together and stretching his arms. "Thank you, but my talents are wasted interrogating servants. Let me know when the bloodshed starts."

The faerie had not gone far. It seemed she had tried to flee into the woods, but the guardians had got wind of her importance, and chased her into a tree.

We stood below the tree—an alder, thankfully—as the faerie shivered above us, alternately muttering to herself and wringing her hands. She was perched on one of the higher branches, and could easily have been dragged out by one of the guardians, but I did not wish to take this step unless necessary. She was only a little larger than Poe, and though her appearance did not match his in any other respect, I felt an instinctive desire to avoid harming her. She was clad in a tea-coloured dress and white apron, and on her head was an enormous buttercup worn like a kerchief, two of the petals pinned together beneath her hair. Her face was very red, very shiny, and very plump. She looked, I thought, a little like a lost doll, though not one mortal children would enjoy playing with; her eyes were the usual all black, and she appeared to be a type of faun, with large and intimidatingly sharp black horns that curved backwards out of her head, and legs that ended in hairy hooves.

"A butter faerie," Niamh said. "The queen had several in her service—this one, I am told, had the queen's particular affections due to the quality of her product."

"Fascinating," I said, wishing I had time to make a sketch. My encyclopaedia's entry on butter faeries had been sorely lacking in detail. "I have never encountered one before."

"They're quite rare," Niamh said. "A good thing, I've always thought. They are peevish, half-mad little things, particularly if you remove them from their creameries."

"I did not know they were found in Ireland," I said. "Most of the tales of butter faeries are from Somerset, are they not?"

"Ah!" Niamh said, her face alight with scholarly enthusiasm. "Indeed they are. But once upon a time, as you know, Where the Trees Have Eyes had several doors leading to British faerie realms. One of these, I'm told, led to a pretty corner of Somerset. I theorize that the creatures used to go to and fro before the door collapsed, trapping several of them in this realm."

"Somerset," I repeated. The word tugged at me like a half-forgotten memory, a sense of some missed connection. But what did Somerset have to do with any of this? I did not have time to puzzle it out.

The creature continued to mutter and wring her hands

above us. I could not make out what she was saying, apart from the odd *my lady* and *the milk*, the latter of which she repeated over and over. How on earth were we to get her down? I cannot climb trees—not that the skill set hasn't come in handy for some dryadologists, but I simply haven't the dexterity.

Razkarden, who had been circling overhead, alighted on a nearby branch and fixed his ancient gaze upon me. I had the distinct impression he was waiting for orders, which I pretended not to notice. A crowd of miscellaneous Folk had followed us from the banquet hall, accumulating more Folk as they went, and stood watching us from the edge of the clearing—some even spreading blankets over the grass to lounge upon, as if we were putting on a play. I could not help thinking again that this was a very silly way to conduct vital court business, the outcome of which could either preserve or destroy an entire world, but as before, no one else seemed to think much of it. At least nobody was selling nuts this time.

Wendell had been standing a little back from myself and Niamh, conversing with the Lady in the Crimson Cloak, Callum, and a small group of servants. Now he came forward.

"They think they've found another servant," he told us. "Apparently my stepmother's favourite hairdresser is still alive. That has a nice symmetry with Macan, does it not? Perhaps he also found dead bees in the queen's hair."

"Yes," I said. "Only I do not know how we will convince this one to cooperate. Can we lure her to us somehow?"

Wendell looked up at the tree, and his face darkened. He spoke but one word—"Down"—and suddenly the little faerie was clambering towards us, muttering even more feverishly. Well, so much for my concerns. She was moving so quickly that she fell part of the way and landed on the forest floor in a heap, where she remained, crouched like a wounded bird, panting and muttering. I now heard several *Your Highness*es and *please*s mixed in with the babble.

"Where is she?" Wendell said. His voice was calm, but he suddenly looked so cold and remote that even *I* found him unnerving. The faerie's muttering grew higher in pitch, almost a whine.

"That won't do," I said. "She is absolutely terrified of you."

"Naturally," said the Lady in the Crimson Cloak. She came forward, and the world seemed to redden, the forest shadows spreading like pools of blood. "If she will not speak, we will dash her head against a stone and see if the truth spills out."

"Stop that," I snapped. "Whatever you are doing. You are only making things worse."

Wendell lifted a hand, and the Lady fell back. "Very well, Em," he said. "What would you have us do?"

"Take her home, of course," I said.

The little faerie's "home" was located deep beneath the castle. I had not known there was much belowground, apart from the dungeons Wendell had spoken of, but in fact there was a warren of common fae workshops and hovels, some of which seemed connected to the castle, such as the room full of spindles where three brownies laboured, repairing tapestries and rugs, others which seemed to be inhabited by Folk who had simply decided to dwell there, at the very heart of the realm. Did proximity to the monarch give them access to magics they would lack otherwise? Yet another question to add to the pile.

At first we descended into the earth via a stone staircase, but gradually the stairs became rougher until we were clambering down the sloping and uneven floor of a vast cavern, the dimensions of which I could not make out due to the darkness. Wendell summoned several lights that bobbed above us, which helped, for the lantern posts scattered here and there were few in number. Many doors had been carved into the cavern walls at various heights, accessed via rough-hewn stairs or silver bridges, and the air was haunted with innumerable voices, clanks and thumps, harp song, and echoes. The air was damp, and in the distance I heard the *whoosh* of some subterranean river. I thought of the queen's curse descending on this teeming little city, a jewel box of scientific curiosities, and experienced a moment of dizziness.

The servant leading our procession found another stair, this one narrower than the last, and we ascended a series of hills and bulges in the wall until we came to something that was almost a hallway, but clearly natural, with a great stalagmite jutting out of it, at the end of which was a door. The butter faerie bowed low in Wendell's direction and hurried through the door, moving with the graceful, gliding trot all fauns seem to possess. We followed.

The faerie's creamery was not too deep, happily, or at least it did not feel so; a chimneylike skylight cut into the stone roof admitted the warm gold-green light of the forest. Given the faerie's size, the workspace was expansive—even Wendell, the tallest among us, did not need to duck—with a hard-packed earthen floor and an array of shelves, some of which held blocks of butter wrapped in paper and twine. In the middle of the workshop was the butter churn, beside which was a tin bucket of milk with condensation forming on the side—which I think is what the faerie had been worrying about, for she immediately rushed over to it and carried it into her cellar. The air was cool, on the edge of cold, and the smell of the place made my mouth water. Not only of butter, but thyme and lavender, strawberries and honey, which the faerie used to flavour some of the blocks. Those on the nearest shelf had leaves tucked beneath the twine—basil, I think.

"What do you see?" Niamh asked eagerly.

I attempted to describe it as best I could, conscious that this was the sort of discovery that would make a dryadologist's career, even if they were to accomplish nothing else. I felt another wave of dizziness.

"Now what?" Callum said. Wendell was tapping the toe of his pointed boot against the floor.

"Give her a moment to settle in," I said. "She's had a fright. She probably thought you were going to torture her. Is that not what your father would have done, Wendell?"

Now that the milk was returned to its proper place, the little faerie seemed much calmer. She went over to a cupboard with a lock upon it, fishing about in her pockets until she located a key. From within she drew out another block of butter wrapped in cloth, which looked to me like all the others on the shelves, only the faerie handled it as tenderly as if it were her child. She went to Wendell and held it out, bowing deeply.

Wendell's mood had shifted, as it was wont to do, or perhaps he had taken my admonishment to heart. He knelt before the faerie and said in a light voice, "Thank you, little one, but I will not deprive you of your prize handiwork. I need only one thing, which you know. You need not fear the wrath of the old queen, for I shall protect you. Will you help me?"

It was an image that made me wish for my notebook and sketching pencils. Wendell wore only a few silvered leaves in his golden hair, his tunic was cut simply and his cloak was an ordinary aristocratic-looking thing—not the one with the beast living in it—yet any who beheld him would have known him as a monarch of Faerie. It had been happening gradually after he returned to his realm, and now that we had been apart a few days, I could see it clearly: not only was he more at ease in himself, to an extent that was not remotely human, but there was a sense that everything around him, the air included, seemed to bend in his direction. I suppose that, if Barrister is correct,* it had something to do with Wendell no longer being entirely *Wendell*—or not *only* Wendell—but the source of every enchantment that held his realm together. And there he was, kneeling before a trembling, dirt-stained faerie barely as tall as my knee, who was clutching a block of butter.

The faerie seemed to feel some of this as well, for her entire attitude towards Wendell changed. Her red face became even redder, and she bowed many times, looking suddenly more eager than afraid. She put away her butter first, then rummaged about on one of her overcrowded shelves, shoving aside several glass jars of honeycomb. Shyly, she moved back towards Wendell, head lowered, and placed a small tin in his hand. She muttered something in a rapid patter of Faie and Irish.

He stood and handed the tin to me. Nervously, I lifted the lid, and found within a handful of empty snail shells about the length of my thumb. They were highly distinct, leaf-green with pointed domes that made them look almost aquatic. Each whorl included a stripe of pure silver.

"She says they were my stepmother's favourite," Wendell said. "She would deliver them to the little one to be cooked in butter."

I nodded slowly. "Have you seen this species before?"

"As a child, yes. They have long been considered a delicacy

---

* Letitia Barrister's article "The Lost Kings of Sardinia," published in the *European Journal of Dryadology* (1895), argues that the collapse of the Faerie realm located in one of Sardinia's mountain ranges resulted from the death of its monarch, who had no heir. While several of the nobility attempted to claim the throne, they were, for reasons unknown, unsuccessful, and the realm slowly disintegrated. Perhaps this is why so many Sardinian tales depict the courtly fae as dangerous vagabonds more likely to steal the preserves in your cellar in the night than carry you off into Faerie.

by the nobility, and for this reason they have gone extinct—or so I thought. They are cousins of the snails we have around here, in the forest, and can be just as vengeful, in their way."

I shuddered. "Where are they found?"

"They are island-dwellers exclusively. The little one knows not how my stepmother came by them."

"Islands," I repeated. A little shiver went down my back, as if a ghost stood just behind me. "But there are no islands nearby."

Wendell shook his head slightly. "My realm extends to the edge of the land and the shallows of the sea. There we have a scatter of many islands—hundreds of them, if one counts the shoals and rocks. The trouble is, I know little of the coast, other than that it stretches for miles."

Wendell went back to speak to the butter faerie, and Niamh pulled me aside.

"There is one thing in all this that concerns me," she said in a low voice.

I knew what she was about to say, but affected not to. "Yes?"

"King Macan's successor," she said. "The new king, the one who defeats the curse upon his kingdom and marries the mortal woman. He dies in the end."

"Yes," I said. "But there is no reason to suppose every detail will be repeated in our situation—for it is not so, is it? The curses are different; the setting. Besides, I discovered an iteration of the tale in which Macan the Second lives. There is no consistency on that point."

Niamh worried her lip. "*One* iteration?"

My composure cracked a little further. Niamh seemed to sense this from my silence and put a hand on my arm.

"We will not let her take him down with her," she said. "We will just—keep an eye out for bees, hm?"

17th January

I've not had much time for journalling these past few days. Now it is dark, and I am alone here by the fire in our bedroom; Wendell has once again gone to the royal forest to do what he can to stop the spread of the curse. The area is too big to burn without the entire hill going up in flames, and the gardens with it. We have abandoned any attempt to locate or burn other corrupted groves, though we know they continue to appear throughout the realm like diseased sores. Refugees have begun to arrive at the palace by the dozens, Folk of all descriptions from brownies to solitary courtly fae, many of whom, intriguingly, have the look of brownies in all but height, often being clad in woven moss and other flora. They are encamped in the gardens, the pavilion, wherever there is space for them. If I look out the window, I can see the flicker of their lanterns and campfires like tiny stars.

All our energies remain focused on finding Queen Arna.

The old queen's hairdresser turned out to be *my* hairdresser, the wrinkled faerie who daily—and often painfully—twists my hair into plaits and chignons. He was a dour, scowling creature who—I had convinced myself—was voicing innumerable insults about my lifeless hair behind my back, but he did exceptional work, which I assumed was why the queen had favoured him so. Perhaps, being half mortal, she had been similarly deficient when it came to cosmetology, and relied on him to help her blend into the sea of beauty that is a Faerie court.

The hairdresser was not as averse to divulging the queen's secrets as the butter faerie. In fact, he looked coldly pleased to be brought before Wendell, and not at all surprised.

"My pay is low for the quality of services I provide, Your Highness," he said, and I realized he had been planning for this moment.

"Is it!" Wendell said, sharing an exasperated look with me. "And in what coin did my stepmother pay you?"

"Tarry seeds," the brownie said, an odd sort of hunger in his eyes. "And a silver melon at midsummer."

"Naturally," Wendell muttered under his breath, looking put out for some reason. Were tarry seeds or silver melons difficult to acquire? I meant to ask him, but I forgot. I have not been getting much sleep these days.

"Very well," Wendell said. "Your pay shall be doubled."

The faerie drew himself up to his full height—a little higher than my waist. I could not help admiring his confidence. But then, I suppose, when one possesses a singular mastery of a trade, one is less worried about losing one's employment—or one's life. "Tripled," he said.

"Tripled," Wendell agreed, looking half amused and half irritated. "But if you persist in wasting my time while my realm comes apart, you shall receive not one seed between now and the day you die, which may arrive much sooner than you were imagining."

The hairdresser frowned at this, some of his confidence ebbing. It was clear that he was considered a lord in his particular domain, and unaccustomed to mundane worries about his physical safety. However, he also seemed pleased with the outcome of his haggling, though in a self-righteous sort of way, as if he had only been given his due. I found his triumph annoying, given how frequently he jabbed me with pins or yanked my hair so hard he pulled out strands. But then I am not the easiest of clients to make over into a queen.

The faerie bowed low. "Your Highness, I know not where the old queen has gone. However, I can tell you there was one problem with which we struggled, the two of us, which remains a mystery to myself. You see, the old queen's hair was sometimes tangled with thorns."

Wendell's eyes narrowed, and I felt that ghost-chill down my back again. "Thorns," he repeated.

"Yes. It did not happen often, but I remember each occasion well, for the thorns were devilishly tricky to remove—one less skillful than myself would have had to cut them out, I'm certain." He paused, as if to give us adequate time to process this triumph. "The queen would sometimes spend a day or two away from court, taking with her no servants, and none knew whither she went. But always upon her return, she would summon me, and I would spend an hour or more picking thorns from her hair. They were curious little things. Double-barbed, like horns."

"Nothing sinister in that at all," Niamh muttered from the table beside us, where she was taking notes. Wendell dismissed the creature, and we gazed at each other.

"That makes two," he said, and I nodded. Orga, perched on the table in her tucked-away posture, paws hidden beneath her umbral frame, gave me a look that seemed to have more disapproval in it than is customary with cats. I affected not to notice.

18th January

After having located our first two clues so quickly, I was certain we would soon find the third. But this has not been the case; though we have interviewed dozens of servants, none have had any information to offer. All served the old queen at one point or another, but none were her particular favourites.

"That is the problem," I told Niamh this morning. We were seated in the banquet hall, Wendell pacing once again by the windows. "In the Macan story, it is his personal attendants who are key to unravelling the mystery of his hiding place. But so few of Queen Arna's personal attendants are left. And the gardeners know nothing."

"This is why we should consider the soldiers," Niamh said. It was an argument we had been having for days. Niamh thought the scope of our search unnecessarily narrow, and that others in the queen's employ—soldiers included—should be questioned.

Wendell finally stopped pacing to gaze out the window. His hand was bandaged again, his face pale, for he has used his blood to hold back the tide of the queen's curse. He has not been sleeping enough, either, to make up for it, but insists upon prowling the edges of the curse until the small hours of the morning, hurling enchantments at it. All of which have proven useless.

"Read us the story again, Em," he said tiredly. Orga tapped his leg with her paw, and he knelt to scoop her into his arms.

I saw little point in it, but I did not argue, merely opened my notebook to the page where I'd recorded the cobbled-together tale. I confess I am growing thoroughly sick of "King Macan's Bees." As an artefact of dryadology, it has its merits, but I keep encountering new, sinister bits of subtext. Macan the Second's betrayal of the First's hospitality, for instance—respect for hospitality is important to the Folk, to the extent that violations are seen as monstrous; no doubt this was meant to be interpreted as a reason for the second Macan's downfall. Just deserts, in other words. I cannot help remembering how I poisoned Queen Arna at her table.

Wendell gazed into the forest, stroking Orga absently. "What about the boggart?"

"What about him?" I said.

"Well, why not ask if he knows anything?"

"Ask—a character in a story," I said slowly, wondering if the effects of little sleep had done him more harm than I had thought.

"*Our* boggart," Wendell said. "We have one in my realm. He dwells—"

"In the Gap of Wick," I murmured. I had known that—Snowbell had mentioned it once, the first time I visited the Silva Lupi.

"Good Lord," Niamh said. She had been flicking through the book before her, and now she slammed it shut with a laugh. "How did I not think of that? But he was your father's servant, was he not?"

Wendell shrugged. "Why not turn over every stone? He continued to serve my father—if one can call a boggart's allegiance *service*—after he married my stepmother, so he was hers too, for a time. At least until she had my father murdered. I assume that put him off her, though I know little about the creature—he was asleep for much of my childhood. I have no idea if he can help us; perhaps it was after he left that my stepmother began constructing this hideaway of hers. Likely we would be wasting our time in seeking him out."

Niamh rubbed her hands over her face, still chuckling to herself. "No, Liath, I think you may have solved it. For it is just like the story, is it not? The third clue does not actually come from the gardener; he points the way to the boggart, who shows them the bridge. The third clue."

My thoughts mirrored Niamh's, but what I felt was not entirely relief. "It is—very like the story," I agreed.

"Then let us depart immediately," Wendell said. He lifted Orga to his shoulder and motioned to one of the servants. "Ready our mounts."

18th January–late

Night has fallen, bringing with it a gentle scatter of rain. I do not mind the rain here, at least not anymore, for Wendell has woven some new enchantment into my poor old cloak that renders it impervious not only to rain but to damp, so that I am untroubled by either sweat or condensation. I sometimes picture the garment as an overstuffed couch, liable to burst at the seams if yet another enchantment is crammed into it.

The Gap of Wick lies in the hinterlands of Wendell's realm, rather like the nexus used by the fauns, but farther to the north, where the Blue Hook mountains cluster together in a confusing topography of peaks and escarpments. No barrows lead there, but Orga found us several shortcuts—I believe she knows Wendell's realm better than anyone, including its king—doors *within* Faerie through various groves and standing stones, which cut the distance in half. Thus we will only need to spend tonight out-of-doors; tomorrow we will make haste for the queen's hideout, and put an end to her.

If the creature did not deceive us. If the other clues we have gathered prove true.

If I am not leading Wendell to his doom.

I brought my grandfather's journal with me on our journey—

I am not certain why. I feel uneasy whenever I open the thing, and it is not as if I do not already have enough to be uneasy about.

As I have been unable to ignore the parallels between my grandfather and me, so too do I find myself seeing echoes of Wendell in my grandfather's mysterious "she." Like Wendell, "she" is golden-haired, her tresses impossibly soft, more like the fur of some delicate animal. She is vengeful in a way that puts me in mind of the Macan story; any and all who offend her are slain. When angered, she becomes a "storm of wrath" and cannot be reasoned with.

My skin prickles when I come to this part.

So many have died by her hand that she is haunted by avenging ghosts wherever she goes, my grandfather writes, quite conversationally. *So familiar is she with Death that she has seen its door, felt its wintry chill. She can kill so swiftly that her enemy has no knowledge of what has befallen them, or so slowly they feel as if they have died a dozen times before the end comes.*

He carries on in this disturbingly poetical vein for several paragraphs, complimenting his dearest's murderous temper with the same warmth as his praise for her golden tresses. This "she" is violent; unfathomable; capricious.

No, she is not like Wendell. But are they entirely unalike?

The Gap of Wick

 is a pass between two mountains, jagged and green with patches of bare sandstone, their peaks shrouded in cloud. The surrounding countryside is open, with only a few groves of yew scattered here and there, and most of these contain several attentive oaks, as if the ghastly things also enjoy the isolation. It is a desolate place that feels less empty than *forgotten*. A great many standing stones dot the landscape, some singular, others running in parallel lines. It is unusual for a boggart to choose such a place to settle; most of their ilk crave companionship.

The clouds parted ahead, revealing a stone tower atop the nearest foothill. It was tall with a tessellated roof and an odd miscellany of windows, and the lowest floor was an open courtyard with immense arches of no architectural period I could recognize. If I gazed at it long enough, the structure seemed to shift slightly.

"We'll need to walk from here," Wendell said, swinging down from his enormous horse. With us we had brought only Lord Taran and two guards, and they followed his lead, leaving their mounts to browse the heather. I reluctantly dismounted Red Wind—while I am still half in terror of the creature, I have grown to appreciate her smooth pace over the course of our journey. I patted her nose and she rewarded me with a tremendous snort; my hand came away wet.

The ground was pockmarked with oddly-shaped holes. They were cut vertically into the lumpy ground, and sloped down into blackness. More worryingly, the turf was scattered with bones—animal, I hoped. I could make out a number of whitish lumps in the distance that I took for sheep, though there were no farmsteads in the vicinity.

"Bogles," Wendell explained. "They've made tunnels beneath the heather. Bloody pests! And look, there is a door to the mortal realm over there." He pointed to a tall standing stone like a jagged fang, which was bent at a strange angle.

"Their visit to Faerie was of short duration," Lord Taran said, eyeing the bones.

I was aghast. "These are all human remains?"

"So it appears," Lord Taran said. To my surprise, he looked irritated by the sight—hardly the appropriate response to murder, but incongruous with my perception of him.

"The bogles will not trouble us," Wendell said. With that, he unsheathed his sword and stomped up the hill. I half expected him to start slashing at bogles left and right, but instead he simply tapped on the ground with the tip as he went, like someone politely knocking at a door. This had the opposite effect of knocking, however; not one bogle emerged. Indeed, as I followed him up the hill, I heard several soft clicks and creaks, as of small doors closing, and caught the occasional glimpse of a little hunching figure with long, grabby arms disappearing into the landscape like some form of scuttling insect. There was something uncanny about the creatures that put me in mind of the tree fauns, or the sheerie Wendell and I fought last year, and I was happy not to get a good look at them, though less than pleased to be tramping about inches from those grasping limbs.

"Bloody mountains!" Wendell exclaimed after we had been hiking uphill for perhaps forty-five seconds. "I had my fill of them in the Alps. Well, we are in my realm, so I may do as I like with the tedious things."

Before I could ask what this meant, Wendell made a gesture that was like patting an invisible dog. I felt absolutely nothing, but the wind lessened. I thought this was all he had done, until I looked up and found the tower immediately before us. The foothill we had been ascending now barely deserved the name, and was little more than a rise in the landscape.

"The boggart may not thank you for that," I said, in my usual attempt at nonchalance in the face of his impossible power.

Wendell made a face. "I would not thank him for my sore ankles. If he likes mountains so much, he can relocate to some godforsaken, glacier-infested height. Wait out here," he added to the guards, then he wandered through one of the arches, gazing about himself like a tourist. Even after what I had just seen, I had to tamp down an urge to caution him, for this was a boggart we were about to confront, not some household brownie.* Lord Taran grimaced and followed more slowly, his sword drawn at his side, so at least one of them had some sense.

The courtyard was empty, just a lot of stones with moss and wildflowers growing between them, and a high ceiling where the wind groaned. I wondered if the upper stories of the tower were furnished, and then I thought, *And what sort of furnishings does a bodiless entity require? Baths and wardrobes?*

"Perhaps we should—knock?" I said dubiously.

"He knows we're here," Wendell said.

"He wants you to grovel, no doubt," Lord Taran said. "A boggart's arrogance knows no bounds; they fancy themselves above kings and queens."

---

* The scientific debate over the classification of boggarts has raged for decades. At present, the most widely accepted systems place them with the common fae, though many among the younger and more forward-thinking generation of dryadologists contest this, with Louis Meyers proposing an alternative system that classes both boggarts and Faeroese *hessefolk* with the courtly fae. Consider that the primary distinction between courtly and common is one of appearance: courtly fae can pass for mortals, while brownies and trooping faeries cannot. Yet most dryadologists also accept that the courtly fae possess magics the small Folk lack, and here we arrive at the crux of the debate, for boggarts are immensely powerful. Though the true limits of their magics are unknown, the Balfour boggart once relocated an entire village, while the rival boggarts in the medieval Falkirk tale "The Blind Hens" performed various escalating feats, including making a forest burst into song, the sound of which could be heard all the way to Glasgow. I know of not one bogle or brownie who has ever cast an enchantment of a similar scale. Indeed, Meyers argues that a boggart's powers may equal those of some faerie kings and queens, and that they should be considered "free-ranging monarchs." Given this, and the fact that boggarts may assume mortal guises when they choose, and often do, it seems self-evident to place them among the courtly fae. And yet! They are in nature very close to household brownies, given their attachment to mortal (or, in some cases, faerie) families, which they hold very dear and will protect with their lives. In this I am reminded of Poe and the Ljosland brownie concept of *fjolskylda*.

Amidst these complexities, our classification systems begin to feel outdated and parochial. Thus boggarts are another example of the blurred boundaries that exist between the Folk, much as we scholars try to herd them into tidy categories.

This was so rich that I actually snorted. Lord Taran gave me a narrow-eyed look.

"Grovel, hm?" Wendell said. "Well, it's all one to me. But what manner of grovelling would such a creature prefer? I know."

He lifted a hand, and the space was abruptly filled with silver mirrors, flashing from every wall, with some even set into the floor like tile.

"It's just a glamour," he said. "Pretty, though, isn't it? What do you think? Too much?"

"A bit," I said, eyeing my hundreds of reflections.

"Oh, I don't think so," Lord Taran said, with a smirk in my direction. "You know, Your Highness, Callum and I had a great many mirrors at our reception—they are lovely as wedding décor."

"Really?" Wendell said thoughtfully, and Taran went on to describe their placement and framing at length. I gritted my teeth and pointedly ignored him.

"*Stop* that," said the boggart. Because, abruptly, there was a boggart standing before us.

At least, I assumed he was a boggart. A boggart's guises are so convincing that there is little to distinguish them from whatever creature they have counterfeited, apart from one thing: like my Shadow, they leave no footprints. The person before us appeared to belong to the courtly fae, but the longer I gazed at him, the more disturbed I grew. For he was not his own person, but an assemblage of Wendell's and Lord Taran's features—the one's golden hair, the other's sharp cheekbones—as well as some I eventually recognized in the faces of the guards standing outside. It was as if the boggart had been formless for so long he had forgotten the shapes he had once worn, and so, in a pinch, had borrowed from the faces he saw before him. Or perhaps that had always been his habit. I noticed he had not deigned to sample my features, surprising me not at all.

Wendell, either not noticing or not caring about this deeply unsettling form of appropriation, swept his cloak to one side in his usual dramatic fashion and bowed to the boggart. "Forgive me," he said. "Only I thought you would appreciate a little adornment for your tower."

"It's a ruin," the boggart said in a peevish voice that had a great deal of Lord Taran's aristocratic tenor in it. "I like it that way. And I could not care less about silver—I am not of your realm."

"As you wish," Wendell said, and the mirrors vanished.

"As you say, you are not of my realm," he went on. "So I cannot command you. But you have served my family for generations, as I understand it. And so I have come to beg a favour, placing my hopes in old loyalties."

"Yes, yes," the boggart said. "Let's have a look at you, shall we?"

He folded his arms and paced around Wendell, examining him from every angle with a frown, even bending to examine his knees from the back. At one point, the boggart brushed his golden hair from his eyes in a gesture that was so like Wendell's that I felt briefly queasy.

"You have only grown more like your mother," the boggart said at last, looking disappointed. "The first one. I did not care for either of your mothers. The first was a dull little thing, the second a clumsy half mortal. *This* queen seems no better." He came closer to me, looking me up and down as a glint of mischief came into his eyes. "But mortals can be entertaining. And they do not break as easily as some think."

Wendell's expression went from one of bemusement to towering fury with such abruptness that both Taran and I fell back a step; Taran afterwards looked as annoyed as a cat following a moment of gracelessness. There came a terrible rumbling sound, coupled with that same wet rustling with which I am all too familiar, as if the attentive oaks were uprooting themselves en masse and lumbering in our direction.

"You are speaking to a queen of Faerie," Wendell said, and it seemed as if the rustling leaves were in his voice. I suppressed the urge to take another step away from him.

I don't know what would have happened next if the boggart had not backed down, but back down he did. He held up his hands and laughed.

"I see it now!" he cried. "Yes, yes, you are your great-grandmother all over again. I was terribly fond of her. In fact, she has always been my favourite. A pity her eldest son slew her when he grew tired of waiting for the throne. Ah, but I came to love him too."

The bloody rumbling noise had stopped, but given Wendell's expression, I still felt it prudent to interpose myself between him and the boggart. I tried to organize my scattered thoughts—I am well-read on the subject of boggarts, and have encountered them on two occasions myself, and thus I was not overly nervous to take the initiative in the conversation.

"You are indeed correct," I said. "The king is like his great-grandmother in many ways."

"Really?" The boggart looked even more delighted. "Does he have a fondness for iced pears? We would eat iced pears together on many an evening, the queen and I."

I pretended to be astonished. "But there is nothing he likes better than iced pears! Unless it is music."

Now, this was not exactly a stab in the dark, but I was betting on my understanding of boggarts, and their bone-deep yearning for kinship, to see me through.

"Music!" The boggart clapped his hands together, positively beaming. "Yes, yes! She delighted in her harpists in particular—she would often steal gifted mortals and keep them even after she tired of their songs, for she would have them killed and stuffed, then put on display with their instruments in their hands. She had quite the collection by the time she was overthrown."

In retrospect, I am pleased with how quickly I recovered from this. "How—alike indeed," I said.

The boggart continued to look Wendell up and down. I was relieved, though not overly surprised, to see that his murderous rage had vanished as abruptly as it had appeared, and he was now watching me with amusement.

"Iced pears," he murmured.

"Yes," I said, giving him a pointed look. "Were you not rhapsodizing about them at tea the other day?"

He smiled. "I was, wasn't I?"

"Very well," the boggart said. "I shall help you on two conditions. The first: that I shall be allowed to return to the castle and live among you."

I did not like this condition at all, but Wendell replied before I had the chance to. "Of course you shall," he said. "You were always welcome. I understood you left of your own accord when my father was slain and his bloodline overthrown."

I could see this was exactly the response the boggart had desired. "Well, one prefers to be invited," he said primly.

Wendell inclined his head. The boggart was so pleased he dematerialized for a moment, and when he reappeared he looked more like Wendell—he was even wearing his clothes.

"The second," the boggart said, "is that you hold a great banquet to mark my return. This banquet must have at least two dozen harpists, as well as cannons you will fire when I enter the castle. At midnight, there should be a procession of the court's finest drayfoxes, all adorned in silver and jewels."

"Good grief, but that's a lot to remember," Wendell said.

"Very well, you will have your banquet. Once my stepmother is dead and the realm is healed. To do that—"

"Yes, I know," the boggart said. Now that he had what he wanted, he seemed to have lost interest in the conversation. "You wish to know where she is. I can help you with one detail only: her hideaway is an island."

"But we knew that already," I interjected. "Because of the snails." This wasn't how the story went—the boggart was supposed to give us a *different* clue, not one we already had.

Wendell's brow was furrowed. "How do you know this?"

The boggart burst out laughing, as if he'd been suppressing it before. "Your face!" he crowed as I glowered at him.

He disappeared for a moment, flitting through some crevice in the ceiling to the upper levels of the tower, and when he reappeared, he had a piece of fabric in his hand.

"The queen told the king that she liked to wander the realm," he explained. "But she always came back smelling of the same thing: sedges and mossy stones. I knew she was sneaking away to some secret fortress. One day, she returned with a bloody knee—the queen was clumsy, as all mortals are. She bandaged it with this."

"Sailcloth," Wendell murmured. He showed it to Lord Taran, whose eyebrows shot up.

"Sailcloth?" I repeated, nearly beside myself with impatience.

Wendell turned towards me, but he seemed lost for words. Finally, he said, "This is from—one of the boats. Our boats. Uncle?"

"Yes," Lord Taran said, handing the cloth to me. "Many of the nobility take to the lake on warm summer days." He saw my blank stare and clarified, "Silverlily."

"*What?*" I snatched at the cloth—it was of purest white, with tiny silver stitchery. "How is that possible?"

The boggart began to laugh again. "Under your nose!" he crowed. "All this time, right under your nose. Oh, I begin to like your mother a little better."

"But—the first clue. The snails. Silverlily has no islands," I protested, angry and indignant. It could not be. Surely I would have worked it out by now, if Queen Arna was hiding on the bloody *lake*. The lake I had been gazing out at each day, furrowing my brow, expending all of my mental energies searching for hidden clues to her whereabouts.

"True," Lord Taran said. "And yet, the creature must be correct—that is where we shall find her."

Wendell, characteristically untroubled by paradoxes, clenched the sailcloth in his fist and bowed to the boggart again. "Many thanks, old one," he said. It was difficult to read his reaction: anticipation, certainly, and something else I couldn't name, but that was very near to the fury he had shown earlier, honed to a point sharp as a faun's horn.

"So long as I have my banquet," the boggart said, and then he was simply gone.

"Wendell," I said, because I still couldn't tell what he was feeling, and it made me nervous. He appeared lost in thought and didn't reply, simply put his arm around my waist, and we left the tower.

I had to suppress a scream when we stepped outside, for there was an oak not five feet from the door now, glaring at me, and three more beyond it in the garden. Oh, how I had hoped I had mistaken that rumbling noise.

Lord Taran, behind me, was muttering curses under his breath. He drew his hood over his hair and gave the oak a black look. "Hurry up," he muttered at me, and together we made haste to pass beneath the overhanging branches and regain the sunlight.

19th January

I must write it down. For it is in writing that I will discover a way out. A door within the story. There is one. It cannot end here.

Yet some stories do.

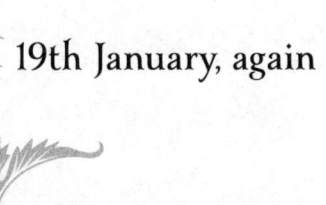

19th January, again

Enough of this. I will force my hand to move, and my mind to think.

We awoke early this morning in our makeshift campsite a few miles from the boggart's lair, whereupon Wendell wasted no time in tracing a path back to the castle grounds. I suspect he reshaped geography itself, as he reshaped the boggart's hill, for we reached the castle in less time than it had taken us to travel to the boggart's tower even with Orga's shortcuts. When we stood upon the lakeshore only a few hours later, Wendell was pale and trembling lightly, as if he had run a great distance on little sustenance.

"What now?" Lord Taran said.

"Take a boat out and look around, I suppose," I said, still dubious about the whole thing. I did not believe we would find Queen Arna on the lake, though a part of me also *hoped* we would not, and I could not be certain where the first began and the other ended. At some point, it felt as if the story had galloped away from me, or perhaps it had galloped away *with* me, and I was barely holding on. Wendell had led us on a path that ended at the eastern edge of the lake, where a dock lined with glass lanterns—extinguished now, in the afternoon light—stretched out into the water. Alongside it were ten little boats large enough for four passengers each, perhaps, with wooden frames over which had been stretched the skins of animals I didn't recognize—something with short black fur. Each had two sails, stowed now.

No islands had materialized in the time we had been away. The weather was out of humour, the sky a miscellany of patchy white and hulking grey clouds, all hurrying along as if late for an appointment, and the skin of the lake was wrinkled with tiny waves, which plashed against the shore and set the boats rocking.

"We will go alone," Wendell said.

"Naturally you will," Lord Taran said, exasperated. "I do not like this. I do not think it will end well."

"It will end," Wendell said, "one way or another."

"No," I said, shaking my head. "No, I will not have any of that portentous faerie nonsense. We are not going."

He stared at me. "Emily! It was you who found me a path to my stepmother. Now, perhaps the boggart has led us astray and perhaps he has not; either way, we must search the lake."

"I do not want—" I stopped, not knowing what I was saying. I did not want to follow the Macan story anymore, that was certain. It was proving *too* helpful, and now I did not trust it— as Niamh had pointed out, the end was not a happy one. But what could I say? That Wendell should allow his realm to be consumed by his stepmother's curse? Yet I found myself framing the idea into an argument—we could return to Cambridge, look for another way to rid the realm of his stepmother. The memory of the soft light and leather-and-parchment smell of the dryadology library filled me like hunger. And truly, what on earth was I doing here in these ridiculous clothes, acting the part of a faerie queen in one of their stories?

"I must go," he said softly, and it took a moment for the meaning to sink in.

"Damn you," I breathed. "You would leave me behind?"

"Not by choice," he said, taking my hand. "Never. Em—"

I yanked my hand back, too angry to allow him the satisfaction of an apology. Letting him face his stepmother alone was insupportable. Grimly, I forced my mind back to "King Macan's Bees." Had I not thought my way out of such impossible problems before? Had I not faced Queen Arna once already? Why could I not do so again? This was an academic riddle, and who was more skilled at untangling those than I?

Something burbled out on the lake, and a dizzying terror nearly swept me off my feet.

Wendell murmured a few words of goodbye to Orga, whom he held in his arms, instructing her not to follow us. She gave him a sleepy-eyed stare and allowed him to hand her over to Lord Taran, who looked astonished.

"Have we made peace, fell warrior?" he said. I too was surprised that Orga would allow Wendell to leave her behind so easily. The cat gave no sign she was aware of either of us, only watched Wendell inscrutably.

We said no more to Lord Taran, and clambered into the nearest boat. Well, *I* clambered, nearly overturning the thing; Wendell moved as gracefully as always, and easily righted us. He loosed the sails and we were off, the prow parting the silvery waters and their blurry tree shapes.

There came a yell from the dock, and I turned to see Taran staggering back, clutching his face. Blood spilled through his fingers from a row of deep gashes. And then there was a dark shape sailing over the water towards us in an impossible, gliding leap.

Orga grunted as she landed in the bow, and then she turned

to lick her back, cool as anything, as if to imply that gouging Lord Taran had been merely one item on an extensive agenda.

After a startled pause, Wendell began to laugh. The sound was welcome, lightening the dread that clung to me like cold damp.

19th January, *again*

    I'm unsure how much time has elapsed. I came back to myself just now, the pen still in my hand—I had descended into a blank haze, during which I simply stared out the window. Someone is knocking softly on my door—Callum, most likely, or Niamh. Why don't they leave me be? I don't wish to see anyone.

Why have no ideas come to me? I refuse to believe that all my studies, my vast knowledge of folklore, could fail me at this moment.

But I must pick up where I left off.

Wendell allowed the wind to carry us across the lake, and then he tacked south, taking us down an arm of Silverlily, which blocked the castle from view. Tree-shadow fell over us and I breathed in the smell of sedge, and then we sailed out into the open again. Dragonflies darted past and crickets murmured from sunny patches of grass, for the shadows were lengthening as the world moved towards evening. Something gurgled intermittently below the water, releasing clouds of bubbles, and occasionally it seemed that a dark shape, too large to be a fish, darted beneath the boat. Apparently the nobility were not the only ones who sailed upon Silverlily; to our left was a tiny canoe being rowed at a furious pace by a brownie in a grey cloak, and here and there along the bank I saw other miniature watercraft pulled up onshore or moored to overhanging tree limbs.

"Why have you not taken me boating before?" I said, only half in jest. The sun had come out, and with it my mood grew more optimistic. The view of the tree-lined banks was lovely, the forest darker and even more full of mysteries from this distance, and the wind was pleasantly cool against my skin. I felt as if I had come to the centre of something.

Wendell smiled. "I understood you'd taken a dislike to lakes after that field study in Sweden a few years ago."

"That was more a dislike of water elves, as well as unscrupulous fishermen, such as those who rented me that leaky rowboat," I said, scanning the water. "Where shall we look first? I have one or two theories."

He gave me an anxious look. "You are not still angry with me?"

"Naturally I am," I said, glaring. "But it is an illogical anger, for you are only trying to save your realm, and anyway I was the one who found you that bloody Macan story, thus I have as much cause to be angry at myself for thrusting you into this danger. So I have chosen to focus on the challenge at hand rather than indulge such a counterproductive sentiment."

Wendell began to laugh. He leaned on one hand, his shoulders shaking, as the boat rocked slightly from side to side.

"Anyway," I said, trying and failing to avoid blushing. Such a look he was giving me! "Perhaps we could start at the tip of that little peninsula and work our way out—"

"Emily," Wendell said, perching on the seat across from me and taking my hand, "we have other business to attend to first. More important than finding my stepmother."

I could only blink at him. "What on earth is more important than that?"

He took my hand. His eyes were greener in the dappled sunlight and emerald murk of the lake. "Will you marry me?"

I can't think of a time when I have been more confused. I believe I stared at him for a full minute, waiting for him to explain himself. "That question has already been answered," I said at last.

Then I realized what he meant and my pulse spiked with another surge of terror.

"Oh God," I said. "Now? *Here?* With—" I waved at nothing in particular. "All *this*?"

"It is far from ideal," Wendell said with a sigh. "I had been hoping for something lavish. I have always thought that if I was to marry, it would be in the castle gardens, or perhaps upon the shores of the Hanging Pools. But I have found myself wondering: is that what you would prefer? You are not much for public displays, unless they involve notes and lecture halls."

I drew a deep breath, trying to calm my racing heart, but it would not be calmed. "I do not like your timing. You are thinking of the story. Of Macan the Second's end."

"Yes," Wendell said, gazing at me steadily. "I must think of such things for your sake, for you are first in my thoughts. I have no intention of dying today—please understand that. But if things go awry—as you must allow they may—I will not leave you defenceless. My people recognize you as a queen of Faerie because I have told them that is what you are, but the realm does not recognize it. Not yet."

"Old-fashioned, is it?" I was trying to joke, but it only came out sounding strangled. And yet, against all odds, I felt my pulse slowing. Perhaps it was due to the lulling environment of the lake, or Wendell's obvious nervousness, something I have observed in him only rarely, but that makes him seem very nearly human.

Wendell answered me seriously. "I suppose so. But then, Faerie does not really recognize *marriage*. That translation from the Faie is only a clumsy approximation." He seemed to think. "Mortals, I've observed, sometimes marry for very silly reasons. The Folk do not, because one cannot marry someone who does not match them. The word has a connotation of accepting one's fate."

"You are trying to calm me with a linguistics lesson," I said.

He smiled. "Is it working?"

I let out a breath of laughter. "Then—you propose we marry by the old traditions? A simple declaration?"

"Why not?" he said.

It was a strange thing. I had been viewing the marriage question with such trepidation—the ceremony, the spectacle, all that came after it, in the form of this strange and beautiful kingdom that would thence be half mine. And yet, as I sat there upon the lake amidst the tree-shadow and reflected light and the dragonflies tussling with the wind, I no longer knew why I had been so afraid. Likely it was also the threat of Queen Arna hanging over us like a guillotine—well, the prospect of imminent death tends to put things into perspective. It was not that my worries *vanished*—no magic could manage that. I only realized how much smaller they were than the world that lay before me. A world that I wanted, even after all I had seen, and amidst such a thicket of danger. I wanted it very much. And I especially wanted to share it with Wendell.

"All right," I said. "How does this work? Must I stand? I warn you, my balance is unsteady in all forms of watercraft."

Wendell blinked for a moment. And then his expression flooded with such delight and relief that I was taken aback.

"You thought I would say no!" I exclaimed, batting away his hand in indignation. "Good grief. And you are always boasting about how well you know me."

He laughed again, a sound that echoed across the lake, and it seemed the trees were stirred by it, raining their leaves down upon the lakeshore. He rubbed a hand over his face. "I didn't think that," he said. "I didn't know *what* you would say. It appears you still have the ability to surprise me, Em."

I rolled my eyes. There was an echo of nervousness in his gaze, and I decided I'd had enough of that. Additionally, he was looking very handsome just then, with the sunlight picking out at least a dozen shades of gold in his hair, so I took hold of his cloak, thumb looping through one of the buttonholes, and drew him towards me.

"Well, come on, what must we do?" I said when at last we broke apart, breathless. I hoped this tradition would not involve lengthy speeches. I have not improved much when it comes to putting feelings into words.

"Nothing," he said. "It's done. Look."

I followed his gaze to the lakeshore. A hundred tiny lights dotted the forest—more than a hundred. A thousand? They kept appearing among the shadows, different in size and luminance depending on the lantern. I hadn't realized the forest was so full of Folk. And among the trees, the silver faerie stones began to glow.

"All this for a mortal queen?" I muttered, flushed and overwhelmed.

"Too much?" Wendell made a gesture, and the faerie stones dimmed, retaining only a faint luminescence. "That's as much as I can do. The small Folk will keep to their traditions—they would be greatly offended if I ask them to put their lights out before morning."

"Very well," I said. It was easier to bear without the faerie stones, which I've always found eerie, the way they hang untethered among the treetops like a strangely shaped mist. I know the curator of Cambridge's Museum of Dryadology and Ethnofolklore would give her eye teeth for just one of the things—none have ever been smuggled into the mortal world, and their form and size makes them unique among faerie stones. We drifted for a time, watching more lights flicker to life.

"What is that?" I said.

We had floated towards the southern bank of the lake. Now we were not far from where Ariadne and I had sighted the castle for the first time, mirrored in the glasslike water. The lake was shallower here; I could see the algal hue of the rocks at the bottom. And something else.

I reached into the water and seized the edge of the weed. It was long and ropelike, with clusters of leaves branching off the main stem that looked like curls of red-brown hair. I gave it a tug, expecting it to come loose, but it was firmly rooted to the lake bottom. Pain spiked through my hand. I examined my palm—it was coated in tiny grains of green pollen, and two black thorns were embedded in the skin.

I showed Wendell, and he removed his sword and sliced off a chunk of the weed. He swore as he, too, cut his hand on the thorns.

"Two barbs," I said.

"Yes." He dropped the weed back into the lake. "They could easily tangle in one's hair, if one went for a swim."

My heart thudded in my ears. "We're not far from shore. You could swim the distance easily. You might not take a boat if you didn't want anyone to know you were out here."

We shared a look. Then Wendell adjusted the sail, and we drifted towards the darkest patch of weeds. I saw nothing unusual in the immediate vicinity. Some of the faeries visible on the shore had settled down on the bank—to see what we were up to, I suppose.

Wendell allowed us to drift for a moment through the wide

patch of lakeweed, then sent us along the perimeter before plowing into the wet leaves again at a different angle. The weeds made a *shhh, shhh* sound against the hull, along with the faintest scratching. I began to worry that the thorns would tear a hole in the skin.

Then the boat came to a stop with a gentle *thunk*.

"I would ask if that was a rock," I said. My heart was thundering so excitedly now that I felt breathless. "But something tells me I don't need to."

Wendell scanned the water, but there was nothing to see—only weeds and darkness. He grimaced. "I don't much fancy a swim in this muck, but I must risk it, I suppose. What do you think?"

This last was directed to Orga. She gave an unimpressed grunt and hopped up onto his shoulder.

Then he stepped off the prow of the boat.

There was no splash, for he did not fall. He merely vanished, in a similar manner to how he is always vanishing in and out of trees. Quite horribly, in other words.

He reappeared a second later, landing in the boat with a thump that made it rock a little from side to side, evidently having taken a leap out of the nothingness he had vanished into. Having not yet gotten over the first shock, I gave a heartfelt "Goddamn it, Wendell!"

"I'm sorry," he said, looking a little stunned himself. He grabbed my arm and pulled me to my feet. "Em, you must see this. I was expecting—and still I cannot quite believe—"

And the bloody man yanked me over the side of the boat.

I stumbled onto solid ground, and Wendell caught me before I could fall. He was blathering on at me before I'd found my bearings.

"Queen Anne's Isle!" he kept saying. "This must be it—we tell stories of it, but I never thought—then there truly *is* a lost castle! And there are no Folk here, that I can see—how then am *I* here? How in God's name did she find it? But *look* at that oak!" This was followed by a series of colourful exclamations in Irish.

I gazed about. We indeed stood upon an island, very small indeed, something upon which, in the mortal realm, one might expect to find a lighthouse, or perhaps a single lonely dwelling. Only instead there was a stretch of shore and a small, roofless castle that looked more like a Norman keep than anything else, which is not the same as saying that it looked like a Norman keep. It had large windows and tall stone walls that had been mostly overtaken by ivy. Within the castle grew a grove of trees, including at least one attentive oak, which towered above the rest.

I looked back at Wendell, who was still exclaiming over the story. I felt a glimmer of amusement, to see a faerie so delighted by a tale come to life, but it passed quickly, and fear descended again.

"All right," I said. "What is this about Queen Anne's Isle?"

He gave me an apologetic look. His hair was in great disarray from how he had been rubbing at it in his excitement. "Queen Anne's Isle is said to have been created by the realm itself to protect a runaway mortal queen—the only other fully mortal ruler before you, Em, that this land has known—from her wicked husband, who wished to slay her so that he could marry another. It is said she lived out her days here in peace—not that many were left to her, for she was elderly when she fled. They say Folk cannot find it. I suppose my stepmother found a loophole, as a halfblood."

"And you only found it because I was with you," I said, feeling a sense of satisfaction amidst the terror; I will never stop enjoying the solving of some faerie mystery. I wondered briefly how I might compose a paper on the subject—disappearing islands are a motif in the folklore of many countries. It was a comforting line of thought.

"Well, it's good to know I shall have a bolt-hole when you eventually tire of me," I said. "And the teacups I leave scattered about. Weren't you complaining of that the last time you were in my office?"

This was comforting, too. Perhaps if I kept making light of things, I could simply skip over the fact that we had come, at last, to Queen Arna's refuge. Was she watching us now from one of the windows? I carefully avoided looking.

Wendell did not reply, merely continued to stroke Orga, still draped about his shoulders and looking wary. With his other hand, he laced his fingers through mine and led me up the bank. Because the island was so small, it did not take long to realize that there was a problem.

"Hm!" Wendell said after several minutes had passed, during which time the castle grew no closer. I looked back, and there was the boat rocking gently against the shore only a yard or two away.

"Interesting," I murmured.

"The island dislikes my being here," he said, glaring at the castle. "I am like a splinter it wishes to expel from itself. What to do? I have a feeling that simply waving my hand and tearing the castle to pieces will not go over well."

"It is obvious what we must do," I said, already examining the ferns and grasses. "Think of the story."

"Which?"

"Macan, of course. Of our three clues, there is one we have not yet found a use for."

"Ah," he said, and we began to scour the greenery, pushing ivy aside and looking beneath ferns, as if we were foraging for mushrooms. The enchantment that prevented us from reaching the castle was an intriguing one: it seemed bound to the trees scattered a few yards above the waterline. They formed an uneven sort of perimeter we could not pass.

"There," Wendell said at last.

The snail was half hidden by a fallen branch and glowed lightly in the shadows descending over the isle. At the sight of us, it seemed to start, and withdrew into its shell, then poked its head back out cautiously.

"Now what?" I said. "Might the shell possess some magic, that we might break this enchantment and find our way to the castle?"

"Perhaps," Wendell said musingly. He reached into his pocket and withdrew the shell the butter faerie had given us, one of those snails the old queen had cooked for her supper. He knelt beside the snail, which may or may not have been watching us—I am no expert in snail anatomy, but its antennae had swivelled in our direction.

"I suspect you have little affection for the one who shelters in the castle," Wendell said. "Many of your brethren have vanished into her pockets, haven't they? And thence to her supper plate. Show me the way, for I am her enemy, and I shall deliver to her the fate she deserves."

The snail's antennae began to twitch. It glided off, and Wendell and I—well, I would say we fell into step behind it, but as you might imagine, it was a moment or two before we were even certain the creature was moving towards the castle.

More snails glided out of the shadows to join the first. And more. And more. Until there were hundreds surrounding us on all sides. Together we left the shoreline and passed under the boughs of the first trees, moving steadily over the castle lawn, which was overgrown with ferns and ivy.

"They are making a path for us," I murmured. "That must

be it. *They* can pass through the enchantment, and as long as we are within their company, it cannot hinder us. And yet how did they organize themselves so quickly?"

"Oh, I imagine they have been waiting to betray my stepmother," Wendell said. "And long would they have waited, for they are patient creatures above all else. I would not be surprised if they have kept a watch on her since she came to this place, and upon the shore, hoping that her enemies might find a way here. That creature did not need much convincing, did it?"

I said nothing. I told myself it was ludicrous to be intimidated by snails, but I could not quite believe it. Yes, I could have outrun them if need be—outwalked them, really—or even crushed them beneath my boots, but there was something about the air of intractable menace that surrounded them, and the sense that should one or more fall, others would only rise from hidden folds in the lawn to take their place, which left me frightened of each step I took, lest I tread upon a single antenna.

It took us perhaps half an hour to reach the castle, moving in a series of slow half steps that at first felt ridiculous, then irksome, then sinister, surrounded by our tiny, faintly luminescent bodyguards. During that time, Wendell was uncharacteristically quiet, only murmuring occasional reassurances to Orga, and I found myself catching his mood. I glanced about at the deepening darkness, the glittering lake beyond. We stood in the shadow of the castle, and the air was cold. The distant shore of the lake seemed to lie behind a thin mist. I could see the lanterns still, but there was something melancholy about them now, the promise of company one could never reach. I thought of an old woman living out her last days here, the memories of what had once been all around her.

"It's a lonely place," I said as I lifted a boot to take another slow step. "When was Anne's reign?"

"Long ago," Wendell replied. "Even before my father's line—one of his ancestors, an age or more ago, stole the throne from a cousin, who was descended from Anne's unworthy husband another age before. I expect her bones still lie here, somewhere. I hope there was someone to bury her."

We reached the castle and a pair of tall oak doors. Their hinges were ornate but rusty, and one of the doors had a sag. Yes, surely many generations had passed in the amaranthine eyes of the Folk if even the enchantments that had created this place were worn with age.

We took our leave of the snails then, bowing low to show our thanks. Wendell knelt to talk quietly to the one he had spoken to before—how he could tell the difference between them, I don't know. Afterwards he hesitated upon the threshold, one hand on the stone wall. Orga hopped to the ground and looked up at him.

"My stepmother has only a little magic," he said to me. "Her power has always lain in her ability to charm and deceive. I don't know if she may, somehow, have charmed the magics of this island into protecting her. Let me enter first, and then I will call you."

He seemed to think I would argue with him, but I had no interest in being blasted in the face by some foul enchantment. "You may enter first," I said, "but do not think you may enter *alone*. If you venture beyond my sight I will be very cross, and chase after you."

"A fire-breathing dragon at my back! No, I would prefer to avoid that. Don't worry, Em, I have as little desire as you to face this alone."

Satisfied, I went back to what I had just been doing—

scanning every inch of flora in the vicinity for bees. The insect life seemed to comprise mostly beetles and ants. Wendell pushed the doors open and stepped through.

He had been honest in one respect; he went only a half dozen paces before he halted. But he did not call me.

"Wendell?" It came out more annoyed than I truly felt, for I was trying to focus on anything but the fear roiling my stomach. I passed through the doors and stood beside him.

He did not move, and I thought he was merely overwhelmed by the tarnished grandeur around us. The castle was one open space, though divisions were implied by lines and clusters of trees here and there. It was roofless, like the banquet hall of our castle—or, more accurately I suppose, it was roofed in dense layers of leaf and branch and enchantment, which kept the elements away. It consisted of the great hall in which we stood and a wide staircase at the back, which led into the tower that backed onto the hall—I could just see the outline of it through the foliage. Was Queen Arna up there, I wondered?

At the centre of the hall was the largest attentive oak I had ever seen. Its trunk was too wide for ten men to link arms around, and its roots bullied their way up through the floor. Its upper canopy was obscured by the other trees, but several lower boughs were visible. Many of the eyes that stared at me with anger or fear, envy or disdain, were rheumy, with wrinkled lids, and I think some were nearsighted. They squinted and seemed to have trouble fixing upon us.

Wendell still had not moved. He was staring at something on the other side of the hall, but I could not work out what it was; there were too many trees in the way, offering only a partial picture. There was a splash of coppery red, an edge of something plaid—fabric? And, just visible past the trunk of a birch, a single pale foot.

I walked forward slowly. The sound of the wind moving through the trees faded, and all I heard was my thundering heart. Wendell followed, then took my hand and pulled me slightly behind him.

At the far end of the hall was an ornately carved four-poster piled high with blankets, including the plaid one I had glimpsed, which spilled onto the floor. Queen Arna lay upon the blankets, still clad in queenly finery, though it was now tattered and stained. She was dead.

There was no room for debate on this point. She had taken a dagger and stabbed herself through the chest. It had happened recently—within the last few seconds, I thought, for her body still twitched. She had heard our voices outside the door. Her eyes did not gaze in our direction, but stared sightlessly at the canopy.

"She knew I was come to kill her," Wendell said. His tone was oddly conversational, but his face was flushed, his eyes wet. "So this is what you've chosen. Vengeance is so important to you, that even in death—" He gave a soft laugh and rubbed his face.

I pressed his hand. I still remember the feeling of his cold fingers against mine. At the time I was thinking, surely he could not be *sad*. Not about her.

"I know," he said, giving me a rueful smile. "I had wanted to say goodbye."

I surveyed the room. It was a romantic place to die at least. I could summon no more compassion for the queen than that—well and good that she had died by her own hand, I thought; spare Wendell the grief of killing the woman who had raised him.

I touched the queen's arm, then drew back immediately, for it was still warm. My hand, where it had brushed the bed, came away bloody, and I hurriedly wiped it on my dress. Her blood dripped to the ground in a steady patter like little footsteps. Orga licked at the puddle, and I picked her up.

Something odd was happening to the queen's body. Her bare feet were darkening to the greyish-white of the birch trees and growing knots, while moss crept up the side of her neck. Something moved in her hair—a host of aphids and small white moths seemed to be making themselves at home. Was this how all monarchs died? I thought of taking my notebook out to make a sketch, but shuddered away from the prospect. Perhaps Danielle de Grey was correct—there are things in Faerie that are not meant to be known.

"Then the curse is lifted," I said. "Is it? What do you feel? Must we do anything else? We could collect the queen's blood, I suppose." I looked at her strange outline—it was not an appealing prospect. And was it still blood, or had it become sap?

Wendell was gazing at me. One of his faerie looks again, and yet, to my astonishment, he was not entirely opaque to me this time, and what I saw in his eyes made me still. What had he said? The queen had killed herself for *vengeance*?

The queen's body ceased twitching. And the world was suddenly changed, and a great many things happened within the space of a heartbeat. I will record each of my impressions now, hindsight allowing me to piece them out:

A swirling miasma of grey descended upon the castle, like a cloud slowly lowering itself out of the sky. A tendril touched my shoe tip, and I leapt backwards with a shout, for the sensation was like the brush of a hot brand.

Orga began to yowl in a voice I'd never heard from her before—it was closer to the cry of a mortal cat than I had thought her capable of.

Wendell lifted the steel dagger his stepmother had used and drove it through his chest in one swift, impossibly quiet movement, and the motion was familiar to me, somehow, the angle—it was how he had stabbed the woman with the raven-feather hair. There was only the faintest rustle as the fabric of his cloak parted, then he wrenched the dagger free in a shower of blood bright as rubies.

As the curse descended upon us, something wrapped round my stomach and flung me backwards—I caught a glimpse of glaring eyes, felt the brush of something soft and wet against my arm. I hit the trunk of the attentive oak, and the castle vanished.

19th January, still

What happened in the moments after is a complete jumble; providing a true account of my thoughts and perceptions would be impossible. I must straighten things out in order for these events to be legible.

It was, at least, easy enough to work out what had happened to me, for when I lifted my head, I found myself on the mainland, not far from the castle gardens. I glanced up and saw that I was resting against the bole of another attentive oak, smaller than the monster in the queen's castle. So: the tree had flung me through itself an instant before the curse would have destroyed me, and I had emerged here, some miles away. Apparently I now possessed the ability to use trees as doors, little as I had ever wanted to.

I lay there for some time, growing wetter and wetter, for it had begun to rain. I wished that Shadow were with me—it is strange, but I felt his absence more keenly, in that moment, than Wendell's. I wanted the dog's warmth, the softness of his fur, his cold nose against my hand. I am not certain I understood what had happened to Wendell at all; in place of grief was a kind of blank incomprehension.

As I gazed up at the canopy, I realized that the forest was

still alight with lanterns, the silver faerie stones still aglow, which I regarded with an absurd disdain. One of their monarchs had perished; why did these Folk not have the decency to turn their lights off? So a part of me was aware of what had happened, I suppose, but it was a distant, intellectual part, securely walled off from the rest of me.

Callum believes it was no more than ten minutes before he and Niamh found me, having been summoned from a meeting of the Council by one of the tree brownies, who had been understandably distressed by the sight of their queen sprawled on the forest floor in a motionless heap. According to Niamh, all I could do at first was complain about the faerie lights. She could get no sense out of me regarding what had happened, though they knew—they knew. For the corruption had vanished from the hill behind the castle, and now here I was, alone and with blood on my dress, babbling insensibly. Callum, however, said it was Orga who confirmed his fears. For I had been holding her tight to my chest the whole while, and she was not attempting escape, but had curled herself into a silent, motionless ball against me. She was less substantial than she had been, her golden eyes anchoring a form that was little more than a spectre.

Callum helped me back to the castle. It was only when I stepped out from under the boughs of the attentive oak that I realized the sky was clear. The tree was weeping.

I must find a way out. I am very tired.

What do I know? Wendell sacrificed himself to heal the kingdom; the kingdom is now healed. We know this, for Lord Taran's scouts have confirmed that the curse has been lifted from not only the hillside but several other nearby groves. He has sent more Folk to confirm it does not linger elsewhere. But of course it doesn't—Macan the Second healed his realm, and then he died. And now Wendell has done the same.

What else? That when Wendell's stepmother took her own life, she gave Wendell no other way out. As the source of the curse tearing the kingdom apart, her death should have lifted it, as in the Macan story. However, unlike Macan, Wendell's stepmother was a halfblood, and I should have foreseen that she would introduce complications, for halfbloods slip more easily out of the patterns of faerie stories. I should have foreseen it. For what healed the kingdom in the Macan story is not the old king's death, as I had assumed, but his *murder*. The ancient notion of a sacrifice carried out by the new monarch. Wendell could not sacrifice his stepmother; her suicide prevented it. So he could only sacrifice himself. Or me, I suppose. I wonder if I would have suited.

No doubt she had planned it this way all along, as one governed by spite and vengefulness would. I should have foreseen it. Probably she hoped Wendell would not find her, that he would be so distressed by the suffering of his realm that he would simply take his life and put an end to the trouble he had caused her. But if he *did*, somehow, confound her low opinion of him and track her down, of course she would not allow him the upper hand. If she was to die, she would force her enemy to follow her. I should have foreseen it.

21st January

I have burnt the pages that followed that. They are little more than gibberish—lists of stories that I intended to consult, half-baked theories. Crossings-out and ink blots from where I drifted in a state of half-sleep.

When I awoke, I was hunched over my journal, and it was the wee hours of the morning, still dark. My legs were nearly numb and my neck was sore, as I'd fallen asleep in a slump in a chair by the bedroom window. A little over a day had passed since Wendell's death. I hadn't slept at all the night before—at least I don't think I had. My memory of that day and night is as blurred as my time in the snow king's court.

Someone was knocking at the door. It was a gentle, hesitant sound, as if the gesture required effort. I stood, still half asleep, trying not to look at the bed where Shadow and Orga were curled up together. They watched me as I passed on unsteady feet, and I realized they had been there all day, sometimes napping and sometimes not, but aware of me at all times. Once Orga had assured herself that I was not going to keel over, she put her head back down and closed her eyes.

I expected Niamh or Callum—perhaps even Lord Taran. Instead, the hall beyond the door was darkened and empty.

I stood there for a moment, blinking. A little shiver went

through me—I'd been reading my grandfather's disturbing journal entries late into the night, putting the book aside in favour of some academic tome only to pick it up again, irresistibly drawn back to the tragedy of it. For companionship, perhaps, in my own tragedy. I could hear my grandfather's voice in the text.

I closed the door. Likely I'd imagined the knock, groggy as I'd been, or it had been Niamh or Callum again; each had come by multiple times. I had locked them out, and had heard them muttering together outside the door, sometimes with one or more councillors, until Lord Taran's voice had ordered them all away. Taran, at least, had understood the importance of the work I was doing.

At some point I'd dropped my grandfather's journal, and it lay facedown on the floor by my chair, pages bent. I picked it up.

Oddly, though, as I glanced down at my grandfather's writing, I wasn't thinking of him. I was thinking of the butter faerie, and that sensation I'd felt when I'd learned she had come from Somerset, where once there had been a door to Wendell's kingdom. It had been a feeling akin to hunting for a word on the tip of my tongue. I had it now—perhaps my sleeping mind had solved the mystery.

Exmoor was in Somerset.

Did that mean the now-broken door in the Silva Lupi had led to Exmoor, to the very landscape where my grandfather had met his doom? Possibly. *Not likely,* my rational mind replied. But still—it was an odd coincidence.

At that, I felt another tremor. *Coincidence* is not a word to be taken lightly in Faerie.

I turned back to my grandfather's journal, fingers trembling against the pages. My interest had been reframed, and now I reread each word of his sojourn in Exmoor, stopping each time I could not make out his shorthand until I'd untangled it, rather than skipping over these parts as I'd done before. This was no longer merely a family heirloom, a tragic story no more relevant to my plight than one of Wendell's novels.

When I'd finished, I sat and stared out the window for a long moment. The weeping rowan tapped its dark berries against the pane.

Then I stood. I opened the door again and listened—Wendell's apartments seemed abandoned. But then I heard the faintest of noises in the bathroom. When I made my way there, I found it empty.

Empty—but very clean. A mop leaned against the wall by the bath, and half the floor was damp, as if the mopper had been interrupted in the middle of his task.

"Are you there?" I said. "I need to speak with you. Will you show yourself?"

There came a rustling noise behind me. I turned and found myself facing one of the *oíche sidhe*.

We gazed blankly at each other. Or, rather, *I* was blank—his face was inscrutable.

"Are you the one I spoke with before?" I demanded—I did not intend to sound rude, but I've no doubt that's how it came across. Ordinarily, I attempt to sand down my bluntness, but it did not even occur to me then.

The creature gave no sign of offence. "I am he."

I gazed at him. The faerie looked so much like Wendell had, back in Ljosland, that I felt an inexplicable surge of fury, and I wanted to scream at him, to strike him with my fists. The feeling vanished as abruptly as it came, leaving me breathless and sick.

"I'm sorry," I said.

I don't know what he thought I was apologizing for. "Does Her Highness have need of me?" he said.

"Yes," I said, trying to put myself back together. I don't know why I'd thought of this creature first. There were others who could help me.

No—I knew why. He made me think of Wendell.

"You know all the rooms in the castle," I said. "You know where the nobility dwell."

He nodded with the faintest of frowns, knitting his many-jointed fingers together in front of him.

"I wish to speak with the Lady in the Crimson Cloak," I said. "Will you take me to her?"

The housekeeper not only knew the way to the Lady's room, which was located at the other end of the castle and down a staircase, then up another staircase, but he knew that it had a back door. We went through a storage room crammed with silken cloaks and gowns that seemed to be in varying states of decay, some only a little musty, others furred with layers of dust, then through a vast and echoing bathing room that seemed designed for communal washing, off of which was a narrow door to the Lady's bedchamber.

This was empty, shadowed, and spare, with only a wardrobe, dressing table, and bed clothed in blacks and whites. Naturally, the floorboards were covered in many dark stains.

"She does not like us to clean those," the *oíche sidhe* said, and for once I could read the emotion in his face—pure disapproval.

"Hmm," I said. I had taken the Lady's theatrically gruesome appearance for glamour, but now I wondered if this was entirely the truth. She has at times put me in mind of the gallows-goblins; I wonder if she counts one or more of the creatures among her ancestors.* Wendell's kingdom is not known as a realm of monsters for nothing, and why would his stepmother have cared if one of her courtiers had a morbid hobby, so long as it did not affect her own interests?

Stepping gingerly over the stains, I sat in the chair at the dressing table. "Thank you," I said to the housekeeper. "You may go."

"May," he repeated, a faint question in his voice. "I may also remain, but in such a way that she will not notice me."

"Do as you wish," I said. Perhaps I should have responded better to his kindness, but I had no capacity to think of anything but the revelation contained within my grandfather's journal, and the desperate hope now lodged in my throat like a splinter of bone that might twist and choke me at any moment. The *oíche sidhe* went to stand against the wall, and when I looked back, I could barely see him. If I focused, it was just possible to make out his greyish outline against the darkness; if I did not, my gaze slid across the wall as if he were nothing but a stray hook or nail.

I waited. After perhaps half an hour, the Lady entered the room.

She stilled at the sight of me sitting there in the shadows, but she did not flee, as I'd half feared she would. Instead she

---

* In some stories, gallows-goblins haunt those jails where condemned prisoners are held before execution; they take pleasure in killing the miscreants themselves, usually in some bloody fashion, unless the prisoner can prove his or her innocence, after which the gallows-goblin will whisk them to safety by magic. In most tales, however, gallows-goblins are less arbiters of justice and more generalized terrors; they delight in murder and bloodshed, often lurking at lonely crossroads in the wilderness, where they choose their victims based on a shared characteristic (for example, farmhands with red hair). The former type is found primarily in France and its border regions, while the latter is widespread throughout Western Europe and the British Isles, leading some scholars to speculate these are separate entities entirely. Both varieties of gallows-goblin, though, are described as having blood upon their hands and feet at all times.

removed her cloak in one smooth gesture and hung it from a hook, where it began to drip on the floor.

"Well," she said, brushing her bloody hands over her black gown. "You've worked it out, then."

"I have."

"What do you wish to know?" As she spoke, she moved towards a tea trolley beside the main entrance that must have been set out for her by a servant; it held a pot, its spout lightly steaming, and a single cup. Into this she poured the tea, adding sugar and cream, her movements unhurried.

"You wish to know why I was exiled?" she went on. "*That* is a long story—or perhaps you only care about why I came here, to this court? There was once a door that connected my realm with this one—ah, but I can see from your face that you knew that already. I destroyed the door after I came through, so that my enemies could not follow me."

She handed me the cup. The handle was bloody now, and the tea smelled of smoke. I held it without drinking. Curiously, my hand did not tremble at all, and I realized that I was not afraid of her. I felt—nothing. Or nothing where she was concerned, at any rate. All my focus had attenuated upon one thing, and surrounding this was a vast, wintry stillness that was not quite the same as calm, but which I could put to the same purpose.

"I have not come to speak of the past," I said. "My grandfather's journal said you communed with ghosts and had seen the door to Death. Is that true? Take me to it."

She settled herself upon the edge of the bed and folded her hands in her lap. Her lips were very red, and she watched me in a way that was distinctly predatory. Yet still I felt nothing under her regard.

"You do not wish to speak of Edgar?" she said. "Why I left him?" Her eyes were too large for her face, and without her cloak I saw she was slim—unnaturally slim; I felt she might turn sideways and slip from my sight.

"No," I said. "Only tell me if what he wrote was correct. Have you truly seen so much of Death that you have learned how to travel there without dying yourself? Or was this empty poetry?"

"He bored me," she said.

At this, my hand clenched slightly on my knee. "Is there a door?"

"Will you have me killed?" she said. "Have you already ordered it? If I flee now, shall I be hunted for the rest of my days?"

"Yes," I said, "if you do not help me."

She seemed to consider this. While she did, I sipped my tea.

"You have his journal," she said slowly. "Yes—I remember him scribbling in it. Then that is how you knew who I was?"

I nodded. "I did not realize it on my first reading, because the possibility that his mysterious captor might be in my midst did not occur to me—for one thing, the courtly fae do not generally travel between realms as the common fae do. And for another, I did not know there had been a door between Exmoor and this world. Once I did, I began to wonder . . . I examined my grandfather's descriptions of his beloved more closely. They accord perfectly with yourself. He referred to your apparel only once, when he noted you liked to dress in red."

She smiled and brushed her hair back from her face. It was indeed golden, though the ends were stained with red. "He doted on me so," she said. "More so than most of the others. How I miss him! I always do, after they are gone, no matter how they tired me in the end."

She had accepted my explanation, and so I did not feel it necessary to clarify that I had *not* been certain she was the faerie who had so bewitched my grandfather—it had been a theory, supported by their similarity in appearance as well as nature. She had given me the proof when she had entered the room and understood why I was there.

"If you do not help me," I said, "Lord Taran will see that your victims are properly avenged. You have slain many Folk, but I wonder if you see yourself as a match for him."

Her response to this, a slight stiffening, was answer enough. It was an empty bluff on my part—I'd spoken to no one except the housekeeper before coming here; entirely ill-advised, I can see that now, but I was then possessed by a single-mindedness so complete I think I could have traversed a field of embers without flinching if it brought me closer to my goal.

"Killing is why I exist," she said finally. "It is my only love. I used to struggle with my temper, but now I embrace it. You cannot fathom how many I have slain, both mortal and Folk. Why should a little nothing like you be the end of me?"

"You know why," I said. "Because it would be a fitting conclusion."

She gave me the sort of look that reminded me of Razkarden when he sizes up a potential meal. The shadow in the room seemed to deepen, redden, and grow damp, a slippery damp I felt through my shoes. I only waited. "Well?" I said.

She seemed to deflate slightly, and the illusion vanished. "You wish to find the door to Death?" she said, a slyness entering her voice. "Very well. I will tell you how. But I must be allowed to depart this realm unharmed."

I could see she expected me to protest or bargain with her. "Done," I said.

Her lip curled. "Such a dull little thing," she said. "You have no spirit worth breaking, I see. You are not like your grandfather at all."

"And you are not as frightening as you think you are," I said. "Tell me."

She did. I listened carefully, asking for clarification as often as necessary. I had not brought my notebook with me, but it did not matter—every word I committed to memory.

When she drew to the end, she asked in a mocking tone, "Is there anything else I can do for you, Your Highness?"

I stood and placed my empty teacup back on its tray. "Run," I said.

21st January–later

I am so scattered I can barely recollect where I left off, though it was only a few hours ago. Well, I have oriented myself as best I can—as always, writing helps. Sometimes I feel it is the only thing that prevents me from coming apart.

Wendell's body had been carried back to the castle, along with the body of the old queen, and placed in a room that was open to the lake. It was large and empty save for an intricately carved stone dais—more heads enmeshed in brooklime—upon which Wendell and his stepmother had been lain. A rainstorm had moved in, bringing gusts that rattled through the canopy, and the sound of waves striking the lakeshore washed over the room. The light was dim but warm from the few flickering lanterns hanging from hooks on the walls.

I had collected Shadow, naturally, and he kept so close that I could reach a hand out and stroke his warm fur at any moment. The *oíche sidhe* had led us here and he remained by my side, though I had not asked it of him.

We three were not alone. Along the wall opposite the lakeshore was a long stone bench. Lord Taran was seated there, his legs stretched out before him and his hands folded in his lap, seeming lost in thought. He didn't glance at me when I entered. On the opposite end of the bench sat two brownies wearing jaunty red hats with feathers in them, who seemed to be arguing quietly about something. Razkarden, along with three other guardians, sat upon a perch high in the ceiling that looked as if it had been made for them, hunched into their feathers. A courtier I vaguely recognized stood crying before the dais—when she saw me enter, she bowed her head and went outside, seating herself on the short, broad staircase down to the lake, where she continued to cry. A number of other courtiers and common fae sat out there, alone or in small groups, some holding murmured conversations. As with most other things in this realm, it seemed that mourning was an activity carried out in a collective, disorderly manner.

I hadn't known what I would feel, seeing Wendell's body, and was unprepared for the magnitude of the shock. For a moment, I simply could not draw air into my lungs. I stumbled over to the bench and sat beside Lord Taran. The little housekeeper stayed by the door, his face impassive, the only sign of emotion the hand clenched on his rag, which had gone white.

Lord Taran did not offer comfort, merely gave me a look of wry resignation. I was glad for this, for it was much more steadying than having him put his arm around me or something equally dreadful.

"They brought them here together," I noted when finally I regained my breath.

"Mm," Lord Taran said moodily. He now had a scar upon his face—three narrow but deep lines that ran across his cheekbone from the corner of his left eye. "Well, she was their queen, wasn't she? I am trying to decide what to do with her. I would like to remove her head and place it on a pike—but then I have also considered giving her to one of the attentive oaks to dismember, and inviting the realm to watch. The trees would enjoy that."

I examined him. "You have been here some time?"

"It's an important decision. A person can be dismembered only once."

I tapped my cheekbone. "Why have you not used a glamour?"

He glowered at me. "The Beast of the Elderwood's mark cannot be hidden by glamour."

I hid my smile—imperfectly, I admit. "Where is Deilah?" I said. "I thought—someone told me she would not leave Wendell's side." I could not remember precisely who—many things about those first few hours following Wendell's death were blurred.

"Oh, she hasn't gone far," Lord Taran said, rolling his eyes. "She was in hysterics, sobbing all over his body. He is 'dear brother' to her now, apparently. But presently she is wandering the forest, wailing and tearing at her clothes. I hope she stays out there."

"Poor child," I said, though in truth I was finding it hard to summon much sympathy, monstrous as that sounds—after all, here were her mother and brother lying dead beside each other. And yet something about Deilah's inclination towards dramatics had the effect of muting the warmth I might have felt for her.

"Children are more trouble than they're worth" was Lord Taran's opinion on the matter.

I finally allowed myself to look directly at the dais—it was several yards away in this large room, which was both helpful and not helpful. I could not see Wendell's expression, for his head was tilted slightly to one side, but I could see the transformation that had overtaken him. He had not been changed into fresh clothes—indeed, I do not think his body had been attended to in any way—and yet, while I could still make out the dark shadow of the wound in his chest, the blood was gone. He was not half covered in moss, like Queen Arna. Instead, some form of dense, creeping vine grew from his chest and from another wound at the side of his head, which he must have sustained when the queen's curse descended upon us, after which the castle—I had been told, for I had not seen it—had split in two, and the enchantment hiding the island from the Folk had shattered. The vine had wrapped itself numerous times around his eyes and temples, so that he seemed to be wearing a strange mask made of leaves and tiny white flowers. His skin, in places, had the rough texture of oak bark. I suppose I should have found the transformation horrifying, but I could not help admiring the beauty of it.

"We shall have to remove him to the forest soon," Lord Taran said. "Before he puts down roots, like his father."

"His father became a tree?" I said. I knew I should not just sit there, for the Lady had emphasized that I had only a narrow window of time to act; yet in that moment, hope was a living thing, and I was in terror of losing it.

"No," Lord Taran said. "An apple sapling grew from his mouth. It is very large now—you can see it, and the old king as well, if you take the east-west path behind the castle. You have to look closely, though, for his body has turned to root and bark. Liath's mother's end was more dignified, I thought. She is now a mound of grass and mushrooms upon a hill in the castle gardens, surrounded by rows of cherry trees. The old king put a bench there."

I did not recall noticing either feature. But then, there had been times that I had noted odd shapes in the trees and mounds of the forest floor. The impression of limbs, sometimes, or faces in the bark. Had these, too, been the remnants of long-dead Folk? Was this why I sometimes caught the whisper of voices in the rustling leaves? Did only monarchs succumb to this process?

I did not ask any of these questions. For the first time in my life, I was weary of answers.

"You have kept everyone away from me," I said. "Thank you."

Lord Taran shrugged. "The realm can survive without a monarch for a time. Your councillors are, at present, insisting that you remarry as soon as possible. Options have been proposed, debates had."

"Really?" I said, almost absently. I found that I was amused by this. How was it that I of all people kept having faerie husbands thrust at me?

"I am about to do something mad," I said.

He looked interested. "Indeed?" He glanced at the housekeeper standing silent and motionless. "I do not believe the floor is in need of scrubbing, but then I am no judge of such things. Do you wish me to leave you be?"

"No," I said. Against all odds, I found his presence comforting. "What are you doing here, anyhow? You don't care for Wendell."

He shrugged. "I was bored."

"You were bored," I repeated flatly.

He took no interest in my reaction. "I am bored most of the time. Bored of politics and adventure and feasting and quarrelling. Of vengeance and loyalty. I have learned there is one thing a person never tires of, no matter how long they live. And that is being in love. All else is ash and ember."

"Wendell loved his home," I said. "That is why he gave his life for it. I suppose he would agree with you."

Lord Taran regarded me thoughtfully.

I felt able to stand again, and so I made my way slowly to the side of the dais where the housekeeper was, his head bowed. I had told myself I would not look at Wendell, but I found this impossible. His expression, what I could see of it through the vines, had nothing at all in it—no fear or anger, nothing that could have told me what he had been thinking the moment he had sacrificed himself. Had he known it would come to this, despite his assurances to me? If not, how had he made the decision so quickly? He still wore the silvered leaves in his hair.

I squeezed my coin, which I used to carry with me to ward off enchantment. Its familiar, pocket-warmed roughness was steadying. The housekeeper watched me.

As the Lady had instructed, I looked for the door in Wendell's shadow, which spilled over the edge of the dais. It was oddly shaped, spiky from the leaves and vines. Part of the shadow was darker than the rest—was that the door I sought, or simply a flaw in the stone? I squinted harder, cursing myself for not asking the Lady more questions. She had said that the door would be easy to see, if I knew to look for it. I imagined I was hunting for a faerie door—for it *was* a faerie door, in a sense.

"I think I see it," I said, more out of desperation than conviction. "But how do I go through?"

The housekeeper's masklike countenance slipped momentarily, and he looked astonished. "You cannot. No mortal can take *that* door."

My heart was thundering in my ears. Ridiculously, I felt my face redden and my throat grow tight, as if I were a child about to throw a tantrum. "But the Lady told me—"

"The Lady wanted you dead," he said.

We gazed at each other for a moment. I said, "I need to get him out."

The faerie nodded. "I will go," he said with as little ceremony as he said anything.

"But—" I stared at him in astonishment, a dozen objections rising within me. For some reason, the one that came out was "*I must get him out.*"

Because of course it must be me. Wendell was my responsibility. Moreover, he was *mine*. I had taken us on the journey that had led him to this, his body cold and half hidden behind a leafy winding-sheet. Who was this small grey faerie before me? I knew not one thing about him, other than that his days were spent tidying rooms, not venturing into other worlds.

"You cannot be proposing to go alone," I said.

He gazed at me, his face unreadable once more. His hand was at his rag again, passing it absently through his fingers. "He is one of ours," he said.

Then, before I could move or speak, he stepped forward and opened a door—I thought I saw a flash of it, just for a moment, a thing of gossamer and darkness in the left side of Wendell's shadow. And he was gone.

22nd January

The moments that followed the housekeeper's disappearance were spent in a state of agonized expectation.

For the faerie to reappear. For Wendell to reawaken. For *something*.

"What is happening?" I demanded of no one in particular, pacing back and forth. I don't think I've ever felt more frustrated, for I had no stories to guide me now, no academic knowledge to fall back on whatsoever. Morning arrived, and it brought an improvement in the weather, the clouds beginning to break, the steady rain fading to a sunlit drizzle. Mourners came and went, bowing in my direction but otherwise ignoring me, none seeming to sense the significance of what was happening.

Lord Taran's response, when I told him what I had done, was one of flat disbelief.

"There are no doors to Death," he said. "The Lady was mistaken—or, more likely, she invented a story to allow herself time to flee. The housekeeper has gone somewhere else, perhaps another realm, and gotten himself lost. Perhaps he is too embarrassed to return."

"Not *Death*," I corrected him. "The Lady told me there is a place, half in this world and half *elsewhere,* where the spirits of the Folk linger for a time before they are truly gone. Only a short time—she said that I must make haste if I wished to pull Wendell out. She had never done anything of that nature herself, but she believed it was possible."

Lord Taran only gave me a pitying look. Fortunately, Niamh arrived shortly thereafter and I was able to lay the matter before her.

"Emily!" she exclaimed, holding up her hands. "I'm glad to find you have left your rooms. But you will need to slow down."

I forced myself to go back to the beginning, trying to keep my voice steady. It was not easy. Not only because of my excitement, but I felt lightheaded—I could not remember the last time I had eaten anything. If Wendell had been with me, he would have been appalled and not left off nagging me until I'd had some toast at least.

"My grandfather believed that the Lady in the Crimson Cloak knew of a door to Death," I finished. "I have his journal—though he was only a hobbyist, he was quite well-read. He cites several sources in arguing—well, essentially, for the existence of faerie ghosts. But I am not familiar with the names he references."

Niamh took the journal from my hand, pausing to allow the braille enchantment to work, then ran her finger over the page I had marked.

"Robbins?" she said musingly. "I wonder if he means Archibald Robbins at the University of Amsterdam. He was seen as an iconoclast in my day; his theories concerned interactions between the Folk and the spirit world. A few reputable scholars still believed in ghosts back then and would debate whether some stories concerned ghostly or fae protagonists, but Robbins went further than many were comfortable with."

"I've never heard of him," I said with some indignation. I had thought myself familiar with the work of all dryadologists within the last century.

"He did not publish much before his death—which was nothing suspicious; he took a fall somewhere in Scotland. The Grampians, I believe. What little he did write was mostly retracted as scholarship evolved." She paused. "Helen W.W. could be a reference to Helen Worthington-West. She was before even my time. Wasn't she at Cambridge?"

I made a frustrated sound. "Of course! How did I not guess that? Bran Eichorn co-authored several papers with her. But then I have never bothered much with the writings of the spiritualists."

"Not much value in it, except in tracing the development of dryadology itself," Niamh agreed. "One might as well study phrenology. Still, my research supervisor—a lovely man, but very much the product of an older era—encouraged me to read Worthington-West. She had some intriguing theories about bogles, or bogeys as they termed them then, but on the whole I found her ideas outdated and rather sensationalist. She presented a paper at a conference in Paris—it may have been ICODEF, before it was called that—in which she claimed to have interviewed a household brownie who had visited the afterlife and spoken with her recently deceased mother. Apparently this matriarch provided her daughter with instructions on what to serve at her funeral reception, including a recipe for lemon scones."

"What!" I exclaimed. "Where was this published?"

"It wasn't, unsurprisingly. I only know about it because my supervisor was at the conference. There was quite the backlash." Niamh paused thoughtfully. "All this is to say that the Lady's claim regarding doors to some sort of spiritual limbo, your grandfather's references to ghosts—such things are not entirely without context in the field of dryadology. Certainly the Worthington-West school would not have been surprised."

I gave a weak laugh and sank back onto the bench, resting my head in my hands. "I had thought that reading the histories of great faerie monarchs would prepare me for whatever Wendell and I would encounter here. Instead I should have spent my time on ghost stories."

"So it appears," Niamh said. I could tell that she was skeptical, if not outright disbelieving, but nevertheless her voice held a trace of hope. I noticed for the first time that her eyes were red and shadowed, and I recalled that she had known Wendell from his boyhood.

"And what does this old misanthrope have to say about your theory?" she said, adopting the familial, teasing tone she often used with Lord Taran, which always gave me a shiver of trepidation.

"Nothing whatsoever," he replied. "I have no use for the arguments of scholars. And I am not so much a villain as to offer false hope."

"That's plain enough," she said, her face falling a little. "How long has the little one been gone?"

Despair settled over me. "Two hours, perhaps."

"You must eat," Niamh said, placing a hand on my back. "You are trembling. Come with me."

"I cannot."

She sighed. "I will send for breakfast, then. And you *will* eat it, if I have to force it down your throat myself."

Despite my weakness, I was sickened by the smell of breakfast when the servants placed it before me on a tray. Still, I made myself eat a few spoonfuls of egg and a piece of toast—

I could not countenance the strawberries or spiced porridge—knowing that Niamh was in the right.

The morning turned into afternoon. I sat and watched the dais, or wrote in my journal. More Folk flitted in and out. Lord Taran departed, then returned. I do not think he came to see if I would succeed, but rather how long I would hold on to hope. Not once did he press me, though. Callum came and sat with me, and though I knew he meant well, I found his presence hardest to bear. He looked at me with an understanding I wanted no part of.

Ivy continued to cover Wendell's body. It was twining about his hair now, too, so thickly that only the odd clump of gold could be seen squeezed between the leaves. Moths fluttered about the flowers, a snail made its slow way across his chest, and I caught sight of the odd cocoon being spun and the dark skitter of a spider. I wanted to brush it all away, but I couldn't. I couldn't touch him.

As the day slipped into evening, I dozed off, Shadow snoring against my feet. I was startled awake by a cavalcade of flickering lights, which spun once around the room and were gone before I could even pinpoint what variety of faerie they were.

I lifted my head, trying to shake off the nebulous unease that accompanies awakening in an unfamiliar place. The room was empty apart from a solitary brownie upon a ladder, who was lighting the lanterns, but a few Folk were still gathered outside on the stone steps—I could hear the murmur of their conversation.

I reached down to pet Shadow. But at some point, as I dozed, the dog had gone to lie next to Wendell's body. I felt my eyes begin to sting. But then I noticed that the beast was not dozing—though his head rested on one paw—but gazing fixedly at the corner of the dais.

The hair rose on my neck. And I realized something else. Shadow had not howled.

I went to crouch beside him, placing my hand on his head. Black Hounds are known for their haunting howl, which they let loose in the presence of death—or, in some stories, around those who are soon to depart. Yet not once since we entered the room with Wendell's body had Shadow made a sound.

"What, my love?" I murmured. Shadow was not staring at the place where the *oíche sidhe* had vanished, but to the left, around the other side of the dais. Which was where Wendell's shadow would have been now, were there light enough to see it.

"The door *is* in his shadow," I murmured. I had seen the housekeeper go that way, but it still felt impossible, even amongst the many impossibilities of Faerie. "Isn't it?"

The dog took no note of me. His world was that of smells, not theories. And while he had never demonstrated any particular aptitude for locating faerie doors in the past, perhaps because he saw them as unexceptional features within the shifting tapestry of scent, his nostrils were twitching now. He stood.

"Shadow," I said warningly.

He stood there for a moment, simply looking at nothing, and I thought that was the end of it and he would lie back down again, as he did whenever he sighted a rabbit on the campus lawn, remembering the effort it would require to catch it. Then the dog made a motion with his snout that was like lifting up the hem of a curtain. And then he stepped *into* the shadow, and was gone.

"Shadow!" I lunged forward, but caught only a few hairs of the dog's tail. He could move quickly when he wanted to, which was not often.

I am not proud of this, but my immediate reaction was not

to send for help, or to charge after him. Instead, I slumped against the dais and burst into tears.

I was crying like a child, heedless of the noise I was making. I heard the murmur of Folk around me, and felt small hands patting my face, my hands, caught the flicker of wet black eyes and leaf-woven hats. I ignored them.

After a few moments, someone pulled me into their arms—not at all gently—and held me in a tight grip. Too tight. It was a faerie, which I knew from the way she smelled. Many people assume the Folk, the courtly fae in particular, will smell like roses, but in truth they smell like mortals, at least on the surface. I suspect it is a part of their glamour, for beneath this is the smell of rainforests and river reeds, moss and algae and leaves decaying into humus. A green smell, not always pleasant, noticeable only when one is very close.

The faerie held me so tight it was almost a wrestling match to get away. This was surprisingly effective at calming my sobs, for my misery was eclipsed by irritation. It was Deilah—but I had guessed that by her golden hair, which she had shoved my face into.

"Poor thing!" she cried. "I should have stayed to comfort you—we could have comforted each other."

I made no response to this—she was still gripping my arms too hard and gazing at me with an excited sort of despair that I found more exhausting than pitiable. Deilah wore a mourning cloak, which for the Folk of this realm meant a cloak woven with thorns that pricked at your arms and throat, and her dress was a torn and filthy mess. Her hair, too, had pinecones and bits of mud stuck in it, as if she had hurled herself down on the forest floor multiple times. She was, on the whole, a pathetic sight, her eyes painfully swollen, as if she had not left off sobbing for days, though she would have been more pathetic if she did not give off the impression of having taken part in her dishevelment. The mud on her cheek, for instance, looked as if it had been smeared on by a finger, and as someone who had traversed the forests of Wendell's realm several times now, I did not quite understand how one would come by so many tears in one's dress, unless they went looking for blackberry bushes to fall into.

Still, she was here, and so I babbled what had happened. Her eyes grew wider and wider as I spoke.

"Where is the door?" she demanded, whipping around to scan the room. Her instantaneous belief in me did not inspire confidence—quite the opposite, in fact; I felt a shadowy premonition that Lord Taran's skepticism would soon be proven right. With their only ally a querulous ragamuffin, anyone would doubt their cause.

"Somewhere here," I said, pointing to the dark place where Shadow had vanished.

She patted the dais, then pounded on it, as if she might tear the stone apart. Finally she sagged back, panting. "Call him," she demanded.

"What?"

"Call your dog!" she cried, looking at me as if I were the stupidest person on earth. "Perhaps he cannot find his way back! Have you just been *sitting* there?"

Much as I wished to, I did not bother pointing out that I had been far more occupied in saving Wendell than someone who had spent the last day staggering about in the forest, wailing. I saw no reason not to follow her advice, other than the fact that it was rather mad—a largely immaterial detail in Faerie.

"Shadow!" I cried.

"Louder!" she urged.

I called louder. I called until my throat was hoarse. I nearly fell over when I heard a distant, warbling howl.

Shadow.

"Here!" I yelled. "Shadow, here! Come!"

The howl came again—closer? I did not know. I could not tell exactly where the howl was coming from. Eerily, it seemed as if it were beneath us, reverberating through the floor.

"What does he like to eat?" the girl demanded, crouching at my side with her knees up in the lithe manner of a small child. We were both staring hard at the blank stone, and if that were not enough to make me feel I was going mad, the girl's inane question was.

"I thought you were supposed to be clever," she snapped in response to my expression. "Or is that just in comparison with my brother? Nobody thinks *he's* smart, that's for sure. Dogs see by smell."

Of course they did—of course. No sooner had I told her about Shadow's preference for raw meat—of any variety, but the smellier the better—than she was snapping her fingers imperiously at the servants, who ran off in disorderly haste, some crashing into each other. I became aware that a crowd had gathered behind us, common and courtly fae craning to see what we were fussing about. I don't think they had any clue what was going on, but they were muttering excitedly among themselves nonetheless. The brownie selling nuts was back, which did not help my growing feeling of hysteria.

Several servants returned, thrusting plates of meat into our hands. I stacked them beside the dais like a gory offering at a sacrifice, and suddenly the howling was much louder. I shouted until my voice broke, and then I was toppling over backwards, knocked flat by the large and hairy shape that had plowed into my chest.

I made a strangled sound, half sob and half shriek, burying my face in his fur. The dog was pulling something large and grey behind him, which turned out to be the housekeeper faerie, whom Shadow had been dragging along by the ankle. The dog dropped him as unceremoniously as he would a bone he'd tired of and leapt on me again, his tongue swiping at my face. Something strange happened next, and it is only by looking back at the memory that I am able to smooth it out, to see the details. The *oíche sidhe* had been pulling something, too—I thought it was a lantern, in the moment, or nothing at all, just a reflection off one of the room's silver mirrors. But whatever it was, it vanished when the faerie came spilling out of Wendell's shadow and tumbling across the room.

"What happened?" I demanded of the housekeeper when Shadow had calmed somewhat and noticed the vast pile of his favourite victuals, to which he delightedly applied himself. The faerie was moaning—no wonder, for Shadow had not been gentle, and his leg seemed to be bleeding.

"The king," the faerie murmured. "Where—? I lost him—"

I knew I should have been paying more attention to his injury, but I could not help demanding, "What do you mean? Did you see Wendell?"

Deilah screamed. She surged to her feet and threw herself upon the dais, where Wendell—

Where Wendell was sitting up.

He had pulled the ivy from his face—there was still a great deal in his hair, along with a small flock of butterflies and moths—and was looking very cross. He shoved Deilah away with a cry of "Ah! You're filthy!" and began yanking at the vegetation at his chest, vines that speared his cloak and twined round his fingers.

"Look at this!" he exclaimed to no one in particular. "My poor cloak! Bloody thorns have ruined it. I cannot mend what has been reduced to threads."

He gave up with a curse and looked around, blinking confusedly at the crowd staring at him in frozen awe, before his gaze finally landed on me, whereupon his face lit up. "Em! What on earth has happened?"

I leapt on him then, babbling nonsensically, and a roar arose among the gathered Folk—mostly positive, I believe, though as before, some were less than pleased by Wendell's return, for a few went stampeding down the steps, shrieking. The forest erupted in lantern light and a cacophony of melody that hurt my ears, as various musicians began jostling with one another for the right to celebrate Wendell's return the loudest.

Wendell did not ask any more questions, merely held me in his arms as I babbled and cried—perhaps I was making more sense than I thought, or, more likely, his memory was returning to him. Several of the moths were crushed between us, their dry wings leaving streaks of dust against my cheek. At some point, Shadow managed to hop up on the dais, slobbering all over us both, and then he sprinted from the room like a pup. He returned moments later with Orga dangling from his mouth by her scruff, hissing and spitting and generally promising imminent pain to her captor. She managed to get in a slash across Shadow's face, and the poor dog dropped her.

"Orga!" Wendell exclaimed. "Leave him be, dear."

She started comically at the sound of his voice, and I expected her to leap at him as Shadow had done, but naturally she had to express her fury and indignation first, and circled the dais, yowling at her master at the top of her lungs. Wendell reached for her, but she only swiped at him with a hiss.

"You miserable brute!" I exclaimed in disgust, but Wendell only laughed. I could not stop myself from touching him, as if from one moment to the next he might vanish—his face, his chest, where now there was no wound, only a greenish discolouration, like a grass stain upon a piece of cloth.

Razkarden alighted soundlessly at Wendell's side, making me jump, and rested one of his hideous legs upon Wendell's knee. Wendell smiled and rubbed the creature's beak. "Happy to see me again, old friend?"

I examined him, looking for some sign of difference, but he seemed entirely himself, and as fresh as if he'd awoken from a nap. And if there was a certain enigmatical quality to his gaze, it was no more pronounced than before, and I was used to it anyway.

"What happened?" I murmured.

He tossed another piece of ivy aside. "I barely remember! It seemed as if I were in the forest. But it was odd. It was dark as a winter's night, and cold—worse than that bloody ice court. I kept wandering, but nothing was familiar. I passed Folk, but it was as if they did not see me. And then—" His gaze fell upon the *oíche sidhe*, whom one of the servants had helped into an upright position. "You sent him, didn't you? He said you had."

"Yes," I said. "In a way. Mostly he sent himself."

The *oíche sidhe* staggered to his feet. He bowed to Wendell and myself, then brushed the wrinkles from his clothes before saying, "Forgive me, Your Highnesses. I failed. I found the king, but I could not find the way back out. I thought we would wander for eternity, until the beast arrived."

"Was that Shadow?" Wendell gazed in astonishment at the dog, who was contentedly gnawing at a bit of gristle, slobber pooling below him. "Good Lord! I thought it was some eldritch monster come to feast upon my soul. When he pounced on us, I thought it was the end."

He reached down and rubbed Shadow's head. "Good boy!"

The dog licked him, then went back to his dinner.

"Can you stand?" I said. Wendell put his arm around me, and I helped him to his feet. He wobbled a little at first, brushing leaves and flowers from himself, much of which fell away with little roots attached. He knelt before the housekeeper, whose head was still bowed low, and murmured something, placing his hand on the side of the small faerie's face.

Then he stood, shrugging off his tattered cloak, which I helped him with. I felt a strong need to fuss over him, which I don't think I've ever felt before. If only it had ended there! Wendell gazing at me blissfully, those damned butterflies still in his hair, though many had departed, flitting off into the cooling twilight. In a moment, we could summon Lord Taran and the other councillors—summon the entire court—to show them that all was well. Their king had been returned to them. This could become a controversial anecdote in my book, one that my fellow scholars would praise and rage over, some accepting Wendell's resurrection as a logical extension of the illogic of Faerie, others painting me as a twentieth-century de Grey, each according to their disposition and professional jealousies.

"I know that look," Wendell said. "This will become a rather sensational paper, won't it? I can see you already drafting the abstract."

I was suddenly more furious with him than I had ever been. That he would make light of all this! "If you think," I said, "that you can do something like this again—without consulting me, without even a *thought*—"

"I know," he said quietly. His tone froze my anger, and I saw that his eyes were damp. "I would never have put you through—that—if I had seen a single alternative. But you are wrong in one thing: I *was* thinking of you, Em. You were my first thought, as well as my last."

But then there came a surge of disquiet, mutters and gasps that rippled through the watching Folk like a stone thrown into a pond.

A motley crowd of Folk had gathered around Queen Arna's body. I hadn't been paying her any attention, and at first, I thought they were attempting to move her somewhere, and was about to command them to leave her be. And yet, no one was holding the queen upright—had she been placed into that odd slump, her hair all over her face? Some of the common fae were poking her, or sniffing at her skin. A brownie lifted her arm as if to examine it, and some of the moss fell away. But the arm kept moving, and the creature leapt back with a startled squeak.

Queen Arna opened her eyes. At first, she gazed listlessly about, and then she gave a choked cry, hands fluttering as if she were trying to cover her naked body. But she was fully clothed still in the soiled finery she had worn in the second castle. Her face was drawn, and she looked, in that moment, neither human nor Folk, but like a frightened, slightly feral animal.

"She followed you out," I murmured. "Somehow—but then, why not? You died in almost the same moment. Yes—why not?"

Wendell had gone still. Every ounce of his attention focused on his stepmother—it was as if the room were empty but for them.

"Let us put her in the dungeon," I said with an urgency I did not fully understand. I only knew on some fundamental level that we could not kill her. It was the same certainty I had felt in the royal court of the Hidden Ones, when I had found myself at a crossroads: slay the wicked king, or choose a different ending to the story I was caught in.

Wendell appeared to consider. Dread settled over me, because I could see he had been overtaken by the darker aspect of his nature, and would at any moment erupt into some unhinged fit of violence. The watching crowd seemed to sense this, too, and shrank back. So it was a shock when Wendell replied calmly, "You're right, Em."

I watched him warily. I do not particularly enjoy talking to him when he is like this, and almost would have preferred him to pull out his sword and start stabbing things. "I am."

"I will not kill her," he said, still with that terrible calm. "Instead, I will lock my stepmother away where she cannot harm you, or me, or the realm. But it shall be a cell with no door, in a land without paths. She deserves no less than that."

He made a gesture I had seen once before, in St. Liesl, and had hoped never to see again, like brushing aside a cobweb. And then it was as if the world had been ripped in two, and between the halves was a column of swirling darkness. It was a narrow opening, a gap, but it seemed to have no beginning or end, disappearing through the floor and ceiling. The gathered Folk wailed and shrieked, trampling one another in their haste to flee.

Wendell's stepmother tried to run. But, as Wendell had been, she was unsteady on her feet. She fell, and he caught her. She opened her mouth, to scream or plead—I never found out. Before she had recovered her balance, Wendell spun her around and pushed her almost gently into the Veil.

5th February

Time shifted when Wendell died, falling out of tune with the mortal realm. What felt like two days to me was about a fortnight for Lilja and Margret, judging by the calendar on the wall of the cottage. I wish I could work out a way to explain this fear—it would greatly unburden me, but I suspect they will only look at me as if I am a puzzle they cannot solve, and can they be blamed for this? I should feel only happiness now that Wendell is returned to me—as happy as they felt when Wendell and I retrieved them from the Hidden Ones, restoring them to themselves and each other.

But I am getting ahead of myself again. Before I speak of the cottage, let me return to where I left off.

Wendell's first inclination upon waking from the dead was, naturally, to throw a party. At this he failed, for a party was already unfolding. A troupe of musicians had established themselves on the lakeshore below the gardens, where there is a large pavilion; another was set up in the banquet hall, which, when Wendell and I arrived, we found already bursting with a chaotic array of food. There were oysters from the southern coast, whole roasted trout, a bubbling vat of caramel for dipping apples, and bread loaves positioned randomly about the room, as well as the queer blue sandwich cakes that were a court favourite—the blue came from blueberry preserves and a sharp cheese, which were layered with a sweet cloudlike batter. From the look and smell of the things, they should have been dreadful, but I had already acquired a taste for them.

Naturally, everyone wanted to talk to Wendell, who was ever in his element in such a circumstance. Few among the courtly fae were interested in hearing from either myself or the *oíche sidhe* who had restored Wendell to life, which was no great surprise, and I did not mind standing silently at Wendell's side like a shadow. But he kept bringing the conversation back to me, declaring that he would still be dead, and the kingdom in tatters, if not for his queen. He was convincing enough that this had the effect of transforming the disdain of the courtly fae into amazement when they looked at me—a questionable improvement; I never had the sense that there was much warmth in it. I was a puzzle to them now, where before I had been a triviality.

It had all happened so quickly that I found myself swept along with the festivities and Wendell's pure delight, which I could not very well begrudge him. After all, his beloved home was whole again, and his stepmother properly out of the way. It felt very much like an ending, and my trepidation was still a formless thing; I did not know how to name it.

"I must speak with you," I said, stumbling a little over my words—I was inexpressibly weary by that point.

Wendell stopped midsentence, gazing at me with surprise that shifted almost instantly into guilt. He waved the courtiers away.

"I'm sorry," he said, leading me out of the room. "I should have known you would find all that tedious."

"You need not apologize," I said, smiling at the earnestness in his expression. A lightness overcame me; I felt as if I would never *stop* smiling. "I would have preferred not to drag you away from the party. I know you wish to celebrate your stepmother's defeat, but—"

"What?" Wendell said, staring at me. The butterflies and other crawling things had abandoned his hair, thankfully, though several spiderwebs remained, which made an odd contrast with the silvered roses two of the servants had added to the golden waves. "Do you think *that* is why I am in such a good mood? Oh, Em."

"Your brush with death, then," I said. "I don't wish to imply that I was little affected by it, that I was confident all along that it was impermanent. I was not. I have never felt—" I was unable to finish the sentence, and I realized abruptly that I was shivering again, despite the warmth of the castle. "But Wendell, there is something not right in all this—"

"My brush with death!" Wendell said, with nothing more than exasperation in his voice, as if he were resurrected at least once a season. "Emily, Emily. Do you not know the main reason I am so happy? We were *married* not long ago—a mere hour or two, to my recollection. Or did you forget?"

I stared at him for a long moment.

"I'm afraid I did," I said at last.

He began to laugh. It went on so long that he had to lean against the wall, wiping at his eyes.

"There was rather a lot to distract me!" I said hotly.

He eventually recovered, though his face was still red, and the roses had become tangled in his hair. "Might I suggest a different form of distraction?"

I gave a soft laugh. My thoughts were in disarray. I wanted to argue with him; I wanted to touch him again, to assure myself once more that he was real. I needed to *think*. But then he smiled at me in such a way that I found myself saying, "I have no objection."

I allowed him to lead me away from the party and halfway up the stairs before the nagging voice grew too insistent and I pulled him to a stop. He turned to look at me with a question in his eyes.

"You must pull your stepmother out," I said. "What you did to her—it is all wrong."

"Wrong?" Wendell looked baffled. "Em, she would have torn the realm to pieces. She nearly killed you on that island!"

"I don't mean that," I said. "She deserves the fate you have given her. But the story is wrong."

The words sounded hollow—I knew they were true, but I did not know *why* yet, and how could I explain it to him, when I could not explain it to myself? Still, though, he waited patiently for me to finish.

"Don't you trust me?" I demanded at last, frustrated.

At that, his expression grew solemn. "Naturally I do. If you believe some misfortune will befall me because I was too harsh with my stepmother, then I will expect it. But Em, I cannot— I *will* not—watch her poison these lands again. Nor will I watch her threaten *you*, which she has done now on two occasions. I will suffer whatever fate awaits me to avoid putting you in danger again, and when that fate arrives, my only regret will be that I did not savour her defeat longer. I wish I could watch her now, stumbling about in that accursed place."

His expression was dark, an echo of his former fury, implacable as a storm. I knew, in that moment, that I would never convince him.

I rose early in the morning, long before the sunrise. I watched Wendell sleep for a moment—he had burrowed himself into the blankets as usual, so that only half his face was visible. I brushed the hair out of his eyes—I doubted he would awaken anytime soon, given that he had more than made good on his promise to provide me with a *distraction*. The clothes we had worn were scattered all about the room, and my mouth felt bruised, but pleasantly so.

I kissed his temple, then I rose, bathed quickly in the ever-full and steaming tub, and packed a bag. I put in it my books, my journal, the draft of my manuscript. An ordinary dress, none of the faerie-made gewgaws.

I motioned to Shadow, and he bestirred himself from the rug at the foot of the bed. Orga, who lay in a nest of quilt beside Wendell's head, gave a low hiss.

"Ungrateful wretch," I muttered. The cat only glared at me, as at home in her hostility as ever a cat can be. I had thought we were making progress in our relationship, but losing Wendell seemed only to have cemented his place at the centre of her universe, a dynamic that admitted no interlopers. When it was clear to her that I was merely going to leave, not attempt to drag him along on some new misadventure, she put her head back down, dismissing me from her consideration.

I was not so lucky with Razkarden, however. I had not known he was perched just outside the window, which was open a crack, among the boughs of the weeping rowan, but a flicker of movement alerted me. We regarded each other for a long moment, during which I felt transfixed by his ancient, haunted gaze. I swallowed uncomfortably, for surely he read treachery in my stealth and would give me away, waking Wendell. But he did not, only watched me, and after another moment, I resumed packing. He kept as silent as I, rustling not one feather.

I paused to leave Wendell a note. I wrote only that I needed to spend time with my books—alone.

Then I left the castle, and then I left Faerie.

When I stepped into the mist of Corbann, I let out a sigh. Not precisely a sigh of relief, for I was still greatly troubled in my mind, but one of recognition. The Folk were not of this world, they could only impinge upon it. Here, their ways and perils were not so immediate, and more easily muffled behind layers of scholarly theories.

Many doors to Faerie are surprisingly easy to break. If one is bold and unafraid of the consequences—a foolhardy boldness in many cases—one has only to crush the circle of mushrooms, or cut down the grove of twisted trees, that connects our world to theirs. I did not need to destroy anything, I merely lifted the first of the unnaturally shiny stepping-stones and turned it upside-down. I think this would have been enough, but to be on the safe side, I flipped the other stones too. The bottoms were covered in mud and insects—perfectly mundane. I was satisfied.

I hoisted my bag, and Shadow and I made our way to the cottage door.

6th February

Naturally, I told Lilja and Margret all.

"He will follow you" was Lilja's first response. "Surely there is more than one door between Faerie and Ireland. He could use another."

"Of course," I said. "But he won't. He will be too afraid of my reaction. More likely he will pester me with letters." I gave a bark of laughter. "At least there is no post today—it is Sunday, is it not?"

Margret and Lilja exchanged a look. We were sitting in the kitchen this morning as a fire crackled in the next room and a thin, chilly rain tapped against the window. I had arrived at the cottage before they had awakened; it was earlier than it had been in Faerie, near midnight rather than dawn. So, after writing in my journal, I had tried to sleep for another hour or so—tried to. I had mostly just tossed and turned in the narrow bed.

"What?" I said.

Lilja merely shook her head, then rose from the table. She went into the other room and returned with a bundle of letters in her hand.

"We did not open them," she said. "Though we wished to, as we could not understand why he would think you were here, and we were worried. But we thought they might be under some enchantment."

I stared at the bundle she pressed into my hand. Wendell's ridiculously graceful writing stared back at me.

"Of course," I murmured. "When he died, the enchantment he used to match the flow of time to that of the mortal realm was broken. A fortnight passed here, while he lay dead, so when I left Faerie, I also stepped forward in time. And yet when I *did* leave, time advanced in Faerie to match the mortal realm—I wonder if he attached the enchantment to me somehow? He must have. Well, hopefully he has repaired things properly, so that I shall not return to find him a century older. Or will I return to find that only ten seconds has passed since he sent his last letter? It could go either way, I suppose; these things are never consistent."

I felt a pang, that I had been away from him for so long—from his perspective, anyhow. But there was nothing for it. I looked up to find Margret and Lilja staring at me.

"Erm," Margret said. "I still don't see— You only just *got* here. These letters have been arriving for days."

Lilja put her hand on her wife's, and Margret trailed off with a sigh. She gave me a rueful look.

"It's like that apple tree he gave us, isn't it?" she said. "It flowers and gives fruit all year long, even when the snow is deep enough to touch the boughs. I can appreciate the apples, but only if I don't think about them too much. If I start, I fear I will never *stop* thinking, if you know what I mean."

I put the letters down. I was too unsettled to focus on them now, anyway. "I'm sorry," I said. "I am ruining your holiday with all my melodrama."

Margret laughed. "You would not be our Emily if you were not trying to solve some faerie mystery. We expected something of this nature."

"Yes," Lilja said. "Well, perhaps not *quite* of this nature. I still don't understand why Wendell is not dead. It is said in our stories that is one thing their magic cannot overcome."

"As far as I understand it, he wasn't truly dead," I said. "Not by our mortal definition, anyway. The spirits of the Folk do not depart immediately, but linger for a time in some in-between realm. It is only for that reason that the housekeeper was able to recover him."

Lilja nodded peaceably—I don't think she found this particularly helpful. "A good subject for one of your papers," she said.

I gave a soft laugh. "Yes."

Lilja poured me another cup of tea. "How long will you stay?"

"As long as it takes me to solve this," I said.

They exchanged another look. "What do you need to solve?" Margret said. "This Queen Arna is dead. I agree with Wendell on that—she deserved no better fate, and perhaps a worse one."

"No," I said. "Something is wrong. In every version of 'King Macan's Bees,' the second king is punished for murdering the first. It has become more and more clear to me that Wendell is caught in that same pattern—too many details parallel the Macan story. Our plan to murder the queen was always the wrong one, much as I cannot see what else we could have done. Stories are the architecture of Faerie, more powerful than magic, more powerful than kings."

"I thought you said there was one with a happy ending," Lilja said.

I rubbed my eyes. "Yes. There is *one* version of 'King Macan's Bees' wherein the first king dies and the second king and his mortal wife live happily ever after. But even that—I don't know. There is something off about it. I wonder if perhaps it was mistranslated."

Lilja was nodding. "Or someone's grandfather decided it

needed a better ending. That's what my *afi* would do. He loved all the old tales of the tall ones, but if it ended in misery and suffering, he would change it. That drove my mother mad—'disrespectful,' she called him. Yet we mortals can change those old stories, can't we?"

I thought of my own grandfather, left to die upon a lonely heath by his faerie love. "Sometimes we can," I said. "If we are not ensnared ourselves."

I shook off my dark thoughts. "In any case, I can think better here, without distractions. And Wendell—well, he will only argue with me. We do not see eye to eye on this."

"Are you certain you cannot convince him?" Margret said.

I didn't need to think about it. "Yes."

Lilja nodded, frowning. "I would not want to be on his bad side," she said slowly. "I know you believe he is different from the king of our tall ones. But there have been moments—only a few, mind—when I am not so certain."

I had no answer to this, and we drank our tea in silence. Shadow, stretched out by the fire, grunted and bared his teeth in his sleep, likely dreaming of rabbits.

"Can we help?" Margret said. "I am slow at reading English, especially the writings of scholars. But perhaps we will notice details you miss."

I looked at them, both smiling at me encouragingly, and felt the knots inside me loosen, just a little. "Thank you," I said. "I—I would be very grateful to have your help."

When I was at Trinity in January, I collected several dozen iterations of "King Macan's Bees," all of which I brought with me to Corbann. Most I had copied myself, which meant that Lilja and Margret were frequently asking me to translate my inelegant scrawl.

After two or three hours, I rose to pace by a window, scowling down at my notes. Lilja stretched and stood. Margret was in the kitchen, attending to the bread she was baking for lunch.

"I need to rest my eyes," Lilja said. "Would you care to see my progress on the carving?"

I would have preferred to continue my work, but felt it would be boorish to say no, so I followed her to her workshop.

"Wonderful!" I cried. She had nearly finished the carving of Poe—only his feet remained. His fingers were perhaps not quite as long and sharp as they are in reality, but then it is difficult to do justice to such a thing without the aid of enchantment. I looked up to find Lilja regarding me.

"It is good to see you in your old clothes," she said, smiling. "I did not wish to criticize, for you looked lovely in those faerie dresses. But I had the sense that they were not very comfortable."

I gave a short laugh. "That is an understatement. Though I should note that the dresses were quite comfortable in the ordinary sense. It is more that *I* was not comfortable in them."

She tilted her head. "Then why bother? Are you not a queen of Faerie, to dress as you please?"

I toyed with Poe's needle-fingers, wondering how to respond. Yes, I was a queen of Faerie—and I wished to appear so. To match. For where had I ever matched before? At Cambridge, yes—I matched with the old stones, and the dusty libraries. I suppose that, in Faerie, I had wished to match with the Folk. A foolish aim indeed! I wondered at myself now. Yet I suppose that one cannot spend one's life half in love with Faerie without wishing to be part of it, to wonder if it might feel like home in a way no mortal place ever had.

Instead of burdening Lilja with all this, I simply said, "The Folk love glamour and beauty."

Lilja nodded thoughtfully. "I suppose. Although in our stories, they love—what is the word in English? Misfits? Yes, they love misfits just as well. Hermits and tinkers, wanderers and poets—more tales revolve around such people than the glamourous ones. Is this only in Ljosland?"

"Misfits?" I echoed, smiling slightly. "No—it is not only there."

Lilja shrugged. "Well—you know the Folk best." She turned to show me another carving, and then Margret called from the kitchen that lunch was ready, sparing me from further rumination.

As the afternoon advanced, I was startled out of my perusal of a story fragment by a knock at the door. To my astonishment, it was Niamh. At her side was a strange little grinning woman I recognized as her spriggan attendant, under a glamour.

"He sent you to spy on me," I said.

Niamh shrugged. "Of course."

I groaned. Lilja came to the door then, followed by Margret, and gave a delighted cry to find Niamh there, whom I had told them so much about. This was followed by a round of introductions, as well as the usual commiserations about the weather and offers of refreshments, and together we retreated inside to the kitchen.

"You needn't have bothered to close that faerie door," Niamh said once we were settled with coffee and some of Margret's spiced bread in front of us. "There is another not far from the castle that opens onto a village on the coast called Dunmare. The journey to Corbann took me two hours."

"I surmised as much," I said. "But I did not want to make it easy for him to follow me. I wished to emphasize my desire to be left alone."

"Oh, he has well understood that!" she said with one of

her heartiest laughs. "I have never known him in such a state. He alternates between declarations that he will set forth after you without delay—armed with numerous silly presents to convince you to return—and moaning that you will only burn him to cinders for his presumption. I believe he has worn several grooves in the castle floor from all the pacing he does, and he routinely terrifies the servants by snatching dustcloths and scrubbing at things himself, or refusing to let the tailors mend his clothes—he is up half the night, hunched over those sewing needles of his."

I put my head in my hands. "I feel terrible," I said honestly. "I did not realize that I would be away so long, by his reckoning. He must think I am furious with him."

Niamh waved this away. "The Folk, most especially the nobility, can endure a little disappointment in love now and then. It is good for them, for they are far too used to getting their way on that front. Anyway! He told me to pretend that I wanted to aid in your scholarly research—which is, in fact, very much my desire; I have no intention of sending back any reports about you."

"You may rethink that," I said, and explained the nature of my disagreement with Wendell.

"Ah," she said, nodding calmly. "It was a grim fate Liath doomed his stepmother to. I would not be surprised if there are consequences."

I let out a slow breath. "I was worried you would take his side."

"Whatever for?"

"I don't know," I said. "I suppose because I have no actual evidence to support my concerns. Only an—an instinct."

"*Instinct* is often all we dryadologists have to go on," Niamh said. "Ours is one of the least-understood fields of scientific study."

I shook my head. "It is unscientific to rely on gut feelings. Wendell was right in refusing to release his stepmother."

Niamh gave a bark of laughter. "Emily, the king is behaving exactly like every faerie monarch in every story. He will do as he pleases, particularly if that pleasure involves some nasty form of revenge, and pretend as if *consequences* is not a word that exists in Faie. This is why their realms are so often in chaos, governed by patterns and cycles from which they cannot escape, despite all their magics. It is plain to any dryadologist worth their salt, but he cannot see it, because it is not in his nature. We must help him in this, you and I."

And just like that, I had three assistants, one of them a celebrated expert in Irish folklore.

Niamh had brought her own stack of books, and together we settled in for a day of research. Lilja had been examining what she termed "the Macan story with the happy ending," which was contained within a Victorian anthology of tales from Ireland's southwest, paired with scholarly commentary.* After another hour or so, she handed me the book, saying, "What do you think about this one?"

I glanced at the page. "That's a story fragment—the early Victorian dryadologists loved collecting such scraps of faerie lore, mostly from decaying Dark Age manuscripts, and putting them together like puzzle pieces. It was a popular pastime for a decade or two. Little of scientific value came of it."

"Really?" Lilja said. "Because there's a footnote—Professor Smith thought this was the true conclusion of the Macan story, though no names are given to the protagonists."

"What?" I snatched the book away from her and scanned the page. She was right—ordinarily I read footnotes, but in my haste, I had ignored most of Smith's.

---

* Dr. Enid Smith, *Folk Legends and Wonder-Tales of the Irish Peasantry*, 1812.

"Bloody footnotes!" I muttered.

After considering Dr. Smith's reasoning, and cross-referencing the fragment with another version of the Macan story, I was able to confirm to my own satisfaction that her theory was correct. In the end, we pieced it together, though I almost wish we hadn't. What follows is the second and final act of the "happy" Macan story, or what I have formally termed the Smith variant of "King Macan's Bees." It picks up after the second Macan slays the first.

King Macan the Second ruled for many seasons with his mortal wife, who vastly preferred him to her previous husband, and for a time, all was well. But as the years passed, Macan grew increasingly convinced that he had not, in fact, killed his predecessor. He heard Macan the First's voice in the rustle of the river reeds, and whenever a bee went past, he would say, "There is another servant of the old king, sent to spy on me."

Macan's wife grew worried about him, and so she tried to prove that Macan the First was, indeed, dead. She brought her new husband several of her old husband's teeth, which were all that remained of his body, and even took to wearing them about her neck, so that Macan might remember each time he looked at her. At first he was soothed, but then he said, "And yet, cannot a man live without his teeth? This proves nothing." She then captured several bees and commanded them to speak, so that they might tell her husband they were not spies, merely the last of the summer honeybees. But the king only praised them as excellent liars, and ordered his servants to kill every bee in the mound. Now, one cannot kill every insect in any place, and thus the only result was that the bees grew to hate the new Macan, and took every opportunity to sting him. This only solidified his belief that the old Macan lived, and had sent his servants to torment him.

Eventually, Macan the Second grew so terrified of the dead king that he began to suspect that every visitor, no matter how humble, was in league with Macan the First. Initially, he turned them away, but his wife was afraid of the old laws and ordered that every wayfarer be welcomed into the castle. Unbeknownst to her, Macan the Second had each guest slain in the night, then ordered the servants to tell his wife that they had decided to leave early.

When eventually his wife learned the truth, it was too late; she had grown old, despite the magics the king had employed to slow her decline, and she no longer had the strength of mind to alter the currents of the king's humours. One morning, he woke to find her cold at his side. King Macan's grief only worsened his paranoia, and he became convinced that his wife had died not of her own mortality, but from some poison administered by Macan the First or his allies.

The more guests King Macan killed, the more he came to enjoy the game of it; he liked playing the role of dutiful host, spoiling his guests, only to find novel ways of killing them ere the morning came. He began not only welcoming visitors but luring them in, using all manner of faerie tricks to entice mortals and wandering Folk to his castle, telling himself each time that they were spies of Macan the First, and thus deserving of their fate. He also had many of his servants and relations executed, until all but the stupidest and the most depraved dared remain at his side. The forest, poisoned by the king's enmity, withered as the years passed, and the river dried up, and all small Folk perished or fled.

Thus the realm of Macan the Second became a cold place, cruel and desolate, like so much of Faerie. And if any mortal should stumble into King Macan's mound, they must go back the way they came, and ignore the tempting lights of the castle, lest they remain there evermore.

After I pieced the story together and smoothed the edges, I gave it to Lilja to read first. She was quiet for a long moment afterwards, and then said, "This is what will happen to him?"

"I doubt Wendell's story will follow precisely the same course as Macan the Second's," I said. "But yes, I think it quite likely that this act of vengeance towards his stepmother has set Wendell—and the realm itself—upon some path to ruin. Perhaps it will lead to madness; probably he will grow more and more vengeful, finding excuses to hurl *other* enemies into the Veil. It is also possible that Wendell's story will play out differently, and he may escape Macan the Second's fate."

"But you do not think so," Margret said, watching me.

I made no reply, and Lilja nodded grimly. "What is to be done?" she said.

"We must change the story somehow," I said. "I have found a version of the Macan story that has given me an idea—in it, the mortal queen seeks aid from the boggart, asking him to heal the bee stings inflicted upon the second Macan. The boggart refuses her, but it makes me think: perhaps I should consult with the creature. Who can say what insight he may possess? He has known Wendell's family for generations."

Niamh leaned back in her chair, folding her arms with a slight huff. I waited, recognizing this as a universal precursor of scholarly objection.

"You place too much importance on the Macan story," she said bluntly.

"Too much!" I exclaimed. "Has it not been remarkably predictive? The three servants, the second castle—"

"I do not deny its usefulness," Niamh said, "but attending too closely to a single story to understand a Faerie realm or its Folk is, as Bennett has argued, fruitless parochialism. Do dryadologists these days ignore his treatise on comparative histories?* We must look for *patterns*."

I digested this. "Very well," I said, leaning back in my own chair. "What pattern do you see?"

"A great many—I have, after all, spent years immersed in the folklore of this part of the world," she said. "One might say I have *become* the folklore now—ha! But one element in particular stands out. You are not going to like it."

"Go on."

"A great deal of the tales concerning the Irish Folk centre on the heroism of ordinary mortals," she said. "I can think of five originating in County Leane alone in which a mortal travels to a foul realm to rescue some faerie lord or lady who is held prisoner thereat. And this is just off the top of my head. Imprisonment, rescue, a journey into darkness—you see it everywhere, even in the most ancient of tales."

"But Wendell does not need rescuing," Lilja said. "You've already rescued him. Or that housekeeper did."

"She doesn't mean Wendell," I murmured, gazing at Niamh. I could see only one way to interpret what she was saying.

She tapped her fingers against her cup and eventually added, as the silence stretched on, "I warned you that you wouldn't like it."

"Then I must rescue Wendell's stepmother," I said. "Well, no difficulty there. I shall simply march off to the Veil and do it now."

---

* Francis Bennett, *A Protohistorical Approach to Folk-Lore*, 1849.

"*Could* you?" Margret said, looking horrified.

"Your cloak," Lilja said.

I shook my head. "Wendell removed the piece of the Veil from my cloak. He was afraid his stepmother might escape through it."

We had another moment of silence, mulling over the image of a deranged faerie queen creeping out of my hem.

"Is there a door?" Margret said. "Like the other faerie doors, perhaps?"

Niamh was already shaking her head. "There are no doors to the Veil, and no paths. Only a monarch of Faerie can summon an edge of it, through which one may pass. Thank God for that—it is a hellscape, a wasted desert of nightmares." She paused, a longing look stealing over her face. "Also enormously fascinating, from a scholarly perspective."

"Only a monarch," I murmured. A terrible realization settled over me like a layer of frost. "Yes—I recall Wendell saying that."

Lilja's eyes widened. "I see what you are thinking," she said. "*You* are a monarch of Faerie! Does this mean you can find a way there yourself?"

"That is not what I was thinking," I said slowly. "I am a monarch, yes, but I am mortal. Look at Queen Arna herself—she cannot escape the Veil, despite her royal title; it must be because of her mortal blood. No—to rescue Queen Arna, I would need the assistance of a faerie monarch. Not a mortal, nor a halfblood."

Niamh shook her head. "Liath will not release his stepmother. He is adamant on that subject."

I gazed at them, wondering how on earth I could convince them of my sanity after what I was about to say. I have my own doubts on that score, I'm afraid. But what else am I to do?

What other avenue is there? And indeed, there is a neatness to it—a return to a beginning.

It is madness in every other respect, of course.

"Wendell is not the only faerie king of my acquaintance," I said.

8th February–very late

Ah, I am weary. Ordinarily my field studies give me plenty of cause to go wandering in various forms of wilderness, but I have not had much reason for exercise since our stay in Austria. Only a short entry this time, and then sleep.

I departed the cottage with Shadow as soon as there was light enough to see my way. With me I brought nothing but the necessities: my journal, pen and pencil, Wendell's letters, a little water and food, and snowshoes. These last I borrowed from Lilja and Margret, along with a pack. They wished to accompany me at least part of the way, but I said no.

"I will travel no faster with company, and possibly more slowly," I said. "And as I have said, this could be a pointless endeavour. I may just have to come back."

Eventually, they relented, and Margret allowed me to hug her goodbye. At first I thought Lilja would not forgive me, for she left the room without another word, wiping tears from her face. But Margret went after her, and after a few moments they returned together.

"I wish you would reconsider," Lilja said, her voice still teary as she hugged me tightly.

"I'm sorry" was the only answer I could give her. I did not

see any way to heal the rift between us, so I turned away before my own tears could fall.

"Take plenty of notes," Niamh said by way of goodbye. And with that, Shadow and I left them.

I had not wanted to bring my faithful beast with me. Rather, I *had* wanted him with me, but I had not wanted to burden him with such a dangerous and wearying quest. But I do not think Shadow would have countenanced being left behind again, not after Austria. Indeed, he seemed to sense what I was about, and was stretched out in front of the door this morning, watching me with a look he might have borrowed from Orga, it was so judgmental. I knelt to rub his face and assure him that I would not be leaving him, and once he understood I was earnest, he rose to cover my face in slobber.

I had hoped to reach the mountain before nightfall, but the short winter days and Shadow's deteriorated fitness—as well as my own—proved significant hindrances. The English translation for its name is, ominously, The Bones, and it is the highest mountain in County Leane, in addition to being the only peak high enough to receive a winter snowfall of any significance. The route there is deceptively straightforward from Lilja and Margret's cottage, merely a pathless expanse of hilly moor, but when one actually attempts it, one finds oneself constantly at war with heather and other bristling shrubs, as well as patches of boggy wet where the sunlight has struggled through the vegetation, and treacherous ice where it has not.

I made camp last night around suppertime, having only reached the base of The Bones, because it had grown too dark to see my way. The mountains at my back were sharp as broken teeth against the starry winter sky, and my breath rose about me in clouds.

I removed my cloak and gave it a shake, as I'd watched Wendell do, and when I released it, the thing transformed into a tent, complete with blankets and an altogether silly number of pillows. Once I was settled, I lit a candle and read the first of Wendell's letters.

> To: Dr. Emily Wilde
> Sruth Cottage, Old Road
> Corbann
>
> From: Wendell Bambleby
> Faerie via Dunmare
>
> Dearest Emily,
> It has been more than a day since you left. You see I have refrained from writing immediately, just as I have refrained from following you. Please tell me that you have forgiven me! Yes, you are using your research as an excuse to go away, but I know that you are, in fact, angry that I have not freed my stepmother. Em, when I promised to grant your every wish, should it be within my power, perhaps I should have specified that wishes of a suicidal nature are to be excepted. I know my stepmother; she shall never leave off seeking power, and it is you she will now see as her greatest enemy, not me. You cannot make a pet of her, as you have other faerie monsters, for she is wily beyond measure, and will find a way to escape any cage. She is probably dead by now anyway—the Veil is a terrible place.
> I cannot help thinking—for that is all I have done since you have left, mull over every word and glance that passed between us when we were last together—that there is another reason you asked me to spare my stepmother. You wish to interview her for your book, don't you? Em, there are villains enough in every corner of my realm for you to interrogate. Come home, and allow me to round up a few. The hag-headed deer have a queen, you know.

Terrible Folk, the Deer. And not one scholar has ever laid eyes upon them.

Yours eternally,
Wendell

"That is unfair!" I exclaimed to the letter. Now, if I *had* gone away from him in a fit of pique, this indeed may have lured me back, as he clearly knew. I had mentioned to him more than once in passing that these hag-headed deer, mysterious as their ways are even to the rest of the Folk, were a subject of particular interest to me. And they had their own court within Wendell's realm, did they? I had never heard of such a thing.

Shaking my head, I turned to the next letter.

To: Dr. Emily Wilde
Sruth Cottage, Old Road
Corbann

From: Wendell Bambleby
Faerie via Dunmare

Dearest Emily,
I had the most intriguing conversation today with the boggart. He has witnessed the reigns of several of my ancestors, you know, and has all sorts of opinions about them. One can trace the building of this castle, the construction of the paths and barrows, the alliances and power struggles between this lord or that lady, through his reminiscences, if he is in the mood for talk. Indeed I have never met an individual in possession of so many stories about our realm, excepting perhaps my churlish uncle. Who knows how long we may have access to his wisdom, for boggarts spend so much of their time asleep, and are near impossible to

wake even if you are a king of Faerie; he may decide to take a nap tomorrow, for all I know, which will last the next decade or more. Please come home soon, or send me a letter, at least.

Love always,
Wendell

"I see what you are doing," I muttered. "You needn't be so obvious about it."

>To: Dr. Emily Wilde
>Sruth Cottage, Old Road
>Corbann
>
>From: Wendell Bambleby
>Faerie via Dunmare

Dearest Emily,
It has been three days since you went away! This morning I decided I'd had enough and made ready to set off after you, if only to plead my case. But then I was struck by a dreadful vision of each time you had glared at me for poking my head into your office at Cambridge, interrupting your fiendish clacking at your typewriter, and I felt my heart fail me. A hundred Emilys, all glowering away, and still this, I think, would be a warmer welcome than the one I would receive for interrupting your research in Corbann after you expressly told me not to.

And yet I believe I shall have to brave it. Oh, it is wonderful to be home again—I would never deny that; I find my realm even more lovely, more perfectly suited to happiness and comfort, than even I remembered it. Truly, I pity Folk who live elsewhere, for there can be nothing that rivals the beauty of these forests and hills. And so, Em, when I say that I am wretchedly ill at ease without your company, that I feel as if I am missing a limb, that I cannot be content even amidst the wonder of my realm, you will understand the depth of my feelings. Surely you must miss me a little as well? I know your heart by now, Em; it is not all stone and pencil shavings, as you are wont to pretend.

Perhaps I will come to Corbann tomorrow. If you will not at least write, I don't think you can roast me for interrupting your labours. Or can you?

All my love,
Wendell

The rest of the letters continued in this vein, alternating between complaints, entreaties, and various attempts to bribe me into returning, generally by dangling some scientific discovery before me. I put them beneath my pillow, cursing him for his histrionics, and also for the effect they had upon me. That I should feel guilty for leaving him, when I had done so only to attempt, yet again, to save his ridiculous neck! I punched the pillow several times, then attempted to sleep, then dragged the letters out to read them again.

I worried I might have some trouble with bogles in the night, for I had noted several faint trails and holes in the ground that reminded me of the terrain below the boggart's tower, as well as one of their discarded cookpots. But Shadow and I were left alone, and enjoyed a surprisingly restful sleep.

Lilja and Margret had told me there was a rambler's path up The Bones from the eastward side, and I was relieved to come upon it without much trouble. The going was much easier after that, despite the steepness of the ascent, and we reached the snowpack by late afternoon.

I allowed myself a rest at that point, for I was sweating despite the cold gusts that swept across the height, and my legs protested the haste with which I had made the climb. Shadow had matched my pace throughout the day, hobbling along determinedly at my heels, and now he lay at my side with his paws on my leg, panting but still alert, as if determined to prove me right in bringing him along. I drank from my flask and ate a little bread, and slowly the pounding in my head subsided. I would have liked to admire the view, for I was half encircled by mountains, the land in the other direction tumbling down to green heathland and the village of Corbann, shrunk to tiny squares of white. However, there was something particularly precarious about the place, the mountain flank steep and slippery with scree that made me quake imagining the return journey. I had the sense that few ramblers ever came this way, and I wondered if this was owing to the pitiless wind, which nearly knocked me over when I tried to stand, or some faerie beast that haunted the place. Either way, I had little desire to linger.

My fingers trembled lightly as I withdrew the pendant I always wore from beneath my collar. It was a small coil of bone as far from key-shaped as possible, and yet that was precisely what it was.

I had no idea if my plan would work. I had to be in the winterlands to use Poe's door—did this place count? It certainly had more winter in it than anyplace else in the vicinity of Wendell's realm, and was far less hospitable, a characteristic shared by all places called *winterland* I'd yet encountered.

I held the key before me, pressed between my thumb and forefinger, and made my way up the snowy slope, feeling alternately hopeful and extremely foolish, particularly whenever my foot slipped and I was nearly sent tumbling back down the mountain. I wondered dolefully if anybody in the village would see me, a tiny speck, if I was to fall to my death, or if I would simply become another mysterious disappearance to add to the dryadology annals. What an inconvenient time to meet my end, given all that I was in the middle of! But then, what person who meets an untimely end is *not* in the middle of their own to-do list, all of which simply turns to dust after, whether the items consist of mundane errands or the preservation of a faerie kingdom.

I was wrapped up in morose thoughts of this nature when my foot slipped—not on ice; it felt as if the mountain slope itself shifted by a fraction of a degree. I stumbled forward, catching myself just in time, and when I looked up, I was no longer in Ireland.

There was the familiar spring, bubbling away, plumes of sulphurous mist dancing over the surface. There was the grove of trees at the edge of the forest, stunted by their northerly latitude, there the view of the winter-dark sea choked with ice.

I allowed my lightheadedness to overtake me, and sank to my knees upon the snow. Shadow, who had been close at my heels, sat beside me with a huff. For some reason, perhaps because I had been hunched forward for the last several hours, fighting the pull of gravity at my back, I still felt I could at any moment go tumbling down from a height.

I began to laugh. I was as lighthearted, in that moment, as if my quest were over, when in fact it had only begun. I looked about for Poe. His aspen was as fine as ever, its bark as pure a white as if someone had polished away any imperfections, and it was in leaf despite the season. A thin wisp of smoke drifted from one of the knotholes, and the winter glade smelled of baking bread. One of the villagers—Finn, I guessed—had cleared a little path in the snow from Poe's tree to the spring.

Something made my gaze drift upwards, and I realized there was a face directly above me, peering down, belonging to a creature who sat perfectly still upon a bare bough. It was perhaps two foot in height, the grey face of a skeleton with an overlarge mouth and glistening needle-teeth, which were bared in my direction. In spite of its face, its body was quite fat, and was wrapped in something that resembled several stitched-together owl carcasses, poorly cleaned. Its fingers dangled from either side of the branch like thin black rapiers, ending in deadly points, twice as long as the faerie was tall.

I stared.

The thing stared back.

When it began to emit a horrifying hissing sound, like a rusted-out kettle boiling over, I screamed—most unlike me. Ordinarily I am better at controlling my nerves around the Folk, even such Folk as this, but the thing's appearance was so hideous and so unexpected in this place where I had thought to find only an old friend.

I staggered back and nearly fell into the hot spring, my hands slamming painfully against the warm, wet stones that lined the perimeter. The creature swayed in the boughs as if gathering itself to pounce, and I drew in my breath to shout the Word—the one that granted a temporary invisibility, that is, not the one for lost buttons. I did not know if it would save me, but it would confuse the thing, and perhaps that would give me time to come up with something else. Shadow placed himself in front of me, growling—I'm not sure he could make out the beast in the tree, nearsighted as he is, but he readied himself nevertheless to challenge whatever had alarmed me.

Into this charged tableau came Poe, emerging from his tree-home with a teetering basket of iced cakes in his arms. He gave me a wide grin of welcome, looking pleased and not at all surprised by my arrival.

"I saw you from the window," he said, taking no notice of the hissing monstrosity above us. "Fortunately, I just finished the day's baking, so everything is still warm."

"There," I said, unable to be more articulate as I pointed with a shaking hand.

He glanced up. "Oh, yes!" he exclaimed happily. "Mother is visiting!"

"Good God" was all I could say in response.

Hsssssshaaaa, said the thing in the tree.

"That," I said, when at last my heart had slowed somewhat, "is your mother?"

Poe handed me the basket of cakes and tugged at the hem of my cloak, his small face alight with happiness. "How wonderful! All my family is here together. Almost all. Where is the golden prince? He is not ill again?"

It was just like the little brownie to accept my sudden appearance as perfectly expected; it has been some months since we have seen each other, and yet to him it is ever as if a mere day has passed. The cakes smelled of apple and peppery spices, and I took one without eating it; my stomach was still unsettled from my fright.

"Wendell is quite well," I said unsteadily. "But he is busy with his kingdom. He sends his regrets that he could not be here."

Poe looked simultaneously relieved and astonished. "Really? Oh, but he does not need to visit—though of course I would be honoured," he added hastily. "As would Mother! She could hardly believe it when I told her that we could count a lord of Faerie among our *fjolskylda.*"

What Poe's mother truly thought of her royal family member, I never knew, for the only reply from the tree was a tetchy sort of growl. I looked up, and found that she had vanished.

"She likes to stand guard over my home," Poe said contentedly. "For she agrees that my tree is the finest in the forest, even finer than the lovely willow in whose bole I was born and raised, and she fears that some jealous enemy may vandalize it. I do not think this likely, do you? For even if I *had* enemies—and I hope I do not, for I always go away and hide when someone wants to argue with me—they would only fall in love with my tree straightaway, and be unable to put even one scratch on it."

I suppressed an urge to look about to determine where exactly his mother had got to. "She has—very long fingers."

"Oh, yes," Poe said. He glanced down at his own needle-fingers, which were also lengthy, though nowhere near the size of his dam's. "Mother is old. I hope one day that mine will be as bountiful as hers, but Mother says I should not wish for things that may never come to pass, but be content with what I have today. She can spear a seal with one thumb, which would be useful, wouldn't it?"

I could not begin to formulate a reply to this, so instead I said, "I have come on an errand for Wendell. An urgent one. I would appreciate your assistance, as would he."

Poe looked suddenly terrified. "Yes—yes. Oh, is he wondering about my tree? I watered it all summer, and I have collected any leaves that fell—I keep them in a very safe place!"

"Wendell is confident in your skills as the tree's custodian," I assured him. "I have come—" I could not get it out at first. "I have come to speak with the king."

Poe's eyes had gone perfectly round. "Oh, but—" He fell back a step, vanishing abruptly into the snow, then reappearing closer to his tree. "But you must not," he said in a low, desperate voice. "He is worse, far worse than the golden prince. I mean—" Terror filled his face again. "I did not mean that! The prince is so very noble and kind, and his attentions to my tree have—"

"Shh, it's all right," I said soothingly. "It's all right. You need not worry about Wendell. And as for the snow king, I will go alone to beg an audience; you need not accompany me. I only wish to learn his whereabouts."

Poe was shivering. "I don't know," he said in an unhappy voice. "The high ones travel hither and thither in their carriages, and at night I have heard their voices singing from the deep places of the forest and upon the mountain peaks. But the king and his court come only rarely to the coast. They prefer the glaciers and snowfields."

I felt a stab of disappointment, but tried to conceal it. I should not have expected Poe to know the whereabouts of the Hidden king. Perhaps the villagers of Hrafnsvik could help me—I owed a visit to Aud, in any case.

"They leave offerings at the king's tree," Poe said, after a moment's silence. "The mortals do. They leave them, and someone takes them away."

"The tree," I said.

9th February

I slept surprisingly well in my tent after my arrival at my new campsite, despite the unwholesome atmosphere. Now, with the morning sunlight falling upon these pages, veined with birch-shadow, I feel I can continue my account of the journey, even as every rustle of the wind through the branches makes me start and whirl around, my pulse leaping in my throat.

He will come. Won't he?

Despite my weariness after my trek up the mountain, I wished to depart Poe's grove immediately, but he first insisted on showing me several adornments he had added to his tree. His visitors have included a variety of migratory birds, and so he has taken the finest of their fallen feathers and hung them from the boughs with a bit of twine, sometimes adding small rocks and jewels left as offerings for him by the villagers, which together make a pleasant clinking sound when the wind moves through them. He then gifted me a fine loaf of bread woven through with the Ljosland sheep's cheese of which I am so fond, in addition to the cakes. Thus supplied, I donned my snowshoes and ventured forth into the darkening woods.

I worried I would not remember the way to the Hidden

king's tree. After all, I had ventured there only twice during my stay in Ljosland. But my scholarship saved me, for I had drawn a map to accompany a recent paper I wrote on the subject, and the memory was still fresh in my mind. I first located the river upon whose bank the tree could be found, which I followed downstream for several hours until I spied the elbow bend.

I did not recall the forest of Kyrrðarskogur being such an eerie place—perhaps it was because the first time I'd come this way, I had been with Wendell, who had kept up such a steady stream of complaints it had deadened any otherworldly atmosphere, and the second time I had been in such a state of dread and pain that I'd paid no heed to anything else. The river whispered beneath its prison of ice, and the violet glow of twilight painted unexpected shadows upon the snow. The forest had the same brooding quality all forests possess in winter, and was alive with small noises—some fae, some not—but when night fell and the green aurora began to ripple behind the boughs like the spectral twin of the river I was tracking, it assumed a distinctly unwelcoming quality. I was an interloper in this inhuman landscape, and were I less learned, and not in possession of an enchanted cloak, it would not have taken some faerie beast to end me, merely the fact of the place itself.

And then we came to the tree.

It looked as I'd last seen it, its trunk white as bone and split open in a long seam, the edges folded slightly like the lapels of a cloak. Not one leaf remained to hide the twisted branches, which were immensely tall and wide, encompassing a far greater share of the canopy than seemed correct, given the narrowness of the hollow trunk, which was only large enough to encompass a single person. As before, I had the sense that the other trees had shuffled backwards to get away from the thing, for a ring of starry, emerald-smudged sky was visible beyond the tips of its branches.

Shadow sniffed the air, looking alert, but he did not whine or show any other sign of distress, as he'd done during our first visit to this place. I saw no evidence of faerie activity, nor of the offerings Poe had mentioned. I saw no footprints, either, though perhaps the inhabitants of Hrafnsvik and the neighbouring villages had not left anything for the Hidden king since the last snowfall.

I did not step inside the tree, which struck me as more likely to end badly than not, but I did venture a wan "Hello there!" or two in the hopes of drawing out any faerie observers. I received no answer. The place was still and silent.

I removed my cloak and shook it until it transformed into a tent again, then rummaged about in the folds, wondering if Wendell had thought to supply it with other camping essentials, and naturally I was not disappointed. I found several pegs for securing the structure to the ground in high winds, yet more pillows of different shapes and sizes (good grief), a small cookpot, and, at last, tucked into a fold I was certain I'd searched before, a piece of flint.

I gathered a few fallen branches and built a fire that I hoped was a respectful distance from the king's tree. Shadow's dinner was dried meat and melted snow, while for my own repast I toasted some of Poe's bread over the flames, pairing it with the last apple I had brought with me from Lilja and Margret's cottage. And then, the winter king showing no sign of materializing in my midst, I went to bed.

9th February—late

Well! Shadow and I have spent the day alone, and night closes in again. We will depart tomorrow morning, I think, for it seems unproductive to linger in this desolate wood any longer. Perhaps neither the king nor his servants visit the tree anymore, and it is some bogle or brownie who makes off with the villagers' offerings.

I confess it is not only practical considerations that make me wish to depart. This is an unpleasant place to linger alone. The air has a heaviness that I have found, as the hours pass, increasingly easy to associate with malice. I am frequently reminded that the Hidden king was trapped here for centuries—has the tree somehow retained a memory of his fury and despair? More and more does its trunk seem to resemble a gaping maw frozen in an eternal scream.

Not only that, but I grow increasingly convinced that there are voices coming from the tree. I cannot make out what they are saying, for they speak in echoing whispers, as if their words have travelled a great distance, but I am certain that it is Faie. I have spoken to the tree—because why not speak to the thing; it is so uncanny—explaining that I am the snow king's former fiancée (God) come to seek a favour. Naturally I have also given him many compliments, explaining that I would not have presumed to trespass upon his domain had I not been certain of his kindness and magnanimity. I am not at all convinced this will suffice to save me from meeting an unpleasant end. After all, the king was told I was dead, and few faerie lords respond well to being tricked.

Enough with these ruminations! I have done too much of that today, as well as fret about Wendell being upset with me, which is not a subject I recall devoting much attention to in the past. I have read his letters perhaps a dozen times—well, what else is there to do in this haunted place?

Perhaps I should scratch that out. He would never leave off teasing me.

I will attempt to sleep. I can only hope the bloody tree allows it—I hear it now, whispering inside its shadowy recess. God knows what it is saying.

11th February

The next morning I awoke to the certainty that something terrible had happened. It was an odd feeling, like waking from a nightmare, without the relief that consciousness ordinarily supplies. Shadow was sitting up, staring silently at the tent flap, his body one long line of tension.

I unbuttoned the flap—it took me several tries, for my hands were shaking. The Hidden king stood just outside.

He was as magnificent and terrible to behold as I remembered. His hair shone like dark jewels, his face all sharp lines, each at precisely the correct angle for beauty. He wore his white crown, shards of ice coated in frost, his necklaces were of jet and opal and sapphire, and over his black silk tunic and boots of pale reindeer leather he wore a fur cloak—Arctic fox, by the look of it. Held loosely in his hand was an enormous sword, unsheathed and glittering. There were pearls woven into his hair.

"Have you come to kill me?" I said. My voice was so hoarse I am surprised he heard; it seemed to have been carried off on the cloud of breath that rose before me.

He pursed his full lips, looking regretful. "Indeed, my dearest. I am sorry it has come to this."

His voice was as lovely as I remembered, rich with an edge of roughness, like the scrape of ice crystals blown by the wind. He'd often seemed to me to have only the most tenuous of connections to the cares of the living, and to be at any moment on the precipice of lifting a hand and sweeping whole villages aside in an avalanche or drowning the country in a days-long blizzard, having no reason at all for doing so, as nature does not, only the purest form of caprice.

"Will you not at least tell me why?" I said.

He looked puzzled—or, rather, he arranged his features into an expression of puzzlement; rarely have I had the sense that he is truly touched by feeling, with the exception of the feral delight I witnessed when his traitorous queen was brought before him.

"I was told you had perished, beloved," he said. "You *should* have perished when you fled my court—how could a mortal girl survive my winter, unless she was in league with the queen and my other enemies?" He examined me. "But first, I wish to know how you escaped, for I am very curious."

I clenched the coin in my pocket—not to ward him off, I am not so foolish as that, but merely because the habit was steadying. "Perhaps I will not tell you," I said.

He gave the faintest of shrugs. "You shall eventually."

I forced myself not to flinch at that. I had never been comfortable in his presence—how could I be?—but I was even less so now, for I was not swathed in enchantment that wore away my fear and memories, as I had been in his court. He stared back at me, and in his eyes I saw only winter, its power and indifference.

Fortunately, my mind had not been idle during the long trek through the Irish countryside and up to the peak, nor during the hours I'd sat in that winter forest. I had surmised that he would think me a traitor and wish to kill me—though naturally I'd hoped to avoid such a circumstance.

I burst into tears.

Or, at least, I gave it my best effort. I made a great deal of noise, certainly, and I screwed my face up into what I hoped was a convincing expression, but I have never been much of a crier, and crying upon command is simply a lost cause, even with my life at risk. Fortunately, the cold made my nose run, so that part at least was authentic.

When I looked up, I was pleased to see him eyeing me with something closer to genuine puzzlement, his lip slightly curled—on account of the snot, most likely.

"Forgive me, Your Highness," I bawled. "But I did not wish to leave you. He"—another snuffly inhalation before I burst out—"he forced me to marry him! He stole me away to his dreadful kingdom, which is so wet and dark, and smells of green, rotting things, nothing like the loveliness of your court. I have only now managed to escape, and you must help me get my revenge—you must! Please, I beg of you. I have—I have longed for you every day."

Ordinarily, my acting skills are dreadful, but fortunately I was in such terror of him that simply dwelling upon my very real emotion sufficed to send me into convincing hysterics. And, as I have noted on numerous occasions, the courtly fae think so little of mortals that they are not difficult to lie to, particularly if one frames it as an appeal to their vanity.

"Who is this blackguard you speak of?" he said, almost gently.

"He was a prince when he came to your realm," I said. "An exiled wanderer from the summerlands. Now he has slain his stepmother and taken her throne."

A violent look came over his face. "Him! Yes, the queen's accomplices spoke of him before they were executed. He helped smuggle her into my court the night she attempted to poison me. I scoured my lands, but could find no trace of him, nor could I determine the reason for his interference."

"It was because of me," I said in a miserable voice. "He has always desired to marry me. When he learned I had fallen in love with you, he was very angry."

The king scanned my face. "Indeed?"

I had expected him to doubt me, but something about the polite disbelief in his eyes was a little galling. "He was in love with my sister first," I invented. "She was a great beauty, with a singing voice that could charm the aurora. When an illness took her, it drove him mad, and he swore he would never marry another but her own flesh and blood."

"Ah," the king said. "She had no other siblings?"

I gritted my teeth. "No," I said. "I wish to kill him, but I cannot do it alone. How could a mortal girl overthrow a king of the Folk? His sole equal is his stepmother, and he has imprisoned her in the Veil, over which only monarchs have power."

The king nodded. "You wish for me to summon the Veil so that you may rescue your husband's enemy."

He had understood this part more readily than I had anticipated, and I wondered if there were stories in Ljosland that followed similar patterns to those in Ireland—mortals embarking on impossible quests for the sake of some tragic romance. No doubt there are—scholars have only recently begun to turn their attention to this country.

"Once she kills him," I said, eyeing him in what I hoped was a sufficiently moony way, "and I am made the happiest of widows, I can return here, and we can at last be wed."

He gave a long sigh, tapping his toe against an ice-covered stone. I could see him running through all that had happened and the story I had given him, weaving it into past events like the missing threads in a tapestry, tweaking the pattern here and there as his self-regard dictated. He glanced down at his sword with a considering expression.

And thrust it back into its sheath.

"My darling," he said. "I have married another, for which I offer my humblest apologies. She is a noblewoman as lovely as the winter dawn. I would prefer not to kill her." He frowned, looking only somewhat put out by the idea. "Still, you have first claim upon my hand. I prize loyalty above all things; nothing is more noble."

I did not like the misgiving in his eyes, so I hastened to say, "I am aware the Veil is dangerous. But perhaps you know of other mortals who have gone and returned thence?"

His expression cleared a little. "Oh, no," he said. "A mortal would likely perish within moments of setting foot upon those blasted sands."

I nodded in resignation. "It is as I feared. Still, I must try."

A smile touched the corner of his mouth as he regarded me. "What nobility of character you possess!" he said. "Yes—you would have made a worthy wife."

I was not at all offended to hear him speak of me in the past tense. "Then—you will do as I beg? You will summon the Veil?"

He nodded. "I would not deprive any mortal of such a quest, which I can see is born of loyalty and self-sacrifice." A thought seemed to strike him. "What an endearing ballad this will make! Even the most fearsome among my courtiers will weep to hear it."

"I will make every effort to return to you, my lord," I said. My voice shook, which no doubt he interpreted as passionate feeling.

He made no reply, but stepped close to me, close enough that I could count the white tips of his teeth through his parted lips, trace the bounds of the shadow beneath his fathomless eyes. Some of the pearls in his hair bore traces of their undersea genesis, imperfectly round and flecked with seaweed. I stiffened but managed not to fall back. Shadow growled so low in his throat that I barely heard it, but felt the vibration through the ice and snow.

The Hidden king tilted my chin up and brushed my lips with his, which sent a wave of cold cascading down my throat, as if I had swallowed glacial meltwater. I could smell his scent—no, *scent* is not the right word. The Hidden king has no scent, any more than newly fallen snow has; rather, he carries with him tiny eddies of cold like left-behind scraps of winter storms, which sting the skin and make breathing painful whenever he draws too near.

"Good luck, my dearest," he murmured.

I could not meet his gaze, for it was too terrible to endure at close proximity, but he did not seem to expect this. He stepped back and lifted a hand. Perhaps unsurprisingly, he is less expressive in his gestures than Wendell, who likes to wave his hands about when he does magic in what I have often supposed is an unnecessarily showy way.

Abruptly, a pillar of darkness appeared before us, which was less a pillar than a door that parted the grove, shoving everything to either side. It was a door filled with rippling shadow that I knew—because I had visited that world once, briefly—was wind laced with sand, painfully sharp. I smelled decaying bone, ashes, char.

In the end, I don't think I could have stepped forward into that abyss had I not been so certain the king would have killed me if I turned back. So I suppose I have that to thank him for.

"Come, my love," I said to Shadow. The dog gazed at the Veil with the same vague interest with which he gazed at any faerie door, or at least those that promised a certain variety of smells. This, too, steadied my resolve. I paused only to draw my scarf up over my mouth and nose and excavate a handkerchief with elaborate silver embroidery from my pocket, which I held out for Shadow to smell. It had been Queen Arna's; Niamh had fetched it for me.

I stepped into the Veil with Shadow at my side.

I have never experienced a sandstorm, but I imagine the sensation would be similar. Yet in the Veil, it was less the feeling of sand than of ashes, eternally churned up by a dry, frigid wind. It was strong enough to nearly knock me over, and I adjusted my weight, leaning into it.

Looking around me was futile. The world was too dark to see much, apart from a vague impression of little hills rising about me, and possibly mountains in the distance. I was forced to keep my gaze downturned to protect my eyes from the stinging ashes.

I knew I could not linger long in this place. It was difficult to breathe, for one thing, and already I felt that sting in my exposed skin and extremities that presages frostbite. I made every effort to focus on the mundane details—the sensation of my shoes crunching on the ashy sand, my breath whistling through the fabric of my scarf. Anything to keep my mind off the wasted faerieland unhallowed enough to unnerve even the likes of Lord Taran. For the most part, it worked. Yes, the place was a horror, but it was like any other horror long anticipated—the reality is never a match for the imagined version, and thus comes almost as a relief.

Shadow turned to me. He had shed his glamour and had grown to at least twice his normal size, his snout distended and his ribs poking through his fur. His eyes flickered like embers—quite unnerving, but also helpful, in that context. He threw back his head and let loose a deathly howl.

I became aware that there had been a great many noises I

hadn't initially noticed, but did now, in the contrasting silence that followed Shadow's howl. Skittering, scuttling noises; odd chirps and groans, like some form of prehistoric bird. I saw nothing alive—or did I? For the darkness seemed to twitch, gathering shape and then fading away. I told myself that it was just my eyes playing tricks, but I found no comfort in this.

I clambered onto Shadow's back and wove my fingers through his fur. "Quickly," I managed to choke out. Shadow began to run, so swiftly the uneven, half-seen topography passed in a blur. Each of his strides became a bound, and we covered untold distances. The dog paused to sniff the ground every once in a while and then we were off again, charging headlong through the impressionistic shadowscape. The sky was starry, I think, but it hurt too much to look up at it. Shadow's paws, when they touched ground, often crunched—on what I never did see, nor cared to.

It wasn't long before he found her.

Before us was an odd sort of pillar of rock, all protrusions and jagged edges. Atop it was something that resembled a bundle of rags, but I knew better. Shadow gave a satisfied huff that I recognized, even if it had more of a deathly rattle in it than usual.

"Your Highness," I called, and the bundle of rags stirred. Queen Arna lifted her head and gazed down upon us, incomprehension in her face—what I could see of it. It was not only the darkness that obscured her features, but filth, her skin grey from the ashes, her hair a torn and ragged tangle that made her resemble a doll some child had taken scissors to. She also smelled dreadful, all the more so given the contrast with the uniform scent of desiccation that was all that remained in this world.

She opened her mouth and croaked something, waving her arm. At first I thought she was trying to attract our attention, as if not fully convinced we'd seen her, but then I heard that uncanny chirping sound to my left. Shadow lunged at something I never saw, and there was a louder crunch followed by a sort of whistling sound, as of air funneling through a narrow gap. The darkness twitched all around us and Shadow howled again, a terrible, unending sound that made my mind fill with images of waiting graves.

The darkness was still until the last of the echoes faded. Then there came another chirp, followed by a series of moaning gasps and dry clicking noises.

"They—" The former queen's voice was too rasping to make out any more. I realized the truth a heartbeat later—whatever these creatures were that haunted this waste, they had surrounded the old queen, who must have clambered up the pillar to escape them.

Shadow howled once more, but the creatures seemed to be mastering their fear of him. The darkness was full of moans and scraping sounds, as of things dragging themselves forward over the sand.

"Jump down!" I hollered.

Scarcely had the words left my mouth, however, than the old queen was acting on them. She drew herself onto her hands and knees and lurched forward, unbalancing the topmost fragment of rock. She struck a protrusion as she fell, and the entire thing began to topple. It was not a pillar of rock, I realized then, but an unwieldy tower of bones. I could not imagine how the woman had made it to the top in the first place, but such questions were for another time. She half fell, half tumbled to the ground, landing in a heap at our feet. At the same moment, something horribly skinny, with jaws as long as my arm, lunged out of the dark and snapped at her hair, wrenching out a hank.

I shrieked and Shadow started back. I just managed to grab

hold of the woman's wrist and yank her half onto Shadow's back before the dog broke into a run. The bone tower crashed behind us, spilling vertebrae and teeth that clattered after us as if giving chase.

Then we were careening back the way we had come, Shadow filling the wasteland with his howls. I barely managed to stay on his back, and Arna did not manage it at all—I was able to hook my arm through hers beneath her shoulder, but her legs dangled free, one foot intermittently striking the ground. Likely I would not have had the strength to maintain my awkward grip, but she had grown skinny as a river reed since we'd shared poisoned wine at her table, and also I was highly motivated not to drop her for fear of having to turn back.

Shadow moved more swiftly on the return journey, though I could not see what he was running towards—either the door was not visible from this side or my eyes were too stung by ash and soot to make it out. But nothing could deceive Shadow's nose, and abruptly the smell of decay was replaced by that of forest, and I was falling forward onto snow, taking deep gasps of winter air laced with frost that had never tasted so pleasant.

12th February

It's difficult to know precisely how long I spent in the Veil—certainly it seemed no more than an hour. But when I returned it was nearing twilight, which did not surprise me. I could see it was the same day, for a few tiny embers still lurked below the burnt wood of my campfire. The door to the Veil had vanished, and the grove was empty—the Hidden king had not bothered to wait for me, which was a relief. Most likely he assumed I was dead, but it was also possible that he simply was not interested enough in the outcome to trouble himself. After all, I had promised to return to him once I'd done away with Wendell, and what reason did he have to doubt me? He'd swallowed the story of my undying love for him.

Well! I do not think I shall be able to return to Ljosland, for I do not see him forgiving me a second time.

My exhaustion was beyond comprehension, and I could scarcely manage to build a fire. Arna lay insensible in the snow; I constructed the fire close to where she lay, left a little cup of melted snow beside her, draped her in a blanket from the tent, and hoped for the best. Then I staggered into the tent with Shadow and was asleep before my head touched my pallet.

Should I have been more concerned that Wendell's stepmother would murder me as I slept? I don't think so. Not only on account of her weakened state, but because she had nothing to gain by my death, and everything to lose should Wendell learn of what she had done. He had proven himself greater than she, for he could control the Veil, and she could not. I did not believe she would be in a hurry to return to the place.

Such bloodless calculations concerning my physical safety in the company of a vengeful faerie queen had not pleased Lilja and Margret when I described them before I left, but they were enough for me, and my sleep was untroubled.

My stomach woke me sometime before dawn, growling ferociously. I devoured half of Poe's cakes and all my remaining water, then scribbled out the previous journal entry—yes, I am aware that making this a priority might sound strange. But I was in such scholarly terror of forgetting anything I had seen that I knew I would not sleep easy until I had written it down. I believe I fell asleep again with the pen in my hand. Oh, how Wendell would mock me if he knew! And yet I have so many ideas for the papers I will write about Dark Faerie, as I have decided to call it—indeed, I could write a book on the subject! That the Folk are in such terror of the place makes it inherently fascinating, and yet, now that I have ventured there, I am not convinced there is anything particularly exceptional about it. In fact, one of the O'Donnell brothers' stories speaks of a faerie realm where it is always night, inhabited by monstrous Folk. As do several Russian tales—the names escape me at present—and one from the Welsh Marches.

Lord, I am rambling. The papers can wait—for now.

When I woke again, it was late morning, and Shadow was still asleep at my side, snoring lightly. It was a fine Ljosland day: the sun was out, setting little jewels of light amidst the snow, and the wind was still, the boughs quiescent. I found the old queen awake, but lying in a heap beneath her blanket. She had added wood to the fire at least once in the night, for it still flickered.

"We must return to the door," I said, and explained to her about Poe and the key he'd given me. She made no reply, but pushed herself upright and sat looking very small and forlorn, as well as younger than she'd seemed to me before, at the height of her power—only a few years older than I. I couldn't tell if she was in shock or contemplating some foolhardy plot to escape.

I returned to the tent to rouse Shadow, and was terrified to find that he would not wake immediately. I had to shake him several times, murmuring his name and rubbing at his ears in the way he liked, my voice increasingly desperate, because while I had known his time was approaching—oh, yes, I had known it, and woken in dread many a night to listen to his whistling snores at the foot of the bed—I could not accept that it would be now. But at last he gave a grunt and opened his eyes. Once he saw me, he heaved himself to his feet, as if determined to establish that he was as hale as ever, and licked my face.

I hugged him, my vision fogged with tears of relief. How I wished we were at the end of our journey! I murmured apologies and praise, rubbing Shadow's neck. How dear he is to me. I cannot write this without feeling my eyes well again.

After I returned the tent to its former iteration and stamped the fire out, Arna allowed me to help her stand. I held out Poe's key, and a heartbeat later we were in his grove again.

Poe was nowhere to be seen, nor was his mother, thank God, though the grove was filled with the smell of stewed apples.

"Would you care to bathe?" I asked the queen, motioning to the hot spring.

Again, she made no response, only watched me inscrutably. I found this unnerving—apparently, no amount of soot or stink will make me easy in the old queen's company—but affected indifference. I helped her undress and step into the spring. I did the same, scrubbing myself quickly to end the awkwardness of the experience, then dried myself with one of the blankets. I'd brought one clean dress with me; the tent contained no spare clothes, but after fishing about for a while, I unearthed a stylish bathrobe of black silk and dense flannel that I supposed Arna could wear.

The old queen, meanwhile, after scrubbing herself from head to foot with some of the abrasive sand at the bottom of the spring, sat there, motionless and sweating, for a full ten minutes.

"Erm," I said at last. "We must carry on. My friends are waiting for me. They will be worried terribly."

"I thought I would never be warm again," Arna murmured, and I realized she was weeping. She did not wail or blubber, merely let the tears flow down her cheeks. After a moment, she buried her face in her hands.

Now, I have never been skilled at responding appropriately to tears, and in this context I was completely at sea. Fortunately, the old queen collected herself and clambered out of the water. I helped her into the robe, and she murmured her thanks.

"Why did my son send you, instead of coming himself?" she asked. "Was it a test?"

This took me only a second or two to parse. "Ah," I said. "You think he has demanded that I prove my worthiness to him as a wife by rescuing you from the Veil. That would indeed be a familiar tale. But, in fact, he had no knowledge of my plan."

I explained the situation to her—my fear that Wendell's

story would follow the second Macan's if he murdered her. I'm afraid I couldn't help making the whole thing sound scholarly, referencing other tales and papers I'd read, as if I were defending myself against a skeptical peer reviewer; such is my impulse when I am nervous. I could not tell if she understood me or not. Ridiculously, her primary reaction was to look hurt by the news that Wendell had not forgiven her. "He wished to leave me in that place?"

I considered and discarded several blunt responses to this. Instead I replied simply, "He believes you will never stop seeking revenge."

The former queen shook her head slightly. "I am done with vengeance," she said. "I am done with thrones. I am reborn."

I absorbed this dubiously. I had hoped she would be grateful to me—Folk rescued by mortals usually are, in the stories—but I'd expected to have to bargain with her to secure an end to her hostility. I said, "Let us go home."

She acquiesced without argument, and I took out the key again. Unfortunately, I had no idea how to proceed from there. It was easy enough to arrive at Poe's tree from somewhere *else* in the winterlands, but how did I tell the key I wished to return to that scrap of winter in County Leane? When I walked round the side of the tree, I found myself back in the foreboding quiet of the Hidden king's grove, gazing at the smoking remnants of our fire and the indent in the snow where the tent had lain.

When I returned to Poe's tree, I knocked upon the bole. I thought I saw a curtain twitch—sometimes I can see the windows in Poe's tree, and sometimes I cannot. Then, abruptly, Poe was standing before us, bowing repeatedly in Arna's direction and babbling apologies.

"You wish for me to show you the way?" he said in a squeak,

without any prompting from myself. "Yes, yes—Mother and I shall miss you! But with royalty, naturally—important business cannot wait—a great many demands upon you—"

And he went charging around the side of the tree. Arna, Shadow, and I had to run after him, and between one step and the next, we were returned to the lonely Irish peak with the village of Corbann visible in the far distance.

We made it off the mountain before darkness fell, but only barely. Arna moved slowly, and frequently required me to assist her over obstacles and down steep sections of trail. It was not a bad thing, though, for I was still very worried about Shadow, who seemed so weary as to be almost in a daze: he would fall back on his haunches abruptly, panting and staring at nothing, before seeming to start back to himself and hobbling after me.

I had hoped that Arna would maintain a dignified silence, but there luck was not on my side. Much to my chagrin, after seeking a few more details about how precisely I had managed to follow her into the Veil—including my history with the Hidden king, about whom she seemed remarkably incurious—I found my relationship with Wendell interrogated.

Every particular was sought. The old queen wished to know where we had met; the development of our friendship and whether we had truly begun as academic rivals or if there had not been some feeling there from the start; whether he had met my family and friends and the nature of their opinions of him; how Wendell had proposed. She seemed scandalized that we had been married with so little ceremony, and I was forced to remind her that this had been necessitated by the direness of the circumstances, namely her having poisoned the king—

dom and made designs on Wendell's life. This landed with very little impact.

"Still, he must be planning a grand celebration," she said. "When my late husband and I wed, the revelry lasted so many nights one forgot when it had begun."

"I am not much for revelry," I said irritably. We were descending a tricky slope, and I would have preferred to focus on my feet rather than on conversation, particularly this one. I could not help adding, "I wonder at your sudden interest in your son's happiness, Your Highness."

I thought she would not reply at first. Then: "He is a different person than I thought he was."

This confirmed something I had noted and wondered about: the former queen's manner of speaking of her stepson had fundamentally altered. I knew from Wendell that his stepmother had been dismissive towards him in his youth, sometimes ignoring him entirely, other times doting upon him in a condescending manner more suited to a pet. It was as if, in foiling her plot and dooming her to torment and death, his character had acquired a new dimension, one that she might respect. If this might not seem an obvious foundation upon which to build some semblance of maternal affection, I can only note that maternal affection is often a complicated subject in faerie stories.

When it grew too dark to continue, we made camp within a little circle of standing stones. I was not worried about bogles now, for they would know Arna, just as Poe had.

"I meant what I said," she told me as we hunched close to the warmth of the fire, each wrapped in a blanket. "I have no interest in the throne now. I wonder at my obsession with it before—what need has one for power, nor for anything besides the wind, so clear and sweet-smelling, and the green earth beneath one's feet?"

She stopped and gazed at the sweep of the land. I noticed that she had missed a spot of ash below her right ear, and that her palms had blisters and scabs she was scratching absently at. "I will take up a small cottage, I think, and live alone, offering this wisdom to any Folk who visit me."

I mulled this over. Naturally I suspected her vow might originate in practical considerations, not sincerity of feeling—she knew as well as I that the game was up. She had no hideout remaining where she could lurk and scheme, and no allies left in a realm she had tried to ruin, among Folk her magic had poisoned. More materially, she had no control over the Veil; Wendell could return her to it if she so much as spoke the word *vengeance*. But I decided that it mattered little whether her reformation was genuine; a self-serving motive would work for us just as well, Wendell and me, and I was not above flattering her for it, in the hopes that she would eventually come to believe in her nobility, and grow more zealous in its affectation.

"I have never heard of a monarch abdicating the throne of their own free will," I lied.[*] "The Folk cling to power and rarely have the strength of character to put the needs of their servants before their own."

She eyed me, and I reminded myself that she was half human, and thus not so easy to deceive as other Folk. "Or the sense of self-preservation," I added.

---

[*] Though uncommon, a handful of stories feature faerie monarchs installing a chosen heir in their place. The Russian tale "The Snow-Wanderer," for instance, tells of a queen who wishes to live among mortals, whom she imagines as having simple, carefree lives. This queen gives the throne to her daughter, who rules until longing for her mother sends her on a quest in search of her, which ends in bloodshed when she finds the queen slain by mortal hands. In the northeast region of Ardamia, a place particularly prone to avalanches, many locals believe that a specific cave in the alpine is occupied by a very peculiar hermit—a queen of the courtly fae who abandoned her war-torn realm to her squabbling children partly to punish them, and is presently occupied in building herself a private castle by tunnelling into the mountains, which is supposedly to blame for the unstable nature of the terrain.

She smiled at that. "Do you not recall our conversation the day we met?" she said. "I am not Folk, and neither am I mortal. I am only myself."

She lay down beside the fire, wrapping herself in the blanket and drawing it over her mangled hair. I almost rolled my eyes—this sort of melodrama was clearly a family trait. But in truth, I was a little sorry for her. Not because of what she had suffered in the Veil—she had well deserved that—but because I could not imagine existence as a halfblood in Faerie to have been easy, and I sensed a litany of slights and injuries behind her refusal to identify with either of her parents' bloodlines. It must be wearying to exist in such a state of permanent self-denial. This did not justify what she had done, but it made her company marginally easier to bear.

"You are welcome to share our tent," I told her, for the wind was picking up, greedily snatching at what little warmth the fire gave off. After all, even singular beings are not immune to cold.

She made no response, only shivered and drew the blanket tighter to her. I sighed and went to bed, grateful for Shadow, who curled up against me—the dog is like a furnace with legs.

Sometime later, however, I started awake at the sound of rustling from the other side of the tent. The former queen spent a moment muttering curses at the pillows, which I had piled up on that side simply to have them out of the way, before she finally arranged her pallet to her satisfaction, and seemed to fall asleep. I regretted my kindness then, as her proximity made it easier to second-guess whether she might think twice about her newfound high-mindedness and strangle me in my sleep, but I had Shadow at my side, and as always, this gave me courage. I slept.

12th February—late

I woke before Arna this morning to fine weather, the sky clear and the winter's chill dulled at the edge, hinting at the coming spring. Ideal for camping, I suppose, but I was eager to reach the end of my arduous trek across three worlds and back, and woke Arna shortly after I finished jotting down the previous journal entry. I doubt I need describe the storm of feeling that greeted my return to the cottage, not to mention the arrival of the woman who had murdered Wendell's family, ravaged his kingdom, and brought about his death. Still, I'd explained the necessity of this circumstance, and never has there been a greater sign of Lilja and Margret's trust in me than their acceptance—grudging and antipathetic, it's true—of Wendell's stepmother as their guest.

Lilja was blunt. "Do we need to bind her?" she said, examining the forlorn figure before her, still dressed in a bathrobe. I could see from her face that she had no complicated feelings about this particular faerie, that Arna perfectly accorded with her opinion of the courtly fae. "We could send for metal wire from the local shop."

"That won't be necessary," I said, guiding the old queen towards one of the kitchen chairs.

"I respect the old laws of hospitality," Arna said. "Unlike

some." Here she gave me a cutting look that I found too absurd to be galling, which isn't to say she was not getting on my nerves by this point. I occupied myself with fussing over Shadow, helping him settle himself by the fire upon his familiar blankets.

"Would you like to take tea?" Margret said with more warmth. Margret, I have noted, appreciates having novel company to test her baking on—even, it seems, if they are murderous relations. She puts me in mind of Poe in that respect.

Arna shrugged. She looked around the cottage, seeming amused by what she saw, or simply by her situation. "Why not?"

"Oh good!" Margret said. "I made local fare this time—apple cake. I had the recipe from one of the shopkeepers. I thought the queen might appreciate it more than our foreign baking."

"I am no queen, my dear," Arna said, looking pleased to have the opportunity to display her humility, as a child would a new toy. Unfortunately, she seemed inspired to take this even further, and rose to help Margret prepare our tea. Margret seemed to wish to stop her, but the former queen has an innate imperiousness that I doubt will ever fade. The results were as one would expect from someone who has drunk a lot of tea but never made it: the former queen added so many leaves to the pot that it took on the colour and taste of tar. I had been looking forward to hot tea more than any other thing after such a gruelling quest and found myself so unreasonably piqued that one would think tea represented the greatest of the old queen's misdeeds.

Leaving the three of them to make small talk, I ventured outside and turned the stepping-stones back over. I knew we should return at once, to spare Wendell any additional fretting, though a part of me wished to tarry. I could not fathom his precise reaction to what I had done, but it was difficult to imagine it being positive.

When I returned, I found that Arna had cast some form of glamour upon one of the paintings on the wall. What had been a portrait of a woman in an antiquated dress smiling faintly at the artist was now an intricate pattern of wildflowers and seashells, with a naked couple cavorting in the centre.

"Already there is a difference," Arna was saying, gazing appraisingly about the cottage. "Mortals give so little attention to the beauty of their environments. The effect upon one's well-being is significant, which they would realize if only they opened their eyes."

I could see from Lilja's face that she did not appreciate the change one bit—I believe the painting had some sentimental value. I gave her a look of silent appeal, and she let out her breath and said nothing.

"We must go," I said.

"Yes," Arna said, pushing her chair back. "I must face my son sometime. I would prefer not to lengthen the anticipation."

I realized she was trembling lightly, which quelled a great deal of my annoyance. I had not expected her to be frightened.

We took our leave of Lilja and Margret, who for once did not seem sorry to say goodbye, though both folded me into a tight embrace at the door.

We ventured across the garden and down the stepping-stone path. I expected to emerge in the forest of Wendell's realm—that was where the door had led most recently. Instead, I found myself in the castle, where the door used to lead. Specifically, Wendell's and my apartments.

I blinked, staring at the now-familiar hallway. Shadow gave a huff and kept walking, glancing over his shoulder in puzzlement when I did not follow.

"He put it back," I said blankly.

Arna looked about. "This is unexpected. Why would he put a door to the mortal realm here? It's dreadfully unsafe to have a door opening onto one's private chambers. What if assassins learn of it?"

Good Lord. "Let us find Wendell," I said through my teeth.

"One moment." Arna pressed a hand to the bathrobe, and a glamour unfolded over it. Now she was dressed in a midnight gown as loose and silky as the robe had been, but embellished with pearls and a silver-embroidered pattern of songbirds and vines. She did not alter the tangle of her hair, but it had silvered vines in it now to match those on her dress. Her feet she left bare. Perhaps she thought the overall picture was one of humility, because she was nowhere near as elaborately clothed as she once had been, though she had sacrificed neither taste nor elegance at this altar.

Two servants appeared at the threshold of the corridor, perhaps having heard our voices. There they froze as if struck by some enchantment.

"Where is the king?" I asked.

They stared at me, mouths agape. Then, "The Grove," one said in a tremulous voice. The other fled.

"Oh dear," Arna said, though she did not look displeased.

"Shall—shall I send for him?" said the remaining servant.

"No," Arna answered in her calm, imperious manner. "We shall seek him there. It is fitting that I should abdicate power at the foot of my old throne."

Now, the fact that I refrained from pointing out that power would not be abdicated on her say-so, for she had been thoroughly overthrown already, or that, as the present queen of the realm, it was *my* opinion of the situation that mattered, represented a remarkable display of high-mindedness on my part, I believe. I was mollified somewhat by the hesitation of the servant, whose gaze darted in my direction. I nodded.

My first priority, of course, was Shadow, and so after summoning a servant to fetch him his favourite victuals, I took him to our bedroom and helped him hop up on the bed, which ordinarily he can manage without assistance. He was asleep almost immediately, but I stayed at his side another moment, gently rubbing faerie salve into his joints—it is a new concoction made by one of the castle brownies, and has proven remarkably effective. He twitched with pleasure when I did his knees.

Arna and I continued through the castle. Many Folk fled at the first sight of her, including the poor tailors in the dressing room, who launched their handiwork and needles into the air with a flurry of squeaks and pushed and shoved at one another in their haste to be gone. Yet just as many mastered themselves enough to return, following behind us at a safe distance and muttering amongst themselves. We accumulated Folk as we went, both servants and courtiers, courtly and common fae. In fact, once we alighted at the foot of the staircase, it seemed as if everyone in the castle were trailing after us. The stairs were clogged with a long river of Folk, some elbowing others aside to achieve the best vantage.

"Good grief," I murmured. I'd had more than enough of feeling like the heroine in a stage performance. Yet perhaps it was better this way—the more onlookers, the greater the likelihood the events of the day would be accurately remembered and retold.

Once we gained the forest path, our audience had swelled to such an extent that Folk began clambering into the trees to keep us in sight. Two young women in elaborate court dresses giggled and shoved at each other from the canopy, their skirts hiked to their thighs. Another man slipped and fell to the ground, landing on the path before us, where he screamed and scrambled aside as if we might blast him to cinders where he lay. I had never seen so many Folk assembled in one place, and was so unnerved I only barely kept my countenance; they seemed to tangle together like a forest within the forest, a vast conglomeration of leaf and moss and fine silk, beauty and monstrousness. Snowbell materialized out of the chaos, snapping his teeth at one of his brethren who had attempted to follow him.

"What an adventure!" he crowed, leaping onto my shoulder and preening, as if he too had returned from a perilous quest in a haunted otherland. Well, at least somebody was enjoying the attention, I suppose.

One would think Arna noticed none of them, for her stride remained purposeful and unhurried, her gaze never straying from the path. And perhaps she did not, for she had served as sole monarch for more than a decade, and as queen longer than that, and was doubtless used to the ridiculous habits of her subjects.

And then we had come to the Monarchs' Grove.

It had not been spared the queen's poison. The mist was gone, but the trees were blackened, as if from wildfire, and yet their leaves remained, dark and tattered, so that the grove seemed to have more shadow in it than it had before. The towering oak whose roots made up our thrones had not been touched, however. It was whole and quite healthy.

Wendell was seated upon his throne, one hand resting on the arm as he leaned forward with a frown, doubtless having heard the approaching tide of Folk. Razkarden perched on the back of his throne, hideous legs unfurled, watching me with his unfathomable gaze. Orga was in Wendell's lap, and he had his other hand on her back, which was arched slightly, as if she were prepared to pounce on whatever threats might be drawing nigh. Snowbell gave a little start at the sight of her and leapt to the ground to hide behind my ankle, though he bared his teeth all the while. As I do not generally prefer the beast to be within close range of my extremities, I found this behaviour distracting, and only just restrained myself from kicking him away. Behind Wendell stood Niamh and several guards, and before him knelt a courtier, who must have been in the middle of seeking some favour, and who now stared in our direction with a terrified expression. Other courtiers crowded together at the opposite side of the grove, and I caught flashes of green disappearing into the forest—brownies fleeing from the tumult, I assume.

Wendell wore his possessed cloak, which gave a grumble into the silence that had fallen, and a crown of silvered rhododendrons in his hair. Against the backdrop of greenery and blasted stumps, he was as arresting as ever, but very pale—I could tell at a glance that he had not been sleeping.

As the eyes of the assembled Folk fell upon me, I realized that I had forgotten to change back into my queenly attire. I still had on my old shift and winter wellies, as if I were returned from fieldwork in the countryside. I was even more dishevelled than usual from my adventure, for I had lost a bootlace somewhere along the way, and I did not even want to imagine what my hair looked like. My journal poked out of one pocket, my notebook another, and my fingertips were smudged with ink. I looked every inch a scholar, a none-too-reputable one at that, and not one millimetre a queen.

And yet, somehow, this seemed barely to register on my audience. The Folk stared at me as much as Arna, with an avidity they had never displayed before. Perhaps it was the contrast I made with themselves, perhaps something else. The Folk respect power above most things, after all, and perhaps there was power in abandoning my fumbling attempts to please them, as if I were above it all, even if I did not feel that way.

In any case, I was not used to commanding their attention, and on the whole was not certain I preferred it.

Nevertheless, I pretended as if none of these thoughts existed, and drew my shoulders back. I had prepared my speech, and practiced it mentally several times. "Forgive me," I said to Wendell. "I have gone against your wishes. I do not believe I had the right to do so in this case, as she is your stepmother and it was your family she took from you—not to mention your kingdom. Yet I cannot abide the thought of losing you, either now or in future. I know you will wish to send her back to the Veil. But I can only ask that you listen first to—"

He closed the distance between us and wrapped me in his arms, and I could not speak.

"I was terrified you would not return," he mumbled into my hair. "Will you go away again? Please say no."

I touched his face, which I realized was wet. I drew back to look at him.

"I will not," I said. "I'm sorry."

He only pulled me to him again, gripping me so tightly I suspected he did not believe me. Someone started strumming a harp, some romantic ballad, but was almost immediately shushed by at least a dozen voices. I wanted to suggest we continue the conversation in private, but naturally, none of the other protagonists in our impromptu stage drama paid any heed to the innumerable eyes upon them.

Arna, at my side, fidgeted with impatience. "Your wife is not the only one come with apologies, Your Highness." She went down on one knee, bowing her head low. "I surrender myself to your judgment. I am cured of my desire for a throne—indeed, for anything that is not the humblest mode of existence, as nothing could please me more than the sunlight upon my skin or the birdsong in these trees."

Wendell drew back, swiping his sleeve over his eyes, and squinted at her irritably, as if she were another self-important musician inserting herself where she wasn't needed.

"How in God's name did you get her out?" he said, looking at me with such bafflement that it teetered on the edge of amusement.

"You don't wish to know why first?" I said, unable to stop smiling. It seemed highly inappropriate, given the circumstances. Yet Wendell was gazing at me with such an expression of delight, awe, and relief, and showing not the slightest indication of flying into one of his fits of temper, nor any evidence that such a tendency could exist in one so light of heart, that I almost wished to laugh.

"Oh, I know why," he said. "Some scholarly tome told you that you must rescue her, did it not? And so you have trusted in that, rather than the evidence of your own eyes, which proved my stepmother deserving of every punishment a mind could invent."

"You accuse *me* of illogic!" I said. "I expected to return to find you very angry with me."

He barely seemed to hear. He looked from me to Arna, and I *did* see a flash of temper in his gaze then—but only a flash. "You have risked your life for her. Haven't you?"

"Ah," I began nervously. "Somewhat, I suppose."

"Somewhat," he repeated. "Somewhat, Em!"

"I had every confidence in my abilities!" I protested, and I told him how it had come about: my research, the journey to the mountain, Poe, the Hidden king's assistance. When I came to *his* role Wendell looked so faint it seemed briefly possible that he might pass out. When I told him how Shadow and I had travelled through the Veil, he stood in complete silence for a long moment, staring at me. Then, abruptly, he pulled me into his arms again.

"You must allow your stepmother to live," I said. I was about to launch into my reasoning, for I still had my speech to finish, but he forestalled me.

"Yes, obviously," he said, pulling back to draw a handkerchief from his pocket and blow his nose.

"Obviously?" I said, puzzled and a little flustered.

He finished blowing and waved a hand, tucking the handkerchief away. "Good Lord, Emily! You think I would risk you doing something like that again? Name your demands and they shall be met."

"I—" I stopped, feeling oddly put out that I could not deliver my speech as I'd intended. "I have only the one."

He studied me. "All the time you were away I spent worrying that you were unhappy here."

"What?" I said.

"Well, I could think of no other reason why you would leave me for so long. Please put my mind at ease. Are you?"

"Am I what?" I was beginning to feel as if the conversation were a wayward wind blowing me off course. We were supposed to be speaking of his stepmother! She stood not a yard from me; I could tell that she, too, had expected to occupy the bulk of Wendell's attention, and was displeased to find that this was not so.

"Are you unhappy here?" he persisted. "I have made a number of improvements, such as hiring additional bookbinders—and I realize that I have neglected that all-important room, the library. Now, I will not use the word *theft*, as it is entirely inaccurate in this case, but if we were to borrow the contents of the dryadology library at Cambridge and make copies—"

"I am not unhappy!" I interrupted. To my surprise, I found myself laughing a little—he looked so dreadfully earnest.

He seemed relieved and glanced at his stepmother with more contempt than hostility. I hadn't thought it would be easy to convince him, and in truth, it hadn't been, but now that he had given way to me, he seemed almost to have forgotten why he'd been so adamant before about killing her. Leaves rustled overhead and I glanced up; to my dismay I found the boughs above us crowded with Folk, the largest number being brownies, black eyes glistening, but also some courtly fae less cognizant of their dignity, adolescents in the main.

"You should not forgive me so easily," I said. "At least not without an explanation."

I launched back into my speech, offering evidence to support my certainty that his decision to punish his stepmother would come back to haunt him, relying on my extensive knowledge of story patterns, as well as the discoveries regarding the Macan tale I had made at the cottage. I broke off when I saw that he was regarding me with a look of pure exasperation.

"Em," he said, "if your aim is to convince me to allow this murderous lunatic to run free through the realm, you need not importune me further; it shall be done. But do not ask me to see the wisdom of it."

"Your Highness," Niamh said, looking as if she had been suppressing objections that could not be held back any longer. "Your stepmother has done great harm. Are we truly to accept her assurances that she will not try for the throne again? I agree she should not be tossed back into the Veil, but surely she should be held in the dungeons at least."

"How much simpler it would be to kill her," Lord Taran said from behind me. I had not noticed he was there—he had blended into the nebulous crowd of Folk—and turned to find him regarding us with a droll expression.

"Simpler, perhaps," I said. "But not necessary. Now that

she is caught, surely you can set enchantments upon her that will circumscribe her movements. Her powers may also be bound, though given that she is no longer queen, those must be greatly diminished already."

Arna only shrugged at this. "What need have I for magic when I can have the smell of trees after rainfall, the melody of water tumbling over moss and stone, the warmth of a summer's day, and the quickening chill of an autumn twilight upon my skin?"

"Good Lord," Wendell said.

"And I shall not *run free* anywhere," Arna went on. "My aim is to take up a quiet little cottage somewhere out of the way—you may choose the place, Your Highness, and have me spied upon at all hours if you wish. The Veil has taught me wisdom, where before—I know now—I had only canniness. I wish to pass this wisdom on to other Folk."

Wendell's only response to this speech was to turn back to me with a look of aghast disbelief.

"I believe she may be sincere," I said. "After a fashion."

"Very well!" he said. "If you wish to make a pet—or, as I suspect is more likely, an object of scientific study—out of the greatest villain our realm has ever known, I shall not stand in the way. I should have known you would appreciate such an opportunity more than any material gift I could give you."

"Your words are pretty, sister," Lord Taran said, "even unexpected—I say that as one who knows you better than any other. But I don't believe you have changed, myself, for you have nothing to gain from it, and everything to gain from pretending. No doubt in time you shall manage to convince other Folk, enough to make some of them forgive you, perhaps. As you know, there is a way out of every enchantment, if one looks hard enough—and if one cultivates the right allies."

He looked at Wendell and me. "She will never stop being a threat if she is allowed to live."

"Perhaps that is the way it should be," I said. I wondered if it was the lack of enemies that drove Macan the Second mad—if it is the cause of other instances of madness among faerie monarchs. Perhaps being too powerful, too unopposed, is a curse in and of itself, leading to boredom and dissipation, and the invention of imaginary enemies whose powers to torment are less limited than those of flesh and blood. Another paper there, I suppose.

Lord Taran glanced from me to Wendell and shrugged. "You are listening to the whims of your wife, and for that I cannot fault you."

"Whims!" I exclaimed, but Taran had already turned away, seeming uninterested in pursuing the argument. I knew that I had not convinced him at all, or rather I had not convinced him for the reasons I had intended.

Wendell gave me an anxious look, as if fearing some discord remained between us. "You are certain you are happy here? You have no idea how the question kept me up at night."

He was so worried that I could not help teasing him. "Only one thing shall make me happier."

His anxiety seemed to increase. "Oh, yes? Please let it not involve my stepmother this time."

"You still have not given me a tour of the kingdom," I said. Despite the continued annoyance presented by our audience, I felt the relief of homecoming, the anticipation of rest and familiar comforts, wash over me like sunlight. "Was I not promised a map to every province and a key to every door?"

"Oh, Em." A smile broke across his face. "I believe you were."

19th February

Tonight we dined at Lilja and Margret's—overdue by several days, for I knew they had been anxious for news. Wendell tells me I should stop thinking of the cottage as Lilja and Margret's—they will be leaving soon, after all, and though they have already promised to return in the summer at my insistence, the cottage will soon be my domain alone. I do not know how much time I will spend in the mortal world, but I can't deny that having the option of escaping the absurdity of Faerie is comforting; it is one of the best gifts Wendell has given me.

On the subject of gifts, Wendell informed me as we made our way down the hall to the faerie door that he had a surprise for me that evening.

"Is that necessary?" I said with a sigh. "You know I prefer *not* to be surprised, as a general rule."

Wendell paused to speak to the small brownie who had run up to him clutching a mug of coffee—these days, Wendell is rarely without a retinue of common fae, who trail after him bearing delicacies and gifts they have made. I am unconvinced that all this fawning is good for his ego, but it is a remarkable thing nevertheless; the small Folk are more accustomed to hiding from the courtly fae, particularly in this realm.

Wendell is kind to them at least, and if this kindness remains mixed with some amount of condescension, this is still more improvement than I expected from him.

"You must allow me a little fun once in a while," he said, following me through the door to Corbann. "I have been so looking forward to this."

"Well, if you must." We walked to the cottage gate, and I paused to wait for Shadow to catch up. He has been doing a little better since our grim quest, but I still worried about him. When at last he doddered up to the gate, I knelt to rub his neck.

"Come, dear," I murmured, my chest filling with a familiar ache. "You shall have your usual blankets by the fire, and first choice of all the courses."

He licked my hand and his tail gave a solitary thump against the grass.

I turned to find Wendell gazing about the garden with a distracted frown that I recognized well. "You are not thinking of apple trees, I hope," I said. "Lilja and Margret seem happy to have escaped that unnatural thing you gave them in Ljosland."

"But it is such a drab little place," he complained. "Even as cottages go. I could add a pear tree, at least."

"No," I said.

"A strawberry patch."

We spent the next few minutes bickering about it until at last I suggested that he summon a wisteria. He beamed in a way that aroused my instantaneous regret, but it was too late; he placed his hand on the cottage and tapped his fingers against the stone. A vine erupted from the ground and clambered up the wall with an unpleasant, excited sort of energy, splitting itself as it bent around the windows and door until it looked like a many-fingered hand itself, crooked possessively about the cottage. Flowers dangled like fat purple lanterns, dewed petals limned by the hearthlight of the windows.

"Much better," Wendell said.

I gazed at the place in silent awe. After wrestling with myself for a moment, I said, "You could add one or two more."

He looked delighted. "That was exactly my own thought!"

I watched as he summoned more vines, taking his time with the placement. It was not so much the flowers themselves I appreciated, but the magic trick. I do not think I shall ever grow tired of that.

Lilja threw the door open at our knock and welcomed us with hugs, followed by Margret, and took our cloaks to hang on the rack. The cottage was filled with the scent of roasted pheasant and more of Margret's baking—which, I can say without prejudice, has only improved with time, and is not far from rivalling Poe's.

Naturally the evening began with everyone talking at once, Lilja and Margret full of questions and Wendell full of compliments regarding their improvements to the cottage and the aromas emanating from the kitchen. Shadow, meanwhile, was so happy to see his friends again that he overturned the tray of toasted cheese Margret had prepared for hors d'oeuvres. Somehow I managed to interpose a summary of recent events amidst the chaos.

"Then the queen is—under guard?" Margret asked. We had settled ourselves at the table, apart from Lilja, who was stirring the pot of soup. "But free to roam about?"

I could guess the source of her anxiety. "She is unable to leave Faerie," I said. "Wendell has bound her to the realm. So you need not worry about her showing up in your garden again."

"She has not left her new home, nor tried to," Wendell said—I could see this still surprised him. The old queen had acquiesced to her humble living arrangements—a small house on the other side of the lake, tucked between two hills well-endowed with pretty meadows—without a single complaint, and, indeed, with a great deal of smiles and admiring little speeches. She had a garden, which she spent most of her days tending, a well, her own cow, and not one servant—though she had several guards and innumerable spies among the common fae, Snowbell among them. Ever delighted to be useful, he visited me daily with updates on Arna's activities, also voicing his anticipation of the day she would attempt to flee, at which time he intended to gnaw the flesh from her ankles.

Wendell believes it is only a matter of years, if not months, before she takes up scheming once more, but I maintain my opinion that the old queen has reformed. He did not see her in the Veil. And perhaps Arna, being half mortal, can escape the patterns her faerie ancestors have been powerless to resist. To which Wendell only replies that mortals can be just as prone to cycles of foolishness and self-destructive villainy as the Folk.

Well, time will tell whose argument carries the day.

"Then Ariadne and Farris are not here?" I enquired. "I wondered if they might be delayed; there are so many connections to make from Cambridge, and the ferry is not always reliable."

"Actually, they arrived early," Lilja said. "More than an hour ago. They just popped down to the village—"

As if we had summoned them, the door opened and Farris Rose stepped in, bearing a bottle of cider. In his wake trailed Ariadne, who had been walking with one of the village youths—for naturally she had already made a friend. I was embraced by both the new arrivals, after which Ariadne also gave Wendell an impulsive hug. Farris, not making eye contact, greeted him with a curt "Hello" before stalking past, which was the politest he'd been to Wendell in months.

"Was your journey a pleasant one?" I enquired.

"Oh, yes!" Ariadne exclaimed, before launching into a list of the research questions she wished to tackle during her stay. The two would spend a week in Faerie as our guests, to which Farris had acquiesced with a sort of grudging excitement. I could tell he did not wish to be any guest of Wendell's, and yet he could not resist such an immense scientific gift, and thus his annoyance was partly with himself, in his betrayal of his principles.

"Hello there!" The door opened, and Callum pushed his head in. "May we come in?"

Lilja hurried to the door, greeting him and Niamh with smiles and thanks—Lilja and Margret had asked that no faerie food or drink be brought, but Callum had offered to play for us and had his harp with him. Meanwhile Niamh had brought several sketches of Wendell's realm drawn by one of the dozen or so mortal artists who dwelt in the castle, so that Lilja and Margret might gain some sense of the place without having to set foot there themselves.

Dinner was a merry affair. The conversation was rather scattered, which does not ordinarily suit my preferences, but among those I knew so well I did not mind it. Farris and Niamh had much catching up to do, for though I had told him she was alive and well in the Silva Lupi, they had not yet reconnected, and were immediately nattering away like the old friends they were, Farris occasionally forgetting his dignity enough to have to wipe his eyes with his sleeve. Ariadne was full of questions as always, but she also formed an instantaneous accord with Lilja and Margret, who were not much older than she. Within the space of five minutes, it seemed, they were inviting her to their house in Ljosland, to which Ariadne—I note with some melancholy—may travel freely without fear of the Hidden king. Even Callum, who is ordinarily of a quiet nature, was comfortable enough to tell several stories of his youth in the coastal village of Kilmoney, and of his early years in Faerie with Lord Taran.

I did not regret our decision not to invite Taran—who in any event had professed himself wholly uninterested in attending—in deference to Lilja and Margret's discomfort with the Folk, and particularly such Folk as he. Margret, after all, still bears the mark of the Hidden Ones on her forehead, and in odd moments I have noticed her gaze grow distant, until Lilja brings her back to herself with a gentle word or touch. Yet I could see they were fascinated by Callum and Niamh, mortals who had not only ventured into Faerie and lived, but remained themselves and unbroken.

"I still cannot imagine the likes of our wee ones as royal councillors," Lilja said. "Do the small Folk truly have an aptitude for it?"

We had told them of our new Council, which now contains an equal number of courtly and common fae—chief among them the little housekeeper who saved Wendell—as well as several mortals. Never before in Wendell's realm—nor any other, to his knowledge—have the common fae been invited into the upper echelons of Faerie's political structure. The results, in my opinion, have been rather mixed, but still it is a nice thing from a symbolic perspective.

"As much as any faerie has," I said. Approximately half of the Council remains entirely useless—particularly the mortal poet and one Lady Thorns and Thistles—and yet I can't help suspecting, given comments made by Wendell and others, that this is an improvement on the general average. Faerie councils, like faerie monarchs themselves, seem not to have much practical utility, other than, perhaps, as a tiller guiding the wayward impulses of the king or queen, yet I have seen no evidence that the councils themselves are any less wayward.

Once we had finished our meal and established ourselves in armchairs by the fire with mugs of chocolate or tea, Wendell leaned forward abruptly, rubbing his hands together. "Now then! I fear I can wait no longer. The anticipation is too great!"

"Oh God," I said. "This is that surprise you mentioned, isn't it?"

"Surprise?" Margret echoed, looking both pleased and nervous; Lilja seemed more of the latter. Ariadne covered her mouth with her hands, nearly vibrating with excitement, and I realized that she had learned of this "gift" from Wendell, and been anticipating it—when, I knew not.

"You needn't worry," Wendell said to Lilja. "It is merely a wedding gift for my Emily. One I have planned for a very long time, but which has unfortunately been much delayed due to unforeseen circumstances."

"Your death?" I said.

"Among other things. The Deer took a great deal of time to root out."

"The Deer?" I frowned. "Not the hag-headed deer in the rhododendron meadow?"

"The very same. I had to request Lord Taran's help to remove them—he has an odd sort of accord with them, or as much as any person *can* have with such magniloquent brutes, and he was only too happy to help."

This did not do much to inspire anticipation. "Was he."

Wendell stood, as if he were about to give a presentation. Instead, to my surprise, he knelt by the fire next to Shadow, who gave a thump of his tail in acknowledgement.

"You see, Em," he said, rubbing behind Shadow's ears, "that particular meadow is one of the oldest parts of my realm, and home to a number of strange and venerable Folk. Including perhaps the only other personage of mixed courtly and common fae blood in the land, besides myself, of course, a woman of bogle and courtly fae ancestry. An unpleasant sort, as you might imagine! Yet I have long known she is the keeper of several of the ancient Words—you know two of them yourself, which places you already in rare company, for most Folk do not know even one."

"Yes," I said, a question in my voice. "Though most Words, in my understanding, are of low value, like the Word for button-summoning."

"Ah," Wendell said, "and has that one truly served no purpose? Most of the Words are of that nature—silly knickknack things on the surface, but useful in unexpected ways. Now, some time ago, I took Shadow to see several brownies expert in animal husbandry—"

"What!" I said. "When was this?"

"Last summer," he said. "A month or two before we departed for Austria. You were at that conference in Edinburgh—"

"On faerie markets," I cried, absurdly outraged. "I asked you to mind Shadow while I was away. And you took him to a—a doctor?"

"Of a sort," Wendell went on, looking only more self-satisfied in the face of my outbursts.

"We have Folk of that nature back home," Margret said, half to Lilja. "Do we not? Hilde and Sam say they live in their stables. They've never had a sick sheep or lamb in all their years of farming."

"Such Folk exist in almost every region," Farris said. He leaned back in his chair, folding his hands over his stomach. "They are a type of household brownie—though they are not always popular with farmers, for some are known to endow their beasts with peculiar gifts."[*]

---

[*] The Belgian story of the egg-laying goat is perhaps the most famous example, but many others exist.

"These brownies dwelt at a livery stable in Hertfordshire," Wendell said. "They also tend to their masters' hunting dogs, who are reputed to live curiously long lives."

My heart began to thrum in my ears. "I've not heard that story."

"It's a small part of the local lore," Wendell said. "More of a footnote, really. I have been searching for such brownies for the past year or two, and never enter a village without making enquiries of the inhabitants—a visit or two to the local pub, usually."

"Wait a moment," I said. "You were planning my wedding gifts *before* I accepted your proposal? Before you had even *asked*?"

Niamh snorted, while Lilja and Margret seemed to be smothering laughter. Only Ariadne took my side, patting my hand while continuing to smile in anticipation. I felt as if I were back in Faerie, with every private moment turned into a spectacle for public entertainment.

Wendell held up his hands. "My intentions were honourable, I assure you. Why cannot one be prepared for every outcome? And in any case, this particular gift was for Shadow's benefit primarily."

"Good grief!" I said, too overcome to be more articulate.

"'Prepared for every outcome,' he says," Niamh said with a laugh. "This one has not once been thwarted in love. You should have seen him in his youth—fawned over by all and sundry. The Folk are already possessed of healthy egos; you can imagine how much more swollen his grew for his early successes."

Wendell gave her a wounded look. "In fact, Niamh, I was half convinced my dear Emily had never met a man whose attentions she was less inclined to humour. I was astonished when she deigned to consider my proposal."

"Indeed?" Niamh rolled her eyes. "You should have turned him down at first, Emily. It would have done him good."

"I'm beginning to see the wisdom of that," I said, but I was too impatient to needle him further. My heart was thrumming in my ears. "What did these brownies tell you? I'd no idea such Folk could help a Black Hound."

He took my hand. "Shadow is ill, Em. Some congestion in his blood—that is how the creatures described it. An illness of age, which they might have prevented before it set in, but which they could not cure."

I sank back against my chair—I had not realized I was leaning forward, my body rigid with tension.

"However," Wendell continued, "I did not lose hope at this, for the information was useful. I'd heard rumours that this half-bogle woman, who aptly calls herself the Wordmonger, had amassed a great collection of forgotten Words. Including one intended to cleanse the blood—used mostly, I suspect, to rid the body of alcohol, and thus its aftereffects. Perhaps one of the most useful Words ever invented! And I thought to myself, why should it not be useful in this case? The Words have more than one function, and it stands to reason that their effects should be stronger in beasts. If ever I regained my kingdom, I told myself, I would venture to the rhododendron meadow to interview her as soon as could be."

"A hangover remedy!" Niamh exclaimed. "You thought to cure the dog with *that*?"

"I already have," Wendell said. "Come here, Em."

I knelt beside him and placed my hands where he indicated. I felt Shadow's heartbeat—with which I was acutely familiar, for the old dog liked to sleep pressed against my back at night. I didn't notice the change at first. But then—

"It's stronger," I cried. "Wait—is it?" I listened again. "Yes—I'm almost certain that it is!"

"I will teach it to you," Wendell said. He spoke the Word, slowly and softly. I felt the magic in the air, there and gone like an errant breeze; the Word had a presence when Wendell spoke that I could never give to it. Shadow gave a huff and licked his hand, his expression more alert than I had seen in a long time. I repeated the Word, adding it to my little collection.

"We should speak it now and then to keep the illness at bay," Wendell said.

"He—" I stopped. "He has seemed better, these last few days." I could not say the word *cured*, for it felt like a falsehood. Shadow was still blind in one eye; his preferred pace remained slow and lumbering. He had sought the hearth and blankets Lilja had laid out for him with all his usual enthusiasm to be off his feet. There was no dramatic transformation—the effect had been so subtle as to be barely noticeable. Wendell had not snapped his fingers and turned Shadow into some strapping immortal beast.

"He is an old dog still," Wendell said quietly. "There are no magics to restore youth in creatures doomed to age—only glamours. But I thought, if I could grant him another few years of health, which he may spend in your company, and in roaming his favourite paths, and napping by the fireside—"

"It's enough," I said, then buried my face in Shadow's fur, unable to control myself any longer. In truth, it *wasn't* enough—no finite span of years ever could be. And yet it was a gift beyond measure.

When at last I had my emotions in hand, I looked up to find both Ariadne and Lilja brushing away tears, while Margret rubbed Lilja's shoulders. Niamh nodded her approval, for once having nothing to tease Wendell about, and even Callum, who is ordinarily a little hesitant around Shadow, being, like Wendell, more given to cats, was blinking rapidly.

Only Farris seemed unmoved, and yet he spoke not a word to dampen the moment, merely regarded Wendell with a sort of repressed antagonism.

"This deserves a celebration," Callum noted, removing his harp from its case. "What do you say?"

As none of us had any objections, he began to play, the music scarcely louder than the wind outside at first, as if they were two halves of the same melody, then swelling into a familiar song. Shadow lay his head in my lap, and I held him so tightly one would have thought I had lost him, as I had Wendell, only to find him again.

1st March

Cambridge slept beneath a blanket of tousled cloud, a few stars peeking here and there through the folds. Our footfalls seemed oddly loud against the stone paths, the echoes more pronounced, as if our return after so long an absence jarred slightly against the beloved topography of the campus. Razkarden and two other guardians flitted through the trees above in their owl glamours, ever shadowing our progress.

Our journey had not been long, for Wendell had commanded the tree fauns to repair one of the ancient faerie doors that once linked his realm with Britain, as another of his extravagant wedding gifts to me. Last year, his stepmother had repaired this particular door temporarily, to send assassins after him, but it had collapsed again afterwards, faerie doors being prone to fragility if not used regularly. It did not lead to anywhere in Cambridgeshire, unfortunately, but to a quiet patch of woodland in the New Forest, which meant a train journey of several hours, with connections, to reach the university. But still it was an excellent shortcut, eliminating the need for the ferry, and Wendell has encouraged Folk to go to and fro regularly to ensure the door does not collapse again. I am uncertain if this increase in faerie activity will be appreciated by the inhabitants of that part of rural Hampshire, but it will give the dryadologists of the South something to scratch their heads about.

We reached the dryadology department, which was not as quiet as I'd hoped it would be. A small group of students was ensconced in a corner of the common room, a heap of books, papers, and coffee cups testifying to the urgency of their industry, likely connected to the present midterm season. Two faculty offices at the end of the hall had lights on, as did—unsurprisingly—Professor Walters's. There came the abrupt sound of shattering ceramics, and I turned to find one of the students staring at us as if we were ghosts. Her companions, though, were too occupied with mopping up the coffee she had spilled to note our arrival. Otherwise, we managed to reach my office without attracting much attention.

"It's very late," Wendell said with a yawn, as if I didn't know; we'd planned our timing in advance.

"I won't be long," I said.

Wendell gave another dramatic yawn and roamed about the office, gazing out the window or adjusting a book slightly, which caused the dust upon that shelf to vanish, before throwing himself into the armchair by the window to wait. Shadow flopped down at his feet.

It was indeed late—only a few moments shy of midnight, according to the grandfather clock. We had chosen that hour for our visit so as to encounter the smallest number of scholars, for neither of us had much interest in being waylaid by inquisitors, of which there would be many in the department. My lengthy stay in the Silva Lupi is now widely known, while Wendell's identity is by now so widely gossiped about—Farris Rose, in refusing to answer questions regarding his knowledge on the subject, has only inflamed the gossip further—that it has largely elided the difference between rumour and fact. All this has been an enormous boon to my career. It seems almost every day some new conference invitation or request for scholarly collaboration arrives at the cottage in Corbann, which is to be my primary mailing address in the mortal world for the foreseeable future.

One would think I was past being flattered by conference invitations, given all I have seen and done. But I am not.

"You should give up your office," I said. I selected two books from a shelf, pressed them to my chest for a moment like old friends, then added them to a little pile I was making. "It seems unfair, as it is the largest in the department apart from Farris's, and you have no plans to return."

Wendell shrugged. He had taken up my encyclopaedia—I keep several copies in my office—and was absently flipping through it. "It's nice to have a bolt-hole, should I need it."

"Should your stepmother chase you out again, you mean. The odds seem rather slim at this point."

"Who knows? There is always Deilah. She is very young. One can only guess if she shall turn out a good-natured ally or a monstrous villain."

I murmured assent. Deilah gave every appearance of the doting sister now, but if there is one thing predictable about the Folk, it is their unpredictability.

"I don't wish to get too comfortable, Em," he said as he slouched into the armchair with the book in his hands.

"You have the love of the common fae," I pointed out. "And not only because they fear you. You have now sought their assistance on numerous occasions, showing them a respect in doing so that the courtly fae never bestow upon them. That makes you considerably more comfortable than most monarchs your realm has known."

One of his sunniest smiles broke across his face. "I am, aren't I? And whom do I have to thank for that, I wonder?"

I kept my eyes on the bookshelves. "Your grandmother?"

He laughed. Professor Walters, just down the hall, cleared her throat emphatically, as if we might somehow have forgotten about her presence, with her slamming her books about as she always does. How a person engaged in such quiet pursuits as reading and writing manages to make such an interminable racket is a mystery I shall never solve. I suspected she was hoping we would remember her enough to stop by her office, thus sparing her the indignity of having to open the conversation with two scholars half her age and, in her estimation, less than half as accomplished. But Professor Walters is a Classical dryadologist, and like many of those specializing in the Greek Folk, much given to snobbery; it is as if such people believe that the discipline's origin in Greece gives them a corresponding precedence over dryadologists of other subspecialties.

"I've thought it over," I said. "And actually, I would prefer to visit the Blue Hooks first."

"What!" Wendell cried. "Not more mountains, Em, good grief! Have you not had your fill of the bloody things?"

"It's just that Niamh was telling me about the most peculiar creature who dwells in a cave below one of the southern peaks," I said. "A banshee who has taken a vow of silence! Either that or she is under some curse; her screams are transmuted into the stones, which levitate into the air. It would be quite the phenomenon to witness. I am familiar with only one comparable example—a rather sketchy account from Hungary—"

He listened to my summary, then sighed and leaned his head against the back of the chair. "In a realm filled with pleasant forests and hills, she has to drag me into the *mountains*," he intoned to the ceiling.

"And don't go ordering them to lie flat or something

equally ridiculous," I told him, to which he only frowned, so I knew the thought would have occurred to him at some point.

"Let's go," I said. "I want to return those books before we leave. I wish the dryadology library closed at night so that I could simply slip them through the mail slot. One of the night librarians holds a grudge against me."

"Entirely unfounded, no doubt," Wendell said. "Nothing at all to do with your habit of keeping books until they are monstrously overdue."

"I would not call it a *habit*," I protested.

He raised his eyebrows at me.

"I may pick up another volume or two while we're there," I added grudgingly. "Well, I don't know when I'll be back."

It was true enough—Wendell and I would spend the next several months travelling his realm. *Our* realm. I must get used to that. I would take copious notes all the while, no doubt filling several of the ridiculous journals the bookbinders kept churning out, and stumbling across so many research questions it would take me ten lifetimes to tackle them all. And after that, who knows? I have my compendium of tales to finish—I plan to gather stories as Wendell and I travel, adding them to the small hoard I've already collected. My presence is not required in the mortal world until October, when I will be delivering a presentation on several key findings in my mapbook, which shall be published in a month's time. When the Berlin Academy of Folklorists sends you an invitation to their annual conference, you cannot say no.

I looked up from the book I was flipping through to find Wendell regarding me with a smile that made me blush. "Don't hurry on my account," he said.

"Do you not want anything?"

He seemed to think it over. "No—ah, but wait a moment. I

wonder if I left my blue scarf . . ." He rose and wandered off, leaving me alone with Shadow's whistling snores.

I glanced about the office. It looked as it always had; nothing had been touched in my absence apart from a few books—I'd given Ariadne permission to borrow what she needed from my personal collection, and no doubt Professor Walters had helped herself to a volume or two. I drew a deep breath, inhaling the familiar scent of leather and parchment, ink and dust. My reflection showed in the casement window against the dark lawns beyond—I wore one of my old brown shifts beneath my cloak, having given away the entirety of my queenly attire to Deilah, for when she grew into them, though I'd taken to wearing a single silvered leaf in my hair along with a little cluster of bluebells, which glinted in the lamplight.

It will still be here, I told myself. *You can still return, whether it be in one month or many.* The thought was a comfort, quelling the jangle of anticipation within me. I had been greatly looking forward to my travels with Wendell, but I couldn't deny the trepidation that came along with it; I have felt the same at the start of many an expedition. The thought of the desk awaiting my return, the well-stocked bookshelves, the manicured view and quiet reflection these four walls afforded—it made me feel easier about what lay before me.

Wendell returned with the aforementioned scarf slung triumphantly about his neck. I woke Shadow, and the three of us made our way to the library.

About the Author

HEATHER FAWCETT is the author of the Emily Wilde series, as well as a number of books for children and young adults, including *Ember and the Ice Dragons, The Grace of Wild Things,* and *A Galaxy of Whales.* She has a bachelor's degree in archaeology and a master's in English literature. She lives on Vancouver Island.

heatherfawcettbooks.com
Facebook.com/HeatherFawcettAuthor
Instagram: @heather_fawcett

About the Type

This book was set in Legacy, a typeface family designed by Ronald Arnholm (b. 1939) and issued in digital form by ITC in 1992. Both its serifed and unserifed versions are based on an original type created by the French punchcutter Nicholas Jenson in the late fifteenth century. While Legacy tends to differ from Jenson's original in its proportions, it maintains much of the latter's characteristic modulations in stroke.